TIME
THIEF

TIME THIEF

ECLIPSE BOOK ONE

Lindsay French

Podium

Podium

TIME
THIEF

CHAPTER ONE

I shivered on the march to the Prophet of the Valley, my tunic loose with no armor and my body light without weapons. The boots of my fellow captives trampled earth as dark as a winter's night sky into a slurry of mud.

After nearly a decade of fending off the conquest of our enemy, our village had finally fallen, and I had failed at what mattered most. My hands curled around a sliver of empty space that should have been filled by my bow.

The baritone hums of the villagers lining our path vibrated beneath my skin. Pounding drums hijacked my heartbeat, thudding within my chest, my temples, my soul.

It was a ridiculous sight—all these people draped in dark robes and gathered around us as we neared the village. What made them hate us so much? We'd only ever tried to live. Their Prophet had been the one to start this feud by taking over the Valley. Even so, I blamed myself, because I had once wielded as much power as he had and should have been able to stop him.

I had long since cursed the day my cowardly instructors on the Mountain of the Gods sealed my power, but never before had I cursed myself as badly as I did now for failing to break free of the limitations they placed on me. The so-called gods gave the instructors the ability to cut off our power for a reason, and no one had ever regained theirs once that happened. They said it was impossible. Still, I could accept no excuses. Not one day had passed since losing my power that I had not fought to free myself. If I had succeeded instead of failed, then our innocent wouldn't have been captured and our warriors would not have fallen.

"Heretics!" The women snarled at us from beneath pale hoods gleaming with the glow of fire. The whites of their eyes burned red. Each held a torch between laced fingers, nestled against their hearts. One stared into my eyes. "Burn! Burn! BURN!"

One snap and I could have shot an arrow through her gaping mouth if I had my precious bow. And with my power, I could have struck her dead in an instant. The Prophet and his followers were hypocrites for using powerful demons to capture us when he was the most notorious demon hunter in the peninsula. I longed to crush his throat.

The thirst for vengeance gave me the strength to drag my heavy body forward. We'd walked throughout the day and night before nearing the Prophet's village. Along the road leading to his gates, men stood over the women's shoulders. Their faces were shadowed by black hoods that drank up the shadows of twilight, their mouths closed so their hums sounded as if they came from beyond—from the gods themselves. Their stares never shifted from us. Blood dripped from their eyes like tears, cracking at the edges as it dried.

I could think only of my adopted nephew, Rune, and his little fingers disappearing from view as the demons stole him away from our village into the night. His young voice screaming my name echoed through my mind.

"Max!"

The coarse rope that tore at my skin was nearly as grating as the glare of the Prophet's faithful lining our path. What crushed my lungs with anguish, though, was how my best friend's form ahead of me punctuated the twilight, how far away Leif felt. The same bonds that kept me from reaching for my people also tethered me to them, so I couldn't help but love what I hated.

I hadn't prayed since Dad died and the instructors at the Sacred School so poorly filled the void he left. I hadn't prayed since I learned the truth about our world, about the gods, about how nothing at all was as it seemed. Now, such desperation clawed into my heart that I lifted my face to the expanse above and I prayed a prayer I didn't believe to gods I believed in even less.

Let this not be real.

Tears wet my cheeks. A touch of warmth where none could be found.

I searched for a response in the space where navy sky and dark earth melted into one, where the barely visible spread of stars above us crashed into the glow of snowcapped mountains. It was easy to see why our people turned this direction to pray, with how the towering terrain appeared to guard our Valley from the rest of the Skia Hellig Peninsula, as if we were divinely protected. But I knew what was on the Mountain of the Gods.

We'd drawn so much closer to it while on this march.

The air ahead glowed brighter and brighter with red and orange haze until the domineering wooden spikes atop the wall of the village appeared. I craned my neck to see up to the guards posted like statues every few feet, their crossbows steadied against the stone edge. No one else in the Valley had defenses close to rivaling this.

Rune's pleas for help blared in my mind. His fingers reaching, straining.

I lowered my head.

The haunting tones of the villagers beyond the walls died as we entered the gate, replaced by an eerier quiet. Wooden, multistory buildings lined the cobbled road, leading all the way to the gently sloping hill near the back where the temple rose over everything in sight.

I squinted, eyes stinging from artificial brightness of lights atop steel poles. It'd been so long since I'd been around electricity. As a child, I'd stood on jagged rocks along the shore and watched the sparkles of sunlight glitter off each ripple, like our own daytime stars. Dad had dipped to run his fingers along the water and lamented at how the light scattered. How he'd never catch the sun's rays like the Prophets did.

Our young world was like a small child with the feet of a man. Awkward and deformed. Deformed by an incredible power we weren't ready for.

Fury flushed through my veins.

The Prophet of the Valley—that damned Eskel the Ruthless—would pay for what he'd done. I'd make sure of it.

Sometimes, the faintest inklings of my power kindled within me, out of reach, but warm like a flame. The heat of it burned within me now.

Our line turned right to a wooden stage tucked into an oval courtyard. The Prophet stood in the center with a thick canvas sheet stretching behind him and a coarse rope in his left hand. Seven disciples stood like statues at the base of the stage, wearing the same dark cloak as their leader. Above them, the Prophet held a spear with his free hand, face shadowed by his hood as he watched us. I knew his image so well, and even better, the nausea it filled me with. Sealing my power had not ended the visions that haunted me. And it was those very inky black eyes that I saw in those visions every time. Strands of black combed through the straight gray hair creeping out from his hood, lying beside the wisps of his beard. An image I had never been able to escape.

The guards forced us into a line before him.

I swallowed down the hard knot of fear lodged in my throat.

The slender man towering over us spoke. "I am the Prophet of the Valley," his voice boomed. Echoes of his words bounded around us. "The gods awakened me in the night with a vision of their enemies' faces no more. Ash and charred skin replaced their blaspheming mouths."

Beside me, Leif's hands twitched into fists.

"We will cleanse your people with your lifeblood. In two weeks' time, when darkness falls and the moon consumes the sun, we will seal the souls of your innocents and cleanse the Valley with a mass sacrifice."

An eclipse was coming. The Prophets always knew when they'd come, but closely guarded the secret. This was really it. My entire life, visions of the eclipse and the Prophet had loomed over me. Visions of my blood pooling on the stage as I died. I could not leave my people behind like this. I wouldn't. I would save them.

Burning washed over my entire body, out of my control.

The ground beneath me darkened into wood planks. The dirt I stood upon looked like a layer beneath another. I shifted slowly into that place, caught between now and a future I'd long dreaded.

No! I had to stay here. As much as I wanted to escape, going there was even worse.

Fire that no one else would be able to see licked the tips of my fingers. The flames burned up my hands and over my arms. I winced in pain, holding back my scream.

The Prophet's inky eyes stared into mine here in his village and in the place that haunted me in my visions—the same eyes from two different times.

The village snapped back in place. No flames. No heat or pain. I was among my people once more. A gasp shuddered my shoulders. The terror of a death that had loomed over me since childhood clawed for the softest parts of my soul, sinking into flesh torn open time and time again. As swiftly as I'd slipped into the future, my mind drifted, the tightness in my body faded, the fear blurred, and I could hide so deeply within myself that no one would be able to see me. Not even myself. Couldn't think about it. Couldn't feel it.

But I could survive. I could survive anything, no matter how it shredded me.

My people needed me to stay strong.

"You will be a sacrifice to the gods," the Prophet said. "Then your people will go free." He ripped the rope down and the thick canvas fell to the ground in a wave.

There stood our people: the children, the elderly, the innocent. The young mother and her sons who lit the town lanterns every morning, the old man who loaded my bag with sweet bread when I went to train, the children—so many children—hiding beneath the arms of every adult. Our innocents stood with hands clasping one another, mouths closed obediently, tears shining against the red of the torchlight, though none of them dared utter a sound.

And sweet Rune, clinging to his daddy on the stage, staring at Leif beside me, silently begging for their family to be put back together again. Begging me to keep my promise to protect them, always.

Of all the lies I'd ever believed or told, this was the worst.

Tears blurred my view of them. Beside me, Leif leaned forward, as if physically drawn.

"Step out of line, and it will be your people who pay." The Prophet marched off the stage, abandoning us with his threat and our innocents out of reach.

Fire smoldered within me with nothing to burn except my tender insides.

I would kill him. No matter what it took.

It would be a slow, miserable death.

CHAPTER TWO

Shackles rang like temple bells. Four warriors knelt in a circle on the dusty ground in the cell across from mine, shaking their shackles as they chanted in prayer.

I wouldn't break it to them that the gods had never been concerned with our suffering, despite that their endless supplication woke me every time I dozed off.

"We have thirteen days left." Leif's gruff voice managed to soften the hardness of the dirt floor. "Just thirteen before we're sacrificed at the eclipse. No one wants to spend it listening to this."

He should leave them be. We were all terrified. I'd managed to numb myself to it while in this cell, like when I'd wash blood from my hands in the winter after a long battle. That was the most dangerous pain. The kind that was too damaging to even feel.

It was also when I fought best.

A draft crept in through tears in the thatched roof. I shivered. The jailhouse had cells lining both sides of a wide hallway. They'd separated our eighty warriors into groups of ten with guards posted in the hall. Except our cell was the only one with a guard inside. One who'd brought in a sharpening stone and a leather bag of weapons, and, yes, tended to swords while we sat only a few feet away. Our shackles were linked and anchored to the ground, so we couldn't get close enough to steal his weapons. Still, daring.

Our best were in our cell: the chief, her commanders, and her most trusted warriors. My two closest friends remained beside me. Leif and Wren. Some of the best warriors I knew. The Prophet may have been afraid to leave us alone without someone close enough to hear our whispers.

Chief Kaid spoke with us now, using a code I hoped the guard wouldn't decipher. It sounded as if she only speculated about why demons would work with the Prophet and how the gods would react. About what the holy ones on the Mountain of the Gods would do. The Prophet hadn't used his own power against us—one of the only limitations the gods placed upon these leaders who had their divine powers. But he'd indirectly done so by having the demons attack. Had he made a pact to stop hunting them if they became his shadow army? The Prophet *had* made such a public spectacle of executing all the demons he found.

Throughout the conversation, the chief's index finger twitched with each word she wanted us to pay attention to.

No moves tonight. We needed to plan. Needed to learn why the demons helped the Prophet and how many more there were. Should not give in to despair.

Normally, Leif would have been in the thick of the conversation, but he only stared blankly at the ceiling. I reached for him and then stopped. No comfort could ease wounds like this. It would be better to focus on making my own plans.

The Prophet of the Valley was the most powerful in Skia Hellig. Though the Fjellfolk of the mountain and the Flatlanders proclaimed their Prophets to be the greatest, all Helligeans feared Eskel the Ruthless more than any others. I only had one option: finally break this damn curse. Even with my power restored, the battle against the Prophet and his people seemed impossible. But I was not allowing my people to die here.

When the instructors, thought of as holy ones by the common man, sealed my power, they forbade me from returning to the Mountain of the Gods where I had trained. To step foot there would mean certain death, they said. The gods largely left our world to its own devices, but my instructors claimed they would intervene in situations such as this. The moment I reached the Mountain of the Gods, it was possible they would strike me dead. I hated that place anyway, and had no desire to return there. I'd been convinced I would find a way back to my power on my own.

But the mountain always had a way of energizing me. Over the years, the inklings of my power had grown, so that even though I could not wield it, I had managed to use trace amounts. The mountain could give me the boost I needed to push through this curse. If the gods tried to kill me, I would simply have to survive. What other option was there? I didn't have time to waste trying to find my power. I had to return to my past and face the curse head-on, even if it meant certain death. It would be better to die fighting for my people than at the hands of the Prophet in captivity.

After what I'd done back then, though, the instructors and the gods would surely do all they could to finish me. My banishment had been the only mercy they would extend. As long as I lived life as a normal warrior and kept all I knew secret, they would leave me be.

The Prophet of the Valley had defied the gods in his own way, though. It was possible the gods would allow me to fight for my people, considering the Prophet obviously had broken one of the only rules they bothered to give us. Prophets were not allowed to wield their power against those who had none. Were my sins really greater than his? But I wouldn't waste a moment hoping for the gods to care when they'd proven to me there was only one thing they actually cared about, and it definitely wasn't us. Not us, not truth, not right or wrong. They'd abandoned us with a power too great to handle, and a world of deceit. No, they would continue to do nothing but watch the chaos they'd created. Nothing, except maybe kill me for returning to the place forbidden to me.

This was on me. I had to find a way to escape. I had to survive the Mountain of the Gods and use its energy to reclaim what had been stolen. It would require careful planning. The Prophet had been clear about what would happen to our people if we acted up. Would the chief even accept me leaving? I'd kept my past a secret, and she'd honored that, making sure everyone else did, too, but this was different. She would never accept what I was. Who could?

Shackles clanked across the hall. I groaned.

"The gods heard you!" Leif roared. "The whole world heard you. They just don't care."

Enough of this.

I kicked the bars so they rang like the shackles. "Stop upsetting Leif."

Wren settled her hands against us both in a silent message to calm down.

The guard in our cell pried his attention from his blades long enough to glance at me. The subtle smirk on his face made my lip twitch. He should be scared, not amused.

"Idiot," I muttered. Though, I wondered if he was good in battle. He wore different clothes than the others, a light gray tunic that resembled what the Prophet's warriors wore beneath their armor. In fact, this could be the opportunity I needed. What better way to plan my escape than to elicit information from one of the Prophet's warriors? He could be valuable.

If his weapons were an indication, then I'd guess he was. The hilt of the sword he sharpened looked perfectly shaped for his hand. The blade flexed beneath a careful strike against the sharpening stone. That was no ordinary weapon. It must have been expensive and crafted for him. Yes, this man wasn't merely a guard, but a warrior. A warrior who'd proven worthy of such an investment. Mining operations were not advanced enough yet to yield all the resources we needed. That steel was precious. I had to try to get to know him.

The sword wasn't very large, though. I was one of the shorter women in Denstar and even I had a larger sword. Odd.

I studied his movements, trying to guess at his technique. Deft fingers gripped his weapon with the delicacy such a blade deserved. He was careful—and strong for having a slender, shorter weapon. Corded muscles wound up his long forearms, disappearing beneath rolled sleeves that were tight against his biceps.

I'd earned a second glance from him, which I figured was rare when he had a weapon in his hand. "Need something?" he asked.

Yes. Plenty, if he'd be willing to oblige. The Prophet's secrets for one. I rose to my knees. "Tell me about this blade."

A grin cracked his expression. He lowered the blade from the sharpening stone and truly looked at me. "That's what was on your mind?"

I twisted my brows. "What else would I want with you?"

My friend Wren snorted. Always ready for a laugh to help ease a crisis. The guard's grin grew.

"Ah." I blinked. He came into focus, not the warrior but the man.

"Ah," he mimicked with a wry smile twisting his full lips.

Dark brown wisps of hair fell over his forehead, as dark as the earth after a long rain. Noteworthy to some, but not nearly as much as his sword. Why should I be surprised at his arrogance when he was haughty enough to sharpen his blades in the same cell as ten of the Valley's best warriors?

I gave the guard a side-eye, with my arms crossed tightly. "You think too highly of yourself as a man. Your value is in that blade. Never forget that if you want to keep it in your hands."

"Who would take it from me?" His eyes fell down my dirty tunic. "You?"

I straightened. "Easily, if all you think about is your manliness."

"Hm . . . I take it you never let your womanliness distract you, not with all that mud twisted in your hair."

I touched the matted dark blond tangles atop my head that strained to break free of my bun. Oh, so the bastard wanted a fight?

But then a twitch of a smile cracked the heaviness of Leif's expression. I knew him well enough to feel it wasn't for the guard's teasing, but for the memory that rose to my mind as well. Rune always brushed my hair in the morning while Leif complained about what a mess it was.

I tried to focus on the guard who'd given me hope of befriending him. My body felt so heavy. "Why do you have a little sword like that?"

He reached into his bag and pulled out an identical weapon, crafted for his left hand. "It has a twin."

I edged closer, forgetting about the shackles until the chain tugged against my leg.

Leif sat up some. "You don't use a shield, boy?"

"I don't need one."

"I've never seen anyone use twin blades in battle," I said. "Only performance."

He turned to sharpen his sword again. "Trust me. These are for battle. It's a shame you've met my swords under these circumstances and not in the proper way or you would know."

"A terrible shame," I said, not as facetiously as it sounded.

"If there's hope for you yet, I'll put in a prayer with the gods."

"Don't bother. My fate has been sealed for as long as I can remember."

"Sounds like a sad tale."

"An angry one, really."

Sparks flew from his sword as it struck the stone. "Perhaps you'll find a way for it not to end here."

I looked for the other guards. Wasn't he worried they would hear? "You don't think I'm a heretic for rebelling against the Prophet?"

"We're all heretics. That isn't the reason some of us are chosen to die."

"What's your name?" I asked.

"Nash."

"Just Nash?"

"Nash the Unknown."

I let myself smile, grasping for the opening this guard had given me. "The unknown . . . Mysterious."

He sat back against the bars. "There's nothing very exciting behind the mystery." But his amber eyes told me otherwise.

"No one has to know it isn't mysterious," I said quietly.

"I'm sure *prisoner* isn't all you've ever been called. What's your name?"

"Max the Sharpshooter."

"Odd name for a girl."

I shrugged. "Max or Sharpshooter?"

He watched me for a moment, a slight smile hugging the corners of his lips. "Max."

"My father named me after his father."

"Is he the one who trained you?"

Warmth from my father's hands on a windy day flooded my palms like I'd slipped back to that time. His voice filled my ear, telling me to look up as he raised my hands to the black sun. Heat grew within me the darker the sun became, as if I'd stolen its rays myself. It was the first and last eclipse I'd seen, back when I lived in lands of mild winters and sweltering summers. The opposite of here. Even in the warmest times, it was still cold.

"My father trained me first, yes. Then I trained with others." I chewed the inside of my cheek.

Nash tilted his head. "Is your father alive? Or your mother?" He nodded at the others in the cell, settling on the chief, who I realized for the first time was watching me. "In here with you?"

I swallowed hard. Surely the chief would see the benefit of what I was doing. "No. Not alive or here. Yours?"

"I don't know. I'd like to think so."

I anchored my arms against my knees. "Nash the Unknown . . . You told me you weren't mysterious. Do you really want to get to know me with a lie?"

A curl fell over his left eye when he looked down. "I'd never lie to you, Sharpshooter. Not when you have a name like that."

"Wise." I plucked my invisible bow and closed one eye, aiming between his eyes. "Might be the last thing you ever do."

Nash's eyes lingered on mine, and I could feel Leif watching us. Could feel his pain. I needed to plan an escape, and getting to know this guard could help. But I'd enjoyed this conversation too much. It didn't feel right that I could feel such conflicted emotions at once. I wanted to retreat; only Leif and Wren were my circle. The people I'd have knelt and prayed with if any of us were the praying type. There wasn't much time. My death beneath the eclipse had been sealed long ago, and soon it would be upon us. I had to save them from sharing in my fate, no matter what.

And I'd start by using Nash the Unknown for my escape, considering he'd seemed eager to give me a warm welcome.

I just had to make sure I didn't enjoy talking to him. Had to remember that when the cold numbed my skin, damage often ran much deeper than I could feel.

CHAPTER THREE

U p!"

Leather boots kicked dust into my face. My comrades groaned at the soldiers rushing our cell, waking us from sleep. Except that I'd had another sleepless night of staring at the ceiling and nudging Wren every time she snored.

I rose onto stiff legs.

"What's this about?" Leif spat on the ground. "We don't die for another twelve days. Are you impatient?"

"Quiet," I whispered.

"Line up!" A soldier jerked my wrist closer and slapped a shackle on tightly. I dug my nails into my palms to keep from lashing out.

Soon they forced us all out of the jailhouse, taking only two groups of our best warriors.

Twilight met us outside, a navy sky splashed with constellations of beautiful white lights. This far north, the sun only truly set for a few hours in the summertime. I loved the midnight sun, but I'd even learned to enjoy the endless nights of winter. It reminded me of things I learned in our science classes at the Sacred School, and I never wanted to forget those truths when so few in my world had the privilege of knowing anything like that.

We continued down the path until we reached the courtyard where the Prophet had stood on the stage yesterday, mocking us with our families held captive behind him. There, he met us again, alone this time.

My skin crawled as I looked up into the face that haunted my nightmares and met me when time and space slipped between my fingers.

I searched for any sign of where they might have housed our innocents, but the entire village was foreign to me. Knowing Rune was somewhere within the village walls both comforted and tortured me. How must Leif have been feeling?

The Prophet's voice boomed like the night before. "The Flatlanders are staging an attack. If we lose, your innocents fall into their hands. You'll fight with us."

That was why they'd chosen a small but effective group of our warriors. Easier to control fewer people. Beside me, my comrades scoffed, shackles clanking as they threw up their hands. But I stayed still. This was an opportunity for me to escape and return home to the Mountain of the Gods for help. If I could convince anyone back there not to kill me, that was. Besides, we hated Flatlanders. They had tried to steal land from us for as long as anyone in the village could remember. I wouldn't mind killing a few of them while I scoped out my escape route.

"I'll have messengers on rotation every hour," the Prophet said. "Any negative report and I will slaughter ten of your innocents."

Brutal. I would need to fake my death in battle, then.

The guards led us behind the stage to a row of sheds. My eyes widened when I entered one and found our weapons stashed in a pile. My shield stood out near the back of the shed, its red emblem burning like fire.

Others shuffled forward in their bonds but I stayed put, turning possibilities in my mind. If I seemed hesitant to fight, falling in battle could be more believable, because I wouldn't be at my best.

"Take up your shield." A guard glared.

I clenched my fists, playing through scenarios in my mind. It seemed better if I pretended to not be willing to enter this battle. Why let anyone know what I was thinking?

Rough hands grabbed my wrists. "Take your shield, woman! Your spear!"

I slammed my bound hands against him. "Why should I fight for my enemies?"

Nash entered beside me, a spear in each hand. "An enemy of your enemy is not your friend in this Valley." He held one out to me. "Fight for your fellow prisoners, not us."

Our gazes met as I wrestled internally with turning the spear on the man near me and fighting for my people to escape now. A foolish impulse.

Without my power, the Prophet would use his to kill me in a second. I knew that. Still, it tempted me.

"Will I fight in bonds?"

Nash took my wrist and lifted my hands between us, hesitating once he'd pushed the key into the lock. "The Prophet is not a forgiving or patient man. Promise me that you'll be wise when I release you."

"Why do you care?"

No answer. He unlocked the shackles and peeled the coarse metal from my tender skin.

Quickly, I turned for my shield and then found the familiar hard leather of my armor, fingers gliding down to the stitching from Leif's repairs over our last training session. Finally, I'd feel like myself again. I pulled it over my tunic and sighed.

"Where's my bow?" I asked the guards when I walked outside.

"You won't need it," a guard said.

"If you want to live, I do."

"Give it to her," Nash said.

The guard groaned and stepped into another shed, beckoning me. Nash must have held some sway to get the man to listen to him. I'd picked a good person to get to know.

I entered the shed and my breath caught. There it was. The beautiful smooth arch of the bow that had saved my ass more times than I could count. It had been thrown carelessly on the ground with dozens of other bows. I could take out a lot of these fools with this.

We gathered outside before the stage where some of the Prophet's warriors now talked in groups. Others were joining us, outnumbering us five to one, and that wasn't counting the guards. Several warriors gathered my people into groups of five and gave us cloth bags with the most basic of supplies. Water, bandages, a small sharpening stone. A guard lit lanterns that circled the courtyard. The Prophet must have needed to spare electricity. The show from the night before may have been a special event meant to intimidate us.

Foolishly, a warrior separated me from Wren and Leif. They might have thought it would make us easier to manage, but it only weakened their war party to jumble our usual formations.

"This is your squad for the battle." The woman was tall, taller than many of the men in the courtyard. "Stay together and follow my lead. I'll be your commander."

As she spoke, a feeling came over me, similar to the sensation of being stared at, only much more intense.

I straightened. Felt her before I saw her or heard her. The haze of power emanated from the temple like heat from a raging fire. It called out to the dormant power trapped within me so I thirsted for it like a woman dying of dehydration. Still, it was a mere pinprick of what I'd felt when our village was attacked.

"A demon!" warriors and guards alike shouted.

Judging by everyone's surprise, I knew the Prophet had not let people in on the secret of his little shadow army. He'd kept his use of demons quiet. I twisted, not bothering to take out my weapons like most of my comrades did. She darted across tree limbs in a flash.

"Don't stand there!" One of the Prophet's warriors pointed. "Subdue her!"

Daring if she wasn't supposed to show her face. The Prophet clearly didn't want his cooperation with demons to be public knowledge.

The torch flames erupted, spewing smoke into the night sky. The guards cried out and aimed their weapons aimlessly, trying to follow the rustle of leaves.

Chief Kaid held up her hand, signaling for our warriors not to engage. I swallowed hard.

The woman they called demon leapt into view, jumping from branch to branch, gracefully bouncing on the balls of her feet. Leaves rattled behind her like maracas. As she circled the courtyard, the smoke danced with her motions, swirling about us.

A harmless trick. Enough to frighten and distract. Demons needed their tricks around the Prophet, though. People said the gods gave power to the Prophets and the demons stole it for themselves. In reality, they were both the same. They both had been given the technology at birth to use their powers. The only difference was who the world accepted and who the world rejected. Prophets trained at the Sacred School and were honored. Demons were outcasts. The gap in power came from Prophets having the best training. That was all.

Nash called out from the center of the courtyard. "Ignore her. She's harmless." He looked through the cloud of smoke with a steady stare. It said a lot about a person to see them react to power. He was more experienced than a common warrior. And the others listened to him, warily looking at one another as they lowered their weapons.

Had he been involved with the demons who captured my people? Hate coiled around my heart. This woman might have been at the village during the attack. And what about Nash?

He waved his hand at her. "Come down before the arrows start to fly."

The leaves clashed. She jumped from the branch and flipped on her way down, landing on her fingertips and toes like a cat. Smoke rose from her as if something deep within her burned. And when I looked at her dusty ash eyes, so deeply red as to verge on black, I thought something really might be.

She waltzed to Nash, clearing the air between them with a flick of her hand. Anger flashed in her eyes and rippled to the torches that beat like a heart.

With the attention on her, I eased closer to Nash, not wanting to miss any exchange between them.

A snarl curled her lips. "I'm not here to play with you, Nash."

"Sure." He tilted his head. "This isn't you playing."

"I hadn't even noticed you were here."

"I told you not to make a scene again. The Prophet won't be happy."

Her gaze wandered down him, her lips forming a pout. "You'll take care of him for me, won't you?"

I raised my brows.

Nash shook his head. "What are you up to?"

"I heard about all the fun you're about to have with the Flatlanders and your captives. Couldn't miss it."

If the Prophet wanted her to be discreet, why had she put on this big show?

"This is taking it too far, Flare. We can talk in private."

She backed away. "Well, I'm really not here for you. Calm down."

When Flare turned, her eyes locked on mine through the gaps in the crowd. The flames of her stare burned through me. A little smirk crossed her face. My heart froze.

Then she moved on, waltzing straight through the smoke toward the temple.

I couldn't move. Did she know who I was? What I was? Was that why she'd put on this big performance? She wanted to get my attention. Tell me I couldn't hide, even. Maybe it was a threat to reveal the truth about me. Or she was calling me weak for not having my power when she pranced about openly using hers.

I wouldn't let her insult me, much less threaten me. "Calm down," I whispered to myself, touching my chest. My thoughts swam. I had to find out more about her, immediately.

Huffing, I cut through the last of the crowd for Nash. He watched Flare as she ascended the temple stairs.

"You have interesting friends," I said, struggling to keep my voice calm. Alienating him wouldn't benefit me.

"She stops by from time to time, usually in the shadows."

"The Prophet rendezvousing with a demon. Imagine that."

"Officially, the Prophet executes every demon he gets his hands on." Nash lowered his voice. "But he shows mercy to our spies."

Anger rose within me. Of course. The demons were his spies. If they were adept at suppressing their power, they would be able to hide among normal people like me. They could be anywhere. No telling how long they had been doing this work for the Prophet. That didn't explain why Flare was flaunting her presence, though. "Doesn't seem like a good idea to make the boss mad."

"Flare is unpredictable."

He knew more. I could see it in his eyes. He understood why she would do something that seemed to make no sense.

I narrowed my eyes at Nash. A woman with power who worked for a demon-hunting Prophet was about as low as a person could get on my list. And Nash seemed to be the only one in the courtyard who knew Flare. He was involved in the Prophet's shady dealings somehow. Maybe even helped capture my people.

This man was dangerous.

"Unknown," I said, voice as icy as Flare was bright.

His gaze turned serious, full attention on me.

"Don't play games with a Sharpshooter." I eased closer so the others wouldn't hear my threat. "There's nothing more dangerous you could do."

"I already told you." He leaned in, too, voice so quiet I could hardly hear him. "I know better than to lie to you."

"What you should know is I'm not easy prey." My lips curled in anger. "I'm the fucking hunter."

"That's what I'm counting on."

What was that supposed to mean?

I backed away, eyes narrowed to slits. I felt trapped.

Flare hadn't picked me out of the crowd by accident. She saw through me. What I was choosing to hold back. Nash saw something in me, too.

What if they both knew my secret? My plan felt impossible as it was. Failure wasn't an option. I couldn't let the Prophet kill our innocents.

Heat flashed through my palms. Had to calm down. Had to before I slipped. The air around me turned cooler, thinner, like a fall day back on the mountain. My breathing came in short spurts. The harder I tried to catch myself, the more I lost myself.

Hands gripped my shoulders. A voice in my ear. Leif. "Lean on me." He held me up. "You're having another spell. It's okay, Max. I'm here."

What if I slipped to the eclipse again? A timeless, inescapable prison.

The heat zipped down my spine and Leif slipped through my fingers. It all slipped through my fingers. The Prophet's village melted from my sight and then my memory.

I stood outside my dorm in the Sacred School on the Mountain of the Gods.

CHAPTER FOUR

One day, I would leave this place and never look back. I picked at the gunky residue on my temple from the electrodes. My head ached from the solid hour the technicians made me spend pushing rocks through obstacle courses with my mind. The harsh lights in the all-white testing room made it hard to focus. At least I was done for the weekend.

I walked past the door to my dorm and continued to the glass door at the end of the hall, trailing my fingers along the pale blue wall. The color was supposed to make it feel like a home. Like children lived here. None of us had been children for a long time. As much as I hated the all-white room, I preferred its bright walls to this lie.

I'd been here since Dad died. Almost five years already. I'd sworn I'd make it out by now.

One day . . .

I sighed and walked out into the courtyard.

"Up here!"

Piercey. I bit down my smile and looked up to the tree branch where he sat twenty feet up.

"What are you waiting for?" he asked.

I looked at the trunk. No low branches to climb. "I'm tired. They had me doing puzzles today."

"Ch-ch-chicken."

I jolted forward, focused the warmth inside me on the muscles in my legs. I jumped higher than I expected and faltered when my foot hit the trunk. I crashed to the ground. "Ouch . . ."

"Weak," Piercey said. "You can do better than that, Max."

I tried again but didn't make it halfway to where I had before. On my third try, I kicked off the tree and grazed the closest branch with my fingers.

"Come on!" I ran for the tree, jumped, kicked off, and caught the branch with both hands this time. Grinning, I focused on my arms and heightened my natural strength as I pulled myself up.

Piercey caught my arm to help me the rest of the way. "I was starting to worry you wouldn't make it."

"Is this your sly way of telling me I need to train more before Monday?"

"Not sure it's sly, but yeah." He nudged me with his elbow. "We can't win our competition without you. You must be ready. If our class wins, we get out of cleaning duty for a month."

"What about you? Why does it all have to be on my shoulders?"

Piercey rolled his eyes. "You know why. You just want to hear me say it."

I grinned and wiggled my legs dangling off the branch. "Come on."

A side-eyed glance and then he muttered the words. "You're better at combat than me."

"That's right, I am." I patted his back. "But you're basically a healing prodigy, so don't feel too bad."

"Gods. Your ego . . ." He took an apple from his pocket. "Saved one for you. It's the sweet kind. Not the nasty ones that taste like nothing."

"Cool." Juice pooled in my mouth when I bit into it. "Mmm."

"If the instructors hear you picking up slang from your shows, they won't let you watch them."

"The instructors can kiss my ass."

He sighed. "You should stop watching so much TV and train more." His voice quieted. "I'm tired of seeing you get hurt."

"Please. The better we get, the more pain they throw at us. Besides, I love to train. I get sick of doing it alone."

"Well, you're in luck, because I'm ready to be your partner today." Piercey pulled his bag off his back and took out his tablet.

I squirmed. "No. I said I would train, not study."

"Studying is training. You won't get good with heights until you understand the concept enough to manipulate it. Like what we were learning about gravity—"

I crossed my arms. "I'm not in the mood to play school. I'm sick of the instructors cramming their shit down our throats."

"You're talented. Smart. There's no reason you can't do this. You just don't want to take anything from the gods, even their knowledge."

I wanted to say that I'd take any resources from the gods if he would agree to escape with me. Piercey had been here two years longer than me. He should have been breaking the walls down. The mountain guard had killed everyone who ever tried to leave without approval. Piercey had panic attacks just talking about it. He didn't see that together, we could do anything.

"They're not gods, Piercey."

"This again."

The words burned on my lips. I wanted to plead with him to leave. Sure, we all ended up here for a reason. Our power had hurt people and we needed help controlling it. But they weren't controlling our power. They were controlling us. I didn't think I would like who they wanted me to become.

Resentment sharpened my voice. "They abandoned our world while they live in a utopia. So, no, I don't want the scraps they toss at us. I don't want to pay the price that comes with it. I'm my own person." I smacked my chest. "Mine. I don't belong to them."

Piercey tapped the base of my skull. "Your implant does."

My nostrils flared. "Watch yourself, Piercey."

"This power isn't magic, Max. It's science. You're wasting your potential if you refuse to study, whatever your reasons are. It's a shame to not become all you could be out of spite."

"Send the stupid research to me if it'll shut you up."

His voice was quiet now. Hurt. "I want to help, Max."

"I didn't ask for it." I met his eyes. "But you're still by far the best person on this mountain. Okay?"

He chewed his lip.

"Piercey, come on." I poked his ribs. "I'm sorry."

He swatted me away, but I poked him again.

"Let me see." I grabbed the tablet from him. "Quantum mechanics and the conscious mind . . . A key to the potential of the neural implant." I lowered it. "I'm falling asleep already."

"Keep reading. This one is good. It talks about how consciousness can affect particles in the superimposed state, and how we can even manipulate gravity with our implant. That's your problem. You strengthen your muscles, but you need to learn how to bend gravity to your will instead."

"I'll read it and practice. I promise."

He smiled but it looked tense. "You know, Max, I'm sucking this place dry for everything I can learn. It pisses me off that it'll be me soaring past you one day, when you could get there twice as easily."

I hated losing. Normally the suggestion would enrage me; only Piercey was different. He didn't see it, but he was better at fighting the gods, even though I wanted it more. I settled my hand on his knee, my voice soft. "You're more than you see. You deserve it more than I do."

His eyes fell to my hand. I tensed inside. It didn't happen often, but sometimes the way he looked at me changed. Normally, it started like this. A touch. Getting too close. Why did I do it when I wasn't sure how I felt about the look that followed? I started to shift away from him when dizziness nearly knocked me from the tree. I grabbed Piercey for balance.

Everything around me flashed to twilight. I gasped, my eyes opening wide. It was night. Night even though it'd been day. A crowd surrounded me, dressed for battle, and a man held me tight.

Pain exploded through my arm and my back. Lights flashed.

Blue sky opened over my head like someone had turned the sun back on. I was lying on the ground in the courtyard.

"Max . . ." Piercey pushed my hair back, eyes wide. "Say something."

"I'm okay . . ." I groaned and looked at my crooked arm. "But I think I broke something."

"I'll take you to get healed."

"Kelvin is going to be so mad. He healed me last week."

"It's okay." Piercey carefully helped me to sit up, supporting my arm. "I've got you, Max."

"I slipped again."

"I saw," he said.

"No . . . like, I was in a different place again. A different time. A courtyard somewhere. I can't remember the rest."

"You need to talk to Kelvin about this. I haven't heard of that happening to someone before."

I shook my head. "Don't say anything. Please."

"Your power is messing with time and space. Doesn't that scare you?"

"Everything scares me." I looked down at my arm. "I've been scared so much in my life; I can't feel it anymore."

A film fell over my world, thickening until the grass beneath me faded to stone. Again, already? I tried to hold on to the world around me, but I couldn't grasp it. Piercey's arms blurred into those of the man; his voice mingled with the other.

"Max." Both of them spoke at once. The boy and the man. Piercey and . . .

"Leif?" I touched my head. My world came crashing back down.

"It's okay." He kissed the top of my head. "You were only out for a minute. Our people covered you."

It'd been a long time since I'd slipped like that. An even longer time since I'd gone back to the mountain. At least I hadn't traveled to any of the bad times there. Every time I traveled there, the feeling of unrealness would linger with me and I had to remind myself that even though nothing in my world was as it seemed, we still mattered. I normally managed to not think about it and would have to fight it off now.

This wasn't good.

"I haven't had one in nearly a year . . ." My skin tingled with pain. The time slips always burned so badly. I squeezed my eyes shut. "My medicine. I haven't thought about it once."

"That's because you only think of others. Never yourself." Leif's voice was hard, but his expression, his eyes, couldn't have been softer.

"We should have thought of it for you," Wren said. "It got left behind when we were captured, didn't it?"

I nodded. "I didn't realize I felt this bad. I was pushing it off."

Wren took my hand, lacing her fingers with mine, her presence as loud as Leif's tendency to shout at me when he wanted to help me.

I hated this weakness of mine. I drew back from them, my arm still aching from the living memory of breaking it. "If I stay calm, it won't happen."

"It's okay, Max. We're with you."

I glanced around. That couldn't happen again. Not with that demon picking me out of the crowd. I breathed in deeply and relaxed my muscles, willing calm into my body.

CHAPTER FIVE

The Prophet's horses kicked up a cloud of dust as scouts took off to survey the battlefield. They'd chosen a massive field half a day's ride from the nearest village. From here, the distant mountains loomed over the Valley from all sides. The tallest peak looked like clouds swelling on the horizon, frosted white against the blue sky.

Leif and Wren stood on either side of me, ready to catch me if I had another slip. The spell hadn't lasted long the night before, and I'd told them I was fine. But they didn't listen. Truth was, I wasn't. The longer I went without my medicine, the worse this would get.

When my anxiety was treated, I felt unbreakable. That assurance was just who I was. Without my medicine, my thoughts slipped from my control. Made me shaky inside, like I wasn't even myself. Piercey had created the treatment back in the Sacred School after he'd studied anxiety. The day I'd escaped, he whispered to me to check the massive hollow of our tree, the one just outside the barrier of the Mountain of the Gods. He whispered it as I begged him to come with me and he promised to always love me.

Every year I found the bags of pills waiting for me. It was how I knew he was still alive. Still on the mountain. Still keeping his promise to love me. I'd never asked for any promises from him, but then, I hadn't asked Leif or Wren either. If Piercey had escaped with me, he would be a part of our circle, too. He was still in my heart.

The hurt tingled in my chest.

Leif drew his sword and inspected it. "This is not the blood my sword thirsts for." He snarled as his eyes tracked the Prophet's people mingling with us as if we were one and the same.

"Don't think about it," Wren said.

I took a tin of black war paint from the pouch on my side and brushed it beneath Leif's eyes like I did before every battle. When I clasped his shoulder and pressed my forearm to his chest, he grabbed my wrist. Settled his forehead against mine.

"My flesh," I said.

"My blood."

I smacked his chest. "This is for Rune and Arn. Remember that."

His eyes misted and tears thickened his voice, but he still roared his words as he always did before battle. "Give them hell, Sharpshooter."

We both shouted as we pushed away, knocking against our group of twenty warriors. They all joined in, our cries ringing out, swallowing the sounds of galloping hooves and the warriors preparing for battle. We belonged to one another, the same flesh and blood, because that was what we'd vowed to one another.

I clasped the head of one of our commanders, Beast. "My blood!"

He held my forearm against himself. "My flesh!"

Wheeling around, I raised my fist and thrust my arm against a hard chest. "My—"

Nash stared into my eyes, war paint absent from beneath his eyes. My people were the only ones left in the Valley who still donned it from the days before the Prophet had conquered the Valley.

I drew back.

"My blade is yours today." He cast a look over our small group. "All of yours." His eyes paused on Chief Kaid's and then turned to mine.

My comrades watched Nash silently. We couldn't be fooled by his well-wishes. Still, I raised my shield in response. If there was any chance I could get him on my side, I'd take that victory, no matter how sick I felt from the worry that he might have helped capture my people. It was only all the more reason to pull him close.

He grinned, drawing both his blades. The sun glinted from his armored forearms.

We moved into formation and I was thankful to have distance from Nash. Hot sun baked the sweat into my neck as I waited. I glanced behind me to the Mountain of the Gods. Piercey would have been training for nearly a decade without me. And he was so smart. If I could survive the journey and find him, he would help figure out how to unlock this power. I had to make it there.

I'd shared my idea for escape with Leif and Wren. They'd tried to talk me out of it, but we'd worked out a plan to make sure some of the Prophet's warriors saw me fall in battle. Leif would take my bow as evidence, because everyone knew I'd never give it up. And I'd escape while the battle still raged.

It still felt risky. What if the Prophet suspected me and killed someone in retaliation?

I didn't have long to dwell on the worry. The battle began like an eruption from a volcano. The Flatlanders moved first, sprinting at us with weapons raised, bodies bounding forward like the waves of the sea. The first shot of energy jolted through my limbs as I tensed my muscles. My body moved on instinct, no longer stiff with worry, but lithe with the hunger of battle.

I sprang toward the enemy alongside our warriors and the Prophet's alike.

I ducked beneath a swinging sword. Stabbed my spear into the groin of the man attacking and ripped it free.

I rushed past before he'd even collapsed, continuing to attack with ferocity, forgetting about everything except each slash, each clash, each thrust of my weapon. Blood soaked through my boots. Streaked my arms. Pooled at the nape of my neck.

I needed to act soon. The battle had sufficiently distracted everyone, so I worked my way toward Wren, veering away from my group steadily enough that it didn't look purposeful. It would be easy to claim I'd gotten caught up in the fighting as I took on one enemy after the next.

I was nearly to Wren as she kicked a Flatlander down and stabbed his side. That was when I saw him. Nash slicing his twin blades in opposite directions, severing a head from its neck. He used the momentum to follow through with his swings, slicing through an arm on the left and across a back on the right. Beautiful. He fought with grace, not wasting a single motion.

Nash was deep in the enemy's swarm with no one to watch his back. His comrades must have fallen as they pushed through. Was he so arrogant as to be this careless with his life? Or too ambitious for his own good?

I sidestepped a Flatlander and ducked beneath a wayward swing from a young enemy warrior, whose round eyes made him look driven more by panic than strategy. I skidded to a stop beside Nash and jabbed at one of his attackers, forcing her attention onto me.

Only then did my mind catch up with my body. Should I have come to Nash's aid when he could end up being a terrible enemy? What if he had worked with the demons to attack us? No second-guessing myself. In battle I had to listen to my instincts and they'd driven me to Nash's side. Enemy or not, he seemed useful.

Another Flatlander swooped low with his sword, but Nash stomped the blade into the ground and simultaneously sliced open his neck. I bashed my shield into my opponent's face in a spray of blood and rammed my sword deep into her exposed gut.

"Thank you." Nash pivoted on his heel and pressed his back against mine. "What's your plan?"

We turned in a slow circle as one, eyeing Flatlanders whose stares locked on us. "Kill the Flatlanders, obviously."

"No." Nash parried an attack, issued a clean strike across a man's throat, and knocked back against me. "To escape."

My breath caught at Nash's question. At the same time, a Flatlander stumbled back from a hit she'd deflected several feet away and spun around to face me. I ripped my dagger from my side and planted it against Nash's right kidney between our backs, all while I slashed for the woman in front of me.

Nash didn't turn, but I heard his breathing slow.

Keeping my blade on him, I kicked the warrior in her gut when she clumsily attacked. Her body slammed back into the blade of her first opponent.

I gritted my teeth. "I warned you—"

"I couldn't tell you with so many listening. The Prophet wants the head of any captive who falls in battle to prove you didn't flee. Be smart."

I withdrew my knife from his back. How did he know what I planned to do? It was a desperate, obvious plan, wasn't it? One that I couldn't chance now that Nash suspected it. I'd have to find another way.

Two Flatlanders wearing helmets with black feathers pushed through their comrades for us. Another with a red feather approached from further back. We'd been noticed. Must have been commanders coming to deal with us.

"You're warning me?" I asked.

The closest officer sprinted for us, sword raised above her head.

"I'm not who you think I am." Nash ripped his blades up.

"We'll see."

I dropped my weapon and shield.

Whipped out my bow and nocked an arrow in one fluid motion.

The commander reared back for a long, full stab of her blade. But I trusted Nash's blades and I aimed my arrow for the Flatlander charging right behind the commander.

Nash slammed both his swords down against hers and knocked her weapon free of her grip. My arrow shot through the open mouth of the unsuspecting man. As Nash wrenched his swords back up, I'd already nocked another arrow, and we followed through at the same time.

Nash's blades thrust through the officer's diaphragm.

My arrow pierced a Flatlander's throat.

Nash defended against the Flatlanders closest to us, while I shot for those who had turned toward us. Though I'd lost my power, I'd worked to salvage the inklings of it that could come by instinct. I unleashed two arrows at once, guiding them with my will as much as my aim.

Footsteps behind me. I threw myself to the ground, rolled off my shoulder, rose back up with my shield, and ducked entirely behind it. Even with my whole body propping up my defense, the whack of the sword drove me onto my ass. I rolled with the momentum and came up on my feet, batting away another hit with my shield.

Nash rushed for my attacker, but I'd grabbed my sword and I deflected the next hit, leaving the man open. We both stabbed him at the same time.

The red-feathered commander pushed a young warrior aside and hefted his battle-ax, eyes shifting between Nash and me. With his other hand, he lifted a large spear and threw it through the air.

Nash slashed it in half and pivoted for the last commander. I shifted onto my toes. Two Flatlanders sprinted from behind him and drove their blades for Nash.

The ax flashed in a glint of the sun. I ducked and jumped backward.

More Flatlanders surrounded us. The fear of it only sharpened my senses as I dodged another blow.

"Max!" Wren burst out in front of me and swung for one of the Flatlanders nearby, protecting me so I could focus on this opponent. Leif was close behind, taking down Flatlanders on his way to us.

No time to check on Nash. I had to hope he was holding up okay.

I parried a hit, but just barely. This man was good.

The red-feathered commander drilled into my eyes with a glare. "You're Denstar."

"Yeah, and you're fucked." I swung with both hands on my blade for the extra muscle and knocked his ax down an inch.

An amused smirk twisted his face. "What coward fights for Eskel the Ruthless?"

Heat flushed my cheeks. My gut. "Can't pass up the chance to kill Flatlanders." I feigned a slash and slid on my knees, catching his thigh with the tip of my sword when he dodged.

"Die a coward's death," the commander cried. He bore down with both hands on his ax.

I didn't dodge. Didn't block. Just stuck my blade through his elbow, twisted, and sent the ax barreling into the ground beside me. The handle grazed my shoulder.

My heart pounded as I jumped to my feet and sliced his head clean from his shoulders. Blood pooled around the red feather. I caught my breath and checked on Wren and Leif as they fought three Flatlanders. More of my people had pushed in to form a perimeter around us. I twisted further, searching for Nash, and noticed his distinct curls in the distance. There he was, outside of the area my people had cleared, taking on two Flatlanders at once. Nash's blades danced so elegantly that his fighting looked choreographed.

Nash thrust his blade behind his head and caught an attack. He struck the hilt of the other's sword with his right sword. Swiftly, he lunged forward, twisted his wrist to lock his sword against the warrior's handle and threw his weight against it, breaking the man's guard. He'd already swung his other blade back up to deflect another hit from the woman behind him.

He was midtwist, slinging his right sword up from a low position and his left over his head, behind himself, when both weapons embedded into flesh. The Flatlanders slid off his blades and onto the ground.

I slowed, having just reached him.

Sweat dripped down the side of his face.

"Are you hurt?" Nash asked, glancing down my form.

"No." I nodded at his bloodied swords. "Just watching the show."

He wiped his forehead with the crook of his arm, his amber eyes almost golden in the sun. "You put on a nice show of your own. And you had my back." Nash pulled a cloth from his pocket and offered it to me. "I owe you."

"Be more careful. You're good, but still mortal." I took the cloth and cleaned my bow, only considering once it was too late that it might have been meant for my face. Touching my cheek, I realized I was covered in mud and splatters of blood. Nash's eyes were on me, a smile on his face in a definite sign that he'd noticed.

My cheeks warmed. I chuckled and wiped my face next.

"I'll be marginally less conceited." He shrugged. "If you start caring for yourself as much as your bow."

I forced down my smirk and backed away.

I needed to tell Leif and Wren about my change in plans. Mostly, I needed some distance. We had only moments before we would need to battle again.

We battled hard together, pushing through until we reached the back of the enemy forces. There I peppered the enemy with my arrows. By the time the Flatlanders figured out what we were doing, it didn't matter. We'd gained too much ground. My arms felt too heavy to even lift, and yet I fought on fiercely until I had to search for another warrior to kill.

"It's over." Leif nodded at the forest where the last of the Flatlanders escaped into the trees. "We won."

The thrill swept through me in a wave of energy. I thrust my blade in the air and roared from my depths, a cry that swelled in my stomach and my chest in pressure. Leif caught my wrist and cried out with me. We fell back, laughing as we lowered our weapons.

It wasn't that we didn't care about the people dead at our feet. Blood mixed with dirt into a gelatinous paste that sucked at our boots, refusing to release us from the battlefield. With each step, we broke free, and that was something to celebrate. We would live another day. Having so precious few left only made me want to roar again. The rest—the sorrow, the guilt, the questioning—could wait until later.

I gathered with my circle beyond the battlefield where the grass was still green and untrampled. The young attended to us as if we were also the Prophet's own warriors. Leif took a basin of water from one of the boys and carried it to our group.

I wet a rag when the grass crunched behind me.

"Any injuries?" a familiar voice asked.

I turned, cleaning the blood from the nape of my neck. Nash stood before me, sweat glistening over his bare chest, dark with dirt and streaks of blood. From what I'd seen, it all belonged to the enemy.

"We're fine," I said, and angled away to avert my eyes. "You?"

"Same."

It was nothing to see a man without his armor or shirt. I'd spent countless days and nights after battle with the men stripping down to nothing. It was so commonplace as to not notice—so noticing now made me burn with embarrassment.

Nash turned to grab a washcloth from the basin of water and I noticed a flesh-colored tattoo weaving down the length of his spine that looked like scars. It was a script. Beautiful letters twisting and climbing up his back like vines. He turned back around before I could figure out what it said.

Leif threw his tunic off onto the armor he'd discarded on the ground, completely naked, as was his habit given his hatred for undershorts. He washed himself with his damp cloth, apparently without an ounce of self-consciousness in front of mixed company. Of course, Nash probably didn't think a thing about it. I wasn't sure why I *was*.

"You fight like a damn demon." Leif looked over my shoulder to Nash. "Never thought I'd say something like that to one of you, but I have to admit it."

Nash took a cloth from the basin on the ground and cleaned his face. "If I fight like a demon, then you fight like one of the gods down here among us."

Leif grinned now and lifted his leg to wash his thigh. "And what would that make Max?"

Nash eyed me. "How is it I haven't heard of you before?"

"Maxy takes great care not to become a legend. She'll let everyone take credit for her." Leif straightened and rolled his neck. "But make no mistake. She's the best of us."

Nash nodded at me. "Sharpshooter. Better than a god or a demon."

It was dangerous talk. This talk of demons and gods. Of things I'd tried to leave behind—had to leave behind.

The past tugged at me in a burn at my fingertips. The Mountain of the Gods seemed to swell in size. I couldn't slip.

"I'm just a warrior." I threw my rag down into the water basin. "Like everyone else."

CHAPTER SIX

The sun set on us drinking with the Prophet's warriors, though it had risen with them guarding us. Tonight, we were all free. All comrades. We'd bled together and that meant something around here.

We'd returned to camp where rows of tents formed a circle around the common area. The cooks had set up tables with fruits and cheeses and even some dried meats. Most importantly, they'd brought plenty of barrels of ale, which had drawn everyone out to mingle, whether they were our people or the Prophet's. I grazed the sampling, picking a handful of berries from a wide wooden bowl.

The sun fell into a blanket of soft pink clouds beside the Mountain of the Gods. Over the years, I'd managed to forget that I didn't belong in this Valley. I belonged on that mountain that loomed over us. Belonged to the place I hated most. My people now paid for the lie I'd told myself, because I hadn't done everything I could to defeat the Prophet.

But tonight there was drink and my wrists were free. Why waste an evening of peace ruminating on thoughts like these? On the coldest nights of winter, we never would shun warmth. I scooped my mug into the barrel and sighed after drinking. Much better.

Plucking the tie from my dark blond hair, I loosened my braid, my freshly washed locks like silk between my fingers. One of the Prophet's warriors had given me a flowing white dress that hugged my waist and loosely clung to my shoulders. I'd earned that gift, apparently, after so many witnessed how I fought. Another reason it would be hard to escape.

Joy I had no business feeling bubbled inside me. Perhaps because my mind couldn't grasp that I had mere days left to live. Every hour felt as the ones before it had: passing. A tiny sliver I could redo again and again.

I scooped another mugful of ale and found Leif and Wren lounging on the ground with a group of our people. Their cheeks looked warm from the drinking, and the loudness of their voices told me they'd had quite the head start on me. I would have to catch up.

I wedged between the two of them and breathed in deeply. It seemed strange that we could drink while our people were held captive. Perhaps we knew that the Prophet's people were watching and that they would see strength in our camaraderie. They would know we weren't easily broken and it was a mistake to take us on. It was that way for Leif, at least. He would never show the enemy an ounce of sorrow or fear. Only wrath or rebellious joy in the face of devastation.

I took his hand and squeezed it tight.

Nothing needed to be said. We'd slept under the same roof for years. Leif would know that I'd just made him a promise, one to protect him and his son and his husband. That our freedom tonight filled me with joy and dread simultaneously, because I had no idea how I'd escape. We no longer needed words. He was my brother. Not the kind born of the same blood, but the kind reborn in it.

Leif shook me. "Max the Sharpshooter! She saved all your asses today. You know it's true." He belted life into our group, into me. He was distracting himself and the rest of us, and I could only be thankful.

Beast smacked me on the back so hard it felt like my bones buzzed. "She almost killed as many Flatlanders as me."

I rolled my eyes.

We recounted the battle, our words twisting more into fantasy than truth. Chief Kaid listened, quiet, but smiling in that strained way of hers that told us she'd hold the pain for us so we could enjoy the night.

I was hanging back to watch the group for a moment when I heard Nash's voice right behind me. "I hardly recognized you."

Turning, I managed a smile. "Who could blame you? I've been wearing dirt like a second skin."

"You did have hair beneath that mud." Nash snagged a strand, his gaze lingering long enough to elicit the sharp patter in my chest.

"You have a way with your insults."

He shrugged. "Maybe I like you in your second skin."

As dangerous as Nash was in battle, he was even more dangerous like this, all cleaned up with his curls full and framing his face just right, his smirk making him look more self-assured than most people had any business being. I nearly retreated on instinct. Was he trying to manipulate me? I would sooner die.

Leif stepped away from his conversation to head for me when Beast, juggling an armful of mugs with frothy ale that sloshed over the top, stopped right in front of him. Just as Leif tried to step around him, I saw his eyes shift to the left. Chief Kaid shook her head in disapproval. Worry clouded Leif's eyes as his jaw noticeably stiffened.

Nash nodded at the barrels of ale. "Want to get drunk, Sharpshooter?"

Chief Kaid had turned her gaze to me. She was giving me approval to befriend Nash, showing me she trusted me, needed me. Leif didn't want me to get hurt, but he should have trusted me, like the chief did.

With my focus on Nash again, I hardened my resolve. This man was my enemy and he could try to manipulate me all he wanted. I'd get to him first. "I really do."

On our way to the center of camp, I quickly glanced down at myself and sucked in my stomach. It didn't take very much for me to pack on muscle or fat. And I always had both, no matter how much I trained. I'd never been thin like Wren. Her long, graceful body looked built for dancing. I always thought I must have been born for war. Some men liked my curves. Some liked Wren's long and elegant line. I wasn't sure what Nash liked. Whether he was feigning interest in me to gain information or if he was different from the Prophet like he claimed.

Half a mug later, I had to remind myself to be worried about it.

"Your sword technique is beautiful," I said. "I'd kill to face off against you."

"Is battle all you think of?"

"I guess you're still thinking only of your manliness."

He ran his hand over his mouth, grin wide. "Such a ruthless woman. But I would love to shoot like you. I've spent so much time on sword-fighting. I need to work on other skills."

"Well." I settled my mug on my lap. "If you teach me a thing or two about your swords, I'll return the favor."

"Would you?"

"Of course."

I was shocked when Nash hopped up, disappeared for a few minutes, and returned carrying two swords and my bow and quiver. A laugh slipped from my lips as he grabbed my hand and led me out to the grassy field beyond the tents.

"Someone's going to fire on me if they see this." I tugged on his hand and slowed our pace.

"You'll be fine if you're with me."

"Why is that? Why do they listen to you?" Couldn't waste a chance to get information from him.

"Same reason your people listen to you. Alright." He tossed the swords on the ground and passed my bow to me. "This looks like a good spot."

I hesitated. "You aren't worried I'll turn this on you?"

"You're not careless. It would be too dangerous for your people if you attacked anyone."

He had a point. "Well, that's true. I also can't kill you before I learn your technique."

"Funny," Nash said dryly.

I lifted my bow with an arrow nocked and drew the string back so my hand nestled against my pillow of hair. Released. "Feel the air around your bow. See how it will flow around the arrow."

Nash moved closer, touching his fingertips to the bow, trailing down its spine until his knuckles brushed my shoulder. My breath caught in my chest.

"We fought together brilliantly today." Nash's voice lowered. "You and me together, we could kill him."

A jolt of shock hit me. He was manipulating me. "Are you playing games with me?"

"This isn't a trick." Nash grabbed my shoulders, holding me firm. It shocked me to silence. "I'm your best shot at taking the Prophet down. Just like you're mine. The woman I saw in battle today would never surrender. Fight with me."

The air was shifting. Waves of heat swelling around me until my skin burned. I had to stop or I'd get sucked in. Would slip to that terrible place where the fire melted my skin.

I ripped away from his grasp. "Why would you kill the Prophet?"

"I want to be free." Desperation laced his words. "Don't you?"

"So stop fighting for him."

"I can't. He's forced me to fight for him the same way he forced you today."

I held my bow against myself. "You were captured?"

"He conquered my village years ago, just like all the others. Not everyone living in his village chose to be there. Some of us were forced to."

"You're a great fighter. Escape."

"I have people, too. You think you're the only one with someone on the line?" Nash shook his head. "The Prophet will never let me go. Don't be surprised when he spares some of your warriors and makes them fight for him permanently."

"My people would sooner die than serve your Prophet."

Nash snorted. "That's why you battled for him today, then, isn't it?"

I caught a hold of his collar and jerked myself up closer to his height. "We'll free our people and then we'll go after the Prophet. We're not waiting around for years for someone to save us."

"Will you?" He pried my hands off him. "If you can't fight now, what makes you think you'll be able to later? The Prophet conquered the entire Valley and forced us all into his service."

"We're only doing this until we can save our people." The pity in his eyes only reflected how foolish I felt as I said the words. This was probably what the warriors of every village the Prophet had ever conquered said. But this was different. I was going to escape. "He has the children." My voice broke. "Rune. He has Rune. Leif's son." I clawed at my throat as images of him tightened my vocal cords. I'd forced myself not to think of him, hadn't I? Just as I forced myself not to see him in the village at first. "I promised him I would protect him."

Nash nodded, looking heavy with the weight of the pain I carried, as though he truly carried his own as well. "The Valley is full of people who feel the same. You think we haven't tried? That we all just gave up once he came for us?"

"We're different." I had no proof to back it up. Couldn't even pretend to have a good argument. I just needed it to be true, because the alternative was unthinkable. Living in service of the Prophet like Nash was unthinkable.

"Your village held out longer than most. That's all."

My fury nearly got the best of me. The only thing that saved him was the truth of his words, because as angry as it made me, I couldn't punish him for my weakness. I had failed so far.

I stared at Nash. "How do I know you're not actually working for the Prophet right now?"

"I'm going to help you escape. That's how you'll know."

The words could have been a punch to my gut. They hit me that hard. "What?"

"I searched the battlefield for someone who looks like you. I didn't find anyone, but I'm going back before dawn while everyone in the camp sleeps. We'll stage a death. You try to escape and I'll pretend to kill you. I can talk the Prophet into not taking retribution for your disobedience."

I crossed my arms, brows furrowed. There had to be some trick here.

Nash sighed. "I've had countless plans fall through over the years. Your people gave me hope. When I saw you in battle today . . ." He ran his hand through his hair. "We can do this."

It wasn't true. He didn't understand the extent of the Prophet's power. If he helped me escape, though, I could return to the Mountain of the Gods for my power and free my people, free the entire Valley, from the Prophet. So I wouldn't tell him how hopeless his plans really were, or that I'd never be able to assassinate the Prophet with this bow, no matter how good of a shot I was.

"Okay," I said.

Quiet settled between us, a stark contrast to the raucous noise of the camp. I couldn't imagine how it would feel to have to fight for the Prophet for years. If Nash told the truth, then it only gave me more reason to fight. I'd been far too narrow-sighted while hiding amongst my people. There were so many stories in the Valley I'd never taken the time to learn.

I studied him. "Who is he holding against you, Nash?"

Pain burned in his eyes. Such deep pain that I couldn't imagine he faked it. His voice sobered. "My daughter."

Shock smacked me. Nash had a kid? I snapped my mouth shut when I realized I was slack-jawed. Nash was old enough for a kid. Of course, he was. I had no idea why it surprised me. Well, maybe because he hadn't once mentioned one. And he didn't seem like a dad. Not with all the flirting. That didn't really make sense, though, did it? Dads could flirt. I just hadn't expected this.

"You're surprised," Nash said.

"I . . . Yeah, I am." If the Prophet had his daughter, then Nash was just like Leif. And Leif would do anything for Rune. Anything. This didn't mean I could trust Nash, no matter how my heartbreak flared as empathy for him, or for how desperately I wanted to offer him comfort. If he truly suffered as we had, how could I treat him coldly?

"How old is your daughter?"

"Four. She lives in another village with her mother."

He didn't offer any more information and I didn't think I should pry. Except, I had to pry a little. "So what's up with you and Flare if you have the mother of your child out there somewhere?" Or maybe I'd pry a lot.

He snorted. "The mother of my child is bound to another man."

"Bound? Not just married?" In marriage, our people vowed their lives to one another, and breaking such a promise would dishonor life here. But being bound meant vowing the next life to one another, joining the gods in death as one soul and not two. It could not be broken. Doing so shamed the entire family, community, and the gods themselves.

"Her family is very pious," Nash said. "As is his. Being bound absolves her of dishonoring the sanctity of life by creating it so carelessly."

The words made my stomach ache for him. Nash was the sin from which the mother needed to cleanse from her soul. It was common to have children outside of marriage, but not for pious families. "What sin did the man she's bound to need to absolve?"

"Choosing the Prophet of the Valley to swear his life to." He shrugged. "No one will speak it plainly, but he clearly regrets this decision."

I would want to absolve myself if I gave my life to the Prophet. Just as we could bind ourselves to another, we also bound ourselves to a community, and the most devoted did so to their leader as well. If breaking the bond between two lovers meant an eternal disgrace, doing so to your people or leader all but ensured damnation. And execution. No doubt about that.

Of course, I knew better than to believe any of it, but it was all my people knew. Though I didn't share their faith, I respected their conviction.

"Anyway," Nash said. "I'm not with Flare."

"Only sometimes."

"You sound jealous."

"You wish."

He smiled. "Maybe I do." Nash nudged my bow. His attitude unnerved me. "Are you going to teach me or not, Sharpshooter?"

"Not for free."

"I have lessons of my own to offer."

My heart fluttered at his low voice. "So . . . You teach me a thing or two about your sword technique and I'll fix your shitty bow skills."

"Oh. That's how you want things to be, then."

Time passed almost as quickly as our ale. I guzzled the last of mine, threw my mug high into the air, and whipped my bow up. Even with the dizziness of drink, my arrow whizzed through the air smoothly, the iron tip glinting before striking its target. Glass shattered and disappeared.

I passed the bow to Nash. "Why is the Prophet working with a demon like Flare when he has disciples?"

He threw his mug and aimed. The shot went wide. "Damn." He sighed. "Demon spies are better than human spies."

I cringed internally at the words *demon* and *human*. The neural implant was the only difference between those with power and those without. It was dangerous to think of demons as more than human, even if they were hunted by Prophets. That was how it started, hurting people less powerful. I worked hard to watch myself for those thoughts that could be so hard to root out. "Why the demons, though?"

"Disciples are too well-known to do the job."

Nash had spoken far more openly with me than I'd expected. "Do you know how many?"

He grabbed another arrow. "No. The Prophet doesn't trust me. I only know because of Flare."

"Has she told you much?"

"Just that she isn't the only one. She controls information tightly. A keeper of secrets." Nash's mouth tightened into a line. "Flare carries the whispers of the gods. I've heard she can even share their dreams of what will one day come to pass. She's learned how to steal powers from the gods that no demon ever has."

My stomach twisted as he spoke. Rumors abounded but Nash didn't strike me as the type to believe in silly stories. "She's been right about the future before?"

"Several times that I know of." He shook his head as if ridding himself of thoughts of Flare, and then settled my bow on the ground. He collected the swords he'd gathered earlier.

"Drunk sword fighting." I snorted and accepted the weapon he offered. "What could go wrong?"

Nash stood sideways to me, blade at his side like an extension of his arm. "Well?"

I lunged forward, but Nash snapped toward me fast as a cobra. I scooped my sword and dodged his advance on the balls of my feet to avoid opening myself up to him.

His eyes caught mine through the snap of our blades.

"You know killing the Prophet won't be enough." I grunted with effort when I knocked away his strike. My world slid off-kilter. "The disciples have to go, too."

"None are as ruthless as the Prophet." He pushed me into a defensive position. "Even if one of them takes over, it'll be better."

"That's wishful thinking." I smashed my heel against his diaphragm, forcing him back a step.

His brows raised but I didn't waste time pretending. I was this competitive. This hardheaded. I brought my blade down hard.

Nash sidestepped, slipped behind me, and brought his sword up around me. Before he could get too close, I drove my own weapon up as a wedge between my body and his. He grabbed my hand over my hilt, carefully tilting my own sword to the vulnerable crook of my neck. Now he was just toying with me. I clenched my teeth.

His breath washed over the side of my face, heavy from our scuffle. One hand over mine, the other wrapped around me holding his sword, we stayed like that for a moment. The steel of my own sword faintly kissed my neck.

"I win," he whispered against my ear. My skin tingled.

I broke free and turned on Nash. "Again."

I'd never faced someone so skilled with a sword. Fire burned in my stomach. I threw myself into my offense.

"We can't kill the Prophet and his disciples at the same time." Nash deflected my strike easily enough that it shot a flash of anger up my spine. "Flare might help us make a deal with one."

"Any disciple who works with the Prophet can't be trusted." I shook my head. "Same for demons."

He caught my foot and knocked it out from under me, ripping my sword from my hand as I fell. On my way down, I twisted and slammed my leg into the back of his knees. He buckled and caught himself on his hands.

"Then how do we kill them all?" he asked breathlessly as he twisted for me.

I bashed my elbow into his side and wrestled for control of the sword he'd stolen from me.

"Shit." He snorted as we both held on tight.

Dizziness had my head spinning. "Wait . . . I need a second."

Nash tapped his fist against my shoulder in a teasing hit. "I think that means I'm winning, then."

I slammed my knee into his side and shoved him hard with my forearms. We both toppled over, where I wrestled with the spinning world around me to push him back down. "Think again . . ." I pounded my fist against his chest.

He abandoned his swords on the grass, locked his arms around me, and flipped me onto my side.

I jabbed my thumbs into the pressure points below his collarbone.

"Ow." He pushed my fingers away. "Okay, a second. At least one."

His arms went limp and I dropped my hands, both of us falling onto our backs.

My legs were still tangled with his longer ones. Neither of us moved. I rolled my head to the side, opening my eyes to his. "I might be able to get help from some friends."

"What kind of friends can kill seven disciples?"

"All you need to know is that if I can escape, I might be able to pull it off."

He twisted my way. "I've been honest with you." His voice was low. Eyes searching mine. "It could get me killed. I deserve answers, too."

"Maybe. We don't always get what we deserve."

I expected anger, but a sly smile crawled onto his face. "Ruthless, again."

My eyes fell to where his chest edged my arm. This man was definitely up to something. I just didn't know whether it was the ordinary pursuits of a man or something more sinister, and I didn't want to be played for a fool.

"I might just be drunk . . ." Nash said. "But I have that strange feeling I get sometimes."

I swore I drew in water instead of air. "What?"

"I feel like I know you from a dream I can't remember." Serious eyes belied the twist of his lips in a smirk. "That sounds crazy, doesn't it? Sometimes that feeling is so strong I swear it's real."

I breathed in deeply, heart pounding. Rune and our other innocents were held at the Prophet's village, and I had no idea if my escape would work. Actually making it to the Sacred School seemed even more impossible. And I was laying here with this man as if I had any idea how to gain the upper hand in a battle like this.

"I do know that feeling," I said. "I hope you don't plan to betray me, Nash the Unknown."

"I hope you don't plan to betray me, Max the Sharpshooter."

We looked at one another long enough that I knew I needed to get some distance before I made a mistake. Pushing myself up and then rising to my feet, I only gave him a furtive glance. "I better go back before Leif and Wren worry."

He stood as well and nodded. "Goodnight."

"Night."

Though I backed away, Nash didn't leave or set his eyes elsewhere. He kept looking at me with that smirk back in place, so brazen, and so confident. If he'd ever felt self-conscious a day in his life, it didn't show one bit.

Very dangerous. I could not let myself trust him.

CHAPTER SEVEN

Nothing dared impede the sun's rays from the face of the gods. Eons of dazzling light saturated their human memories and made them forget the beauty of golden sunlight breaking through the edges of black storm clouds. When they looked upon the storms of our world, it was not greatness nor evil which flashed in their hungry eyes, but the breaking of boredom.

The gods' stares found me in my dreams. The god, actually. The only one I'd ever met. She spoke of hope on top of that mountain. Hope that what the gods learned from our world could save others. To this day, I only saw the breaking of boredom when she looked upon my suffering.

Her eyes flashed and I jolted from my sleep.

It'd been more than a dream. The sensation was undeniable. It felt like Flare, only at least ten of her, raging hot as a wildfire.

I wrapped my hand around Leif's mouth in our tent and held a finger to my lips. His wide eyes found mine. "We're under attack."

Leif didn't need an explanation. He woke Wren and they followed me out of the tent in a crawl. In the dim of night, a soft breeze feathered through the grass we'd trampled during our party last night. The platters, now empty of food, remained on the tables undisturbed. Empty barrels lay on their sides just as we'd left them. Leif looked at me quizzically, but I didn't question myself. Someone was here.

Wren nudged me. A woman slinked through the shadows, carrying what looked like a dagger, and disappeared into a tent that housed some of the Prophet's warriors.

I crept forward when a rush of heat engulfed my body, so strong I thought for sure I'd slipped to the eclipse again. An incredible force ripped me off my feet, straight back between the tents. Leif and Wren only had time to turn before I lost sight of them. I reached my hands forward silently as my body flew through the air.

Tree branches snapped against me. The force jetted me through the woods and slammed me onto the ground in a clearing. Leaves and twigs scattered in a cloud of dirt. I groaned and pushed myself onto my forearms.

Flare stood before me, eyes glowing like embers in the darkness.

I didn't have time for this. The camp needed help. Without giving her more than a glance, I jumped to my feet and sprinted for my people when I slammed into an unseen wall. Pain splintered down my face. Damn it.

"It's not time to leave," Flare said.

I turned back to her. "Let me go."

She burned away the space between us with her fiery gaze. "You can't run from me. You certainly can't hide from me." She strolled to me and breathed against my cheek. "Demon."

I clutched her wrist. "What do you want with me?"

She plucked my fingers from her wrist and pried herself away with a haughty chuckle. "Dear Max . . ."

How did she know my name?

Flare sighed, as if she pitied me, or didn't want to deal with me. "You think you can win any battle if you want it badly enough. That's the curse of the naturally gifted. You don't understand failure."

I grabbed her throat, driving her back, fingers digging into her slender neck. "I asked you a question."

Flare clutched my arm with a broken gasp. Flames erupted from her palm against my skin. I gritted my teeth and held tight, nails cutting into her.

"Answer me!" I screamed in fury and pain. With the smell of my own skin burning, I could have sworn I'd slipped to the eclipse, the flames of that day licking my fingers. I dropped her and smothered my arm with my tunic. There was no time for this. My people could have been dying.

Coughing, Flare backed away from me, drawing her fingers back from the bloody claw marks on her throat. Fear shone in her glassy eyes. I saw all that I needed to in that one look. This was no warrior. Just a woman who wasn't prepared to face death.

"You're afraid of me." I snorted. "Looks like you're in over your head."

"Someone at the Sacred School should have taught you manners." Her gaze flashed down me. "They raised a barbarian."

How did she know about that? The only demons who should have known about the school were the ones who'd trained on the Mountain of the Gods. There were only two routes off that mountain: as a Prophet or dead. As far as I knew, I was the only one to ever forge a new path for myself and it had nearly killed me. Flare didn't look like she could survive at that school, much less make it down the mountain.

My voice came out like a growl. "Who are you?"

Flare covered her neck with her hand and wrapped her other arm around herself. "That's not your concern. Be a good girl and listen for once. I'm trying to save you from yourself."

"You really must want to die today. Let me go. I have to help my people."

"This entire region is in shambles. This sorry excuse for a society keeps producing unruly children like you. Barbaric, angry, violent fools." She raised her chin. "You're better than this. Instead of wasting your life fighting against me, help me make this Valley a safe place to live."

A laugh erupted from my chest. "What are you talking about?"

"Max." She bit off the word like a mother chastising her child, only she didn't look that much older than me. "It can't have been easy growing up with all those visions of your death. The eclipse is only ten days away. There's so little time for you to redeem yourself. Focus."

Nash had called her a keeper of secrets. My heart beat wildly. "I don't trust a word you say. I should kill you now."

Flare eased closer with her hands raised as if she approached a feral animal she hoped to keep calm. "With what power?" She clasped her hands in front of herself. "Even if you could, it would be unwise. I'm the only person who can save you. You and that sweet little girl of Nash's."

I coiled my hands into fists. "If that's a threat against a child—"

"I'm not a monster." Flare sighed. "You and Nash are the ones putting her in danger. The Prophet of the Valley is not the only one you have to worry about. There's plenty of world beyond this Valley and changes are coming. Follow my lead. I'll keep you and Nash on track."

"I'm not following you anywhere."

"It never works. What good came of your rebellion on the mountain? You should have stayed at that school and become a Prophet. You could have made a difference by now. Instead, you're playing mortal with this little tribe of yours."

Rage coiled tight fingers around my heart. "Whose side are you on?"

"There are no sides. You'll understand that when you finally grow up."

I swallowed hard. "Don't act like you know me."

"But I do know you. I know you very, very well, dear girl."

That feeling struck, the same kind Nash had talked about in the field. The familiarity of a dream I couldn't quite remember. The sweat on my neck turned cold.

"That's good." Flare walked closer, holding my gaze. "You're the one who's afraid now. You should be as long as you're not on my side." She cupped my shoulder with a strangely gentle grip. "Don't lash out. I know that's your instinct. Think it through. Make the right decision this time."

I couldn't draw in a breath. "What, exactly, do you want from me?"

"I told you. I want you to help me bring peace. As long as we're ruled by one person, it will always fall to the worst rulers. The type of person who can take control of so many is someone who we don't want controlling anyone. Look at our highways. The roads were paved so that everyone could travel freely and safely. It was meant for trade and growth. Instead, they've become paths of war. The people should be in charge of them."

"How is it that you have the support of the Prophets when you're against them?"

"You think I tell them that? I only give them the truths they want to hear."

"A guarantee that you're only giving me the truths I want to hear."

A smirk cut into her serious expression. "You're quick on your feet."

"That's why I know to never trust anyone else who's quick on theirs."

Passion smoldered in Flare's eyes as she leaned forward. "You're educated. You know that the world doesn't have to be so bloody and hopeless. Your instructors taught you that there are worlds beyond ours." Flare watched me intently. "Ours is so young. Once we needed the Prophets so we could grow beyond little tribes that massacred each other for meager power. Now the reign of the Prophets' must come to an end as well."

I blinked. "Social evolution happens in its own time."

"Why does it have to work that way? Do you want to spend an eon slaughtering one another?"

"World peace sounds great, but you're delusional if you think whatever you're doing in the darkness will lead to that. Who are you here for today? The Flatlanders or the Valley? Will you save my people or watch our enemies take us away?"

"You're still thinking too small. I'm not here for the Flatlanders or your people. I came here for you. The distraction at the camp gave me the perfect opportunity to talk to you."

For the last eight years, I'd focused solely on the Prophet as our great enemy. Whoever this woman was, regardless of her claims that she wanted to help us, might prove to be even worse than him if she had any way of making her plans a reality. I didn't trust her for a moment to bring peace. "Tell me what you know, please. I need to help my people."

"I know you must plan to return to the mountain for help, because you've left yourself no other options. Gather your allies and work with me to free these lands from the Prophets."

It might have sounded as though we wanted the same things, but I knew from the games Flare played with the Prophet that we had very different ideas about what kind of world we wanted to live in. "Let me guess. You won't talk until I deliver."

"Of course not. Now, take Nash with you. I trust him. He'll be an asset to you and he'll ensure my interests are remembered."

If this woman trusted him, then he couldn't have been the man I hoped for him to be. "Fine." Not. No way I'd do anything she wanted. "Now leave, so I can save my people." I would never ally with her. She reeked of trouble.

"Okay, then." Flare took a step back. "I'll find you when the time is right."

"How could you possibly find me?"

"I have the eye of the gods. I can find anyone in the world at any time." She touched her neck and frowned at her bloody fingers. "Now, be good. I'll be watching."

I couldn't speak. As glib as she sounded, I recognized a threat when I heard one, and I knew to take it seriously. Something was very much not right about Flare.

"Oh, and take care of Nash," Flare said. "I'm fond of him."

She flashed a smile and vanished. I stumbled back, searching the area. I'd seen demons move with incredible speed, but that wasn't what she did. One moment she was here and the next she was gone. Not even my best instructors could do that. It shouldn't be possible.

I pressed a hand to my stomach, staving off the nausea. What the hell?

No. There was no time for panic or confusion. The camp was under attack and with Flare gone, there was no one to stop me from returning.

I hiked through the trail of snapped branches Flare had dragged me through with sweat beading over my brow. She shouldn't have taken me so far away. What if I was too late? Their names swelled in my throat. Wren! Leif! I had to clamp down on my teeth to keep from crying out for them.

The smell stung my nostrils first, and then heat flooded the air. Fire. I sprinted through the woods to the field and skidded to a stop. Flames consumed the tents, clawing for the clear sky overhead, the camp glowing red and hot.

I threw myself to the ground to crawl low, despite how my mind screamed at me to run as fast as I could for my dearest friends. My hands ripped away clumps of grass each time I dragged myself forward. Before I even reached the perimeter of the camp, the fire had started to eat into the surrounding field. Sweat doused my body from the heat.

I caught a glimpse of the center of the camp through the tents. The flames crashed over the area as if hitting an invisible dome. Panic tightened around my heart again. Dozens were tied up in the center of the camp.

Chief Kaid sat among them, blood running down the side of her face.

Damn Flare for taking me away. Tears sprang into my eyes.

Where the hell were Leif and Wren?

The grass rustled behind me. I climbed to my knees and twisted with fists ready. Nash faced me, his finger pressed to his mouth.

"How did you get away?" I whispered.

"I left to find the body on the battlefield. I saw the flames in the distance."

How awfully convenient.

"What about you?" he asked. "How did you get away?"

Should I tell him? He might offer information. I decided it was worth the risk. "Flare took me."

"Flare? Why?"

"Trying to recruit me."

A flicker of emotion flashed in Nash's eyes. Concern, possibly. Frustration. Perhaps fear. Whatever it was, he didn't seem happy about what I'd told him. I couldn't begin to guess at what this meant to him when apparently, I knew absolutely nothing about what was going on.

Besides, I wasn't ready to believe his story and that deserved my attention. He may have known this attack was coming. The offer to help me escape could have been a cover the entire time. The heat of anger rolled through me, but instinctively I knew I shouldn't show him I was suspicious. If he was trying to fool me, I might have a chance to catch him off guard by pretending I believed him.

Even so, I wasn't ready to stay by his side during this attack. I started forward but he grabbed me.

"We should do this together," Nash said.

"I don't have time to figure out what I plan to do, much less explain it to you."

"Unless you plan to take on ten demons and a small army by yourself, I'm guessing that you'll run."

I clenched my fists. Ten demons? Were there really that many? "Where's Leif and Wren?"

"I don't know."

Sometimes, when I was desperate enough, I could scrounge the meager amount of power it took to listen for my friend's heartbeats. Straining, I heard nothing, until finally I quieted my thoughts.

I heard the soft patter near the trees, further down from where I'd been taken. One of the hearts sounded so faint. I nearly ran for them but stopped myself. I couldn't let Nash know.

"This is where I last saw them." I combed through the grass to pretend to search. "There are tracks. Stay here and watch my back."

He nodded.

I rushed for the trees in a crouch. A boot hung out past a patch of thistles. Tears filled my eyes. Leif's body sagged against a tree with Wren holding on to him with bloodied hands. Arrows stuck out from his chest, covering his shirt in splotches of blood. Three in total. He must have come after me and gotten chased through the woods.

Wren's face twisted with grief. "Max," she whispered.

"I've got him." I squeezed Leif's hand. "Go be a commander."

Wren was the best tracker we had. She'd follow the Flatlanders and watch for an opportunity to help our people.

"Stay alive," Wren whispered. She kissed Leif's head. "We need you."

Wren grabbed me in a quick hug and took off for camp.

"Alright." I stared at Leif, overwhelmed. I had to stabilize him and move him. What if I could reach more of my power? I'd never come close to the amount I would need to help stop the blood loss. But I had to try.

Leif's eyes opened as I placed my hands on his chest.

"Don't." He grunted through gritted teeth. "No, Max."

I froze.

"You never said . . . So I never asked . . ." He shook his head. "I may not know your reasons, but I do know this. You never use your power."

"Leif."

"I've known you too long not to know, Max."

"I can't use it," I whispered. "It's a curse. Sometimes I can catch the smallest amount. So, quiet. I'm not letting you die. I have to find a way to do this."

"I'll be okay." He smiled at me like he could possibly calm me or placate me.

"Rest and let me work."

"Leave, Max. It isn't safe."

"I'm not leaving you."

He clutched my wrist with a warm, bloody hand. "This is your chance to escape. That was your plan."

I dug my nails into my palm. "Not without you!"

"You have to. Save them . . . Save Arn and our little Rune. Please, save my family."

"We will save them."

He breathed out slowly and then he belted out a roar. I fell back, eyes bulging.

"Come kill me, you cowards!" Leif screamed.

"Stop it!" I clamped my hands over his mouth. "I can take you away and stabilize you when we're far enough."

"I won't last that long." Leif grabbed my hands and pulled them down to his chest. "I love you, girl. Go make us proud."

"No . . ."

Hands grabbed at me from behind. A strong grasp. Nash. I hadn't even noticed him approaching.

"Leif!" I reached for his hand as Nash pulled on me.

"Just go," Leif whispered harshly.

"Come on." Nash tugged.

"Get her out of here." Leif stared past me with hard eyes. "Hurry!"

Nash caught my wrists and pulled my hands against my body, wrapping me up in his arms. He lifted me from my feet as he rushed deeper into the woods.

I tried to wrench away but Nash was too strong. I couldn't budge. Teeth gritted, I kicked his shins, slammed my head back against his neck, managed to rip an arm free as he coughed. The fire that consumed our camp burned within me. All of it. I twisted and punched Nash in the jaw with all my strength.

He dropped me and grabbed his face. "Max!" I'd hoped he would give up, but an arm that felt as unyielding as steel locked around my waist and ripped me back against that hard chest of his.

That was an insanely hard hit. Had I used some power for that? There was no time to figure it out or to fight with Nash. I had to rescue Leif. Boots pounded in the field, drawing closer and closer.

Desperation and fury tore my mind in two.

"Stop . . ." Leif reached his hand for me like I had when Flare dragged me through the woods. "Goodbye." He smiled.

Peace flooded me. Peace from the knowing look on Leif's face. He'd made up his mind. It melted the anger within me into sorrow. Tears gathered in my eyes. A sob wrenched from my chest.

"He'll be alright." Nash's voice whispered in my ear as he secured my wrists again. "The demons can keep him alive. They're taking prisoners. You saw that. Your people are alive. They'll want Leif. He's valuable."

Footsteps sounded near the woods. I had to be quiet or they'd hear. I fell, listless as Nash carried me away, Leif's body blurring in my teary eyes.

"We'll save him," Nash said. "The smart way."

As the ground raced beneath us, it blurred, and it twisted, and it tore in two. The slipping swept the earth away. I had no hope of stopping it. One moment, I was in the forest with Nash carrying me, abandoning Leif with our enemies.

And the next . . . *Fluorescent bulbs burned bright overhead in our training room.*

CHAPTER EIGHT

*M*y instructor knelt in front of me. *"You're wavering."*

I focused on the sliver of air between my stomach and the sharpened blade I hovered above. The skin all over my body burned in pain. The rest of the room, lined with the seven other students in our class, blurred in my periphery. My entire world fit onto the tip of this blade for the moment.

Pain scratched into my hands from using my power for too long. "It's been thirty minutes. I need a break."

"You'll get a break when you deserve one." The instructor's sharp stare switched to Piercey. "Is it healed yet?"

I grunted as I strained to tilt my head to see Piercey holding the little bird with the broken wing. He didn't respond and Kelvin wouldn't stand for it.

"Answer me, now."

"Concentrating." Sweat beaded on Piercey's forehead.

The healthy wing twitched and then snapped.

"Why did you do that?" Piercey jumped to his feet. Tears flooded his eyes. "It's not his fault. Don't take it out on the bird."

"You're right. It's your fault. He has two broken wings now because of you."

Piercey settled on the ground once more with anger tightening his expression. "It'll be okay." He stroked the bird's head with a single finger. "I'll figure this out."

"What kind of healer can't even heal a bird?" Kelvin leaned over him.

Tears slid down Piercey's cheeks. He kept his eyes trained on the bird. Slowly the wings straightened as the bird wiggled on his palm. Healing required mastery of anatomy. It wasn't fair to ask Piercey to heal a sparrow when he had never studied them before. Kelvin was in a mood today.

The point of the knife nicked my stomach. My eyes widened. He was right. I had been wavering. I squeezed my eyes shut and lifted myself higher.

Kelvin studied the sparrow. "Fuse the bones, Piercey."

"You're only making it harder."

"Quiet, Piercey," I whispered. Usually, I was the one losing it on Kelvin.

Our instructor lowered his head. "How will you heal your people in the midst of battle? What kind of healing Prophet will you be if you demand peace and quiet to work in? Pathetic." Kelvin turned for me again. "And you. You should be able to hold yourself over this without breaking a sweat, Max."

I shut out his voice. Never mind that I could shoot a bow better than he could. Or that I could crush all the bones in his body if I wanted to. He wanted to berate me and so he would.

"You have ten seconds to heal that bird, Piercey."

My friend's tears fell onto the bird's wings.

"Six seconds."

Piercey's face contorted. Sweat slid between his eyes.

"Two seconds, Piercey."

The bird's right wing fluttered.

"Now!"

A crushing force slammed into my back and threw me onto the blade.

Pain erupted in my middle.

My hands twitched as I fell onto my side. The knife stuck out from my stomach in a bubbling pool of blood. I couldn't even scream. Shock and pain strangled my voice.

"Max!" Piercey dragged me onto his lap.

The cry finally squeezed out. I threw my head back and screamed.

Kelvin loomed over us. "Heal her. You both have an appointment in the white room in an hour. Don't be late."

"What is wrong with you?" Piercey's voice hitched. "I haven't learned how to work on an abdomen yet."

"You know enough to do this, kid. Like I said, quit making excuses. You think I'm cruel? All of you have killed people with your power. If you can't master it, you're too dangerous to be kept alive."

Kelvin walked out the door as Piercey screamed after him.

My vision waned, closing in on Piercey, so all I could see was his face. Hot blood poured from my stomach and drizzled onto the ground. The other students clamored for us now that Kelvin had left.

"Don't panic . . ." I struggled to find my voice. "You've got this . . ."

And then I passed out.

Bright light shone into my eyes as I squirmed on a cold table. After years of entering the door of the gods, it had lost its mystery. Everything in the room was pure white. The walls. The chairs. The table. Like I was the only color that existed.

"Do you have any lingering pain?" The technician studied me.

"No. Piercey healed me well. Report back to Kelvin on how stellar his teaching tactics are."

Piercey shook his head at me. He sat on a table across from me.

I tore an electrode from my head. "I'm tired of you gluing this shit to my head when you don't need to. Why do you do it? I know this technology is way beneath you. Is it so I have some tangible proof that you can mess with me whenever you want?"

"Max," Piercey whispered harshly. Kelvin had put the fear in him. Well, he'd only awakened my anger.

"Have you been experiencing any other signs of paranoia?" the technician asked, annoyingly unfazed.

My nostrils twitched. "You watch us and test us and poke us. Lie to us. I'm tired of pretending I don't know."

He opened his mouth to speak when the room went dark. I straightened.

Then came a woman's voice. "I think it's time we finally meet."

I rose at the sound of the woman speaking. Piercey hopped off the table and moved beside me, grabbing my hand. I wasn't sure if it was for my sake or his.

After several seconds, the lights came back on. The other side of the room looked completely different. It was pale blue, like our hallway, and it was outfitted like a living room, complete with an ugly floral love seat.

A woman sat there, watching me with sharp eyes. "My name is Dr. Henderson."

"How did you do that?" I asked.

"You have so many questions, Max." Her long black hair laid across one shoulder. "I'm afraid I don't have all the answers you want."

"Don't have them or won't give them?"

"Won't give them." Dr. Henderson smiled. "I've had my eye on you. You're not easily distracted." Her voice softened and she spoke to me the way I imagined

my mother would have if I'd ever known her. "That's why I'm meeting with you and Piercey. You two have been struggling, haven't you?"

Piercey shook his head. "No, ma'am. We're fine."

I was only sixteen, but I was so tired. Tired like I'd lived decades and never got a break. "We're not fine. We're being held hostage at this school."

She simpered. "You'll be released when you can control your power well enough that you won't hurt people anymore."

Shame seared my heart. The eclipse. Not the one that haunted my future, but the one from my childhood. It was as if the two eclipses were entangled, tethered in time, and my entire life existed as a tug-of-war between the two, even now. Dr. Henderson was talking about the people I hurt back then.

I couldn't let her distract me with my guilt. "I'm tired of hearing that excuse. Kelvin stabbed me today."

Dr. Henderson scooted forward. "I'm sorry that happened to you, Max. We give autonomy to the people in your world, including the Sacred School. That's very important. There isn't anything we can do."

"Why? Why do you have to silently watch?"

"There are many things I can't tell you."

Rage made my mouth taste bitter. "Yeah. Because you'd compromise your experiment by making your subjects aware."

She sat back, thrown, but only for a moment. Then she smoothed out a wrinkle in her pants. I imagined she had few wrinkles in her life. "My, my. Perhaps the library at the school is a little too robust for your needs."

"It would be much easier to control me if you denied me an education. You know, like you do with ninety-nine percent of the world."

"You're angry."

"I'm more than angry."

"It's fair. I would be, too."

"This mountain has technology that the rest of our world won't hope to have for thousands of years. The people think you're gods because you come from a more advanced civilization. You let them pray to you while you watch them suffer in silence. I deserve to know why. Why are you running tests on me? What are you trying to learn?"

"Stop, Max." Piercey's voice shook. "The gods won't tolerate dissent."

Dr. Henderson waited until we'd both fallen quiet. "There are worlds like yours all over the cosmos, Max. Young worlds with growing civilizations. We want to learn how to help them develop without having to suffer through all the war and chaos that comes with social evolution."

I blinked. "You're watching us all kill each other to learn how to keep others from doing it? That's the stupidest thing I've ever heard."

Piercey grabbed my shirt and tugged me back to his side. "The whole world is the experiment, not just the school. There'll be more like us, Max. More experiments. More worlds."

A hint of pride shone in Dr. Henderson's eyes. "I can't lie to bright young people like you. It's true. One percent of your population has the neural implant that allows you to manipulate matter at the quantum level. Other worlds have greater numbers with power. I know it's hard, but you wouldn't be better off without us, and this data will save more lives than you can comprehend."

"This is just great." I raised my hands. "The most evolved species in the cosmos are total idiots. Why do you think it's okay to experiment on people?"

"It isn't okay. We can't pretend it's ethical. Still, math doesn't lie. The number of people who will suffer in these experiments is the tiniest fraction of how many people it will save from suffering."

The white walls snapped black and specks of light pierced every inch of the room. Stars glowed in the darkness, growing until raging suns dominated the room. Above us a planet teeming with light green water appeared, and another to our right, one chilled with mountains of ice. More. Zooming past us too fast to see. People popped up on the walls. Children laughing. Children screaming. Rapid flashes of life and death far too overwhelming in number to take in.

"They're all suffering." Dr. Henderson folded her hands on her lap.

I squeezed my eyes shut against the blur of faces, nauseous.

"You can help us end it. My society has long since evolved beyond death. Now it's time for others to do the same."

I struggled to find my voice. "Go help people. Stop experimenting."

"It's not as simple as that." Darkness overtook the room once more and light gradually dawned on the floor, rising up the wall behind Dr. Henderson. A breeze that I could actually feel kissed my cheek and carried in the smell of berries. We stood in a dimly lit forest.

Beside me, Piercey turned in a small circle, marveling at the transformation.

"Sometimes our best attempts to help actually hurt." Her voice was as mild as the breeze now. "We need to prove which interventions are effective at helping young worlds evolve with less suffering. Interventions that preserve a world's right to self-determination."

I clapped my hands so loudly that it made my ears ring. "So moving. You are truly worthy of worship, aren't you, Dr. Henderson?"

Her mouth straightened. White crashed onto the walls, leaving us bereft of all the life from moments before. "I have tolerated your disrespect and foolishness long enough."

"The truth will come out. What do you think everyone will do when they find out? It'll be chaos. Good luck having reliable data then."

Dr. Henderson sighed. "You just don't understand, Max. You can't tell anyone about this. No one can. It would mean the end of your world."

My muscles froze. I couldn't even try to speak.

"The entire purpose of your world is this experiment. If you compromise it, the council will shut it down precisely because it is unethical. Once an unethical experiment is unproductive, it cannot be allowed to exist."

"You'll . . . You'll destroy an entire world? You can't do that. You can't kill us all." I backed up for the door before I remembered there was no door. No escape. I was at her mercy. Beside me, Piercey looked like he had vanished from his body.

"The less you know, the better," she said. "I didn't want to share any of this with you. But I've been watching you. You were going to fight until you got answers. Now that you have them, let your world live in peace."

I gasped for breath. It felt like my throat was closing. "This can't be real. You can't just destroy entire worlds. You aren't gods!"

"We are the gods of this world, child. We created it. We can end it."

Piercey's eyes still looked vacant, but his lips twitched in silent words I couldn't hear. I stared at him, trying to figure out what he said.

"Tell her, Piercey," Dr. Henderson said. "You know the truth. You already suspected it."

A single tear slid down his face.

"Tell her and make her understand why she must stay silent. If you care for her, you'll do this."

He turned to me. His eyes looked like those of the dead. Dr. Henderson had killed the life in him. "They have total control. Our world isn't real." His voice was dry. Monotone. "This is a simulation, Max."

I bowed forward, unable to fully comprehend the words.

"Don't be scared." Dr. Henderson spoke calmly. "You're real, Max. All of you are real people who died as babies in your natural world. We uploaded you here to give you what you lost far too young. It isn't so different from how my people live. We all uploaded to a digital universe long ago. We are the Kethios—the ultimate ascension. It's okay to leave behind our weaker, physical forms."

A hoarse gasp ripped apart my throat.

"It'll stay okay as long as you're quiet." Her voice drifted past like the breeze, the threat buried in softness. "Be a good girl, Max."

My life here mattered. Piercey mattered. I mattered.

None of this was real. But it was all I'd ever known.

And it could slip away at any time.

CHAPTER NINE

For a long while after learning the truth, nothing felt real anymore. Then one day, Leif and his family breathed life back into the world, into me. In my memory, the sun shone brightly on that day, even though I've been told since it was actually cold and cloudy. It was after I had left the Sacred School. The first time Leif took me hunting. That day in the woods, I shot a deer I had to squint through the thick of trees and thickets to see. Leif howled, and danced, and lifted my arms in victory. That was the first time his family and neighbors had meat in a couple of weeks.

It had started with the jolt in my heart when Leif celebrated my shot. Later, when I saw him fill his toddler's bowl with venison stew, when chubby little cheeks broke into a grin, the jolt sparked into something I hadn't felt in a year. Joy.

Our world might not have been real, but we were, and our connections to one another were woven into the fabric of existence, as real, more real, than anything that had ever been. Certainly more real than the Kethios.

"How do you feel?"

I stiffened at Nash's voice. He'd carried me away after I passed out and didn't seem to trust me when I told him my fainting spells were nothing to worry about. We sat on the leafy floor, quiet for the ten minutes that I'd been awake. I searched the green canopy overhead like I would find answers. I not only had to save my people from the Prophet of the Valley, but now from the Flatlanders.

"Max?"

A growl rumbled in my chest. "I feel like I abandoned my heart and soul."

Leaves crunched as he scooted closer. "You honored Leif's wishes."

I crossed my arms atop my knees and settled my head down, turning my face to the side to see him. His jaw was reddened where I'd punched him, swollen enough to notice with just a glance. "Is your face okay?"

"I can tell the world I narrowly survived a direct hit from the great Sharpshooter." He smirked and touched the spot. "I'm fine. But you hit a lot harder than I thought you could. You'll break your hand if you keep hitting like that."

I tucked my hand beneath my knees so he couldn't see it. It wasn't even sore. With that one hit, I'd somehow managed to accidentally draw more power than I had in a while. Still, it was nothing compared to what I'd once done.

"Tell me your plan, already." Nash tossed a pebble at my leg. "I know you've done more than sulk over there."

When I'd been exiled from the Sacred School, I only wanted my power back. Finding Leif's village and falling in love with the people there had come as a surprise. For the first time, though, I wished that instead of regaining my power, I could simply take it away from everyone. Humans could not be trusted with it, and I could do just fine with my bow.

There was no use in thinking about the impossible, though. I was not going to strip the world of power. I needed to focus on saving my people from the Prophet. My only option was to find a way back to my power on the Mountain of the Gods. And perhaps to even reach Piercey in the Sacred School. If he had allies, we could amass enough power to take on the Prophet's forces, and likely Flare. I didn't trust her, at all. Which reminded me that I shouldn't trust Nash.

"I'll tell you my plan," I said. "If you tell me yours."

"Same as before. I want us to kill the Prophet together."

"Your plan is too simple." It was time to be honest about at least that much. "The Prophet has enormous power. More than the best demons."

I didn't tell Nash why that was. The Prophet was exactly like the demons, except that he'd trained at the Sacred School. That was the only difference between Prophets and demons. I saw that so clearly because I had lived as both. Even as a child, they called me demon because they feared my power. When the Sacred School took me in to help me tame my power, they changed how the world saw me. Suddenly, I was not a demon, but on the path to becoming a Prophet. The only difference between those two versions of myself was that I'd been given an education.

One I completely abandoned. When I trained at the Sacred School, something my instructors claimed was an incredible privilege, I'd rebelled against the gods and everything they stood for. The instructors were hypocrites and they abandoned our world to suffer while they looked down on the innocent from their mountain. My stand had cost me everything I'd had at that point. I never regretted it, though. I saw the gods and the instructors for what they were. Frauds. My only regret was that I had not yet found a way to reverse their seal on my power.

"They still have flesh and blood," Nash said. "You don't think an arrow could kill one?"

"Have you ever seen a demon or a Prophet die?"

Nash straightened. "No. Have you?"

"I have. They're very hard to kill. Their survival instinct kicks in and they're as dangerous as what you hear in the legends."

"There's only a handful of Prophets or demons capable of the power you hear about in the legends."

"Normally, yes. Get one of them on the verge of death, and they're all worthy of their own legends."

He quieted. "I've heard stories. I just never know how much to believe. There's talk about the Devourer from fifteen years ago who killed thirty men in battle just by looking at them."

I shifted. "Stories are never entirely true."

"Eclipse." Nash blew a puff of air. "That's who the Prophet says he's saving us from with these sacrifices during eclipses."

My heart hammered at the name. This talk couldn't continue. "The Prophet murders people during the eclipse to control everyone." Heat warmed my palms. I squeezed my hands together. "Look . . . I'm trying to tell you that your plan won't work. You have a daughter to think about. Just listen to me."

"I refuse to believe he's impossible to kill. We have to do this."

The Prophet had finished his training, so I knew for a fact he was more powerful than I had been at my peak. I gave up so much for my dissent. To say I regretted it was too simple. But I hurt, especially now, for the advantage I'd lost. Even if the Prophet had more power, I'd still kill him. I'd kill him because I had to and because I actually had something worth fighting for.

"To kill the Prophet, we need help." Once I told him, I couldn't go back. "I have a friend on the Mountain of the Gods."

That shocked him to silence for a moment. "How do you have a friend on that mountain? It's the deadliest place in the world."

I'd made it off the mountain alive, but, as far as I knew, I was the only one. Before having my power sealed, I'd tried escaping, and while I had been banished instead of executed, no one was offering to help me get down the mountain. I had to do that myself and it had nearly killed me. If I'd followed the rules, I would have been well on my way to becoming a Prophet by now. They wanted me to make myself so small that no one would see me and to live out my days in silence. Well, they had another thing coming. I knew the weaknesses of the mountain. I knew how to make it through. I could do this.

I hardened my voice. "I know what I'm doing. This is the plan. I'm sticking to it."

"Then I'm coming. You won't make it up that mountain alone."

His skills would be invaluable. How could I risk Nash's life, though? He didn't have power and I couldn't assume that I'd be able to protect him. I had no idea if I'd be able to access more of my power or not or whether I'd even get it back. Plus, if he acted as Flare's spy, I didn't want to travel with him anyway. "I'm going alone. You have a daughter. It's too dangerous for you."

"You can't tell a father not to protect his child."

He had a point. If I had a child, I would want to do the same. Still, I didn't want him to come with me, not when he didn't understand what he was getting into. "I'm not taking you. You'll slow me down."

"Bullshit. I'm as good with my blades as you are with your bow. You're still angry with me." Nash softened his voice. "That's why you won't let me help you."

I rose and moved for a blackberry vine a few trees down, picking them with my teeth clenched. He acted like he wanted to help, but I couldn't stop thinking of Flare saying she trusted him.

Nash met me and took a berry from my palm. Lifted it to my lips. "Stop brooding. Eat something."

I pushed away his hand. "Stop toying with me. We don't know each other. Don't speak to me like we're friends."

Nash dropped the berry back into my palm. "I know some things about you. I know how your eyes look when you face death, or when you lose, or when you're drunk."

I scowled. "Now you know the sting of my anger. You're only fortunate it isn't my wrath."

"Max."

"Leif is my brother." I stared into Nash's eyes. "I was unknown once, too. Then he knew me. He became my family."

"If you really wanted to stop me from taking you away from Leif, we wouldn't be here." Nash's voice lowered. "Is that really why you're angry with me?"

"Fine. I'm angry with you because you're a shady liar." My chest tightened. "Nash the Unknown. Even your name is shady."

"I got that name as a boy. I wandered into the village, half dead, unknown by anyone. It stuck."

"I'm not an idiot." That story could have been true, but the name wouldn't have stuck all these years with how good he was with his swords. The Unknown. What could he have done to earn the name except live a life of secrets? "You said the Prophet didn't trust you, and yet he's given you so much freedom. Nothing is free." I glared at him. "You're a spy." Flames awakened in my chest. "You're Unknown because he named you so. That's the real reason you know Flare."

Not a hint of concern crossed Nash's expression at my accusation. "Come on, Sharpshooter. You already knew I was in the service of the Prophet."

"Shameless." My nose crinkled in disgust at how Nash did not even try to deny being a spy. "You excused away fighting for the Prophet, but you've spent years doing his bidding in the worst way possible."

"How is spying worse than whatever you thought I did?"

"You truly have no honor if you don't know." My eyes narrowed. "Unknown."

"My daughter is my honor. I have no shame in that."

"What behavior can't you excuse, then? You gain people's trust and use it against them. Wielding your charisma like a sword. Attacking unarmed, unsuspecting people from behind."

Nash shook his head. "Do you care to know what I actually do, or will nothing stop your self-righteous ranting?"

Tears burned in my eyes. "It was you, wasn't it? You helped him take my people." I would slit his throat here and now if it was true. I would. Heat burned my palms. "You're the reason the Prophet got to Leif's son." I'd betrayed Rune, allowing this man to get twisted up in my heart enough that I even considered trusting him. I could never forgive myself.

His lips straightened. "No. Max, I swear. I would never spy on innocent people."

"You targeted me. Tried to get to me. That's why you treated me like this."

His voice softened. "That's not what I was—"

"As if I'd believe a spy." I spit on the ground at his feet. "I hate spies."

He spit as well. "I won't take your shit. I already took a fist to the face. Not to mention you headbutted me in the throat. I spy on Prophets and their disciples, not the innocent. Not even warriors. You're the one who targeted me anyway. I know you started talking to me because you wanted something."

"I don't trust you." I wanted to scream. "Flare knows I'm going to the Mountain of the Gods. She told me to take you with me because she trusts you. You're both spies. You're both working for the Prophet and double-crossing him. Now she wants you to spy on me."

The fight had fled Nash. I was so blinded by my anger that I didn't notice his shoulders had gone slack, that his face had paled, that for the first time since I had met him fear shone in his eyes. "Flare said that?"

The look on his face stole away my own fight. My voice came out small. "She didn't use the word *spy*."

He ran his hand through his hair. "Tell me exactly what she said."

"I don't have to tell you anything."

"You know what, don't trust me. That's fine." He bit off each word. "I'm not ready to trust you either, Max. I was willing to put my life in your hands and journey with you. I'm not ready to put my kid's life in your hands. You don't get to know everything."

I couldn't stop myself from softening at the conviction in his eyes. "I want to believe you. That's why I can't let myself. How could I possibly trust you?"

He moved closer to me and lifted my hand, prying open my fist. I'd crushed the berries and didn't even realize it. Purple oozed from between my fingers.

"We need to decide now," he said. "Either we fight the Prophet together, or we don't."

His touch was a distraction and he must have known that. If he was a spy, he knew how to manipulate people. There were so many signs that he'd done that to me. He'd never had any real interest in me. I could hear Rune's voice in my mind, begging us to save him. I had to get the truth from Nash, and there was only one way I knew how to get anything in this world.

So, I smeared the berries across his eyes and ripped a sword from his hip. He jammed his forearm between his neck and the blade. Caught my wrist while my fingertips, sticky with berries, grazed his other sword.

"Damn it, Max." His face scrunched as he shook his head, flinging hunks of berries.

I pressed the blade into his forearm hard enough to bite, to let him know this wasn't for show. I'd carve through flesh and bone to his throat if I had to. "If you didn't spy on my people, then who?"

"My homeland." He managed to wipe an eye against his arm and squinted through the remnants of smashed berries. "I was born in the Flatlands, not the Valley. You could have asked without the sword."

"Not when you've already lied to me."

"I didn't lie. Just didn't tell you the truth either."

I scowled and pivoted, slinging the blade down to touch the one still sheathed so I could free my wrist from his grasp. He would have to lose his fingers if he wanted to draw it. "You told me you were off looking for a body when the Flatlanders attacked. That isn't true." Warning filled my eyes when he opened his mouth to speak. "Don't lie again. Flare has put stock in you. She wouldn't have left you to be killed."

"Fine, I lied." Nash wiped his eyes and groaned. "That stings."

Rage flushed through my veins, the pent-up horror of leaving Leif behind strangling all thoughts except for one. Nash had known. I swung for his chest. He dodged backward, and though I'd followed through to block him from his blade, he grabbed his empty sheath instead. Had the audacity to slam it onto the stolen sword I held.

The embarrassment of it distracted me for the fraction of an instant it took Nash to get his second blade in his hand.

"One of us is going to get hurt," he chided.

"Good."

I let my sword respond in a swift arc for his midsection which threw the sheath off to the side. He deflected, something I'd expected. With a skilled swordsman like Nash, my best defense was an offense. Giving him the opportunity to strike would mean death.

He was faster than I'd expected. Much faster than when we had sparred. He deflected a second strike. Quickly snapped his blade against mine in the center so the steel wobbled, vibrating through my hand. A reprimand, and evidence that he knew every inch of these blades. "Max." He narrowed the eyes I'd blackened with berries. "Stop it."

He'd lied. He'd known. He'd held back in a match. Fresh anger bloomed hot in my cheeks. I slashed through a branch overhead so it crashed against Nash in a flurry of leaves, but his blade crisscrossed through the debris in rapid swipes, so he never lost sight of me. Saw my every move as I kicked off the tree and barreled for his knees.

Without the advantage of surprise, he sidestepped, and I changed course, sliding across the ground as I slashed for his ankles. Nash's heel slammed the blade against the ground, almost ripping it from my grasp. Worse, the sword he wielded snapped for my neck. But I threw myself to the side and ripped the blade free.

I barely had time to get my knees beneath me before I was forced to block a strike head-on. The power of his blow shook me down to my bones. It broke my guard and left me open for a killing swipe. I'd known it only took one offensive attack from him to end a match. But I'd never been good at admitting when something was over. So, instead of letting him press the tip of his blade to my throat in a sign of defeat, I snapped my sword up perpendicular to the ground and strengthened it with my arm against it. A dangerous attempt to block his next hit, but a block nonetheless.

Nash twisted on his heel at the last moment so his sword swung away from me. He skidded to a stop and raised his voice. "Are you trying to lose an arm or just break my sword?"

I breathed hard. "Leif could be dead. You knew about the attack."

"I didn't know about the attack. Flare took me away before it started. I raced back to the camp."

"How can I trust a man who spies on his own homeland?"

"The Flatlanders banished me to the desert to die when I was a child." He shook his head. "My sister was sick and I stole from the offering to the gods so I would have something to trade for medicine. That land is not home. I won't let them take over the Valley when the Prophet dies."

I studied his amber eyes, searching for truth or lies. The unfairness of Skia Hellig throbbed in my chest and made me want to comfort him as his words turned in my mind. I'd been exiled before. What if he was telling the truth? Once again, I was left with two options. Either he was an incredible ally or a terrible enemy. I wasn't sure whether I could afford to pass up the chance to have his help, or whether I could afford the risk of having him around.

"You want to prove you mean it? Help me save Leif and Wren and the rest of the warriors."

"Will you try to slit my throat on the way?"

"Not if you don't give me reason to."

He scoffed. "So you really won't apologize?"

I picked up the sheath for his sword and passed his weapon back to him. "The invitation is as close as you'll get to an apology."

He checked his sword for damage and shook his head. "I'm angry with you."

"Great, because I'm angry with you, too."

He paused, staring at me with hints of intrigue clouding the anger. "Just keep your temper in check around my family. We'll stop there for supplies on the way to the outpost. That's where the Flatlanders will take everyone."

"By *family* you mean your daughter and her mother, right? Won't it put them in danger?"

"They live in the country on a farm. No one will know we came. We should make it by nightfall."

If I couldn't decide what to do with him, then it was better to keep an eye on him. I needed to get all my weapons back. If I'd had my bow, the fight would have been over much sooner.

"No more lies," I said, very aware of how hypocritical it was when I hid so much from him.

"Then don't you lie either."

I walked forward and he joined. What else could I do but see where our paths led, as I had in battle, as my instincts told me to do. I hoped that if I couldn't trust Nash, I could at least trust myself.

That had never been easy to do.

CHAPTER TEN

We'd arrived at Nash's family's home soon after nightfall. I sat on plush pillows on the floor with a steaming mug of tea on the short table before me while Nash talked with his child's mother, Trish, in the other room.

This was a nice house, the kind meant to last a lifetime. There was a kitchen and small living area with two bedrooms attached. Canvas paintings of the Valley hung on the walls. Fresh wildflowers fanned from a vase on the table. Enough time had passed for smoke to blacken the wall behind the indoor stove. The Prophet was able to offer people forever homes, with the promise of steady food and protection. No wonder so many served him.

"Sorry I didn't introduce myself properly earlier. I'm Trish." She'd quietly entered the room while I gawked at her house. Long hair lay over her shoulders.

"I should apologize. We've interrupted your day." I stood and bumped into the table. Tea sloshed onto the surface. "Sorry." I stumbled over my apology as I sopped up the steaming liquid with my shirt.

"Oh, I have towels." Trish opened a basket over by the stove.

Of course, she did. She wasn't some barbarian who cleaned up with the clothes she wore. I was a mess. Speaking of which, I looked terrible. Mud and grass stains streaked my dress. There were tiny tears and even specks of blood from the branches I'd hit. I didn't even want to think about my skin or hair.

Trish passed a towel to me even though there was nothing left to clean—except for myself, and I would need a stream or tub for that. Maybe the entire sea.

"My husband is a farmer and a politician," Trish said. "Important business called him away to the Prophet's village. We don't have to worry about him coming home."

Nash had brought us to the home of a councilman? Was he insane? No wonder Trish and her husband had gotten bound. They weren't just pious, but the most loyal to the Prophet.

"I should have mentioned that," Nash said to me. "He's always away at this time."

Interesting. Did Nash come here often when the other man was away? Trish cheating on her husband would be one thing. Betraying the mate she'd bound herself to? I couldn't fathom Nash putting his family in such danger.

Trish clasped her hands in front of her. "What he doesn't know won't hurt him. I wish Nash would make safer choices for himself, but I've sworn to honor him as my daughter's father, and that means making sure he doesn't get himself killed."

"I'm sorry, Trish," Nash said. "I know how you feel."

"Well . . . That doesn't seem to matter to you."

Nash looked away, jaw tightening. For Trish and Nash to entertain any semblance of feelings for one another, they must not have been able to help it. Trish was betraying not just the man she was bound to, but the Prophet they had sworn their eternal souls to by welcoming us. Disgust filled me at the thought of such a vow.

Even if no one ever found out that Trish helped us, surely she believed the gods knew. Protecting Nash was worth the stain on her soul.

Must have been love. Love that could never be. At least, not now that Trish had bound herself to another man.

"Elsie is playing out back," Trish said to Nash, easing the tension they'd created.

Nash nodded and then hesitated. "Take Elsie to the cabin until I return. Promise me you'll stay there."

Trish's voice tightened. "What will I tell him?"

"Whatever you have to. Soon, we'll all be free of the Prophet, including your husband. I know you both want that."

He walked past her without giving her time to ask more questions, and her worried eyes turned to me.

"It'll be okay." I wasn't sure why I said it, because I didn't know that it was true, or that it would even make her feel better.

She sighed quietly and offered a stiff smile before leading me around the house to collect things for our travels. Coin that Nash had stashed here, clothes, food, bandages, and jugs of water. I thanked her and then followed her out of the house, ready to be free from the discomfort of not knowing what to say. I was trespassing on their family time.

Nash reclined on the grass beside his daughter where she played. Tight curls of black hair bounced when she hopped on her knees, lifting two dolls up into the air. She had her father's smile, right down to the dimple. How often had I watched Leif lie on the ground with Rune when he was little and marvel at every move he made?

Pain crawled up my chest to wrap around my throat.

"What's her name?" Nash's voice was low and gentle. He tapped Elsie's doll on the head.

"I told you, Daddy. She's Daisy."

Nash smiled. Elsie seemed to forget about him as her doll got caught up in an adventure. He just rested there on the grass with her, watching every move she made.

I remembered that feeling so well. Being a child and the whole world fitting in my patch of grass. My vision blurred. I could see my father's face as it had been back when he was young and unburdened, or at least when I was too young to see it.

I'd broken my father into shards, keeping each piece of him separate so I'd never have to reconcile the different sides of him. If I ever put him back together in my mind again, I might lose the part that had once been my best friend. I tried to only see that side of him, but the rest forced its way in— shapeless, soundless memories lurking somewhere inside as pressure in my chest.

Nash looked up, then. He'd caught me watching. My cheeks burned but I forced myself to smile to cover my embarrassment.

He took Elsie's hand and led her to me. "This is Max. The friend I told you about. Introduce yourself."

Elsie hopped forward one step. "I'm Elsie. I'm four years old and this is where I live." She reached a stubby hand back toward her house.

I knelt at Elsie's level. "It's nice to meet you, Elsie. Your dad told me so many good things about you."

"Did he tell you I'm fast?"

"He did." I winked. Conversation came as easily with her as it always had with Rune. "He told me you're way faster than him."

Elsie clasped her hands over her mouth and giggled. "Daddy, did you really say that?"

Light as bright as the sun overhead filled Nash's eyes as he met his daughter's gaze. "Maybe we'll race sometime and see." He knelt to pick her up and kissed her forehead. "Listen now. Max and I have to go soon, baby."

Elsie's smile soured into a frown. And then she buried her face against him.

Nash held her head against his chest and rocked her lightly. "I'll be back soon. Promise."

Her voice hitched and she dropped her dolls, reaching her little arms up for his neck, sobbing. "Daddy, don't go!"

Trish stood up to come over, but Nash shook his head and brushed Elsie's hair back. He walked with her out toward the field, speaking to her in words I couldn't hear. My chest hurt watching them. Nash wasn't like my father. He really did love his daughter. Really was a good father. If he was so focused on Elsie, would he really spend time trying to manipulate me?

My soft heart was getting in the way again. Of course he would, if it meant being with his daughter or protecting her. From what I saw, Nash would do anything for Elsie. His love for her made him a risk to my people. Rune needed us as much as Elsie needed her father. More, because he was in danger. I had to repeat it to myself as I watched Elsie's tears soften, watched her melt in her dad's hug and cry herself to sleep as he whispered to her.

None of this meant I should trust Nash. But it was slowly succeeding. My anger, my suspicion, my fear dissipated. It wasn't even a fair fight.

I'd always known I would die young. I wouldn't bring a kid into the world only to abandon them. But I liked children. Thought I'd like to have one if I'd had a different fate. Nash and Elsie made me hurt, for the first time in many years, for the children I'd never have. The life I'd never have. Beneath the darkness of the eclipse, I'd always been destined to die, just as beneath the darkness of the eclipse, the child in me had once died by my father's hands. By my own hands, really. My fate had been sealed long ago.

Nash had hit my weakness. That didn't mean he was trustworthy.

CHAPTER ELEVEN

Trish saw us off while Elsie slept. Sadness wound its way around the short conversation. We left quickly. Quietly. The way I ached to see Rune again made me feel Nash's separation from his daughter too acutely to ignore.

I wanted to squeeze his hand like I would Leif's in such a situation, but I didn't. We were warriors, not friends, or comrades, or anything more. We had roles to play. And we played them well as we traveled through the night and stopped only to sleep a few hours once we couldn't continue.

"Are you bound to the Prophet?" I'd finally worked up the courage to ask. He could lie, but I wanted to see the look in his eyes.

"I'm bound to no one and nothing." He kept his eyes trained ahead. "Only to my child."

"The Prophet allows you to be unbound?"

"I suffered for my stubbornness. Eventually, he gave up."

"What did he do to you?"

Nash stiffened but his voice remained level. "He used his power to carve his name into my body. Then he healed me." He hesitated and glanced at me. "Again, and again."

"Bastard." I gripped my fists. Then my breath caught. "The script along your spine. It's scarring." Images of Eskel's bloodied name carved into his back flooded my mind.

Nash nodded. "If he would have threatened Elsie, I would have relented. But Trish had just been bound and he didn't need conflict with either family. The Prophet will only ever hurt Elsie if it's a last resort."

"I can't believe he would do it at all considering she is Trish's child."

"He won't let me go. He can't. It's not just because I'm an important asset. He would look weak."

I wanted to say something, but what words, especially from a near stranger who'd pulled a sword on him, could ease such a burden?

His voice dropped low. "One day, I'll watch him die, whether by my hand or another."

Nash had many reasons to hate the Prophet. Surely, I could trust he was an ally. "We'll kill the Prophet. I swear it. Just keep yourself alive for your daughter. You have to come home to her."

He said nothing, eyes fixed again, the pain back on his face.

Silence settled. As we journeyed, my heart ached more with every step, ached for Rune left in the Prophet's clutches, for abandoning Leif while he was injured, for whatever danger awaited them at the outpost, for the little girl crying for her daddy back home.

I could only think of how I wanted to set them free entirely, not just from the Prophet, but from the unfairness built into our world, from the gods.

For the first time in almost a decade, I let myself wonder if Piercey had made good on a very old promise, and if there could be hope after all.

My head ached as I walked through the woods with Nash. During the short rest we'd taken, I'd slipped again. This time to my future death that had always haunted me. I didn't think Nash noticed this time. I'd had my eyes closed as I rested against a tree. But it was enough for time to tear at my body and mind and cause both to ache.

It'd been three days since I'd taken my medicine, long enough for the mild dizziness to start, and for my thoughts to become harder to control. I needed to see Leif and Wren to know they were okay. The fears bombarded my mind constantly, humming inside me, humming so deeply my gut buzzed with it. I could face swarms of enemies without an inkling of fear for myself, but one night away from my people and I wanted to curl up into a ball. Every possible way they could die entered my mind, and all felt as likely as the sun setting this evening, no matter how I tried to reason with myself.

Even if they weren't in danger, which they were, I would have still felt uncomfortable with worry. Our circumstances, not having my medicine, knowing it would be days before seeing them, all of it filled my body with the heavy weight of dread.

To make matters worse, every time Nash looked at me, tingles bubbled beneath the unsteadiness of constant worry churning in my gut. Feeling both at once wasn't so different from the tension of being real in an unreal world. The two did not sit well together. The suspicion about him and fear I couldn't trust him warred with the draw to believe his story and not fight the pull I felt.

I whacked a patch of thickets with a branch I'd been carrying hard enough to make my hand buzz.

Nash shifted to look at me. I glanced away, knowing that even if I hid my face, I couldn't hide how tense my body was or how my free hand clenched in a fist. I couldn't unwind my body.

"You okay?"

My eyes burned. Throat ached. "I'm fine."

"Of course, you are."

"I am." My ankle caught in a tangle of thorns and I ripped free.

The kindness in Nash's eyes melted me. I didn't like another person I hardly knew having that kind of power over me, especially when I didn't feel like I deserved it from him.

I knocked another branch out of my path when the sensation of power pricked my skin into gooseflesh.

I wheeled around to an unsuspecting Nash. Of course, he couldn't feel her like I did. The look on my face must have set him on edge, because he drew his blades without even looking behind him.

"Flare." I narrowed my eyes at her over Nash's shoulder. She'd appeared out of nowhere. Just like she'd vanished the other night.

"I thought you were going to the Mountain of the Gods." Flare sauntered toward me. "You took a wrong turn a few hours ago."

"You know I can't abandon my people. I have to save them first."

"You're so easy to get riled up. Of course, I know. That's why I'm here. I thought you should have a heads-up. Wouldn't want you to get startled and accidentally hurt anyone."

"What are you talking about?"

She smiled and vanished again. Then the feeling of her exploded beside me right before her breath hit my cheek and her body warmed my side. "You owe me." The whisper seemed to linger longer than she did.

Flare had disappeared again.

It was dizzying trying to keep up with her. I looked to Nash to ask if he understood any of that, but his eyes were on the path we'd already walked. I heard it then. Faint footsteps.

He eased forward with his swords ready for a fight. On instinct, I listened, as I had so many times before, attuning my senses with my power, and heard the pitter-patter of two heartbeats I knew better than my own. My feet were running before the thoughts could fully form in my mind, and long before the names could escape my lips.

"Leif!" I sprinted as fast as I could. "Wren!"

Every person had a distinctness to the rhythm of their hearts, and I savored my friends' unique sounds as I finally made out their forms approaching.

There was no sign of the injuries that had left Leif wilted against the tree. The distance quickly disappeared between us but I couldn't slow down. I had to reach him so my hands could tell me what my eyes didn't believe. That he was here, alive and well. I slammed into Leif with my arms around him and knocked him onto the ground.

Tears streamed from my eyes onto his shirt as I buried my face against him and sobbed. "You're alive. You're really alive."

Leif groaned on the ground, holding on to me tight. "I missed you too, girl."

I reached for Wren, unable to release Leif, and drew her down to wrap an arm around her.

"Your wounds . . ." I wiped my eyes and nose and then patted Leif's chest and stomach where the arrows once protruded.

He wrinkled his brow. "Yes, please, wipe your snotty tears all over me."

I laughed and smacked his chest. "You're completely healed."

"The healers took care of all our injuries, no matter how minor." Wren smoothed my hair back from my face to get a good look at me. "What about you? Are you hurt?"

"No. Leif opened his big fat mouth and screamed for the enemy to get him. The fool saved me."

"I would do it again," Leif said, voice serious.

"Never again." Tears warped my voice. "Never."

"We have a lot to talk about." Wren met my eyes.

I didn't like the sound of that. Wren had her commander's voice, the calm but impossible-to-deny tone she used in battle and meetings.

"We do," I said. "Just first, tell me how you escaped. Are they searching for you?"

"The demon from the Prophet's village came," Leif said.

"Her name is Flare," I said with a hard voice.

Wren nodded. "Then the Flatlanders released us with our weapons. We brought yours." When she pulled my bow off her back, I immediately grabbed it like I had Leif. "They told us we were free to attack the Prophet of the Valley as long as we didn't interfere with them again, and they let us leave while they kept the others hostage."

"They're using you as a weapon." I twisted at Nash's voice. "You've been a shield for the Flatlanders for many years. The Prophet was too busy in the Valley to turn to them."

Leif eyed Nash. "What do you know of the Flatlanders?"

He sighed and rubbed the back of his neck. When he opened his mouth to speak, I interrupted. "I'll explain everything soon. The Prophet has information on the Flatlanders." I held Leif's arm. "Let's talk on the road."

Nash watched me, looking surprised.

Leif didn't seem satisfied, but he did nod. He would never accept Nash if he knew the truth, not when he was still suspicious of him anyway. I'd cover for Nash, for now. Though I had concerns of my own, I did believe that I could kill Nash myself if he stepped out of line. And I had the help of Leif and Wren now. If he truly hated the Prophet as much as he said, then we needed him. Plus, Flare could cause problems if I ditched Nash. Concern churned in my gut as I reasoned with myself, because it was starting to sound an awful lot like rationalizations, and if I had to keep it a secret from Leif, then maybe it meant I was being a fool.

As we walked, I remembered what Nash had said after we sparred. He felt like we'd met in a dream he couldn't remember. I knew that feeling so well. Maybe it was why I couldn't send him away. Or maybe it was a much more pathetic reason. My head was spinning with worry.

We'd spent two days on the road and still had so far to go to make it to the Mountain of the Gods. After a few hours of anxiety, I'd tried to convince Wren and Leif to return to our people. However, Flare had already told them of my plans to travel to the Mountain of the Gods, and Chief Kaid had already commissioned our trip. Wren took her duty as a commander too seriously. Even without the order, I wouldn't have been able to convince these two to leave me. There was no turning back.

Wren had said that it hadn't been an easy conversation before they left. Our leaders had questions that no one could answer except for me. They had always respected that I didn't want to discuss my past. That was over now. When I returned, I had to answer to the chief, and she was angry with me for withholding so much more than she'd ever imagined. To my surprise, Wren said Beast had been the first to say that they would wait for my return to attack the Prophet, because they wouldn't be able to defeat him without me and whatever I had been hiding on this mountain.

I would have accepted Leif and Wren being angry with me as well, but they weren't. It only fueled the guilt I felt for not telling them about my history. I'd wanted to protect them. Now, I was leading them to the most dangerous place in the world.

"Flare told us you'd agreed to work with her and brought us here." Wren's eyes were on the pink of the sunrise as we walked. Nash had ventured further up the path and Leif hung behind him, refusing to take his eyes off the other man for a moment.

"I am not working with her. She told me bringing you here was a gift." I shook my head. "I think it's a warning. She's showing me what she can do and indebting me to her."

"What about Nash? Do we trust him?"

I smiled at that. *We.* Because if I trusted someone, Wren would, too, no questions asked. Unlike Leif. "Enough for now."

"He won't be easy to take down if it comes to it."

"No."

Wren hesitated, voice gentler now. "If the worst does happen, with him or whatever awaits us on the mountain, we'll need your power."

Pain twisted my stomach. I couldn't bring myself to look at her. "How long have you known?"

"Longer than Leif." She hooked her arm around my neck and leaned on me as we walked, tall and slender. Always there to keep me grounded. "He told me the power is sealed. You'll get it back. I have no doubt."

And that was all she said. No questions asked. No details given. Just a nonchalant update that my circle knew I was a demon and always had known. Great.

Where Leif might have chided me for my shame or tried to make me laugh until I forgot, Wren only walked alongside me and let us be silent together. Though they knew my secret, they didn't really understand. They hadn't seen what I was capable of, but soon they might. What if they looked at me differently? They would always love me. But what if the precious comfort of their acceptance grew dimmer and things shifted? And what if I lost what I loved most in the world?

By the time we stopped to rest for the night, my stomach was in a tangled mess. That didn't seem to matter to Leif, though, because he decided to pounce anyway. Nash and Wren both left to forage before bed while Leif and I prepared a fire. Hardly a minute had passed after they left when Leif ripped the firewood from my arms and threw it on the ground.

"Tell me the truth, now," he said.

I frowned at the wood on the leafy forest floor and then at him. "What?"

"What? You know what." Leif scowled. "Are you fucking the enemy?"

My jaw dropped in indignation. "Obviously not."

"It's not obvious at all."

I growled and shoved him. "Don't be an ass, Leif!"

He swatted me away. "Girl." Warning filled his voice. "I'm not playing."

"I'm not either."

"Then make this make sense. Why is he here?"

Now real hurt spread over my chest. "You think I would compromise the most important thing in the world to me because of that? The only thing I care about is getting our people back."

His expression softened, but it didn't stop him from saying the next part. "You wouldn't do it on purpose." He held up a hand when I started for him again. "Don't. I mean it."

I lowered my fist to my side. "We need all the help we can get. He has inside information on the Prophet and Flare, and he's one of the best swordsmen I've ever met."

"Those all sound like reasons to me to never fall asleep around him. Max, you're not this stupid."

"Wren trusts me."

"Wren is too trusting. You're usually the first to say that."

He had a point. I fell back against the closest tree. "It's my gut, Leif. No matter what happens, I just keep feeling like he's supposed to be here. And don't you dare say it has anything to do with any kind of feelings for him, because it doesn't."

Looking unconvinced, he sighed. "I've always trusted you, but I don't trust him. If he's here, then we're sleeping in shifts. My family is on the line, Max."

"I know." I bit the inside of my cheek. "Look, if we send him back now, then who knows what he'll do? If he really isn't on our side, he could go straight to the Prophet. If we keep him with us, we can watch him and kill him if he crosses us. Is there anything more trustworthy than my bow and your sword?"

Leif grinned now. "Hell no. Nothing. Look, if the time comes, you have to really kill him, though. You can't let your emotions get in the way. And just know if he even looks at you too long, I'm ripping his windpipe out with my bare hands." He lifted his fist in the air like he was imagining it. "Then I'll shove it back down his throat, deep in there, and—"

"Okay." I pushed off the tree. "Damn. I get it."

He picked up the wood and hesitated. "I may have been a little harsh with you."

"You were an asshole!"

"Stop being so childish." Leif groaned. "Shouldn't you have grown up more by now? You're not a kid anymore."

"You're the one who should have grown up by now, you old man."

"I am not old."

"Arn would take my side, you know. He wants you to be more patient with me."

Leif rolled his eyes. "Only a holy man could have enough patience to deal with you, girl."

As much as the bickering could annoy me, I loved it just as much, and I loved having Leif and Wren back with me. When I settled to sleep that night with Leif and Wren both close, I finally had a touch of peace. But it still wasn't enough to keep me from slipping away in my dreams.

CHAPTER TWELVE

*W*ind rushed beyond the Sacred School and tore over the cliff, carrying away pebbles from the rock we sat on.

Piercey stared past the Valley below with eyes still as the dead themselves. He didn't need to tell me what he was thinking about. I could feel it as powerfully as the wind.

"We're real," I said.

"Then we'll still be real when we wake up in the real world."

I closed my eyes. "What is the real world, Piercey? She said her world is digital. Her people all uploaded. There may be nothing physical to return to."

"Don't you want to know what's out there? Where we come from? Who we are?" He turned to face me. "You want to fight to keep this prison they built for us?"

"I'm the one who has wanted to escape the school for years."

Piercey threw his head back and laughed. "Listen to yourself. The whole world is the school. It's all under their control. It's all fake."

"Our life is here."

"What about our life out there? What if we all have families waiting for us to wake up from this world? Who knows whether Dr. Henderson told us the truth when she said this is the only life we've ever known." He reached for my hand then, life in his eyes for the first time since we found out. "Let's be free. We don't even have to fight. Just jump."

I recoiled. Pebbles scattered over the cliff's edge and fell until they were too small to see. "I'm not jumping. Don't you even care that you'll lose me?"

His expression fell.

"I doubt they'll let us remember any of this if we do get to live beyond this world. We'll lose everything we have, including each other. I won't be me anymore if I can't remember my life."

He turned his face back toward the cliff. "I didn't think you'd be willing to participate in their experiment, even if rebellion cost you everything."

"Living is not giving in. Dying is. This is our life. Ours. We should take this world back from them. Not abandon it, abandon everyone in it, to the whim of false gods."

"You can't fight a god, Max."

I rose and turned my face into the wind so it would dry the tears that filled my eyes. "I won't surrender to death, and I won't be her lab rat either. I'm leaving this school. I'm going to live. Maybe I can't take our world back, but I'll take my life back. One day, I'll figure out how to do more than that. I'll figure out how to beat the Kethios."

Piercey lowered his head. "You'd rather fight than be free."

I knelt down and wrapped my arms around Piercey's shoulders. Settled my head against his back. "You feel this?"

The wind roared against us.

"This is real. This right here. If we feel, we are."

Piercey was quiet for a long while. We sat that way with silence and wind between us.

When he spoke, his voice was stripped of emotion. "The white room must be beyond our simulation because the laws of physics seem to be different. If there's a way for the gods to let us in, there must be a way to break in." He squeezed my hands. "If we can break into the white room, we should be able to also break into the infrastructure of the simulation. Break into their control."

I knit my brows. "If we hack into the interface of our world and take control from them, they could physically destroy the hardware we're on."

"Destroying hardware is risky. Do they have a fail-safe? Are we separate from the other simulated worlds they're experimenting on? Destroying us could destroy their entire project. Maybe they would just let us live freely."

I settled my forehead against the back of his neck. "You're too optimistic. Dr. Henderson doesn't look like the type of woman to let go. She'd fight for control."

"But would she destroy us?"

"That's a major gamble."

"Might be better than jumping off a cliff."

Piercey had spent years helping me plan to escape, and still he refused to actually do it. "Would you really do it, Piercey? Would you actually try to take back our world from the gods?"

The quiet that followed said it all.

I sighed. "You always find the answers and do nothing with them."

He glanced behind himself, where I still held him. "I find the answers for you. I can't deny you anything, Max. I've never been able to."

We were growing up. I heard it in his words. Felt it in his strong grip on my arms. This wasn't like when I first came here at eleven and he held me when I was homesick. Or when I pulled him close after he'd failed his first healing test. The children in us couldn't survive long in a place like this. We were growing into more. And my arms around him had grown into more, too, into something he wanted but I never quite did. I should have let go then as I felt that stillness settling between us, only it was hard to let go of the only person who'd never let go of me.

"Stay in this world, Piercey." I held him a moment longer. A moment too long. "Stay in my life."

I made myself release him then and I walked away, leaving him to feel the emptiness of someone letting go. Because if he jumped, he'd let go forever.

"You matter more to me than the world. I'd risk it all for you." I said it softly. So softly, I didn't know if he'd heard me.

The slips to the future and past were getting worse, so every time I fell asleep, I lost my hold on the present. At the very least, I was recovering quicker. This time, not even Leif noticed something was wrong.

It was getting harder to keep information to myself as we traveled. Everyone deserved more from me, including Nash. It was just so hard to make myself share it. I told them pieces of the truth that wouldn't endanger them. I'd been recruited by the Prophet in my homeland on the other side of the world to train at the Sacred School when I was eleven, but I'd run away before becoming one. Nash had asked if the gods gave their powers to me. I'd said I didn't make it that far, even though the truth was that I'd been born with the power. But now they all knew that I had a friend on the mountain who stayed, and would be as powerful as the rest of the Prophets by now.

Nash had been the most persistent in asking me questions, but I'd been persistent in ignoring him.

It hadn't worked any favors in regard to the tension between us. I couldn't stop thinking about how he worked with Flare, which only made me angry again about him serving the Prophet. I understood his reasons, but I couldn't respect them. I would have found another way.

At least, I wanted to believe I would.

The anger would churn with my worries about whether Leif was right and I'd made a mistake, until Nash met my eyes. That instinctive pull to trust him would overwhelm my senses, and I couldn't decide whether that meant I absolutely should not have been listening to myself, or whether I should. I'd always followed my gut in the past.

The next time Nash had pressed me for information, I glanced at the narrow space between us. "You should be careful."

He raised his brows, confused.

"Leif is watching you and he already described to me in detail how he will brutally murder you if you get too close to me."

A grin climbed up one side of Nash's face. "Really?" Nash glanced behind us and I did as well. Leif stared directly at him with his hand resting on his sword, walking close enough that he could reach him with one swift lunge.

"You've made your point," Wren whispered to Leif.

But the man would not be swayed and kept his glare on Nash.

I was surprised when Nash smiled in response and turned so that he could see everyone as he walked backward. "I grew up with a sister." Then, he tapped his left shoulder. "I had a bad wound a few years ago. It's slight, but my flexibility is not quite as good on this side. If you get just the right angle behind me, it can be a problem in battle."

"Are you mocking me, boy?" Leif asked.

"Just giving you reassurances. I can't fault you for protecting Max. If I got to see my sister again, I'd do the same."

Wren's expression melted. "That's sweet."

"No. You think you can charm people." Leif shook his head. "It doesn't matter to me what your intentions are. I won't trust you."

Nash shrugged. "Fair enough." He took a large step away from me to the side, but it only made Leif grumble.

The encounter had distracted Nash from interrogating me, at least. I had to focus on strategizing how to make it up the mountain and get my power back. Perhaps, if I killed the instructors, it would unlock my abilities.

And what if the gods decided to prevent me from even stepping foot on the mountain?

I rubbed my sore neck as we walked.

After another day of traveling, I finally had to break it to the group that to make it to the Mountain of the Gods we would have to cross forbidden lands, and that our method of transportation also happened to be forbidden.

"I don't understand." Leif crossed his arms and eyed me. "It's a beast?"

I held back my sigh. "It's called a train. It transports resources from the mines to factories where things like our weapons are made, and then to the edge of the forbidden land where the Prophet's people move everything on the highways."

Nash scratched his nose with his thumb and scoffed. "You soften it with your made-up words. Forbidden and holy are the only descriptions that matter. The Prophet ensures death for anyone who tampers with those lands."

Leif waved a hand in the air. "Max survived the Mountain of the Gods. She'll teach us to survive the Prophet's forbidden lands. What I want to know is whether the Prophet keeps such a powerful beast under his control all the time? That must exhaust him. Perhaps, it's a weakness."

Nash glanced at Leif. "Exceptional point."

"No," I said. "It's not a beast. It's not alive. It has no mind. It's made of metal, like our swords, and powered by energy, kind of like the electricity in the Prophet's village."

"The closest villagers say it roars like a beast," Nash said. "So loud that it shakes the ground."

Wren nodded. "I've heard of something like this. The Prophet can use the souls of the dead to animate nonliving things and use them for his will."

Leif gave a skeptical look. "That's some made-up shit, Wren."

Her brows furrowed in frustration. "How is it any less made-up than some mindless train beast?"

I snorted and coughed to cover the reaction. "You'll understand when you see it."

"I'm not sure I want to understand," Leif mumbled.

The others nodded in agreement.

I chuckled. "So none of you want to ride the train?"

"No," all three said at once.

"Well, then you really won't like the Mountain of the Gods." I walked backward so I could see everyone. "You could turn back and let me go alone."

"No," Leif said, eyes narrowed.

I shrugged. "It was worth a try."

As we drew closer to the route the train took, the scenery changed. Beside me, Nash's face looked shadowed as he shifted toward the foothills of the Mountain of the Gods where the industrial zone was hidden away. No one dared venture there, not even the most fearless of scavengers and looters. What the Prophet called forbidden was taken seriously, especially with the shadow of the mountain looming over it. Might and reputation were far better deterrents than the best defense. Even the demons feared stepping too close to the forbidden foothills.

Really, it was an area filled with mines and factories run mostly by machines and the disciples of the creators, Prophets who were gifted inventors. Unfortunately, they tended to not be as gifted in warfare, which meant that most creators in the world fell to the control of ferocious Prophets, like Eskel the Ruthless.

The potential of neural implants had been wasted and abused in so many ways, but this was perhaps the worst. An industrialized area hidden from the people and controlled entirely by one cruel man. Although, the palaces on the coast almost infuriated me as much. The most powerful people in the peninsula vacationed to these high-tech retreats, where they could indulge in the most luxurious of pleasures, and the nastiest to imagine. I'd heard of awful virtual reality rooms where the most faithful lived out their most depraved fantasies.

Perhaps we could have cured diseases that could wipe out entire villages, but no, we had to focus on weapons for controlling and pleasures for the pampered. The forbidden lands were cursed in my mind, but not for the reasons that others feared it. Our world wasn't ready for this power, and we didn't deserve it.

I sped up, wishing I could flee my thoughts. The guilt pawed at me, and with it the burning of the eclipse that had always haunted me. I could feel the flames burning my hands. See the Prophet's inky eyes staring at me. Sense death closing in around me.

A shudder squeezed my spine, trying to wring the life from me.

I pressed on with the others until we rounded a bend and saw the first large factory building looming over us. Train tracks cut across the ground before it.

Nash was the first to slow. Leif continued further toward the building, and Wren came to my side.

"Do they have things like this on the mountain?" she asked.

I nodded. "Something like it."

Ahead of us, Nash's hands tightened into fists. "The bastard keeps this all for himself. What storm could tear down such a structure? Children could have better homes if the Prophet is capable of this."

The words settled over us, resonating the same way a voice echoed in the mountains. Trains arrived and departed constantly to keep up with the Prophet's expanding reach. One would come soon and we would have to be ready.

"Forbidden," Leif said. "Forbidden to all but a few."

A faint roar swelled behind us and then the rumbling of the ground began in weak vibrations. Leif twisted, as if ready to face off against an enemy, while Wren studied the possible threat from her war-painted eyes. I watched Nash and how his expression changed so subtly as the massive train charged toward us. For the first time, it occurred to me that having to serve the Prophet and live in his shadow meant Nash had seen things Leif and Wren hadn't. And that, perhaps, shock did not come as easily to him as I expected.

There was no need for defense this far away from any villages and so deep in the forbidden lands. The train pulled to a stop right before a massive door that opened to the factory, where large crates traveled by overhead rails. Then, the train would creep forward, so the next car lined up with the door.

I motioned for my friends to follow as I climbed up the side of a car and hefted myself on top.

Leif clung to the edge when the train rolled forward, eyes wide. "I still do not understand."

I had to turn my face away to keep from laughing.

Once the last car had been loaded, I rolled onto my stomach and held the edge like Leif had. "Don't let go."

The train moved forward, gaining speed every moment until it broke that of a horse, and soared beyond how fast anyone except for me would have ever traveled.

Leif screamed at the top of his lungs with his hair ripping back in the wind. "I don't fucking understand."

But Nash lifted onto his forearms, eyes bright as he looked over the side. My stomach tightened and I grabbed the back of his shirt, terrified he'd fall.

"Careful," I said.

He looked into my eyes, laughing that exhilarated kind of laugh while the curls flew back from his face. "No land will be forbidden to me again."

My heart caught. I gripped his shirt still, unable to let go with how close to the edge he rode. "You're having fun?"

He scooted to the middle of the car and carefully crawled onto his knees, letting his head fall back, his arms raised, his tunic whipping in the wind. Exposed cliffs flashed around us as the train rushed ahead at full speed. Leif screamed in horror again while Nash laughed and unleashed a very different kind of roar.

Wren nudged me with her foot. She'd been so quiet and still, I hadn't even looked at her. "Stop worrying so much."

I bit my lip and looked back to Nash. It did look fun. Sighing, I crawled beside him and closed my eyes against the power of the wind. His arm slid around me, and Leif was too busy clinging for dear life to the edge of the car to notice.

"Does it go faster, Sharpshooter?"

"I think this is fast enough." I laughed.

With the danger we were barreling for, I couldn't believe I was feeling anything close to fun, but I couldn't keep Nash's infectious grin from spreading to me.

So I took the excuse to hold on to him, to let the wind take away my suspicion and fear, and enjoy the exhilaration of how each curve made us slide. Nash and I held on to each other tightly, laughing as we kept each other from toppling over. I could let myself have a short time with my guard down. It felt good to let go of all of my anxiety. It seemed to be something Nash had no trouble doing.

I couldn't decide if he just didn't have the good sense to be afraid. Or, if maybe he had the sense not to be.

CHAPTER THIRTEEN

We hiked through the foothills of the mountain after we reached the end of the train's line. Along the way, I told everyone of the dangers that awaited us: hidden pits with sharpened stakes, a lethal army, perilous trails. The mountain guard would kill anyone who came or left without permission. No exceptions. The only reason I'd ever escaped was because in the earliest days of the school, the instructors had used their power to carve secret passageways into the mountain. None of them connected from the beginning to the top, but it offered reprieve for anyone who lived at the Sacred School if they needed to take an unsanctioned trip down the mountain.

Gentle slopes stretched into towering hills, the dark of fertile land now pocked with gravel and bright with rusty soil, bald here where the carpet of trees had thinned into dead grass and thorny weeds. The Valley was lush with vegetation, but the southeast side of the Mountain of the Gods looked as if someone had painted it in a brushstroke of red. A unique pocket of iron-rich hills and cliffs starved this swath of land. Soon, the inclines would steepen into small mountains that rolled like waves into the giant peaks, and there the cover of evergreen pines would shield us from the sun once more.

We were close. Close enough for the land to cool in the mountain's shadow. As we hiked, the hours crawled by, and the mountain slowly grew above us, until its white peaks took up most of the sky.

"I want to know more about the mountain and the Sacred School." Nash spoke quietly to me.

"I've told you what I can."

"You hold the knowledge and power in your hands and feed me crumbs as you see fit." He pounded his fist in his hand. "I won't go from being the Prophet's lackey to yours."

Pain pinched my chest. "I never asked you to do that. If you don't trust me, then go home."

"I'm not going anywhere. I just want to know what the hell I'm jumping into."

I wiped the sweat from my brow. "Chaos and torment. That's what, Nash. Mysteries you'll never unravel. Get used to it if you want to finish this journey."

He huffed in frustration and walked on ahead of me. Fine. I steeled myself against his dissatisfaction and trekked forward.

I continued the rest of the way in silence, slowing when I reached the unseen barrier surrounding the mountain. Would the gods intervene? The instructors should not have been able to detect me unless I used my power, which of course, I currently couldn't. But I had no idea what the gods were capable of.

I tensed my muscles as I took my first step over and waited for something devastating, like a fireball to shoot from the sky and incinerate me. Nothing happened, though. Another step and I started to hope that I might survive after all.

Nothing looked different over this barrier, not the cone tops of the trees or the dense shadows, but the air here was charged. Already, the warmth of my dormant power felt even hotter than normal.

From this moment on, we would be hunted if anyone caught even a hint of our presence. "We're here," I said. "Stay quiet."

Nash, Leif, and Wren filed into a line behind me, copying my every movement perfectly, just as we'd discussed as we traveled. Harsh rock cliffs and broken patches of grassy land mottled the terrain. I stepped carefully across what looked like a worn path up a slope, but I knew hidden pits lined both sides, with only a thin patch of earth to travel across. I steadied my breath as I put one foot in front of the other.

"Everyone okay?" I asked and checked behind me.

They all nodded.

Once I crossed the path, I held my breath until Nash, Leif, and finally Wren made it to me. There wasn't time to celebrate. Every moment out in the open risked us being seen, and the guards had radios. If I did manage to use my power, they even had detectors that picked up quantum energy so they could track us.

Why the gods had been willing to give such advanced technology to the guards when they claimed not to act in our world made my blood boil. The guards had a mandate from the gods, and I knew their communication and detection devices came from them. Dr. Henderson wouldn't help children trapped at the school, but she would equip people to hunt us down.

I struggled to understand why the guards so fanatically fought to protect the mountain. Piercey had wondered if they were artificial intelligence. But the gods would want to replicate whatever they did here in physical worlds. What had they done to earn such fealty?

There were so many answers left to uncover. I had always wondered if that was the real reason Piercey refused to come with me. So he could unearth all the secrets on this mountain.

We navigated around pit after pit. Finally, we picked up our pace across steepening terrain until we stopped at the base of a towering hillside. Sparse trees grew out from the side, the roots bare where earth had slid away beneath rain and wind.

"We have to get to the top," I said. "Watch the path I take."

"There must be an easier way." Leif gaped at the towering hill.

"Trust me. This is the easy path. Any other way, and we'll have to fight the guards, which means we'd have to keep fighting our way up the rest of the mountain." I gripped a tree root sticking out from the mud and hefted myself up. "Go slow."

We picked our way up the dirt incline on our hands and knees. I tested the ground ahead of us, careful to veer away from any patches of ground that didn't look stable. Leif climbed up right beside me with Wren and Nash not far behind.

Rocks broke loose from Leif's grip and tumbled down the hill. He pressed his head against the dirt, breathing out slowly. "We're all going to die."

"We're not going to die." I dug my toes into the earth and climbed up another foot.

The ground vibrated against my hands; the mountain angry with my arrogance.

Beneath Nash's hands and knees, a massive shelf of earth broke free of the hillside. In an instant, he was airborne.

Fear choked out my breath.

I launched myself down the hill with all my strength and drew my blade as I fell. I reached for the heat inside of me desperately, focusing on the power I felt from this mountain, and struggled to grasp what had been locked away. Traces of it burned inside of me and helped to drive myself faster than Nash tumbled, until he was within reach. But I needed more and I needed it now.

I slammed my sword through the falling debris for the cliffside. Nash caught the hilt of the sword with me, so I released my hold on it to grab him around his neck, fighting against the earth to lock my legs around him.

Nash grunted as he held on to the sword with both hands now, our bodies slowing just slightly more than the landslide. Still reaching for my power, I clawed at scraps of it to help us stop. I managed only to pull out a trickle of it, but it was enough to clear out the mud around us so the sword broke free to stable earth. It nearly ripped the weapon from his hands and me from his back. I wasn't sure whether we held on ourselves or whether that was more power that had saved us.

We hung from the sword as the ground fell away beneath us.

"You're . . ." Nash panted. ". . . insane . . ."

Looking up, I found Wren with her arm latched around a small tree while Leif pulled her over the edge of the newly formed cliff.

Dread filled me. The guards would have heard that landslide and I may have managed to use enough power for them to detect.

I released Nash and rolled as I slid along loose dirt. Nash dropped next and tossed the sword to the side. The mud nearly swallowed it whole.

"You could have died." Nash stumbled toward me, covered in mud. Chunks of it hung from his hair, the weight flattening his curls. "What were you thinking?"

"We're alive. It doesn't matter." I looked up at the exposed cliff. There was no way we were getting back up. "We'll have to take the difficult route." I sighed and backed up to see Leif and Wren. "The passageway is behind you. Travel up the stairs. We'll meet you at the top by the morning. Do you see it?"

I focused on the rock wall, imagined it, and tried to carefully pry open the narrow slit that would allow them through. Damn it, though. It wasn't working. Opening the passageway took so little energy. I had to find a way to access these passageways or we were dead, considering that we'd accidentally announced ourselves to the guards.

Breathing in deeply, I allowed my father's voice from childhood to fill me. Though I tried not to think about him, he always made me angry, and anger more than any other emotion helped me to unleash myself.

"Feel the flame inside you. Let it grow."

Energy flowed out from me, not as something I could see, but feel. Enough, I hoped.

Leif looked back down with wide eyes.

Yeah, he saw.

"Be careful!" he shouted.

"We have to go." I nodded toward the woods. "Guards could be here any minute."

Nash followed me as I sprinted for the wooded hill to our right. This led to an impassable rock wall with only a thin tunnel that was always crawling with guards.

"We'll have to fight." I drew my bow. "There's no way around it."

A tree splintered ahead of us. We both shot to the ground. I rolled off my shoulder and landed on my knee behind a tree trunk. Nash pressed against one ahead of me.

I spun out from my shelter. Immediately released my arrow into the chest of our attacker.

"Flank them," I said. "Dead ahead there's a tunnel through the cliff. Meet me there."

Nash nodded, swords drawn now. "Be safe, Sharpshooter."

I clenched my jaw, thinking of Elsie in his arms. "You, too."

We broke away and sprinted in opposite directions.

The power escaping from the cracks within me might not have compared to what I'd once been able to do, but it energized me now. As I ran, I easily listened for heartbeats. There were five guards already in Nash's path. I couldn't leave all of them for him. My eyes fluttered as I aimed my bow and drove my arrow with my mind. It whizzed between trees, around branches, and flew straight into the heart of a guard headed for Nash.

Despite not being able to use power for so many years, what I could grasp came back to me naturally.

With my hearing attuned, I noticed the stomping of the guards as they all switched directions, running straight for me. They must have been watching their radars and I must have exuded enough energy for them to detect.

A group came into sight. They scattered between the trees, using them as cover as they wove through the woods.

I had to break through this seal on my power. These few hours on the Mountain of the Gods had helped me to regain far more than I had during years of training and struggle. Everything was different here. I could do this.

When Piercey and I had trained at the Sacred School, he had increased his powers by studying the science behind what we did and by actually understanding the code of our world. I'd always felt it, like water I could run my fingers through, or sand I could gather in my hand. It was the same as seeing the visible world versus reading a description of it. Without thought, I experienced it.

Together, we'd made a great team by combining those imperfect methods. I didn't understand exactly why this mountain changed my access to my power, but as I reached for it, I felt as if I could actually touch it for the first time since it was sealed. If only I had Piercey with me to help me get there faster by seeing the world through his eyes as well as my own.

I could not allow anything to hold me back, though. Lifting my palms, I scraped down to the depths of my soul with my will. Everyone was counting on me. If I couldn't do this, it wasn't just Leif, Wren, and Nash who would die here. All of our warriors and innocents would, too. I had to let go of my past failures and my fear that I couldn't do this. I had to kill the curse.

A wave of energy exploded out from me.

The guards flew through the air from the power of the hit. They slammed against their backs and slid across the ground, knocking into each other, into thick trees.

Wow. The rush flooded my body with energy. It was by far the most power I'd managed since losing mine. Even so, it was a pathetic shadow of what I'd once managed to do. I should have been able to instantly kill all of them.

I lowered my head. The burn of my power ate across my skin. This sting was only a taste of how bad it could get. I needed to get used to it again.

To my heightened senses, the subtle twitch of a guard turning his hand for his knife jolted through my chest like he'd slammed his fist into me. My eyes snapped to him.

I bound his hand with my mind. Turned his own weapon on him so the quivering tip pushed for his throat.

He clasped it with both hands. The veins in his arms and neck and face strained like massive worms thrashing to break free of skin.

He shrieked. Maybe they all shrieked. The noise faded into the background for me. I only heard my own blood rushing through me. I felt alive again.

I drilled the knife into the man's neck as I lunged for another guard.

The rest happened fast. Incredibly fast. It'd been so long that I had forgotten how quickly I could move, think, act when I accessed my power.

I snapped the wrist of a woman and drove my sword through her gut.

A flash of power and I closed the throats of two others, strangling their screams into the guttural, gasping sounds of dying animals.

My own fear drummed beneath the thrum of my power. Fear of myself. Of what I could do and had done before. I couldn't hold myself back because of it. I strained for every ounce of power I managed to draw out from myself.

The last one left untouched backed up against a tree and choked on her sobs. The other two had collapsed onto their sides, their movements weaker now. Power rippled across every inch of my body, the burn more like sparks of electricity.

I snapped the necks of the ones I was strangling.

"D-demon." The living guard trembled. "Demon!"

I slashed her throat with my sword. It split in a neat, thin line that opened to the fountain of blood within.

In the old days, I would have killed them all before they could take a breath. This little rush of power had my skin burning and covered with sweat. We were never meant to wield our gift for destruction, and the pain of it was something that took training to overcome and banish. How could I take on the Prophet when I was in such a state from killing five powerless humans?

My eyes snapped shut. We were all humans. I was a human. I repeated it to myself until I was sure I would never forget. Thoughts like that were dangerous. Words like that. They were every bit as powerful as the energy I could use to tear apart a body.

Cold air nipped at my burning skin. No, no, no. It was warm today. My friends needed me. No slipping.

But in the cold air, I heard the whisper of Piercey's voice the last day I'd seen him, so calm and so in defiance of his usually soft spirit.

"None of this is real. Don't hate yourself."

I tried to shake his voice away. The woods blinked blue. The pale blue of my hall as a child. Pale blue streaked in blood as black as the sun during the eclipse.

My instructors' faces blurred against a veil of tears. The twist of their mouths frozen in terror, frozen as snowflakes fell from the hole in the ceiling onto their lips. I'd told them not to hurt Piercey anymore. Told them. "I didn't mean to . . . I thought I had control now . . ."

"No one can control a power like this," Piercey said. "The Prophets are wicked with it. The gods have gone cruel with it. It's the power, Max. Not us."

"I can't stay here." I lifted my bloody hands, eyes wide. "I killed two instructors. We have to go, Piercey. It's time."

I nearly slipped entirely to that day, when I saw the eyes of the last guard I'd killed today on the mountain. Wide hazel eyes stared into mine, frozen forever in terror.

My breath came in broken gasps. I couldn't slow down, no matter how hard I tried. I doubled over, breathing so rapidly that none of it reached my lungs. If only I had my medicine.

In the hot haze of my guilt, Piercey's voice whispered in the woods. Whispered on the breeze.

"You mean more than the world to me, too, Max."

Even though Piercey had said it, he still hadn't come with me. With all the time that passed, the pain of it still burned deeply within me. If it was true, then how could he stay behind? I had stayed at the Sacred School for him even when it killed me. So why hadn't he fled with me? It had felt like betrayal. Abandonment.

If I let myself feel the lost friendship, the slip would steal me away to the past. Or even worse, the future. My legs wobbled beneath me, more from what I'd done than from the fight itself. That power, as limited as it was, would be like a beacon. More would come our way. We needed to make it to a passageway.

I walked forward as I nocked an arrow and used my power to drive its aim through the throat of a guard approaching from the east. Again with another. Another.

Fire flooded my veins. I didn't want to kill these people. It didn't feel right, like I was attacking someone who was unarmed. But if I didn't kill them, they would kill my friends, and I would never make it up the mountain. The guards would never give up on killing intruders. I needed all my power, not these crumbs. Either the journey to the top would help me break free, or I'd force the instructors to break their seal.

I focused on Nash, the strong beat of his heart stilling my own. I sprinted for the pass to meet him and found him there, walking straight through the narrow hall of stone. Nash rolled his shoulders, both blades in his strong grip.

Four guards ran forward. Or at least, four guards had when I entered.

Nash plucked a knife from his side and threw it into the eye of one guard. A long step. Drove his blade straight up through the soft underside of another's chin.

The others pushed forward with their faces red and strained.

Nash sidestepped one swipe and then another from the third guard. I rushed forward to help when he carved his blade through the man's back. Only one remained and Nash rushed him, charging forward like a bull.

The last one raised his sword, but Nash knocked it from his grip with one hit and plastered him against the rock wall with his shoulder so hard that spit flew from the guard's mouth. Blood rushed down the man's legs in a stream. He collapsed into the red puddle on the ground, his stomach open and pulsing.

Nash ended his suffering with a stab into his carotid artery.

"Wow." I looked at each body. He'd used no power. I'd never felt any from him. That was definitely natural. "Nash."

He nodded toward the light at the end of ten feet of solid rock. "Let's go, Sharpshooter."

"Oh, you're going to pretend that was no big deal?" I stepped over a body on my way to his side. "That's how good you are, huh?" His skirmish managed to plant me back in my body, away from those I'd abandoned behind me.

Nash rubbed his side. "Glad we can agree on something."

I rolled my eyes and looked at his side as we continued forward. "And you hurt yourself, didn't you, Nash the Badass. You could have left two for me. You didn't have to slay everyone in sight by yourself."

"It's just a bruise from the fall."

"Let me show off next," I said. "Be a gentleman and give me a turn."

"I figured you'd had your fun, flying down a landslide to save me."

"I need much more fun than that."

Nash smirked. "I'll have to keep that in mind."

I gasped. "Are you really flirting right now?"

"You're the one who was flirting. I merely played along."

"Please." I scoffed. "There's people trying to kill us, you know."

"Not right this second. They're obviously going to ambush us once we make it through. This might be the last flirt of my life. How can I pass it up?"

I shook my head. "What's wrong with you?" I didn't know whether he teased me because it was just how he was, or whether he was trying to manipulate me after all, or if maybe he actually was interested. It made my stomach flop. This was a dangerous game to play. Too dangerous.

But he was right about what he'd said. Out in the open, they would have plenty of room to fight us, and they had numbers on us. They wouldn't send in more guards to get slaughtered. If we continued forward, I'd have to use my power and he'd know what I really was.

Only we didn't have to face that just yet. This path wasn't more difficult because of the battle we'd just survived. It was because of the battles to come now that the guard knew about me. For now, I could avoid the fight.

"You might have time for more flirting. There's a passageway." I moved forward and felt along the rock for the familiar, deep crack. I closed my eyes and focused. Gravel fell from the crack onto my head as the rock widened and moaned until it had opened enough to squeeze through.

"How did you do that?" Nash's eyes were wide.

I eased part of the way through. "It's a door. I was taught how to open it." I nodded. "Come on. It's safe." I slid into the cool air of the passage. Eternal flames burned in the lanterns along the rocky wall. A slight breeze wafted down the tunnel, like we'd stepped into the mountain's own little world.

Nash's hand fumbled through the crevice and then came his head. He grunted as he squeezed his shoulders through.

A narrow hall carved into the rock stretched before us in an upward slope that led to the start of the spiral staircase. "If we hurry, we can make it to Wren and Leif by morning." I closed the passageway and breathed a sigh of relief.

His eyes widened. "We'll be in this tunnel that long?"

"It connects with theirs higher up the mountain." I nodded toward the stairs.

"I'd rather go back and fight." Nash started for the stairs. I couldn't help but smile.

CHAPTER FOURTEEN

Endless stairs.

Absolutely endless stairs with narrow stretches of tunnel that echoed our every breath stretched on and on and on. For hours upon hours, we walked and didn't stop for a break even once we'd been reduced to crawling up the stairs, unable to speak.

We'd both sweated so much that the mud had run down from our faces and necks in dark streaks. Every muscle in my body burned.

Three more stairs and I rounded a bend that wrenched a cry from my chest.

"You hear it?"

Nash perked up. "Water."

We clambered up the last few steps and stumbled down the hall to a natural cave in the mountain. Stalactites reached their spindly fingers from the ceiling toward the floor below. A still pool of water reflected the blue hue of the cave's ceiling. I stumbled for it, collapsed, and sucked in mouthfuls of water so fast I nearly retched.

My stomach hurt from drinking too much. "I didn't think we would make it."

"Me either. I'm going in." Nash pulled his tunic over his head and pried off his shoes before reaching for his pants.

"A warning would be nice!" I turned my face away.

"I told you I was going in."

"Not without clothes," I muttered. Washing away the mud and sweat did sound nice. I bit my cheek. "If you look, you die. Okay?" I glanced over at Nash to find that he'd ventured chest-deep into the water.

He covered a bare shoulder with his hand. "You're the one who's look-ing. Keep your eyes to yourself, Sharpshooter."

I rolled my eyes at his smirk. Even after he turned his back to me, I felt nervous. "You really can't look."

"I would never do that." He splashed water over his face. "Not even if you were drowning. I'd look the other way and preserve your dignity so you could perish untainted by my gaze."

"Oh, shut up." I left my clothes in a pile, so exhausted that even that simple task of undressing felt incredibly tiring.

The relief of the water immediately soothed me. I relished the feeling of weightlessness on my heavy body. Once I felt like I could move my arms again, I unknotted my hair to scrub away the mud.

"They'll try to ambush us higher up the mountain now that they know we're here." I pulled chunks of mud from my tangles. If Rune saw this, he would tease me and say this mess would break the brush. I missed the little guy.

"I figured," Nash said. "I'm getting out now. You can look if you really want to."

"How do you have the energy to be an ass right now?"

"An ass? I'm trying to do a nice thing for you."

I scoffed. "Oh, how generous of you."

"I like to give to those in need. You seem pretty stressed out."

My jaw dropped. I was somewhere between laughing and wheeling around to punch him in the kidney. "You better walk away right now."

"I'll accept a simple thank you, but I wouldn't turn away coin if you're feeling especially grateful."

I dragged my arm across the water to splash him. "You're insufferable."

Refusing to look at him for even a second, I turned away immediately. His laugh both grated at me and made it hard not to smile.

Forcing my clothes over my damp skin took so much effort I could have cried.

I stumbled toward Nash on numb legs and slid down the large rock he reclined against.

"I feel like death," Nash said.

My heavy eyelids slid shut. "Me too . . . We'll sleep here tonight and fin-ish the journey to Leif and Wren in the morning."

The cool air of the cave chilled my wet skin. I shivered and drew my knees up.

Nash opened his arm in my direction. I looked at him suspiciously, waiting for him to make some quip.

"I won't tease," he said.

"If you do—"

"I'll die," he finished for me.

I was too exhausted to feel embarrassed or to appreciate his closeness as I slid against him and drew my legs over his. His embrace wrapped me up.

Never mind. I felt something. Warmth tickled my stomach even though our bodies hadn't yet eased the chill.

"Don't react." His mouth brushed the crown of my head as he whispered. "I lied to you about Flare."

His confession came so suddenly that I almost sat up to look at him, but he held me tight.

"She knows things only spoken in private. Act like we're just resting in case she can see or hear."

It was so hard not to speak. I closed my eyes to pretend I was drifting off, but I had so many questions.

"When I first met her, I thought she was another human spy like me. She was really the first demon to work with the Prophet of the Valley. She recruited the rest."

What kind of power did Flare have?

"Flare used the Prophets to divide and conquer the tribes in our region. Not just in the Valley, but the Kyst, the Flatlands, the Fjellfolk. That's why demons helped attack with the Flatlanders in the night. She's orchestrating this. Now she wants to unite our lands under one head. One Skia Hellig."

Already our young world had more than it should. Roads, steel, villages with indoor plumbing. Our power had paved the way for us to have what took other worlds hundreds of thousands of years to gain, except it was still so undeveloped. Flare didn't care about the suffering that the Prophets caused, only the stability they would bring once formal governments rose to take their place. They were a stepping stone to speeding up evolution so that fewer people would suffer for a shorter period of time.

Just like what the gods wanted for our world. They weren't content to watch countless worlds in the universe evolve naturally on their own. They wanted to master evolution. But just like the gods, Flare wasn't mastering evolution here. Only creating a sickly mutant in place of what otherwise would grow on its own. Had the gods given her special gifts because she believed in their vision?

I couldn't speak, so I dug my fingers into Nash's side where my hand rested.

His voice lowered even more. "One day, Flare will turn on me. I've tried to keep her trust to figure out what she's doing. But she could hurt Elsie. I need to kill her. I've seen people try, but every time, she vanishes the instant they almost have her. She reappears moments later, unharmed. I don't know how to take her out."

Chills darted down my spine. I'd bent time with my power, but I had always been a passenger in time, not a god of it. The control had always eluded me. Flare seemed to have mastered manipulating space-time. The gods must have given her a power I couldn't imagine. Piercey and I had tried for years to help me control it without any success.

Nash whispered against my hair. "If we don't stop her, more lands will be conquered, and countless will die. Those of us who survive will lose the world as we know it. This is bigger than the Prophet of the Valley."

This couldn't be the world we'd leave behind for children like Elsie and Rune. There had to be more I could do. I certainly couldn't sit there saying nothing after he had told me all this. So I eased onto my side, tugging Nash to encourage him to stay close.

I nestled against the rock while he stretched out alongside me, his body turned to cover mine, staving off the chill. My breath caught in my chest when I looked into his eyes. His face hovered so close to mine. Even as I told myself not to think about it, my body wouldn't listen. Every inch of myself was attuned to him, to every part of us that touched and every part that did not. I managed to whisper, not looking away from him even though my cheeks felt hot. "You decided to trust me."

He held my gaze another moment before speaking. "You threw yourself down a cliff to save me. Sometimes it's too dangerous not to trust a person who deserves it. I've been fighting for a long time, Max. I need you."

Did I need him? With my power returning, did I need anyone? My heart told me yes, because throughout my life it had always been the people I cared about who gave me the strength I needed. "I trust you, too and that scares me."

Nash's stare briefly slipped down my face. "The gods, fate, our own will—whatever it may be—something has drawn us together. That's what I keep feeling."

I nodded, helpless to fight the same pull, or maybe just unwilling. Leif would rip both our windpipes out if he saw this. But he wasn't here right now. It was only Nash and me with no one between us. I could no longer pretend that my heart had any reservations. I believed that he was on my side and that I could put my trust in him. Resisting Nash felt as futile as fighting a slip. I couldn't change it any more than I could the past when I traveled there.

That or I'd simply surrendered to the kind of power Nash had. Was I being fooled by a spy who knew how to sway a woman with his pretty face and his disarming confidence? Or did we have a real bond that would be a shame to discard? The questions faded to a whisper in my mind until I could no longer hear the lingering worry. It was too late.

"We'll kill them," I said. If Flare had put the Prophets in power, then she was my enemy. "We'll find a way. I will stop at nothing to kill her and the Prophet."

"We will. I'm in this with you."

With me.

"The gods aren't what they seem, Nash. Nothing is as it seems. Climb this mountain with me, fight with me, stand up to them with me. But the rest is off-limits. Soon, I'll have to ask you to stay behind. I'm not letting you get pulled into this."

"I'm already in it." The hot breath falling against my lips clouded my mind. I simply watched him as he whispered. "Whatever you're holding back, you won't be able to protect me or your friends from it for long. If you're going to trust us, then trust that we can handle it."

An unexpected wave of pain from all that this power—this curse—had cost me thrashed my heart. Nash could not possibly fathom all that I held back from him. "You don't know what you're saying. There's only suffering in my future. You shouldn't get too close."

His eyes reflected my own pain as concern softened his face. If he knew what I really was, he wouldn't look at me like that. "What is it, Max?" he asked.

I looked away. "Something I'll make sure you never have to worry about."

He pushed my wet hair back from my face. "You can let someone protect you for once."

"You can't protect me, Nash." My voice sounded distracted, though, because his hand hadn't left my head, and being close to him quickly wore down any semblance of a remaining defense against him. I lifted my fingers to graze the definition of his jaw, the day's growth of stubble, and up along the sharp angle of his cheekbones.

A strong hand smoothed over my hip and dug into the dip of my lower back. He drew closer and I closed my eyes as he worked his mouth over mine, his lips soft and full.

His closeness amplified every feeling, so even a faint touch felt more like a shout than a whisper, and anything more entirely overwhelming. My palms smoothed down his shoulders and around—

He grunted and caught my hand as I dug into his side. I'd forgotten. I sat up and ripped his shirt up to see where he was hurt. Black and purple bruising mottled his side, stretching in a long swath up along his ribs.

Pain tingled down the back of my arms at the sight of it. "You said it was just a bruise."

"It is just a bruise." He drew me back down.

I pushed against him. "Are you hiding other injuries from me? We need to look out for each other."

"Well, I didn't want to say . . ." Nash drew his collar down, voice serious. "I have a scratch here." He twisted his neck and pointed at a thin scrape. "And here." The teasing smile crawled back on his face.

"Like I said, insufferable."

Still holding my hand, he pulled me close until I could feel his breath against my face. Then he drew my palm beneath his shirt, along his back. "More bruising."

His bare skin warmed my hand. The heat shot straight to my cheeks.

"What about you?" His deep whisper wafted against my ear. His fingers caressed my wrist. "Scratches from the fall." His touch slowly traveled up my arm. "Cold from the water."

I sighed. "My pride because you never stop teasing me."

He turned with me and settled me back down against the rock floor.

I could sink into this. Probably not make it for air. Even though we didn't know each other well and might not know each other for long, it felt like if I let him in even once, it would hurt terribly to tear him back out. Soon, I'd die beneath the eclipse. It would be easier to die alone than to leave behind another person to grieve me. Already, I'd let too many people love me.

Lying here with nothing between us, not even my suspicion, our bodies betrayed our secrets, and all that we might've wanted to hide. His eyes looked wide open to me. I feared what he would see in mine. I didn't let go, but I couldn't let myself draw him any closer either.

I buried my face against his chest and closed my eyes, breathing in my first good breath as he held me. We lay together for a while, not saying anything. Weight pressed me into the earth, not his own or mine, but the weight of total exhaustion. When I tried to say something, maybe to apologize, he hushed me, kissed my cheek, and simply held me as we drifted off.

CHAPTER FIFTEEN

I slept soundly for the first few hours before time tugged and pulled until it unraveled. I resisted, lying there on the ground in Nash's arms. No matter how tightly I clung to him, I slipped in and out all night while he slept. Every time I drifted off, I dreamed of another time, or lived it. I couldn't say whether I was awake or not.

Most slips came in snippets, like of my father when I was young and we were best friends. Later when we weren't. So many things I didn't want to remember about my time before the mountain.

"Get up, Max."

I moaned and covered my eyes with my arm. We'd meditated so late into the night. It couldn't be time to get up already.

"Max." Dad shook my shoulder. "Come on, Maxy girl."

"It's still dark out." Darkness still painted the window. The sun had not yet crested the hill overlooking our cottage. "All the other kids in the village get to sleep until the sun comes up."

"You're not the other kids. They don't have what you have."

I didn't really understand what that was. I'd been going to our Prophet my entire life. While my friends ran through the summer fields, I was stuck kneeling, and praying, and growing the flame inside me.

"Soon you'll be eleven. The Prophet wants to test you before your birthday. You aren't ready. You'll fail as you are now."

I rolled over, twisting myself right out of the past. But I didn't even have time to steady myself before I was falling headlong again.

The old Prophet's face flooded my vision. Not the Prophet of the Valley who'd taken over my future, but the Prophet of my past, from across the sea where wild meadows and endlessly flat plains comprised the world as we knew it, the Prophet who'd taken me to live with him in his temple that day when Dad told him I was hiding my power.

That Prophet's bright eyes stared into mine. And I was lost again.

"Do it, Max."

I turned my face away so I couldn't see Dad or the Prophet. "I told you, I can't."

"Can't?" Dad slapped the back of his hand against his palm so loud it made me flinch. "You can do much more, Max. We need you. Your power can set the people free from the blasphemers who bring the gods' judgment upon us."

The Prophet hadn't yet spoken. Often, he didn't. Instead, he walked to me, lifted my chin, and made me look into his eyes. "Now."

With no hesitation, Dad unholstered his knife and placed it at his throat. He gave me only a second to think before he pushed against the blade and drew a bead of blood. Determination hardened his expression. He shifted, ready to slice his own throat.

I screamed and twisted my wrist, my power ripping the blade free of his grip and throwing it against the far wall.

He reached for his sword next, but I squeezed my hands into fists and focused on his arms so they were tethered in place. Dad struggled but couldn't move. Why would he do this?

Why?

The flame erupted like a volcano in my body. Blind, panicked power ripped at the boundaries of my every vein.

"Max." The Prophet's voice strained. It was only then I realized he was using his own power to hold mine back. "You must breathe, child. Your power is out of control."

But as concern spread over the face of the Prophet, my father only smiled.

I grabbed hold of the world the moment I could and jerked up. My skin was hot. Slick with sweat.

I stared at Nash, wishing it was the daytime and he was awake. Wishing he could say something, anything, to distract me. I couldn't hold on to my time. I just couldn't.

Stumbling up, I walked as quietly for the pool as I could and splashed my face with water, shaking from head to toe. I was heading back to the day. It felt as inevitable as when I'd first lived it. Dad training me until the eclipse. Until the day that changed everything. I couldn't go back there. I couldn't.

I gripped the back of my neck and walked briskly back and forth near the pool.

"Don't slip," I whispered. "Don't slip. Don't slip. Don't slip."

But I did. I lost track of how many times I relived sleepless nights with Dad and my endless days with the Prophet, honing my power. My medicine would have stopped this, or at least lessened it. But I was alone. All alone, trapped in the past, until it released its hold on me so the future could steal me away.

Above me, the moon had nearly consumed the sun.

Pain consumed me. My head fell and I opened my eyes to my bound ankles. Strands of blood rushed down my legs. I would die here. I would die during the eclipse.

A crowd spilled out over every inch of the courtyard before me. Their screams tore into my mind. "Kill! Kill! Kill!" The voices swirled about me. Growing. "Kill the demon!"

Stepping back, the Prophet of the Valley raised his bloodied spear against the dark sky. Black dripped from its tip.

I jolted up, gasping, back in the cave. Nash knelt beside me, grabbing my arm. "Are you okay?"

I must have fallen asleep at some point, because I sat on the ground near the pool.

"Did you faint again?" he asked.

"No. I couldn't sleep." That day that had not yet come to pass clung to me and made me feel sick. I struggled to speak. "I wanted to walk . . . and then I got tired . . . so I slept here."

Nash looked skeptical. "Yeah?"

I nodded. I had to get out of this tunnel. Had to get off this damn mountain. "Let's just go."

Nash studied my face. "Why don't you sleep just a little more." He slid his arms around me and hugged me tight, settling down against the ground with me. "I'll wake you up when we need to leave."

I felt desperate to melt into him, but I remembered the feeling of dying and thought of how soon the eclipse would arrive. How would he feel once I died? How would it feel to get any closer? I started to push him away when he whispered in my ear.

"I've got you. It's okay. Sleep. I won't let go."

Maybe even though Nash didn't have any power, couldn't control time or space, maybe he did have something else. Because I should have slipped again and didn't. It was as if he held me in place.

CHAPTER SIXTEEN

After a morning of long and hard traveling, we had finally reached Wren and Leif, where my journey was rewarded with an earful about how I should have warned them of how awful the walk would be.

"I hope you had as miserable of a time as we did," Leif said.

"It isn't possible for theirs to have been as miserable." Wren furrowed her brows. "They didn't have to travel with you. If you complain one more time, I'm gagging you."

"Don't worry. We were miserable." My legs ached as I stretched them by the exit.

"Very miserable," Nash said. "There wasn't even a single moment of relief."

With my back to Leif, I was able to cast a glare at Nash. To his credit, he didn't flash a hint of a teasing smile, but I knew exactly what he was doing, trying to vex me. Didn't he want to keep his windpipe intact?

"Good," Leif said, voice suspicious.

Wren groaned at Leif. "Would you stop?" She rarely lost her patience.

Ignoring them, I placed my hands against the stone to open the passageway. With all of us weary, but ready to face whatever came, we squeezed outside to a very different mountain than where we'd entered. Towering cliffs surrounded us. The air was cold and the ground moist where remnants of melting snow clung to the ledge we stood on. Soon we would reach heights where snow fell year-round and terrible winds could white out the entire sky.

Dark clouds lingered low in the mountains that blocked our view below, and limited how much we could see of our surroundings. Sprinkles of rain fell for a few minutes as we picked our way along the edge of the cliff. Around the curve, we would need to climb to another ledge, where sloping fields crawled up to more cliffs, and to the lowest peaks of the mountain. There we would face difficult climbs up steep cliffs to reach the next passageway.

We had to make it there, through another section of the mountain, and a final passage that led to the sacred area the guards weren't permitted to patrol. A tram would carry us up to the school. That would be hard to explain to my friends, but not any harder than the train.

Things would only get more dangerous from here. The guards actively patrolled this area. Even though they knew we were trespassing, as long as I didn't use my power, they wouldn't be able to detect me on their radars. Ironic to hold myself back after I'd spent so long trying to regain my energy.

"Do I need to worry?" Leif asked quietly, his whiskers scratching my ear when he leaned in to whisper. I shook him off.

Yes, he should worry a great deal because I definitely had not heeded his advice. "No. Don't start a fight either," I whispered.

"I'm not trying to antagonize you. I'm trying to protect you."

What would Leif do if he knew Nash was a spy? The worry I thought I had shut down churned in my stomach now. That did sound terrible. I softened my voice and looked back at him. "Trust me. Okay?"

Leif's shoulders sagged. "Okay."

It made me feel guilty to see Leif's concern and then mislead him, but he wouldn't listen to anything I had to say about the matter. We needed to keep our thoughts on the task at hand anyway. We were entering dangerous territory.

I eyed the ledge above as we came to the end of the cliff, steadied myself, and felt for the best place to start climbing. The others followed after me as I dug my fingers into a crack and tested an indentation with the toe of my boots. Only five feet to go. This was a short cliff. I breathed in deeply and focused on the next foothold rather than looking back or ahead.

As I strained to reach an outcropping, a noise above the cliff caught my attention. I lowered back to hold steady as I listened. We couldn't wait long. We'd exhaust ourselves. As quietly as I could, I climbed another foot. I heard at least two guards walking overhead.

I neared the top when I braved a peek. Three guards walked along the short trees dotting the ledge. None of them spoke. They all scanned the area with knit brows and swords readied. Lowering, I looked over my shoulder at the others and mouthed to them. "Three . . . On alert . . ."

No point in wasting time. I dragged myself over the edge with burning muscles. There I crouched, easing behind the guards so they wouldn't see me. Nash followed, drawing his blades. Leif and Wren weren't far behind us.

I readied my bow and aimed at the guard farthest away while Nash tiptoed toward the closest. Wren took a dagger from her thigh and Leif grabbed his blade.

One of the guards turned. He opened his mouth. I switched my aim and shot my arrow through his teeth. Nash sprang forward, blades swinging like lightning to rip open a guard's back. Wren's dagger whizzed past me and thudded into the neck of the final guard. All three sank to the ground, two already dead, while Wren's wheezed his final breath.

Leif's eyes scanned our surroundings. "Clear," he mouthed.

"Hide them," I whispered. We had to cover our tracks. Wren and I searched the corpses for useful supplies. When we finished with one body, Leif and Nash hefted him up and carried him to an outcropping to hide the body. The guards checked in with each other frequently, so it wouldn't take long to realize that these three were missing and to narrow the search. Quickly, we hid the other two, and fell into a line as we traversed the mountain.

Slinking past another group, we managed to come upon the large field separating us from a cliff we would need to climb. Either we had to cut through the center, the fastest route, or hug the edge of the field in a tangle of trees. If guards were here, that was where they would likely be, but we would have cover at least. I nodded to the woods to the east. We had no other path to take and would need to fight whoever came for us. This was exactly why we had needed to make it through the first passageway undetected. They'd had all night to prepare for us.

Tightness squeezed my chest. I could only hope we would encounter significantly less guards before finding the next passageway.

An arrow whizzed past us and planted itself in the ground ahead of us. A man on a horse galloped out of the woods dead ahead. It was too late to take to the trees. We'd been spotted.

More guards appeared behind him. Wonderful.

Nash, Leif, and Wren went low as the approaching guard fired another arrow. They'd expect that from me and I needed to be able to shoot.

I jumped instead and nocked two arrows, tucking my knees up high to give them the least amount of space to aim at me. With a snap, I released the arrows, and reached for more before the first two had hit their targets.

Metal tips pierced armor. The arrows drove into the first man's heart and eye. I landed in a roll and peeled off another the moment I came up to one knee. Both hit their marks exactly. A straight shot through the heart of another guard who emerged from the woods.

Guards tore into the field on all sides of us, even from the cliffside.

There was no point in hiding my power from their radars when I needed to know how many we faced. I focused and listened for heartbeats so I could count the enemies. Our area was flooded with them. At least forty, most hiding in the woods ahead.

I glanced beside me where Nash turned in a circle with his swords drawn. He had to make it home to his daughter. And I couldn't let anything happen to Leif and Wren. It was time to reach deeper than before and draw out more of the power locked inside me. Nash would find out who I was. What I was. No longer could I hide from the truth. So be it.

Focusing on the flame of power within me, I prepared another arrow, drew the bowstring back, and let it soar, driving it with more than the force of my weapon but by the power the gods gave me.

It ripped through the man's chest at an impossible distance.

Leif, Wren, and Nash all ran out in different directions, blades clashing with those of the mountain guard. I had to count on them to take out the ones behind me. The woods before me teemed with guards preparing to fight.

I felt the wind hit my cheek a second before the enemy arrow would've split my face. I caught it midair, one hand wrapped around the thin wood. The power of the shot ripped my shoulder back. I steadied myself, clasping the arrow against my heart.

Too close. Where had it come from?

I listened for the heartbeats. Reinforcements had come from a cliff beyond the thin stretch of woods. Snipers I couldn't see. Closing my eyes, I listened, honing my senses, until I heard the patter of hearts. The whistle of breath. There they were. I whipped my bow up and returned their arrow. I didn't need to listen to know I'd no longer hear the pattering or the whistling, only the rush of a dying breath.

Two lines of guards sprinted across the field for us, twenty in all. I couldn't let them get closer.

This was the real reason the instructors didn't want me returning to the mountain. There was something different about this place. They couldn't suppress me or control me here. I had to remember that so I could break myself free. I had to have total faith that I could take the power I needed, a power that was mine and mine alone.

I focused on the burning within me, the flame inside, and breathed life into it. My eyes shot up to the men sprinting for us. I reached my hands out into claws, visualizing the power erupting from me.

One man's neck snapped. Another down the line. Three more after that. *Snap. Snap. Snap.*

Their bodies slammed into the ground in an awful rhythm.

Snap.

Within seconds, I'd killed them all without even breaking a sweat. Wren took on one remaining on the right side of me, out in the field alone. Leif turned, his face serious, three bodies on the ground behind him.

The mountain fueled me. The cracks in the dam inside me widened, the walls beginning to crumble. There was still more untapped, but I hadn't felt this in years. The shock of it, the exhilaration, froze me for a moment.

Wren slayed the last man. And everyone went silent. Everyone, including Nash. I couldn't bring myself to turn and see the look on his face.

The grass rustled behind me.

Wheeling around, I met the wide eyes of a guard as he stumbled back a step, his mouth opened, ready to form the words. Demon.

It wasn't like Nash to leave him alive for this long. Three of the guard's comrades lay on the ground, their blood staining Nash's sword that now hung in a limp grip. Yet this man was still alive. Alive and looking into my eyes just like the woman I'd killed yesterday.

Anger rippled down my spine. With a snap of my bow, I silenced the fear in my enemy's eyes. Still, my own coursed through me, because I couldn't deny to Nash what he had seen with his own eyes. Even if he'd suspected that I had power, witnessing it would change everything. Now he'd see the demon living inside me. I trained my eyes on the ground, unable to meet Nash's stare.

What if it changed things for Leif and Wren to see it, too?

Wind ripped through the silent field, stealing away the last of the guards' breath and the screams they never had time to unleash.

Until finally Nash's cracking voice broke the quiet.

"Demon. That was the last word he tried to say."

I flinched at the name and squeezed my eyes shut, not ready to see what I'd done and what Nash would think of me.

Nash's voice sounded small. "You're a demon."

Pain swept through me. I'd been a fool to hope Nash could be different. Why would he be? He would hate and fear me like so many others. He'd called himself an outcast as a boy, but he had no idea what outcast meant.

"Shut your mouth!" Leif shouted at him from his place on the field, veins popping in his neck.

The blood caught my eye. The still bodies. The judgment within me screamed above Nash's so I had no choice but to look at the destruction I'd wrought. I raised my hand to silence Leif. I could no longer hide from Nash, or from Leif and Wren. I could no longer hide from myself. I lifted my head and faced them, faced the judgment I'd tried so hard to escape.

"All this time you accused me of lying and hiding things. You could have told me. Maybe I could have trusted you then." Nash's voice was solemn, as if the Max he thought he knew had died right before his very eyes. "What's your name?"

I tensed. "You know my name."

"The name the people know you by. Your demon name."

I bit my cheek.

"That's enough," Wren said, walking closer. "Her name is Max. That's all, just Max."

"I took you to my daughter. Who are you really?" Nash's voice blared. "I accepted your silence to my questions about all these mysteries before, but how can I do that now? You lied."

Pain pounded with my heart. "Eclipse. My name is Eclipse."

Nash's expression tightened after I uttered the name Eclipse. Wren stopped walking, face looking stricken. Even Leif stared like I'd taken off a mask and showed him who I was for the first time. I'd thought nothing could ever come between us, but I'd known this could. Right? I'd always known. Who could accept me after what I'd done?

I lifted my hand toward Nash and then looked to Wren and Leif. "Let me explain."

"Eclipse? You're Eclipse?" Nash's shocked stare shifted to the dead littering the field.

I covered my mouth, my eyes burning with unshed tears. My voice cracked when I spoke. "I should have told you all."

"It changes nothing." Leif's voice shook. His eyes were red, but he said the words with enough conviction to make me believe he meant them.

Sorrow flooded Nash's face, and this time when he looked at me, it felt as if he actually saw me again. "I trusted you, really trusted you. I want to believe you. So, tell me everything I've heard about you since I was a boy isn't true."

He'd told me things that put his family in danger. In the morning, he'd held me so I could sleep. If I had trusted him, too, and told him the truth myself, I could have explained without the suspicion. The feeling of his kiss filled me with shame. He'd meant it, hadn't he? He'd really opened himself up to me and I'd stayed hidden.

"Max," Nash said. "Tell me the stories of the Slaughter of Dark Noon are a lie and that you didn't kill those people."

Leif and Wren were watching, too. They would stand with me, but they wanted to know. The problem was I couldn't say it wasn't true, only that I hadn't meant to do it. When I opened my mouth, echoes of necks snapping all over this field filled my mind. Did I even deserve to defend myself?

The world called me Eclipse, the Soul Eater, the demon who would stop at nothing to finally consume even the sun. That wasn't true, but I'd earned the name with something unimaginable I really had done.

The horror I'd felt since that day slashed through my chest like a battle-ax. My eyelids fluttered. Leif started for me, but he wouldn't make it in time. Couldn't help me anyway.

I focused on my black boots to ground myself, but they fractured into the little red shoes I'd worn the day my father died. I slipped into two different times at once, before Nash and my friends on the mountain, and with my father in my childhood village.

No, no, no! Not now.

Tears filled my eyes. I counted the seconds and focused on my feet, on staying in my black boots in the present and not those red shoes in the past. Only a few moments passed, but time drew me in and tried to swallow me whole.

The field dimmed, and our time with it, hovering beneath the skin of this world, harder and harder to see.

Nash stepped back toward the jagged wall of the cliff that had materialized behind him and looked up into the darkening sky. Wren and Leif were nowhere to be seen.

"No!" I wheeled around to see the last of the sun disappear behind the dark moon. I wouldn't go back to this time. I refused.

"Max?"

"Stay still!" I barely choked out the words.

I stumbled backward toward Nash until I could cover him with my body, closing my eyes, channeling myself into the scratchy grass at my ankles in the field. The heat baking the sweat into my neck.

The sun pierced the ring of the dark moon.

Villagers whispered below.

"The light . . ." my young voice said. "Look, Dad! The light . . ."

His voice blared, deep and knowing. "Your strength is greater than even an eclipse. Release it. Release it from within. It'll be beautiful, child. I promise. It's okay." A warm whisper fell against my ear my ear now. "Show them the light. Free them."

The heat of the flame swelled out of control, even though I tried to hold it in, tried to push Dad's voice away. Power erupted from my body. The Prophet wasn't here to stop me this time. Dad's body jerked and froze in the air, his fingers popping first, and then his arms, his legs. I clenched my eyes shut.

Shrieks ripped through the air. Shrieks from Dad, from me, from the villagers below.

Shrieks echoed and grew until they all snapped to silence, and I was the only one left screaming.

I gasped when I blinked to the field and the field alone. I stood in a single spot in a single point in time, back in the present. The wild scent of weeds and woods mixing with the blood of the guards I'd slain grounded me.

"What was that?" Nash asked, turning in a circle to look at our surroundings.

I stumbled forward.

The world started to spin. I lurched and vomited hard. Leif caught me and held me up by my middle.

Nash dropped down beside me and placed his hand on my back. "Can you hear me?"

I nodded, my stomach roiling so much I couldn't speak.

"Hold on to us," Nash said. "Don't go back to that place."

Leif shoved him back with his forearm. "You're the one who upset her and made this happen. Get away from her."

I stumbled away, putting distance between us. "I didn't know you could slip with me. Stay away. All of you stay far away from me." I lifted a shaky hand. "It isn't safe. I can't control it."

What was I doing trying to regain this power that had slaughtered sixty-seven innocent people? Children had died. My stomach heaved again as I remembered clearly what I'd tried so hard to forget. It felt more real than it had since it first happened. No longer did I feel like I was in my body, but like I was trapped in the past on that day.

There was no time for me to break now. More guards would come. And if I lost control of myself, I'd lose my hold on time, on space, on the only thing grounding me in the present.

Even so, Nash's voice haunted my mind. I couldn't shake it.

Demon.

CHAPTER SEVENTEEN

We had wasted too much time on the fallout from the battle. We stole across the field, scaled a cliff, and entered the next passageway without any other guards pursuing us. They hadn't given up, that much was certain. Now they knew their enemy. They'd be preparing for a battle that could take down a powerful demon rather than throwing away lives haphazardly. The higher up the mountain we journeyed, the fewer routes we'd have. There would be no escape.

Leif tried to help me as we traveled up the steep stairs. I was nauseous from the slip. I refused to let anyone near me, though. Refused to even look at them and have to face them.

"Max," Nash said gently. When he moved close to me, I jolted away, terrified I'd drag him through time with me again.

"I told you it's not safe," I said.

"I—"

Leif rammed his thick forearm into Nash's chest and plastered him against the rock wall. "Didn't I tell you to stay away?" Another shove. "If you upset her again and she has a spell, who knows what will happen. She said she can't control it."

Wren turned around from higher up the stairs and sighed. "Let's all stay quiet and give Max time. Let him go, Leif."

Nash had not tried to push Leif away. He just held the other man's stare. Another tense moment, and Leif backed away. I turned my stare to the ground, struggling to keep my mind in the present. I could hear the screams of the guards I'd killed echoing off the walls of the stairs and through my mind.

We traveled quietly after that and slept only a few hours before we left the safety of the passageway for the inevitable battle that awaited.

A burst of icy wind cut through the opening of the passageway and scattered snow at my feet. I squeezed outside, sank into knee-deep snow, and focused on listening for the guards. It was pointless to even try counting. There were too many.

We waded together through the snow, the icy coldness eating through our clothes, making us heavy and wet. No guards approached but they were there. I could hear them assembling more soldiers out there in the white, hear them gathering supplies, whispering in clashes of sound I struggled to isolate.

Up here there was no such thing as flatland. Rolling white clearings would suddenly crash into cliffs or stretch into precarious outcroppings, steepening with every foot closer to the peak. I couldn't see anything.

We were easy targets out here.

Whizzing pierced my ears.

I tuned in so acutely that it hurt, and attempted to create a barrier around us to shield us. The power within me felt like it spurted through the cracks in the dam, most of it trapped within me still, while what could escape rushed out at an incredible speed. Though the barrier wasn't visible to the eye, I could feel it and imagine the edges of it. It was uneven and fading. Come on!

Was all this for nothing? Would I really fail now? Enraged with myself, power burst from me and strengthened the barrier.

Sunlight glinted from hundreds of arrows, all raining down in the sky, glittering in the haze of snow-dusted air. I planted my hands on the ground for support and thought of how helpless I'd felt as the past stole me and Nash away. Or when he'd called me demon. When the people I killed looked at me in fear. Then I imagined little Rune waiting for us to come back to save him. Everything I felt hardened inside me, and I used it to destroy the limitations of my power, not caring if I destroyed myself in the process.

With a scream, I unleashed a wave that knocked away all the arrows.

Shrieking blared in the distance, just like when I'd killed those people during the eclipse. Some of the arrows broke and fell to the ground, but dozens arched back toward where they'd come from. I breathed deeply as they thudded into bodies.

I rushed forward to put distance between myself and the others and sank into knee-deep snow. Focusing on listening for the guards, I gave up in the end. It was pointless to even try counting. There were too many.

No break. Hundreds more arrows came. I created a shield around my friends much more easily now. At the same time, I knocked the arrows away. My eyelids flickered. My body trembled. Hands burned with heat. Even now, I was not as powerful as I had been when I trained at the Sacred School, and the fury of that beat at the crumbling walls around my power.

Flames bit into the sky. This time, I didn't get them all. Some sank into the snow. The fire would move underground beneath the snow if it got hot enough and there was anything to burn. I couldn't risk letting the flaming arrows hit.

"Run!" I motioned at the others.

The next bout of arrows came. How many people did they have? They must have been using some kind of machine. I stumbled as I knocked them away. More fire hit the ground, melting pockets of snow where they disappeared.

Nothing was going as it should have. That awful landslide had set us on this collision course from the start. Grief panged in my chest.

Men rushed for us in the clearing. I'd missed them in all the commotion. I flattened five of them to the ground with a sweep of my hand, but more continued for us.

Nash met one with a powerful swing of his blade, cutting into his chest. Wren and Leif weren't far behind, flawlessly battling against the guards launching their attack. I struggled to defend us from the onslaught while also keeping a barrier around my friends as they fought.

Something cut the air to my right. I snapped it in half and it fell to the ground. A spear. Heads popped up in the snow as dozens of men threw more spears at us.

Even with how the mountain energized me, the struggle to unleash my power overwhelmed my body. It felt as if my skin would melt off. I clenched every muscle, struggling against the agonizing fire burning over me.

This time I destroyed every single arrow. Every spear. They splintered and rained down over us.

The ground beneath me trembled with my power.

I had to find all the men and kill them. They were splitting my focus with this onslaught. I didn't want to spill so much blood, but they wouldn't stop. These people had devoted their lives to protecting this mountain. Killing them was the only way.

Searching the clearing beyond what I could see, I snapped the neck of every person I found. My muscles twitched with the burst of power that broke fragile neck bones. Two, five, eight people. Ten. More. So many more. Pops and cracks every few seconds, my own spine-curling war drums.

All the while, waves of arrows darkened the sky over us. Spears flew; guards rushed for us.

I searched for more to kill, but I couldn't juggle all of this at once. A swath of arrows hit the ground. Sharp pain crackled through my arms in a jolt of electricity from my power.

My father's voice slithered through the past and the whistling wind, tugging at the seams of my control, drawing the deep power hidden inside myself. Fear tangled my limbs, my thoughts. If I lost control, I could kill Leif, or Wren, or Nash. I needed more power, but terror froze my body, colder than the frozen mountain peak.

"Stop it!" I screamed and swiped my hand through the air, throwing the spears into the hearts I heard nearby. "I don't want to kill you!"

More arrows darkened the sky. My body hurt so badly I could hardly stand. How many more were there? I reached within myself for more power, begging myself to open up a door I'd kept closed for so long.

Leif grabbed a man's arm to pull him close as he stabbed his sword deep into his gut. Wren ducked a swing. Nash slayed two in only seconds.

I searched the woods as I destroyed the arrows overhead. But when I tried to catch all the spears, I missed some.

They slammed into the ground all around us.

My eyes rolled back as I struggled to hold off everything that blasted us all at once.

That was when I felt it. The shattering of my barrier. My eyes widened. *Thud.*

A thick spear tore through Nash's chest and knocked him back a step. He touched it with his face contorting. The bloodied tip stuck out through his back, skewering him.

My world froze. Nash's eyes found mine, and then his head fell back as he collapsed onto the ground.

The blood dripping from the tip of the spear sticking through Nash's chest snapped the last thread of reason in my mind.

"No!" My voice amplified, exploding throughout the mountain. Terror took control of my body.

A guard swung for Nash where he lay on the ground. Wren caught him with her blade, crying out in effort.

I turned in a drift of snow as two more spears shot through the air. I knocked them aside without even thinking about it, the power flowing from me increasing as I slowly stepped toward the guards. The ground didn't just tremble. It quaked. The arrows raining down shattered and fell in bits of wood and iron. The snow scattered in a wave that tore through the field, flinging eight camouflaged men into the air.

They hung there, suspended and totally helpless. I hardly heard their shrieks and pleas. The same force that caused the ground to tremble ripped at their bodies. With dozens of pops, their arms and legs snapped like twigs. Next, I heard their ribs crackling like the flames of a fire, the kind that burned within me.

If before I'd managed to break through the walls blocking my power, this time, I pulverized them entirely. The energy exploded from me.

In my mind's eye, my perception rushed across the field with my power, closing in on the faces of guards who I ripped high into the air. Dozens, maybe hundreds, flew up from the ground high into the sky as they screamed.

I couldn't think. Couldn't stop myself. Couldn't control it. The power had taken over and it was spreading.

"Max . . ." Nash's voice sounded so weak.

Bones shattered while bodies jerked in unnatural positions.

"Max!"

I froze, really registering the people for the first time. The eight before me hung in a cloud of misty blood, the tiny beads suspended along with them. Broken bones tore through skin stretched tight. One man's skull had caved in. Another had arms that looked like balled-up cloth. Several were bent backward in half. They were all dead.

Those were only the closest ones I could see.

Blood fell in splatters of rain over the white. Bodies dropped to the ground with a ghastly rhythm.

I'd butchered them.

Fear filled me as I turned to see Nash laying on his side, his eyes half-closed. "Max . . ." Blood darkened his chest and middle. "Stay here . . . Don't . . . don't slip away."

The surviving enemies retreated, leaving us completely alone. They must have had orders to fall back after my last display, or all were too terrified to continue.

I crawled to Nash and reached for him, afraid to touch him. My tears dropped onto his neck and chest. "I'm so sorry. I didn't mean . . ." I bowed my head. The tip of my hair that had pulled from my bun brushed his chest. Nash was right to look at me the way he had. I was Eclipse. I'd spent my whole life trying to outrun the name. It was who I was.

I sat up, carefully taking hold of the spear. Leif slid onto the ground beside me, holding my arm to steady me. It had lodged deep within the base of his chest on the left side.

Wren covered her mouth with one hand and gripped Nash's hand with the other.

"I've got you," I said. With a grunt, Leif and I both ripped it from his body. Nash screamed through clenched teeth, blood pumping from his wound. It took only moments for his eyes to slide shut.

I used my power to stabilize him as best I could. I could stop the blood loss and hold him together, protect him from any bile that might leak inside of him, but I couldn't heal him. That advanced skill was something I had never learned to do. It took a lifetime to master.

We carried Nash through the snow for an entire hour, struggling even as I used my power to aid our natural strength, until I found the cave where I had taken refuge all those years ago.

Once we were deep inside, I collapsed, exhausted from the power, the fear, and the guilt of what I'd done.

CHAPTER EIGHTEEN

Even sitting, my heart raced like I'd run for hours. I rested with my forearms against my knees, working every second to keep Nash's wound closed. We at least had a fire going and Nash was properly bandaged, lying down in his blankets. The burn from my power had settled into a constant pain throughout my body.

The lives I'd taken pushed against me and threatened to smash me into the ground. All those guards, dead.

I could feel the blood splattering like rain. The thought of the warm droplets made me tremble.

No one should have this power. No one. I thought I was finally succeeding by traveling here to get help taking on the Prophet. Flare had been right in her own way. I didn't see the big picture yet. I was thinking too small.

This power needed to be destroyed.

The pain of what I'd done eviscerated my insides.

Nash had passed out several times on the way, but since getting situated in the cave, he hadn't slept.

"Try to rest," I said gently. "We'll continue as soon as the sun rises."

He looked at me for several seconds. His stare made me feel my haggardness. "You're exhausting yourself . . ."

"I can't stop, Nash. You'll bleed out. I'll be fine. Please rest."

Pain strained his face as he reached for my hand. My heart lodged in my throat when he tugged it onto his chest, holding it in both hands. "I'll be okay, Max . . . Don't worry."

I laughed, trying to fend off tears. "You'll be okay if I keep the wound closed." I kept my hand in his, willing him to sleep so he could have rest from the pain and I could see him at peace for a few moments.

Leif watched us, expression tense.

"I'm sorry for what I said," Nash whispered. "I was wrong."

"You don't have to say sorry." I settled on my side next to him.

"Your skin . . . is so feverish . . ."

"It's the power." I pushed his curls back from his damp forehead. "Stop talking and sleep. Please."

His eyes settled shut.

What would we do now? We would never make it up this mountain with Nash in this state. If I left him, I wouldn't be able to keep his wound shut. At some point, I'd walk too far away and I'd lose him, especially because I was still getting used to wielding power again.

A few minutes passed before Leif knelt beside me. "We have to take action soon, Max. He doesn't look good."

"I don't know what to do," I whispered.

"Yes, you do." Leif's voice was too calm. "You just don't want to let us do it."

I twisted my brows. "I don't. What could we possibly do?"

He glanced at Wren and then me. "We have to go on without you and make it to your friend."

"That's not happening." I nearly released Nash's hand to knock some sense into Leif. "You don't know the mountain. They're watching for us. It's certain death. Even if you make it, the instructors may kill you."

"This is certain death." Wren rubbed small circles into my back. "That's why they aren't pursuing us. They're waiting for us to die here. We knew this was dangerous. This is why we're here, Max. If you and Nash had come alone . . . You'd either die with him or leave him to die. We have to continue on."

"It's too dangerous." Panic ripped at my lungs until I couldn't draw in a breath. Nash moaned, his grip on me tightening. I focused on him again. I was losing my hold. Trying to breathe, I glared at Leif. "I won't stand for this. I'll find another way."

"Do you want to leave Nash to die?"

"No one is dying!"

Leif looked at Nash again and placed his hand on his shoulder. Worry filled his eyes. "Boy."

Nash's eyes slid open.

"Don't be weak and die on us. You hear me? The only thing you have to do is stay alive. That's your only job."

The corner of Nash's mouth just barely lifted in a smile. "I will . . ."

"Come on, Wren." Leif stooped and kissed the top of my head. "We'll be back with help."

"I'm not letting you leave." I caught his hand.

"Will you fight me?" Leif tilted his head. "That's the only way to stop me."

"Yes! You know I will!"

"Oh, Max." Wren pulled my hand from Leif's. "You're wasting precious energy. We'll come back for you. Leif has me and I have him. Tell us everything we need to know to find your friend and then have faith in us that we'll return."

My head fell as the tears came. I didn't want to do this.

Time crawled. If Leif and Wren managed to make it up the mountain, the instructors at the Sacred School would know the moment they made it to the tram. It was on sacred ground, which was heavily monitored by the instructors. That would take a day to reach, and they couldn't even use the secret passageways since I wasn't there to open them, so it could take twice that time. This was a foolish plan if I'd ever heard one. I had been exiled. The instructors would happily let me die. In fact, they'd kill me themselves. Wren and Leif had said they'd tell them that they came to beg for help after the Prophet captured their village, and appeal to the instructors to actually hold the man they'd trained accountable. Really, they just wanted to get to Piercey.

It seemed even more foolish now than when they'd first left. This was a plan of total desperation. The instructors didn't care about the villages in the Valley so far below them or they would have done something by now.

I had to find a way to go after them. We'd all die at this rate.

And yet, I had no alternatives. Hours had passed as I kept my hand cupped in Nash's while he slept, watching him the whole time to make sure he didn't die in his sleep.

He moaned in his sleep. I wish I knew how to numb him to the pain. Despite my best attempts, he still bled slowly.

I struggled to keep my grip on my power. My heavy eyelids threatened to close. Sweat dripped down the side of my face. I ached from the burning.

And then I heard hard snow and ice crunch outside. I darted up and drew my sword, eyes wide.

No sounds followed.

I tensed and searched for the pitter-patter of their hearts. It felt like my mind was being torn in two.

There. Three men. Well-trained. I heard it in the steadiness of their hearts despite that they'd come to face the demon who had butchered their forces. Probably the only three willing to face me head-on. They'd have good reason for their confidence, not just because they must have realized I was weakening, but because they were the best.

A spear tore through the air. I knocked it against the cave wall with my power before it had the chance to reach me.

The three charged. I didn't have the strength to take them all at once. The battle earlier and the effort to keep Nash alive had drained me mentally and physically. Panic filled me as I held two of the men in place with my mind and hefted my sword up for the third, leaving him free to venture forward.

"The other two left the cave." One man's voice strained as he struggled to break my hold on him. "Call it in . . ."

The one who stepped toward me lifted his radio but I blinked and crushed the antenna.

"Turn back," I said.

"I must kill anyone who trespasses here. No exceptions."

"That's unfortunate for you."

We leapt forward at the same time. Our blades collided, the little power I managed to put behind my attack making his muscled arms tremble in exertion.

It didn't matter if I had to spill every drop of my blood. I was not going to let them kill us.

I knocked the charging guard a step back, twisted for momentum, and slashed for his neck. He parried and kicked. I jumped back to dodge.

Pain pounded in my temples. The two men hadn't stopped fighting to free themselves. One struggled forward an inch. Terror filled me that I might not be able to hold them off.

I needed to strike the paralyzed men before they broke free.

I deflected the strikes from the man attacking me and then threw my knife past his right shoulder. It plunged into another man's throat, embedding past the hilt and halfway up the handle.

The one I still held back roared as he muscled forward another inch.

I was wearing down quickly. I could feel my hold on Nash slipping. I threw the bulk of my energy into keeping him alive and holding the man in place.

It left me open to the one still attacking. I blocked a hit, barely caught the follow-up, and was forced deeper and deeper into the cave.

His eyes caught Nash. I bashed my forearm against his nose and threw my weight into a piercing strike.

He knocked it back too easily. I was losing strength. No matter how hard I tried, I couldn't compensate.

The man at the mouth of the cave trembled as he inched his hand toward his weapon. The veins in his neck bulged.

The one attacking me feigned an attack and then sidestepped me for Nash. I threw a wave of force against him that shot him against the wall.

The cave shook.

My hold on my enemy broke like a cord snapping. Now freed, the second man grabbed his knife and reared back. He threw his blade through the air. I slashed it down with my own when it was in midair.

The man I'd thrown struggled to his feet. That was when I noticed Nash. He had dragged himself toward his weapons, gasping from the pain and exertion.

His wound threatened to rip open.

I wasn't going to be able to hold these men off. So, I ripped their blades from their hands and sent them flying into the woods. One sliced through a man's arm on its way out.

"Stay down!" I yelled to Nash.

With one final push, I flung the two men toward the mouth of the cave. They slid across the ground.

Turning, I saw blood seeping into Nash's bandages. Damn it. He'd stopped, but he still eyed his blades that lay out of reach.

The two men were on their feet and running to me. I saved my mental strength to fortify my defense. They attacked with their bare hands. I nearly got lost in the flurry of punches and kicks.

One lunged. I dodged. The other grabbed. I swung my blade. I kept them back for ten seconds. Twenty. They were good. I couldn't hit them, even though they were unarmed.

My muscles burned with pain. My knees felt so weak I nearly tripped and fell.

Finally, one jabbed his fist and left himself exposed. I made my move, slicing through muscle and tendon and embedding my blade in the stocky one's shoulder. While I struggled to wrench it free, the other managed to slide past me, barreling for Nash.

I wheeled around and kicked the inside of his knee. He went down, grabbing desperately at me. I tried to use my power to push him back but it was no use.

Screaming like a dying animal, the injured one spun and threw me hard. I managed to just barely soften the blow when I crashed against the wall and then down to the ground.

Nash called out for me. My focus waned as pain vied for my attention. I kept his wound closed but I could do nothing else, not even rise to my knees. He reached an arm above his head and dragged himself forward a few inches, that small progress enough to wrench a scream from his gritted teeth.

The injured one crawled across the ground toward me, growling.

Nash's fingertips brushed his blade. Fresh blood spread over his bandage. The second man reached him and ripped the weapons away. Threw the swords into the darkness of the cave. He reared his sword back, the tip pointed at Nash's throat.

I couldn't do two things at once. Not now.

I released my hold on Nash's wound. Pressured the blade that plunged toward his neck until it snapped like the men's necks in the white field. I slung the broken blade around with my mind. It speared the man's eye. His corpse hit the floor.

The guard close to me wrapped his hand around my ankle.

Blood was gushing from Nash's open chest. I wrapped his chest with a tight pressure, but it was even harder to keep the wound closed now that it had reopened. His body slackened on the ground.

The man attacking me jerked me to him and buried his fist in my gut. I curled up, consumed by the shock of the pain. My diaphragm spasmed. I couldn't draw in a breath.

I needed to end this fight before I lost my energy entirely.

The strain of using my freshly awakened powers over such an extended period of time, combined with my exhaustion from the fight, drained my energy at an alarming rate. I had to end this.

Growling through clenched teeth, I slammed my heel against the guard's wound. He screamed in blind rage, blood pumping from his shoulder.

Off to the side, Nash coughed up spurts of red, choking now as he lay on his back, too weak to roll over. I had to make it to him. Had to.

We would die at this rate. I couldn't let this happen.

My sword lay on the ground, out of reach, so I pulled myself toward it along the cave floor.

The last man left alive was out for blood. He was wearing down fast, but Nash and I were going down faster.

Nash twisted enough to spit out a mouthful of blood. His body fell limp, breathing ragged. I held his wound closed. Only one more. I could do this. Had to.

The guard rose and took me with him, his grip impossibly strong despite his injury. He grabbed my face and gathered my wrists with his other hand, tightening his hold until it felt like he'd crush my skull.

In his fury, my enemy wanted me to suffer as he had. His fingers tightened until my teeth cut into my cheeks, filling my mouth with blood, and the pressure forced black spots into my vision.

Instead of going for the kill, he swung his fist for my gut. I lifted my knees, managing to block the first hit. But the second battered my ribs so hard the pain paralyzed me for a moment. He hit me again in the same spot.

It nearly broke my focus on my power.

I sank my teeth into his hand, funneling my pain into that bite. Hot blood rushed into my mouth. At the same time, he had punched me in the same place again. My ribs gave in like twigs snapping.

Then he dropped me and ripped away from my teeth. Desperation drove me forward as I clawed my way across the ground and buried my fingers in his shoulder wound. We both screamed. Knives of pain hacked at my ribs.

All the while, the life and blood continued to drain from Nash as my hold on his wound weakened.

The guard thrashed as I clawed my fingers deeper into his open wound. He tried to shove me away, but I clung with all I had, digging my nails deeper and deeper until my hand ripped his wound wide open.

The man's head dropped back. He spasmed and cried out. And then he collapsed in a pool of his own blood.

I grabbed my sword and stumbled. Fell to the ground. Dragging myself back up, I struggled to each man and sliced their necks to ensure they were dead.

Exhaustion pulled me to my knees beside Nash.

"It's over." I hardly had enough breath to speak. "Hold still."

Black spots danced in my vision.

"Max . . ."

As the adrenaline faded, the pain flared in my body. Each breath felt like something stabbing me in my side. The brute had broken my ribs.

Unable to sit up any longer, I collapsed over Nash, barely keeping pressure on his wound as I struggled to stay awake.

I could hear the pain in his labored breathing. I was losing him.

"You're . . . hurt . . ." Nash said. "Live."

"Shut up. Elsie is waiting for you." I wiped the sweat from my face and spit out the blood in my mouth. "Trish."

"Trish . . ." Nash wheezed in a breath. Blood covered his lips. Speckled his left cheek. "I want someone . . . who fights with me . . . She gave in . . ."

"Save your strength, Nash."

"I really wanted to survive this . . . and convince you to fall for me . . ." A hint of a smile twisted his lips. "I think I could have . . ."

Tears slipped from my cheeks onto his. "Stop teasing me. You're really hurt, Nash."

His eyes slid shut, voice quiet. "You always think . . . I'm teasing, when I'm serious . . ." The pause was long, so long, I thought he'd fallen unconscious. "I'm sorry I hurt you." Pain gripped his expression. He was only upsetting himself. "You're not a demon."

"It's okay." I pushed his curls away from his face.

He said something, but it sounded like a groan. Nash was slipping away from me. More tears fell down my face. Wet his cheeks. Mingled with his own. I weathered through the pain of bending to press my lips against his and kiss him while he was still awake.

I carefully lowered myself beside him, holding his hand tight. He tried to speak once more, but unconsciousness took him, and it tried desperately to take me as well.

Fire consumed my body. I radiated heat. Nash, though, felt cold and clammy.

Every second stole precious strength from me.

Sleep still clawed at me. I fought it like I fought the guard who'd held me in the air.

How could we survive another hour? A whole night? But we had to. Nash had Elsie waiting for him. And I couldn't abandon Rune and my people in the Prophet's captivity. All these days and my little buddy must have lived in constant fear. Frightened for his life and for his papa who hadn't yet returned.

I had to survive and return these fathers to their children. Striking all else from my mind, I focused on Nash's wound alone.

"Hold on . . ." I dug my nails into his hand.

Every breath hurt like the guard hit me again. The hours passed, and though I had no idea how I held on, I did, each moment feeling impossible. Nash holding Elsie as she cried hovered in my mind through the night. Rune's fingers reaching for help. The coldness of my father's body after I sucked away his life during the eclipse. All these years wanting so badly to see him just one more time, even though it didn't make sense to love him so. It all drifted through my mind, heating my skin each time, igniting embers of power still smoldering within me.

As dawn warmed the cave floor in a glow of yellow, its rays didn't make it to me, and I was shivering with cold. Even the sound of Elsie pleading for Nash to come couldn't draw an ounce of warmth within me. The embers of power were dying. I knew I wouldn't last much longer. It was like drifting off to sleep. My strength faded more and more.

With shaking fingers, I lifted my shirt. My side was swollen and black and blue. But my stomach made my heart hammer. It looked like my bruise had leaked out in my abdomen and spread in a pool of dark purple. Internal bleeding. Neither one of us had long.

Nash was out. Even when I tried to wake him, he didn't stir. His heart beat faintly.

I eyed the dead bodies on the ground. No one had come for me after those three. The guard must have decided it was too dangerous. They'd be watching, probably hoping Nash and I would die here. If we left, they would attack again.

It would be hours still before Leif and Wren made it to the tram. And longer for help to return. We wouldn't make it.

My vision waned. A thin trail of blood dribbled from the corner of Nash's mouth. My hold on his wound weakened each passing minute. We couldn't die this way. There had to be something I could do.

Still, Nash grew weaker. Time only seemed to pass more slowly.

I searched for any power left inside me.

In the distance, I heard someone's heart, too fuzzy and faint to recognize. Had my friends given up and returned? No, only death would stop them from reaching Piercey. It must have been the enemy. I was helpless to stop them from approaching. The guards must have been coming for me now that we were in such a weak state.

Would we even make it long enough for them to kill us?

A form darkened the opening of the cave. I managed to open my eyes but I couldn't even reach for my sword.

My vision blurred as I studied the form approaching us. "Stay . . . back . . ."

"My gods. It really is you, Max."

I tried to make out the image of the man who knelt beside me. I felt him, then. "Piercey?"

"I've got you now."

Leif and Wren approached at his side. They didn't look hurt. How had they all made it here so fast?

I blinked a few times, managing to make out those eyes I knew so well. "Piercey," I whispered. "Bind his . . ." It hurt so bad to breathe. The pain choked out my voice.

The last ember of power died out and I fell limp.

Piercey had him. I had no doubt. He had me, too, lifting me gently into his arms.

CHAPTER NINETEEN

Nash?"

I asked it before I could register what I felt and saw in my surroundings. Before I could even wonder where I was or remember what had happened. All that came in a flash after I uttered his name, and still, I didn't have my answer yet. Was he alive? The room around me blurred.

My heart twisted in my chest in a torturous series of somersaults.

"He's okay. He's in a medical room."

The voice seized the wildness of my heart. That was right. Piercey had come for us.

"You're okay, too," Piercey said. "I started healing you both."

I rolled my head to see him standing in the open doorway with Leif and Wren crowded behind him. Pale ceiling tiles stretched over his head and bookshelves lined the far wall.

Leif pushed past Piercey and ran to me, dropping to his knees, close, ready to help me. "We're here, girl."

My arms felt shaky as I tried to rise up. Piercey held up a hand to stop me and came to my side of the bed beside Leif. "Not yet, Max. I needed to work on you both at the same time. I didn't make it very far before resting."

"He needs it more."

Piercey spoke to me in that slow, calm voice he always used when he wanted to help me settle down. "Yes, he does. And he's getting everything he needs."

I let myself relax into the plush mattress beneath me. The bed was far more comfortable than I remembered anything in this compound being.

The lights in the room were dim and the curtains drawn closed. Beside me, there was a nightstand with books on physics and quantum mechanics. Nothing else. Piercey hadn't stopped studying.

"I want to see him," I said. I would try again to rise, but I knew I couldn't. I'd used all the energy I had and now I was shriveled up.

"That's fine," Piercey said. "Take it slow. Your ribs were badly broken. You're lucky your lungs weren't punctured."

Leif carefully sat beside me and lifted me so I could sit up.

"I really thought we were done for." I squeezed Leif's hand and then nodded at Piercey. "Thank you."

Piercey was quiet for a beat. "I can't believe you're here, Max."

So much time had passed. We'd both changed. Piercey didn't look much like the boy I'd left behind. His beard was full and dark, and he'd filled out his lanky form enough that it would have taken me a moment to recognize him. "Me either."

"Let's get you up." Leif lifted me into his arms and carefully carried me around the bed toward the doorway. I soaked in his comfort.

"Where are we?" We passed a massive desk with a curved screen. It was a nice room. Looked like Piercey lived here alone, though. That made me feel a little sad for him, thinking about him by himself.

"The director's apartment . . ." Piercey pushed a wheelchair in from the living room. "I took over."

My eyes widened. "You run the whole center now?"

"You sound surprised."

"Well, yeah."

"You missed a lot, Max. I'll fill you in when you're healed and rested."

The surprise quickly fell into hurt, though. "You didn't unseal my power."

Piercey helped Leif settle me into the wheelchair and then paused. "I couldn't, but there was no one to defend the seal when you started to break through here on the mountain. It's incredible you managed to do it. Those instructors are long gone."

Did he think I was a monster, too? He didn't trust me down in the Valley carrying a power like this?

"How strange." Leif ran his fingers along the rubber handle while Wren knelt to inspect the wheels.

"I know this is overwhelming," I said, swallowing down the feeling of betrayal.

"Your friend explained a great deal of things to us." Wren chuckled. "Too much. I'm lost."

"He isn't one to spare details."

Piercey crossed his arms. "We should talk before I take you to your friend. Leif and Wren told me about what's happened to your people. I have dozens of graduates I would trust with my life. I'm calling on them to help free your people."

I jolted up in excitement and then doubled over from the pain.

"Calm down." Leif pushed me back against the seat. "We still haven't talked him into killing the Prophet."

Piercey sighed. "Three of my best will take Leif and Wren back to your people and meet the others there."

"We should all go together," I said.

Wren knelt beside me. The permanent war paint darkening her eyelids couldn't harden the softness of her eyes. "We need to get there soon. No one will trust a group of demons if we aren't there to explain. You and Nash need more time to heal. You won't be far behind us."

"They'll be well guarded, Max." Piercey had confidence like I'd never seen in him. It soothed the fear. "We need to work fast. You should say goodbye now."

Wren gripped my hand. She knew how hard this would be for me.

Pain twisted my heart.

I'd said goodbye to Leif and Wren far too many times this week. My heart yearned for them as Piercey wheeled me down the hall.

Now that we were alone, our years of separation and our years together burst at the quiet. "I can handle whatever you have to say, Piercey." Windows lined the hallway. Outside, blustery winds scattered snow in the air, so all we saw was white. So much like the white room.

His voice was heavy when he spoke. "I don't know what to say, Max. So many times over the years I thought about what it would be like to see you again."

"Thank you for always sending the medicine. It saved me."

"I pushed some in through an IV while you were out. You should have relief."

I turned so I could see him. "You know I didn't want to leave you, right?"

"Of course, I know." The same eyes of the boy I'd said goodbye to looked back at me, even though the years had changed us both so much. "I didn't think you'd ever come back. I thought about telling you the instructors were gone now, but I couldn't. It's . . . complicated . . ."

There was much more to the story than he'd told me and it was clear he felt guilty. But as important as the past was and the implications it held for the future, I needed to get him focused on my people. He had a soft heart and he would want to save them. I swallowed down the pain in my throat. "I need your help."

He smiled softly. "I love that you want my help. The thing is, you don't need me to do anything for you. You could kill him yourself."

Shame and anger flooded my cheeks with heat, so I had to turn away quickly. "Your power has grown. Mine hasn't. And the seal, I don't know if it's broken for good, or if I'll lose my power when I leave the mountain."

"I think it's safe to say you broke it for good. I was forbidden by the gods to return your power to you or reach out. They upheld your banishment. But I told Dr. Henderson that one day you'd find a way around these limits. So, I don't think you ever needed me. You had enough power as a child before coming to this place to kill the Prophet."

The reference to the eclipse shot tingles through my body. "That was . . . I was out of control."

"That power is inside of you. I've had my entire life to come close to it. You've always had it. You're holding yourself back."

Was it true? All this time, was it not so much the instructors or the gods sealing my power within me, but my own fear and guilt?

"When I don't hold myself back, people die." The blood raining in the white snow flashed in my mind. I dug my fingers into my side too hard and sparked pain. "I don't want this power anymore. I want Dr. Henderson to take it away from us all."

"We'll talk more when you're well. You're in pain."

I chewed the inside of my cheek. As much as I didn't want to let this go, just talking about the eclipse made me feel defeated. "How did you guys get to us so fast in that cave?"

"I monitor the radios. I knew there was a threat and it was a demon woman. Odds were high it could be you. Your friends got into a nasty fight. I caught it on the radio. That's how I found them. Good thing, too. I would've had to use my power to get to you if I didn't have their help. Taking on an army would have slowed me down."

"It still couldn't have been easy getting to the next passageway having to carry us."

Piercey stopped at a door and reached around me to open it. "I've made more passageways with my graduates. We also installed an elevator system to get down the mountain quickly. You were off the beaten path. That did add some time. But not so much that I couldn't hold the guards off."

He wheeled me into a small room with chairs and benches. It looked like a waiting area. "You held them off?"

"I can only manage it for so long."

I couldn't fathom the power Piercey now possessed. Surely it was far more than what I'd tapped into during the eclipse. It distracted me enough that at first I didn't notice the observatory window at the far end of the room. "Is that . . ."

Piercey rolled me right up to it. Nash slept on a medical bed with monitors beside him and an oxygen mask over his face. I touched the glass. My heart ached. "Is he sedated?"

"Yes. I'll let him wake up after this next treatment, though."

"Thank you, Piercey." I curled my fingers into a fist. "He has a daughter. He has to make it home."

"He'll make it home, Max. Now, rest while I do your treatment."

I closed my eyes. Peace flooded me as his healing power washed over my body like the water in the cave.

If my power was like fire, Piercey's was more like hot springs. Powerful, yet fluid and controlled. No matter how many healing treatments I had in my life, it never stopped amazing me. I could feel a gentle stretching inside. My bones strengthening.

Soon, the pain was only a distant memory.

I stood from the wheelchair and twisted to test out my ribs after Piercey had finished healing me. No discomfort. "You've gotten good at that."

Piercey only smiled as he sat on a bench by the observatory window.

"Are you working on Nash, too?" I asked.

"Yes."

"You don't even need to look?"

He crossed one leg over the other. "His wound might have been severe, but it's a simple fix. It just takes time for the tissue to mend. I can visualize it easily."

"You're just one big hotshot now." I sat down beside him. "Hotshot healer. Hotshot director."

He rolled his eyes.

I paused. "Why did you take the job?"

"Big surprise. You don't approve."

"I didn't say that. It's just that we went through so much here."

"Change is always possible. We don't train children or force them to come here anymore. We give them a home here if they need one, but that's all."

I sat back. "Where do they learn to use their power?" I didn't like how the Prophets had education whereas few demons did, but that didn't mean I wanted no one to have training.

"They get to be kids. They can enroll when they've proven they're mature enough to understand. And our graduates help the world, instead of hurting it."

"Are you sure about that?"

He narrowed his eyes. "Yes. Why?"

"There are people with power all over the Valley and the Flatlands. Powerful ones."

"They aren't mine. I know who you're talking about."

"So you're letting them run wild?"

"What should I do? Start a war?"

"That's what they're doing. Warring against people who don't have power."

"We don't hold people captive here, Max. Or kill the people who can't cut it. There's more people with power because this school has changed."

He was right. I wouldn't want him to continue in the old way. "There just has to be a better way." Piercey had always been about peace. Frustration leaked into my voice. I didn't have time to be angry with him now, but it was there, waiting for me to let myself feel it. I remembered that he was healing and cut myself off. "Sorry. I need to let you focus."

"No, no. We can get our fight over with," he said. "You don't have to wait."

"Not while you're healing Nash."

"I can do both at once."

It'd always been like this with him. No matter how upset I was, no matter how enormous our problems were, we could always put it aside.

"Why did I have to climb this nightmare of a mountain to ask for help? Why weren't you already looking after the innocent down there?"

"I am helping. I'm training people the right way. They're going out and doing the work."

I could hardly keep myself standing. "You're a few days travel from people who are really hurting. The Prophet has total control over the Valley and now he's taken my people."

"If I had known he had your people, I would have acted. Word hadn't made it back to me yet. You have to know that you have never been alone down there." Piercey's eyes looked sad. "I've kept watch over you."

"Excuse me?"

"I was scared for you, and once I got some power around here, I used it to look out for you. I have no regrets."

Was that why my people had escaped the Prophet's grasp for so long? Not because of our skills, but because I had Piercey on this mountain watching over me? "So I'm the only one who deserves your protection?"

"It seems like swooping in to save the day will solve the problems, but there are always consequences for interfering."

It felt like he'd slapped me across the face. "You sound like the gods."

"I have a lot of power now, Max. But I'm still just one person. I don't have any right to alter the course of countless lives. What if I take the wrong approach? It's better to have a multitude. That's why all of our graduates meet regularly and we vote."

"Oh, so did you vote to let the Prophet capture the entire Valley?" I did stand this time, unable to sit next to him while he squandered all this power. "People are dying. And you're just living on top of this mountain, disconnected from it all."

"Says the woman who abandoned everything: her friends, her power, her responsibility." Hurt blared from his eyes. "Me."

"That's not fair. I was banished and my power was sealed."

"I'm talking about before that." Piercey sat forward. "You knew when you told them that you refused to become a Prophet that it would end like this. Your rebellion was always going to end in a curse."

"It was never about us. I'm not going to do the gods' bidding. This power is the curse. Either we all should have it or none of us."

"If you had stayed, it would be you in my position. You would have far more power. So judge me all you want. It is your own fault that you are now too weak to save your people. All because of a pointless rebellion that accomplished nothing. You thought my way was cowardly, but I've managed to actually change things."

Fire burned in my gut. I couldn't deny it, and that made me want to fight him even more. Piercey rarely uttered such provocative words. He'd become bolder. Maybe he believed in the words so much, it was worth hurting me.

"If I remove the Prophet from power, then what?" Piercey asked. "All the tribes in the Valley will war and kill each other like in the old days. Or someone just as bad will take his place. If I try to install some kind of government, it won't belong to the people. It won't work. It isn't as simple as strong-arming everyone in your path."

"Those are all excuses. You can't tell me that with all this time to think, you figured doing nothing is best."

"That's what you've done. Nothing."

I ground my teeth down. "I've lived. That isn't nothing. I took my life and fought for it. Can you tell me you've lived your life? Can you?"

"I'm doing more than you'll ever know. This program is unrecognizable from what it once was. While you've been throwing a fit for a decade, I've worked on the gods. Our world is changing, Max."

I blinked. "Changing. It's all getting worse. Don't you see that?"

"It will get better."

My eyes slid closed. "No, Piercey . . . No, no, no . . . What have you done? Have you made deals with her? Have you trusted Dr. Henderson?"

I sat down on the bench and let my head fall into my hands when he said nothing. Whatever good he thought he was doing, he'd only acted as that woman's puppet. He couldn't really believe he'd done something good with her. I didn't need to know Dr. Henderson well to know she couldn't be trusted.

CHAPTER TWENTY

Piercey's confession about working with Dr. Henderson had rattled me. He put his hand on my back. I nearly knocked him away, but for all my anger, I hurt for him as well. He wanted to help so badly, and he was so good that he trusted the good he saw in others, forgetting the bad was still there.

"Did you agree to not harm the Prophet, Piercey?"

"Not exactly."

I dug my fingers into my hair.

"After the accident—"

"Just say it. Don't dance around it. After I lost it and killed our instructors and blew the roof off the dorms."

He sighed. "Yes, after you killed them and ran, it shook the school. I knew that even after they settled for banishing you and sealing your power, Dr. Henderson could change her mind and have you killed. So, I sought her out. That's how we started talking."

"Did she make you director?"

"Eventually. I understand what she's trying to do. I don't agree with her, but I showed her that I can be objective and scientific. Dr. Henderson wants this program to succeed so badly that she's hidden the negative outcomes so that we have time to fix everything and yield reliable data." Piercey's voice rose. "She's given me so much information."

"Oh, Piercey." Pity won out over the anger. "You can't trust Dr. Henderson."

"I don't trust her. That doesn't mean I can't work with her."

"'Work with her.' You aren't colleagues."

"I'm her apprentice." Piercey spoke the words boldly. "When I'm done with my life in our world, I'm a potential candidate for the council in the Kethios. They've created a whole digital universe, Max. The physical world is just one step in evolution. It took her people a long time to go completely digital. The sheer amount of energy needed to maintain it is beyond my comprehension. But it's real."

I shook my head. "That's so wonderful for them. They'd abandoned us on this planet with nothing except power we don't know how to control."

"I know, but there's a way to work with them. We will join them one day when we die here. Intelligent life from all over the cosmos has uploaded to a much safer digital dimension. All the physical worlds still evolving will one day join. It's everyone's ultimate destination. Our life here in our world is only the start."

I listened with my mouth partially hanging open, unable to interrupt him, because I didn't even have the words to say.

"Max, you were right before. Our life here matters. Physical worlds die eventually. The people who lived in them join the digital universe. We need to make it the best it can be for everyone. I think that if you meet with Dr. Henderson, you can convince her of more change."

I dropped his hands then as if they'd burned me. "I'm not going to work with her. She's been corrupted. It doesn't matter how great her society is. There's something wrong with her. Have you forgotten the way she talked to us? We were only children. Is that how you would have treated confused kids?"

"She's a little on the clinical side."

"The *insane* side, Piercey. You said yourself that she's hiding things in this experiment from her council. And that one person can't be trusted with so much power."

"It's different with the Kethios. Dr. Henderson had to reach enlightenment before taking over the experiment. She's lived tons of full lives in simulations. She is wise, Max."

"If she ever was enlightened, she's lost it. What does she have you doing? You need to be honest."

"Nothing. I pushed for changes in the Sacred School and she agreed to them. I said we needed quiet, inauspicious people with power who can guard the innocent and work for positive change. People who will use their power for medicine and infrastructure, not war."

"Yes, that part sounds great. I want to know about the Dr. Henderson part."

"She doesn't want me to single-handedly upset the balance of the world. That's all. My graduates and I have to agree on political movements. She hasn't forbidden us from doing anything."

"Only because she hasn't had to. The moment you cross her, she'll crush the illusion of freedom."

Piercey shook his head and sat back against the wall. "All you want to do is fight."

"All you want to do is force peace, even when it's false peace."

"Just listen to me for once, Max. Dr. Henderson has to make sure that every single intervention she takes can be replicated in physical worlds, and that it gives the people she's helping the greatest level of self-determination. So she doesn't remove people from the experiment. She builds profiles of who uses their power for good to better understand who it should be given to, but she doesn't take it away from the bad. Only, if someone threatens the experiment as a whole, she will take them out. Max, do you hear me?"

My thoughts all settled. My feelings. I nodded. "Trust me, Piercey. I understand. Dr. Henderson has threatened to kill me so that you'll be her willing servant."

Piercey sighed at my claim. "No. She never threatened that. I just know her. If you keep crossing her, I'm afraid I won't be able to save you. Let's get on the same page and make our world better. Don't be stubborn."

"You're a fool, Piercey. I'm going to prove it to you."

Anger hardened his voice. "What's that supposed to mean?"

"I'll provoke her and let you see who she really is. I doubt you ever piss her off enough to see behind her mask. Her council ought to know she's devolving as she plays god with our world. There's no experiment anymore, Piercey. Dr. Henderson has truly become a god. Our world is for her, now."

He groaned. "We're just not on the same page. I need to share what I've learned with you. That's the only way for us to understand each other. See, we've made war with these neural implants and missed their most basic functions. Things children in other worlds grow up knowing how to do are lost on us." He reached both his hands out. "If you still trust me, I can give it all to you, right now."

I stared at his hands. "How?"

"I have a neural link with my graduates. We can communicate with our minds any time we tap in. We don't need computers. Our implants are linked. But I've never shared everything with someone before. I want you to have it, Max. I want you to have everything I've been through, everything I've learned, every ounce of wisdom I have."

My heart started to pound. "You'll open your soul to me."

He laced his fingers with mine. "All of it."

"Piercey . . ."

"Trust is all it takes." His eyes lowered. Voice lowered. "It doesn't mean anything more than that."

The pain on his face crushed my heart. "Leif and Wren are my blood, Piercey. But you've never stopped being my best friend. Not for a moment." I squeezed his hands. "Take what I have, too. Understand me and I'll understand you."

"If you hold nothing back, I'll have it all. Your every memory and thought."

I glanced at the window where Nash still slept. I couldn't share everything.

"You don't need to save me from the things I already know." Piercey smiled sadly. "I know how you see him, Max. And I know how you see me. It's okay."

Sadness tinged my thoughts. Knowing it and experiencing it were different. "I can't hold anything back?"

"Once you close up, it's hard to keep the rest of yourself open. You don't have to give. You can just receive."

"No. We both need to know everything. Let's do this."

"Linking will give you a weapon I've been working on for a very long while."

"What weapon?"

He lowered his voice. "It's safer to show you."

The look that had always stopped me in my tracks as a kid, made me retreat, burned in Piercey's eyes, somehow brighter than ever. How could he still love me? After all these years? I'd left him behind, but he never left me. I'd had him this whole time.

The other day I'd slipped back to when I fled the Sacred School. I could feel his embrace now, as if that girl I'd been and the woman I'd grown into shared the same body. It'd been different than any other time we hugged. Didn't feel like it was between the kids who'd survived this terrible Sacred School together anymore, but instead the people who'd been quietly growing inside of them. His hands had touched me differently that day. Touched me more like he did now. When he'd pressed his lips against mine, it was the first time I'd ever kissed someone.

It was confusing then. Such an experience, to be kissed and to kiss a boy.

But I'd quickly found it didn't feel right to me. Not with him.

Piercey breathed out slowly and closed his eyes. "It's as easy as opening a door. When you feel me, let me in. I'll do the same for you."

I didn't understand. Couldn't understand. Not until it happened. Warmth spread from his palms into mine, tingled up my arms, flowed into heat that washed over me from head to toe. Everything we'd experienced together filled me as if I remembered every second at once. I could've held back. I could've shut down.

Instead, I opened myself to my friend and I let him in, no matter what it meant for us.

My eyes widened. Our gazes met and his life washed into me. It was the same as waking from a dream and remembering in a single moment who you were. What your life was. All of it there within you.

I didn't have to wonder what this meant for us. I knew. Knew him fully. Somehow knew myself more fully.

"I'd forgotten." My voice came out hoarse. "We really do need each other."

A tear slid down his cheek. The piece of me that had missed him was healed now. The anger over our differences gone.

With our knowledge and experience combined, everything that had been unclear was now so apparent. Piercey really believed that he could work with Dr. Henderson because the influence she gave him helped him turn the Sacred School into an academy of peace and healing. But the fact that she was intervening when she claimed she wouldn't told me everything I needed to know. I had no doubt she was taking action Piercey knew nothing about. The things Flare had said were similar to Dr. Henderson. Piercey wasn't the only partner. Flare must have been, too.

Piercey would know that now. But when we connected, I felt his hesitance still to take action. He was so trusting in the good of others.

He breathed out slowly. "If Dr. Henderson tries to destroy you, you have to use what I've learned. Use the weapon I gave you. I know you'll want to use it regardless, but you know how I feel. The risk is too great if it can be avoided."

Piercey had never stopped trying to learn how to hack into our simulation, because he knew one day I might ask for it, and he'd been right back then. He never could deny me. More than that, he trusted me to do something he didn't trust himself to be able to do. He trusted me to decide whether to use it. And experiencing the way he saw me made me trust myself, too. Because Piercey was the smartest person I'd ever met. If he believed in me, why shouldn't I believe in myself?

I took my friend's hand. "Dr. Henderson taught you how to open your soul to someone so you would do it with me. She thinks you'll change me. She thinks when I see her next, when we see her next, that we'll work with her together." I shook my head. "Before I leave to battle the Prophet, I have to see her, and figure out what she's been doing in the Valley. Otherwise, I don't know what I'm walking into. I'll be wise with the weapon." Although, I could use the threat of hacking the simulation to force her to confess her actions to me.

His expression was hard. Before, Piercey had known not to trust Dr. Henderson, but now that he truly saw from my point of view and witnessed what Skia Hellig truly had been through, he must have understood how dangerous his game was. It had been a lie when she told us she didn't intervene in our world. Even if I killed the Prophet, my people wouldn't be free. Piercey had been right that I had the strength to fight this battle, though it wasn't because of the energy that killed those people at the eclipse. It was because I knew the truth and I wasn't afraid to do something about it.

Dr. Henderson was fucking with our world, and I would stop her at all costs.

"We'll save your people, Max. And we'll find a way to free the people from the corruption of the Prophets, and Flare's manipulation, and the crushing power of our implants. I can't promise I'll kill the Prophet or fight Dr. Henderson. Only that we'll find a way to help everyone. Just tell Dr. Henderson one thing for me. Tell her, I'm with you. No matter what."

I swallowed hard. "I will, Piercey." So that was it. He'd choose me. Neither of us had really had the right approach. It wasn't as simple as killing Flare and the Prophets, or having the gods take away our power. It wasn't as diplomatic as Piercey working with Dr. Henderson to right all our wrongs. As long as Dr. Henderson had so much power over our world, we would never be free to determine our own path. Piercey couldn't deny me. He was letting me follow my heart, despite his misgivings. I'd prove to him that his trust wasn't misplaced.

Piercey gestured at the window. "Nash is waking up."

Opening ourselves up to one another hadn't changed the way we felt. Only deepened it. Deepened it so much that I knew without a doubt I was never going to fall in love with him. Only love him more deeply as my friend. But he was cursed. Cursed with more than that for me. The pain of that burden ate away at me as I looked into his eyes.

"Go ahead," Piercey said. "He'll want to see you."

CHAPTER TWENTY-ONE

I knocked on Nash's door before pushing it open, nervous about all that I still had to explain. When he said "come in," I opened it to him standing at the bed with his back to me, fastening his pants. A button-up lay beside his old, bloodied clothes. The script of Eskel's name laced his spine, woven intricately between his defined shoulders. It was my first time really getting a good look at the scarring, and it ignited my hatred for the Prophet.

"How do you feel?" he asked, glancing over his shoulder at me as he fumbled with the pants. "What a strange piece of clothing."

"Better." I ran my fingers along his spine as my stomach twisted with the desperation for vengeance. Nash hesitated at my touch and glanced behind himself at me. My voice fell to a low threat. "Nothing will stop me from killing the Prophet. I want you to know that."

Nash turned and studied my eyes. "I do."

"My power was sealed by the old instructors at this school. That's why I couldn't kill him before." I looked to the light pink scar along his chest from the spear. The pain of letting him nearly die threatened to close up my throat. "I won't fail again."

"You didn't fail." He spoke softly. "You saved me. You saved all of us."

I swallowed down the knot in my throat, shifting my stare to the ground. "I've been failing for a long time." Before he could argue, I made myself smile. "I need to explain things to you. I thought after I get a few things done we could talk."

"I'd like that."

"Did Piercey tell you anything?"

"All kinds of things that really didn't make sense."

I nodded. "Yeah. I'll explain things better."

The heaviness of what we'd been through over the last few days made my heart feel raw, and that weakness, combined with the fear I'd felt at losing Nash, ignited the longing to embrace him again. I hadn't expected to feel it so strongly. My heart ached, but my breath felt thick in my lungs. The way Nash looked at me told me he felt it, too. Maybe remembering, like I was, when we kissed and fell asleep in each other's arms.

I sighed and stepped back for the door, my stomach burning like my power had ignited in me again. "I have to work on something, so find me in a few hours."

"Work on something or run away?"

He must have thought that challenging me would appeal to my pride and make me cave. And damn it, he was right. I balled my hands into fists. Lying felt too pathetic now that he'd called me out. "Both. Happy?"

"Not particularly." He grabbed the button-up and winced as he slid an arm into the sleeve. "Go ahead, though. Leave me wounded and alone. Bye."

I shook my head, refusing to smile. "You can be such an ass."

He looked down at his twisted shirt. "What is this?"

I bit back a laugh as he managed to get his other arm through the sleeve. The Sacred School was a unique place in our world and they'd honored our past lives by giving us relics of our original time. It had taken me years to figure that out, but now I realized this place held a piece of what should have been our life.

Looking puzzled, Nash picked a leather belt off the bed and wrapped it around his midsection, frowning when it didn't hold the shirt closed.

"That's for your pants." I took the belt from him and pushed one end through his belt loop. "See?"

"No. I don't understand the concept at all. You'll have to do it for me."

I rolled my eyes and reached around him as I threaded it through the loops. Even though I knew he was joking, I did it anyway, enjoying a light-hearted moment and the excuse to feel his warmth. When I fastened it for him, I gave the belt a tug, like I was testing its hold. "Have to make sure that stays in place."

"Look who's teasing now."

"The buttons are what hold the shirt closed." I fastened the bottom one for him. "Are you going to make me do this for you, too?"

"No one's making you do anything, Max. You volunteered."

My face felt warm as I continued buttoning the shirt, my knuckles brushing his bare skin. I knew I needed to leave, but what could it hurt to spend a little more time like this?

When I finished, Nash tugged at the shirt. "Now teach me how to take it off so I know what to do later."

I groaned. "Stop with your insufferable flirting."

"Stop liking it and I'll stop doing it."

"I never said I like it."

"Right."

I pursed my lips. "I'm going to hurt you."

"Finally. I'm ready."

I popped him in the stomach.

"Ow." He brushed my hand away. "I'm still injured, you know. I have two healing treatments left."

"No whining or I hurt you worse."

"Oh. I can work with this after all. Continue."

I jabbed my finger against his chest and met his eyes. "I'm done, Unknown. Don't mess with me anymore."

"Are you saying that in a sexy bossy way or—"

"Nash," I said.

"Fine. I apologize. I would like it to be known that you started it this time, though."

That feeling that had drawn me to Nash, urging me to trust him even when I wasn't sure I could, had only grown hour by hour, taking firm hold of me now. How foolish of me to stay and play around like this when my people were in captivity, and I had so few days left to live.

"Woah," Nash said, lifting my face. "I'm sorry. I thought we were having fun. I should have listened to you."

"We were." Now I'd really embarrassed myself. I turned my face away to hide how my expression had fallen. "There's a reason I don't want to get too close."

The beat of quiet panged hollow in my chest.

"You can tell me," he said, the joking replaced with seriousness.

"You almost died, and it crushed me. I don't want you to go through that." If I said it, Nash would argue with me like Piercey always did. "I don't just slip to the past. I've seen my death in the future. The Prophet will kill me during the eclipse. I just have to make sure that I kill him, too."

Nash took my hands in his. "We'll kill him first and you'll be fine."

"No. There's no stopping it. It's already happened, because I've lived it, even if it hasn't happened yet. Just trust me."

"Piercey told me you would say this. He said you two had used your powers to share your past, and that you would push me away because you think you're going to die."

I drew back. "He had no right."

Nash caught my arms. "He said it was the only thing he would ever share with me and that he had to because it's so important. If you're convinced it's impossible to save yourself, you won't try."

"So what? You're the only one who can convince me?"

"You have to convince yourself. But I can ask. You never give up on a fight. Don't give up on the most important one."

My eyes burned. I tried to look away, but Nash shifted to follow my eyes.

"Don't get closer." Pain broke my voice. "You'll get hurt."

"You were going to die with me in that cave, because you refused to walk away. So how could you ever ask me to leave you?"

I tried to come up with something, only what could I say? It had seemed like Nash would surely die in the cave, but I never would have given up on him. There was no way for me to defend myself.

"It's because you think you don't deserve to be loved," he said. "Deep down, in a place inside of you that you may not realize is there, you think you're not good enough. No matter how much of yourself you give away to save everyone else, it's never enough."

Tightness spread down to my chest so I felt as if I couldn't breathe. "I know I'm not bad."

"But do you believe it? Or do you believe you're what your father made you feel?"

I rubbed my hand over my chest. "I hurt everyone, and I'll hurt you."

"Not true." He bent, even though it tightened his face in pain, and stole a warm kiss. The unexpected taste of his lips melted me.

"Nash—" I pushed against him gently to encourage him to straighten so he didn't strain his injury, but he nestled his cheek against mine.

"I want you to live," he whispered against my skin. "Dying only makes it more important that you live now. If I'm not what you want, that's okay. Just don't turn down what you do want because you're afraid to lose it."

My heart beat so hard and my eyes stung. He'd completely disarmed me and left me defenseless. So be it. I smoothed my hands up his neck and wound my arms tightly around him so my body eased against his. Our noses brushed while Nash worked his palms into the dip of my waist and down my hips, opening my mouth with his own. His kiss seized the breath in my lungs, far more potent than the first time in the cave. I'd meant to only kiss him once, but I was desperately consumed by the need for more. Ironically, Nash saved me by whispering between kisses.

"You realize you almost got me killed in the Flatlander battle? You look amazing swinging a sword around."

I snorted against his lips and drew back, wondering by the light look in his eye if he'd known I'd needed the interruption, even if he didn't want it. "Your teasing has no limits."

"You never believe that I'm serious."

Nash still had a powerful control over me, but this gave me the time I needed to collect my thoughts. It must've hurt him to dip to kiss me when significant damage remained beneath the fresh scar on his chest. "Your wound is still deep." Although, Nash didn't look like he cared about that at all right now. We'd had our chance back in the cave and I hadn't taken it. Now wasn't the time. "We shouldn't get carried away."

"Let me guess, you really do have work to do," he said dryly.

"Well, I do."

With a groan, he lifted his hands and backed up, taking one more glance down my body. "Fine. Get out of here, Sharpshooter."

When I reached the door, I hesitated. "I regret it, you know."

Nash tilted his head. "Regret what?"

"Pushing you away in the cave the other day."

Genuine shock widened his eyes. "You say this on your way out the door?" He ran his hand through his hair. "Is this revenge for all the teasing?"

"Sure." It hadn't crossed my mind, but it felt nice to take the upper hand in this battle of ours.

Soon, I needed to break into the white room and confront Dr. Henderson. What would happen after that, I couldn't say.

"Max."

Hands shook me awake. I rubbed my eyes and sat up in the library to see Nash beside me. I'd fallen asleep after hours of running through the steps to the hack. Piercey had never stopped researching and there was so much here for me to learn, even about my time slips.

The smile crept up before I thought to feel self-conscious. "Hi."

"Did you faint?"

He was worried. I shook my head. "No."

"Good." He sighed. "I had my last treatment. I feel great."

"No lasting damage?"

"None."

I sighed, weight falling off me.

"Piercey told me you're entering the Door of the Gods. I'm going with you." Nash lifted his hand when I tried to argue. "I won't back down on this. I didn't come all this way for you to go alone."

I wasn't going to take him. He was crazy if he thought I would.

"You carry so much guilt and responsibility." Nash took my hand and laced his fingers with mine. "Let me help you."

"I butchered the Sacred Guard. Brutally." My voice was raspy, eyes stinging. "I don't even know how many I killed." I sighed. "I can't pretend anymore. I'm not a normal person."

"You were never just a normal person, Sharpshooter."

Despite his efforts, it couldn't feel like a compliment. "We have more important things to do than assuage my guilt. I owe you answers."

Nash sobered. "Piercey spoke with me again. He told me most people specialize in something, like how he heals people. He said you manipulate space and time, but that you struggle to control it."

"I've never come close to controlling it." I sat back. "This will be hard to take in. But I'll tell you what I can about the gods, our power, my past. All of it. Just tell me if it becomes too much."

Nash and I had talked for over an hour and there was still more to tell him. He'd needed breaks while we spoke, especially when I'd tried to explain that we lived in a simulation. That didn't make any sense to him at all, of course. Sometimes he just stared out the window at the snow. Other times he paced and asked questions. Most of the time, he simply listened. He sat at the table now, looking as though a weight tried to push him down. I'd just explained to him that my Prophet from my homeland had trained me for years and told other Prophets about my potential. So, when I killed the villagers during the eclipse, they brought me here to help me learn to control my power, and turn me into a Prophet.

Then I told him about the day I finally had to act on my plans to flee. "The instructors were hard on us. I lost my patience because they pushed Piercey too far and he hit his head really hard. I used my power to throw one of them through the window. Others attacked to subdue me and I got angry. It was a blip of what happened when I was a kid. I started to slip through time, the power exploded, and I killed three of them. I don't remember it happening. Piercey said that I broke all the bones in their bodies."

Nash had taken my hand after I said it.

"I'd been planning to leave and find other people like me so that we could take on the instructors, the Prophets, even the gods. But I couldn't wait after I killed them. Piercey wouldn't leave with me, though. He told me to go become something great and that he'd be here for me if I ever found my way back. They sealed my power while I was on the run and I spent the years away trying to regain it."

"How did Piercey end up in charge?"

The door creaked and I straightened.

"Sorry to interrupt," Piercey said.

"You're fine. We should do this." I sighed. "We'll talk more, okay?"

Nash nodded.

Piercey's face looked serious. "Do you feel ready?"

"Yes."

Nash stood when I did, staying at my side. "Where's the door?"

"Max will have to lead you," Piercey said. "I should come, too."

"No. We need you here. It's too risky. If anything happens, thank you, for everything."

"If you need more time—"

"I don't. Just focus on me from here to help strengthen me. Hopefully it will work."

"I'll meditate and strengthen you." He looked to Nash. "Good luck." Then back to me. "See you on the other side."

I hugged Piercey, thankful to have him back again.

Then I turned to Nash, my heart full. "You'll be free of Flare and the Prophet. Your daughter will be free. Piercey will make sure of that."

"I'm going with you, Max. Don't act like you're saying goodbye."

I reached my arms around his neck and drew him against me. "If I don't make it back, tell Leif and Wren I love them."

When I pulled back, he tried to grab me, but it was too late. I'd already opened the door and he didn't know how to get to it. Didn't know it wasn't actually a door. And right before he caught me, I pried it open in my mind, still looking into his eyes.

"Max!"

CHAPTER TWENTY-TWO

Darkness, as black and inky as the Prophet's eyes, closed in on me.

Where was the white room that the Door of the Gods had always led me to?

My body felt as though it stood in the library with Nash and Piercey, but my mind wasn't there. My mind was floating in the darkness, floating everywhere and nowhere.

This wasn't right.

Panic drudged up in storming thoughts as violent as the worst lightning storms I'd ever seen.

And then I felt him. My father. I couldn't see him or hear him. But I knew he was here.

No . . .

The gods had closed the door in my face and abandoned me to slip into the past. I searched for my time, clawing back for Nash and Piercey in the Sacred School, as the void dragged me in the opposite direction. I was slipping in slow motion. Slipping to Dad. To the eclipse.

The darkness beneath me shifted into shadowy blades of grass until I looked down upon the hill where I'd once stood with my father. In the sky, a ring of light pierced the black moon, arcs of red burst in faint lines, and the earth fell silent as the source of life and light vanished from our sight. The villagers crowded together to watch the totality, their forms blurred in my mind by a dark film, like I could only see them from the furthest edge of my peripheral vision, even when I looked right at them.

I had to block them from my mind, even now.

Dad knelt before the eleven-year-old me with his arms outstretched. Like a faint mirage, Nash came into view on the hill with them. There, but not. Fear shot through me. Between the father and daughter, beneath the dark of the eclipse, Nash lowered to his knees and met my young eyes with pinched brows. "Max . . ."

I tried to scream. Time and space had swallowed me whole. It wasn't him the girl below saw. Her eyes lit for the man behind him. The one that was really there. Nash was fading, fading even from my sight. He didn't belong here. And I wasn't here. I was dangling between, one foot in the small boot and one on the other side of time.

Pain filled Nash's expression as he watched the old me run right past him into the outstretched arms of the tall man.

"Can you believe it?" The girl I'd once been bubbled with laughter. "The moon swallowed the sun whole."

"It did." My father took my cheek in his hand. "Can you feel it?"

"Feel what, Daddy?"

"The sun." He placed his hand upon her heart. My heart. "Burning in your soul."

"Not yet."

"Focus," he whispered. "Focus, baby girl . . ."

The scream I couldn't unleash burned in my soul.

I could feel what the young girl felt mingling with my own as she looked into Dad's eyes. We brimmed at once with love for Dad and with the rage I'd been abandoned to carry alone. Two points in time converged into one. It felt like the sun burned within me, ready to burst free.

The bastard.

My dad.

Pure chaos churning in the deep of my soul.

"The light . . ." my young voice said. "Look, Dad! The light . . ."

His voice blared, deep and knowing. "Your strength is greater than even an eclipse. Release it. Release it from within. It'll be beautiful, child. I promise. It's okay." A warm whisper fell against my ear now. "Show them the light. Free them."

Nash had faded but I could feel him here with me, here in the heat burning within me, in the timeless mourning of this moment. I wasn't alone. Never was. We'd always been here together, here with her, the girl I'd once been.

The heat of the flame swelled out of control, even though I tried to hold it in, tried to push Dad's voice away. Power erupted from my body. The Prophet wasn't here to stop me this time. Dad's body jerked and froze in the air, his fingers popping first, and then his arms, his legs. I clenched my eyes shut.

Brightness erupted from the small body I'd once inhabited. It washed over the people below in a beautiful array of golden hues and vibrant reds and purples as deep as a setting sun. The power washed over them and tossed them to the ground in waves, leaving their bodies stranded and useless while their souls moved on to what came next.

A wail exploded within me—one that had begun during this eclipse and never stopped. I couldn't utter it or hear it, just felt it, blaring as it always had, battering my insides.

Black snapped shut the curtain on my view of that day. I drifted between the eclipse and now and the nothingness separating the two. Time collapsed in on this one point and exploded forward. Entangled forever.

Memories popped in the black void like bright stars in the winter sky. Hundreds, thousands, millions of events surrounding me.

I couldn't let them distract me. I had to find Nash. My mind reached through a lifetime in the void.

I could see Nash then, watching again from above as he flashed over the void. His smirk the first time we'd met, where he'd sharpened his blade and looked at me. Drinking and fighting in the field. And then I saw us dangling from the cliff. Climbing up the stairs. Tangled in each other's arms on the cold cave floor.

I wanted to warn him of what was coming.

I saw the spear flying for him. The guards racing for us. Nash reaching for me in the library as I faded, catching my fingertips, catching me before I slipped away.

"Hold on!" The words broke free from my silenced mouth and I caught my time by just a thread. Had to hope I'd caught Nash, too.

The void was stripped away and I was alone, kneeling in a pure white room.

Pain racked my chest as I fell onto my hands and forced my voice to croak out of my throat. "Hello?" I wanted to scream the words but I didn't have the energy. "Answer me . . ." I kept seeing the golden hue wash over the villagers beneath the eclipse each time I blinked, flashing against the dark of my lids just as it had over the dark of the void. "I'm here. Like you wanted. You have me right where you want me."

"You think this is where I want you?" Her voice whispered warmth in my ear, even though I couldn't see her, or feel her. "I wanted you to lead. Not shatter on my floor."

With my head still bowed, my eyes snapped up to the place Dr. Henderson had stood in the last time I saw her. I imagined how she'd looked that day. "What did you do with Nash?"

"He's safe."

The white wall beside me faded so I could see him drawing his hands along the perimeter of the room. His eyes stared past me. He couldn't see me.

I clambered to my feet and fell against an unseen wall. "Why did you let him in?"

"He traveled all the way up the mountain with you. It was impolite to leave him behind. I'll let him join, if you promise to be good."

My tongue clung to the roof of my dry mouth. I nodded, holding my breath. I couldn't leave him alone in that room. "I will."

Nash stepped back with wide eyes. Then, he was looking at me. Really looking at me. "Max . . ."

He ran forward a step and I wrapped my arms around his neck. I told myself if I held on tight enough, Dr. Henderson wouldn't be able to rip us apart. That was what I hated most about the power she had over us. That she could take me from the people I loved. Nothing could be more cruel or unfair. The bitterness burned on my tongue.

"You were supposed to stay behind." I clung to him tightly.

"You were supposed to take me." He held my head against him anyway.

Then there was the feeling of a presence behind me. Nash stumbled back, taking me with him.

Dr. Henderson had finally appeared.

"Who are you?" Nash asked.

Her long hair laid over one shoulder. She looked so young despite how many years had passed. It wasn't that she aged well. She looked exactly the same. Same haircut. Same manicured nails. Everything was the same, like years for me had only been weeks or days for her. Maybe hours.

"It's her." I kept my arm around Nash and stayed beneath his. "The god. Dr. Henderson."

"Thank you for the introduction, Max." She studied Nash for a few seconds and then met my eyes. "A little dramatic for my tastes, but it will do."

Whatever. She reveled in the drama. "I know you're not just working with Piercey," I said. "You're up to much more. Tell me what you're doing."

"You still jump to conclusions with so little to support them."

"I know you're hiding the problems from your council." I pulled away from Nash and stepped toward Dr. Henderson. "If you really do care about us, listen to what I have to say. Stop manipulating our world and just give us our lives."

Her expression was so soft, I actually wondered if I'd managed to reach her. "You want me to give up."

"I want you to set us free from the burden of saving the universe. We can't. It's over."

"You, who cares so deeply for your people, would abandon countless who are suffering?"

"I don't know how to help other worlds, Dr. Henderson. All I know is this isn't it. You've made deals with Piercey, and I'm certain you have with Flare as well. You've given her powers that no one else has. Whatever you're doing in my world is an untested intervention that invalidates your own experiment."

"Don't lecture me on the scientific method, child. Once I have your world in shape, then I will be able to collect relevant data. I'm showing you mercy by not starting over in a more developed world."

Rage boiled beneath my surface. I steadied my words. Already, I wanted to fall back on the weapon Piercey had given me. "You're creating suffering, not eliminating it. This power you've given us has been weaponized against helpless people. You should take it away, not play god."

She snorted. "This world has no more suffering than any other world. It's just a unique spin on the usual. You actually have hope. You should be thankful. At least there are people like you with the power to help. You would be just as helpless as everyone else in another world."

Nash shook his head. "You believe your own lies, don't you."

Dr. Henderson sighed. "All people in all worlds ask these questions. Why do bad things happen to good people?" She looked at me as though I was a child who couldn't possibly understand. "At least you get to look your gods in the face and ask. The rest of us spent millennia after millennia crying out to the void. Why? Our cries for help were met with silence as we were tormented by wars, famine, the promise of death."

I scoffed. "You're still crying out to the void. Except when you got tired of the answer, you turned to our world to terrorize us."

She chuckled. "You're the answer to the prayers lifted all over the universe. As I said, dear child, be thankful."

"None of us signed up to be your experiment or your sacrifice."

"No one signs up for the life they're born into. And this life, resented so it may be by you, is infinitely better than the one we salvaged you from. I can hardly imagine it. An infant left trampled in war-torn streets on Earth. Unknown. That was you and Nash both. You were caught in a war that was much bigger than your world, one that consumed your planet, and lost your life before you even got started. We did you a favor by uploading your consciousness. We cleaned up the mistakes and wrongdoings of people who were willing to sacrifice your life and countless like you for their own gain."

My breath caught. "We died on Earth as babies?"

"Very unfortunate. It was a difficult time in human history, I'm afraid. We're still uploading worlds, you know. That's why Earth was one of the planets chosen before others. So, knowing your unfortunate life, knowing that we gave you all you know, is it me you want to scream at? Or is it someone else?"

My fists clenched. I couldn't even wrap my mind around what she'd said, much less my heart. So I gave into the glorious flames of my rage. "Oh, it's you."

She pinched the bridge of her nose. "Have you considered that you don't have the experience to appreciate what I'm doing?"

"The heart knows wrong." Nash held her eyes. "Enjoy your deathless world. Let us live and die as we were meant to. As everyone before has."

Her voice hitched in a rare show of emotion. "My world is not deathless. We carry the burden of all those who suffer and haven't yet found our world. Our empathy knows no bounds."

"Poor thing." I rolled my eyes. "Deal with it. You seem perfectly capable of that."

"I'm fighting against an eternal truth; one I refuse to accept. Death is a virus we cannot stop. Every time we think we've evolved beyond, it comes for us in new and insidious ways." Dr. Henderson lowered her eyes to the floor. "I'll do anything so that one day that won't have to be true anymore. No matter how many lives you live, no matter how much time passes, no matter how well you think you've healed . . . The sting of death is eternal." She met my eyes, tears shining in hers.

I punctuated my words with jabs of my finger. "You're playing god to right some wrong that haunts you. Or maybe you're just bored from immortality and justifying yourself."

"You think you know better than an eternal council? There are ancient beings from the first days of our universe who approved this experiment. I'm a child compared to them. Who do you think you are?"

I slapped my hand against my chest. "I'm a child of the world you created. I am the grief you've caused with your own hands. My voice matters." Heat burned in my palms. I had to breathe to calm myself down before Dr. Henderson realized I had learned how to access my power here. "Let me plead our case before the council. We'll see what they have to say."

Dr. Henderson snorted and then I knew I had no hope of winning her over. Her eyes were cold again. Her body stiff. This experiment had warped her. If she'd ever reached enlightenment in the past, at some point since, she'd turned and gone the wrong way. Death truly was a virus and it had evolved into a god who stood before me.

"Please." I closed my eyes and drew upon all the love I had for my people. Melted into the warmth of Rune's sweet eyes and smile. If it hadn't been for Piercey sharing his experiences with me, I would have used the weapon already. I understood, though, how dangerous it was to change an entire world. Asking was the only thing I could do other than use the weapon. "Please, do not interfere in our world anymore. Watch us in silence. Take away this curse of power from all of us who wield it."

"Keep your pleas. I want you to help me or get out of my way." Fury sharpened her voice and silenced her laugh. Her eyes looked as though they were on fire. "Make your choice now."

I rose back up and stepped close, so close I thought she might feel the heat burning in me as well. She couldn't be allowed to supervise our world any longer. "I'm going to kill your precious Prophet. I'm going to kill your fool of a servant Flare. I'm going to free my people." My voice deepened into a growl. "And I'm going to take this world out of your hands."

Smoke stung my nostrils. Her entire body singed with flames ready to erupt from her skin. The burning in her eyes deepened into a fiery red that devoured the hazel of Dr. Henderson's eyes. They were smoldering.

My heart skipped a beat. Breath fled my lungs. No . . .

"You're—" The words got stuck in my throat.

Dr. Henderson had faded entirely from the person who stood before me. Flare stood in her place. And I saw it now. Heard it now. The same tone in a different voice. The same haughtiness on a different face. The same person in a different body.

Flare wasn't a demon. She was a god. A god who'd walked among us and played in our world.

Heat swelled from Flare's body. "Did you forget that I told you to fear me?"

CHAPTER TWENTY-THREE

Nash and I had moved for one another at the same time. I jumped back and slammed into him while he grabbed me from behind. We had nowhere to run, not in this white room, not in the Sacred School, not in our entire world.

"You foolish, foolish children." Flare stomped forward. "I have given you enough chances."

"Why?" I couldn't draw in a breath. My voice came out as a squeak. "Why do you have this disguise?"

Flare—Dr. Henderson—rolled her eyes. "Why, why, why. I always have to explain myself to you."

What did she mean? She left me wondering all the time. When had she truly explained herself to me?

"I appreciate the sanctity of life," she said. "Rather than scrap this world, I've been speeding up your development until your society is ready for this power, so I can finally gather reliable data. But you always stand against me. I will no longer tolerate it."

I had so many questions, I couldn't think of just one to ask. So I stared helplessly with my jaw slack. Nash's grip on me tightened like he could possibly protect me.

"This was your final chance, Max. I tested you. I figured that's what gods do, right? They test their followers."

My voice shook. "You really are insane."

"I wanted you to see Piercey. He always talks sense into you. So, I let you go to the Sacred School. I really thought after all these years of him working with me, he would be able to turn you around. Now I know there's no hope for you. You're a danger to this experiment, and that makes you a danger to this world."

"Don't you dare threaten her." Nash pulled me beneath his arm.

Flare sighed. "Oh, sweet Nash. You know you can't save her from me. It makes me so sad for you."

I gripped Nash's arm. "He doesn't belong to you, Flare. Not you as a demon or a god or a woman. You disgust me."

"Please. He's a big boy. He can handle a couple drunk nights with me. You're the one who always ruins him. Besides, he did it as a spy. He wanted to manipulate me. Don't feel sorry for him when he simply knows how to use his charms."

"Why do you say *always*? What do you mean I always ruin him?" I asked. "What are you talking about?"

Dr. Henderson had never looked so much like a god as she did in Flare's form, lighting up the white room with her fiery heat, no longer having to hide her power. Vengeance burned in her eyes. "It's not shocking that you haven't figured it out, Max, but I am a little disappointed in Piercey." She glanced between Nash and myself. "I've never told any of you before. I'm not sure I should."

Color sparked over the white wall to our right, and it came to life with a meadow of daffodils. Nash and I stood there together in the image, his hair longer, mine shorter, a slithering scar crawling down his left arm.

My stomach churned. This had never happened.

Then I heard my voice and chills crashed through my body.

"Flare said she can take me through the Door of the Gods without being on the mountain. I have to go."

The Nash on the wall drew me closer. "Not without me."

"Just say bye and stop fighting me."

The look in his eyes was the same as when I'd just left him. "You're so stubborn."

I stood onto my toes and kissed his lips. The room went silent while we melted into each other's arms on the wall.

The left wall flashed with another scene while the one on the right continued to play silently.

"What the hell?" Nash stumbled back a step beside me.

On the other wall, we faced Flare in the halls of the Sacred School. Both of us were splattered with blood. I held a wound on my side while Nash looked like he struggled to stand.

"You'll never win." Flare's voice flooded the room, but it wasn't her speaking here in front of us today. "Stand down."

My stomach lurched. I doubled over, almost getting sick. This couldn't be.

"Enough, Flare." Nash lifted his voice over the movie playing for us. "Let us out of this mindfuck palace. Now!"

The images playing on the screen gave me that feeling. That feeling of a dream I couldn't quite remember.

I didn't want to believe what my mind was screaming at me. Couldn't believe it.

"We've done this before," I whispered. Why hadn't I considered it? This was a simulation. There was no reason Flare wouldn't run it more than once.

Flare's image faded into Dr. Henderson once more. She knelt down in front of me, voice unnervingly soft. "This isn't the first iteration of the experiment. It failed twice. You've destroyed your world both times." Long fingers reached out to my chin and lifted my face to hers. "The council would have wanted to shut you down the first time. I loved your world, though. I saw potential. So I saved you. I restarted your world twice without them knowing. This is the third time you've all lived. I'd hoped you would finally work with me."

I couldn't wrap my mind around what she said. It was way too much for Nash. He sank down to his knees, staring at one of the walls where we had finally let go of one another.

"The first time, when I saw you rebelling, I tried to be kind and win you over with compassion. The second, I did the opposite. I was hard and cruel. This time, I decided to simply be myself. No matter what I do, we always end up here in the end. This time, I even made sure Nash traveled with you so you would come to your senses together."

"It can't be true." Though I knew it could be, probably was, I just couldn't accept it.

"But look at you. You and Nash are such close souls." Dr. Henderson smiled wistfully. "You always find your way to one another. I tried to keep you apart last time, hoping it would help. I've given up on that."

Nash and I had been together before. It felt right to hear it. As disturbing and unthinkable as it all was, thinking about him finding his way to me every time set something in place inside of me. As if we, too, were entangled, our souls imprinted upon each other, bound through space and time and something beyond that. This draw I'd felt, his feeling of the dream he couldn't remember, these were the artifacts of a life once lived and a bond that ran much deeper than what we could remember.

Dr. Henderson shook her head. "I never wanted to kill you, Max. You love this world. You just won't stop fighting me. The first time, you told the world the truth, and chaos descended. The second you tried so hard to kill me that you lost control and destroyed everyone around you. What will happen this time? Will you ruin your world forever? I just cannot allow you to do that, no matter how good your intentions are."

The fight leaked out of me with each word. I'd never lost it before, no matter how hopeless it all felt. But what she said confirmed something in me the same way that hearing I'd always found Nash did. I was a curse. I'd known it since I was a child and I killed those people at the eclipse. It wasn't just in this life that I'd fought so hard that I killed the people I loved. It had always happened.

The world would be safer without me.

I collapsed on myself. Fell forward onto the ground and wept a lifetime—three lifetimes—of grief and failure. I wept for Dad who I loved and hated and had killed. I wept for Nash who I'd always dragged into this disaster. I wept for myself who I'd apparently let down time and time again. I wept so hard that I couldn't breathe, couldn't tell what was happening around me, until the wonderfully familiar arms lifted me, and I fell against Nash's chest.

There was no slipping away from him. He'd always held me, hadn't he?

"Let go," Dr. Henderson whispered. "This is your only hope. The world's only hope."

Nash pressed his mouth against my temple and spoke softly to me like the first time he'd told me the truth about Flare. "Don't listen to her, Max. Listen to yourself." He ran his fingers through my hair and pulled it away from my face. "Listen to me." Nash held my head against his chest. His heart beat steadily in my ear. How had he not broken with me today? This had to be far more shocking to him than to me.

I trembled in his arms.

"Nothing has changed." Nash kissed the top of my head. "We still need to stop her, just like before."

"Nash." Dr. Henderson sighed. "I don't want to remove you, too. I've seen a world without you in it, and Elsie doesn't need to go through that again. Stop this talk."

The black void Dr. Henderson had trapped me in opened up inside of me and swallowed me whole, so I lost all feeling, even as I wept against Nash. My mind and body had separated. I wasn't here. I wasn't anywhere. I was gone.

Nash continued to rock me gently. "You're the only one who stands against her every time. That's what I heard. You're the only one she fears. Her only threat." Nash breathed in my hair. Kissed my face. Held me close. "Stop holding yourself back."

Henderson rose before us, looming over us, darkness shadowing her face. "Maybe you're the only one who needed to die all this time, Nash. So Max will finally break and relent."

Panic threw me violently back into my body. I jerked up, eyes wide and unfocused.

"Don't worry." Henderson lifted her hand toward him. "It won't hurt. You'll wake up in perfection in the afterlife and won't remember a thing."

My eyes snapped to Dr. Henderson. The hottest of fires erupted from within me and flooded the room with energy. Fear flickered in her eyes. I would never let her hurt Nash.

"How are you accessing your power?" Her voice was tight.

"You shouldn't have let me bond with Piercey." The white room shook. Color leaked from the images that had been painting the walls as everything began to melt away. My voice rumbled out low and dangerous. "This is our world. Get the fuck out."

A scream tore from her throat as power sparked like a flash of electricity against her arm.

Nash stood beside me, as fearless as I'd ever seen him.

Dr. Henderson's eyelids flickered. Her hands twitched. As I dug my way into the fabric of this room, through its boundaries, working out into our world, resistance suddenly slammed against me.

The code Piercey had shared with me rolled through my mind as if I'd always known it. This power of mine had always come as an instinct. Now, I also had Piercey's knowledge. I felt my way through the code of the world just as my hands could feel the cool of water, or my ears could hear music, or my eyes could see color. I searched for control of my world instinctively, just as a child learns to walk. And I knew Dr. Henderson was in the interface as well, trying to stop me.

Blood trickled from my nose. Pain popped over my head. Sweat doused my skin.

"You really will destroy it all!" Dr. Henderson cried out with effort. "You reckless, foolish girl. You could eradicate everyone's consciousness if you damage the simulation."

I couldn't stop now. There was no stopping. No questioning myself. I'd started this and I didn't know what would happen if I turned back. But her words tore at me like daggers.

"Max, please." Tears slid down her cheeks. "You'll never get your world back if you destroy it. The work it will take to restore your consciousness . . ." Power zapped against her skin again. I had thought she would've retreated, but she stayed firm, fighting against me. "The stain of death never leaves. Never. If you kill us all, it will stick with our souls, even if they resurrect us!" More tears fell. "Trust me, Max. I know."

Nash spoke against my ear again. Somehow, despite all evidence that I'd only fail again, he still believed in me. "You can do this."

Consequences be damned. Maybe I really was Eclipse, the Soul Eater. Maybe I was nothing more than destruction. One thing I never did was surrender. And I would never, in any life, let this woman kill Nash. If I wouldn't do that, how could I leave the rest of our world in her hands?

I pushed through her resistance with every nerve ending in my body sizzling in pain.

A feeling like slipping filled me. Dr. Henderson met my eyes, sorrow, panic, maybe anguish filling them. And then, just like that, she was gone.

It was all gone.

Nash and I were lying on the ground in the Sacred School, our arms around each other.

CHAPTER TWENTY-FOUR

I stared at the floor, unable to rise. My entire body felt numb. "We're alive." I lifted my hands to look at them. "The world is still here."

Nash gripped my knee. "You did it."

"I felt an insane surge of power," Piercey said.

"We took control of the simulation." I clasped my throat with my hand and rubbed the soreness in my muscles. "Dr. Henderson was fighting me. She disappeared right before the white room did. I think she unplugged. She's probably out in her world right now figuring out how to hack back in."

"She's obsessed with this project," Piercey said. "I don't think she'll destroy the hardware, not when she's been hiding things from the council to keep our world going. She's not going to do anything until she's sure it's safe."

"So we have some time." I hefted out a deep breath. "Who knows if it's minutes or weeks or years. She's smart. She'll take back control eventually."

Nash nodded at me. "That gives us time to prepare for whatever battles we'll face."

It had been four days since we took control of the world away from the gods, every one of them spent traveling. We'd taken the elevator down the mountain and met with Piercey's graduates over his neural link. Val, one of his instructors, had met us after we descended the mountain and rode ahead of us with Piercey, her short auburn hair slicked back in the breeze. Everyone had been quiet today as we prepared for the battle tomorrow.

The Prophet knew that our people were coming to attack and had reinforced his village with warriors from surrounding regions. Piercey had sent graduates to escort Nash's family to the Sacred School to protect them, and a group had kept their eye on the Prophet to ensure he didn't hurt the innocents. It wasn't a promise that nothing would happen, but if the Prophet hurt even one, he'd be inviting an attack. While Piercey and Val had agreed to help us battle, the others wouldn't unless the Prophet started executing prisoners. They didn't have the votes to use the full weight of their group to bring down the Prophet when they worried about who would replace him. But no one planned to stand in the way of Piercey and Val.

What good was their power when they did nothing but watch the Prophet use his to hurt others? I had no use for diplomacy. Not with my people in danger and that snake controlling the entire Valley. But we'd created a good plan on our own. Nash had the idea for Piercey to use his power to shield him in battle so that he could fight against the disciples. Val had interesting strategies of her own. The first day we rode, we had kept so busy with our plans that I didn't have time to feel worried. The second day had been the most difficult, after we'd already made it down the elevator and started our ride toward the Prophet. Dr. Henderson's voice haunted me. As wrong as she was, as much as I knew she needed to be stopped, I wasn't right either. I had three lifetimes of fighting counterproductively and still I had no ideas other than to plunge headlong into the same strong-arm tactics that had ruled every life I'd lived. I was no better than her. She was the god of death and I was her demon of destruction.

This was why I needed to only think about saving my people and seeing Leif walk free with Rune and Arn. My thoughts would be the death of me.

I glanced at Nash as he rode beside me. "We shouldn't stop for rest tonight. We should ride and go straight for the Prophet. We're so close."

"We need sleep to fight well."

"Don't take Piercey's side."

Nash grinned at me. "Don't give me orders, Sharpshooter."

I pursed my lips and tore my eyes from him, before I could linger on the other thoughts that consumed me. With my own eyes, I saw that we'd had something in our previous lives, but I had no idea what it was. Had we met like we did this time and shared something fleeting? Or had we actually been together? Had we had a life together that Flare stole?

"We've squandered four days," Nash said.

Why couldn't he ever let me avoid anything? I tensed. "I told you, wait until after the eclipse." Not only because our focus needed to be on saving my people, but also because it was wrong to draw him any closer when I knew I'd slip away for good this time. We stole the world from the gods, so it wasn't like I would be reincarnated into another life. I'd be gone from this world.

When Nash and I had talked that first night about what to do, I'd told him that we should wait to figure anything out until after the eclipse. He'd looked at me skeptically when I told him, like he knew I'd break, and asked me if I'd ever stop tormenting myself.

He watched me now in the same way.

"Just say it." I couldn't handle another second of his burning stare.

"What excuse will there be after you survive the eclipse?"

I shot my head toward him. "If by some miracle I don't die in two days, then we can talk. That's entirely reasonable. Don't act like I'm being ridiculous."

"You haven't slipped to that future since we took control away from the gods," Nash said.

"It isn't as if I slip to it every day. It's coming."

"If dying during the eclipse is inevitable, then why did Henderson work so hard to take you out herself?"

This wasn't something I could speculate about. I'd accepted my fate long ago. Getting my hopes up now would only devastate me when the day came. "What does it hurt to wait?"

"Because we could die."

I tilted my head, brows raising. "Exactly why we shouldn't do this. You've completely lost me."

"The reason you want to wait is the reason I don't. We could fall in battle tomorrow." He eased his horse closer, voice quiet. "Even if we do, we'll be together again. We've always been together. It's a dream we keep waking from. A dream we keep returning to. Tell me you don't feel it in your bones that we've been here before. That we always end up here."

I couldn't tell him that because I felt it, too, as irresistible and inevitable as every slip I'd ever had. Maybe I wasn't afraid of what would happen if we opened ourselves up to each other and I died. Maybe I was afraid of what had already happened. That every day, every battle we fought, every catch of our eyes, every moment tying this one to the first time I saw him, I'd been slipping into his arms. He'd been slipping into mine.

The fear sharpened inside of me so I couldn't lie to myself. It was too late. Multiple lives too late. If time was entangled between the eclipses, then Nash and I had become entangled as well.

"I won't be strong enough to say goodbye." I gripped the horse's mane.

"It's not time for that." His voice melted the tension in my chest. "Live in this moment. Stay with me, here and now. If we ever do say goodbye, it won't be forever. I'll come to you in the world beyond this one. We'll find our way to each other. We always have and we always will."

His words melted me. "That world is far bigger than our little Valley."

"That won't stop me."

My fear crumbled into sorrow. "If I always find you, then I also always lose you. But that doesn't make me regret meeting you."

"Then don't make me wait another lifetime to have you. Not when the wait since our last life has already been so long. Give me one night. At least one night."

The cruelty that I'd lost him before—no, that Dr. Henderson had stolen us from each other—ignited the fire within me. We had to get to my people to free them and figure out how to keep her out of this world so that we had the chance to live in peace.

That night, Nash used the excuse of foraging to leave camp, and twenty minutes later, I left for the river, hoping it wasn't too obvious to Piercey.

I didn't know exactly what Nash meant when he asked for a night with me, but I was certain I needed to bathe. That much was no mystery.

The river washed away days of dirt and sweat. Cold water prickled my arms and flowed over me in a soft current. I changed into fresh clothes we'd brought from the Sacred School. It wasn't what I would choose for a night with Nash, but it beat the nasty clothes I'd left in a pile on the rocks by the river.

A few minutes after I'd finished, I heard footsteps and I straightened my wet hair over my shoulders. I'd told him to find me at the river. Good thing I'd gotten ready in time.

Nash had washed up, too. He looked handsome in the dim light of the setting sun with his curls full.

"Hi," I said.

He stepped closer. "Hi."

We'd been through so much together but suddenly it felt like my first time meeting him. I'd taken down all the barriers I'd always held between us. There was nothing left to protect my heart from him, nor his from mine. What would I do now? Kiss him? Talk to him? Throw off the clothes I'd just changed into? I had no idea what I'd actually agreed to.

Nash erased the worry from my mind when he reached a hand out for me and nodded at the riverbank. "Walk with me?"

I swallowed down everything I felt and took his hand. His arm came around my shoulders as we sauntered along the water's edge. The sun nestled into a bed of pink, cut short by the Mountain of the Gods in the distance.

"After the eclipse, I want a proper day with you." Nash looked down at me.

"What does a proper day look like?"

He chuckled. "Whatever we want. We can even fight if you'd like. I've never taken a woman training before, but I wouldn't mind an afternoon sparring with you."

I looked down as I smiled.

"Maybe we could go on the river. Or find a village that's having a festival."

Warmth filled my stomach. "I would love that. Any of it."

"Tell me things, not about the gods or power. Things about you."

"It feels like that's all there is to tell about me."

"There's much more."

His nearness and attention had me so flustered, I couldn't think of anything clever or endearing to say. I told him about the normal days in my village that I wanted back, how Leif had seen the potential in me and trained me, that I'd spent years never sleeping alone, and I couldn't wait to make it back home. And he told me about long summer days with Elsie, how she never stopped running when she was a toddler unless she slammed into something and fell over, and that he'd hated every moment he served the Prophet.

"I want to live away from the villages and fighting and politics." Nash laced his fingers with mine as we walked. "It needs to be at least half a day's ride away from any town."

"Half a day? That's pretty far out there."

"I would only have to see the people who I really want to see and who want to see me badly enough to make the trip. That would be just fine with me."

"I haven't thought about where I'd like to end up, but I do like being with my people." I wouldn't mention the eclipse. Not when we were having such a nice walk. "What you said doesn't sound too bad, though. I can see wanting that once you get used to it."

He nudged me as we walked, smirking. "Would you visit me, Sharpshooter?"

"Don't know." I tried not to smile, to give myself away, but it was impossible with my hand in his. "Depends on how tonight goes."

Nash tsked. "Such a bad liar."

I bit my lip, turning my face away. "What about me? Would you visit me?"

"Maybe I wouldn't have to. Maybe you wouldn't be that far away."

My heart fluttered.

"I'm not supposed to say that, am I?" But he didn't look embarrassed or guilty, and certainly not as if he regretted it. His voice was comfortable, words unrushed. "I'm supposed to pretend I need more time before knowing what I want."

His confidence and openness took my breath away. Doubt tried to choke out what he'd said, what he'd meant, but at the first flutters of insecurity, Nash was already dipping my way, his lips already against mine.

All this time, I'd been so afraid that he knew the power he had over me, because that power made me feel like I was at a disadvantage. Most of all, because Nash was too good for me. Too good for Eclipse, the girl called demon, who'd slaughtered an entire village.

Tonight, though, my heart finally felt it. Nash didn't see what I feared he would when he looked at me. He saw something I couldn't. He saw who I'd be if I hadn't spent my life hiding from Eclipse. Maybe that was who I really was.

"Why . . . Why are you so good to me?" I asked.

"It's obvious, Max." Another tender kiss. "Why can't you see it?"

I wanted to say something but there was nothing I could say. We both knew why. It wasn't a question that demanded an answer, but a change in the way I'd lived my life.

So instead, I squeezed his hand tightly as I stepped forward with him. "I think I want somewhere quiet, too. Somewhere I don't have to hide, because there's no one to find me."

Nash smiled, eyes lingering on mine.

We talked well into the night after we circled back to the riverbank and skipped rocks against its dark, glistening water. Nash was talking about his swords and I was trying to listen. I really was interested. Only his shirt hugged his shoulders with every rock he threw, and every word he spoke drew my gaze to his lips.

His voice slowed as he looked at me. He laughed softly. "Are you listening?"

"I'm a little distracted." I couldn't lie to him. Didn't need to anymore.

I took a step closer and his look changed, the seriousness in his eyes again even though he wore that sly grin. "Something on your mind?"

"There is."

"But I have much more to tell you about my sword-sharpening technique."

The soft light of the midnight sun hugged his jawline. I slowly smoothed my hands up to his neck and then his face. "Tell me. I can do two things at once." I kissed right beneath his jaw.

His hands found my sides. "Actually, I've never cared so little about my swords as I do now."

I pulled his face down to mine and I kissed him the way I'd been dying to. Not the struggling kiss after his treatment, or the weary one after hiking up the mountain. I rose up as tall as I could on my toes, plastered myself against him, and kissed him deeply with absolutely nothing holding me back, not even my own fear.

Nash pressed against me so I started to fall back, but he had me. Held me with my toes scraping the ground.

We stumbled back away from the bank to the softness of the grass and the weeds and the wilted leaves that carpeted the earth. We sank down to our knees, our sides, down into a world of our own.

I remembered the night Nash had given that grin of his and told me he felt like he'd met me in a dream I couldn't remember. All of this felt like that. I lived not only in this moment but in those moments long past and forgotten. We'd done this before, many times, and I could only hope we would do it again.

Still, I struggled to accept it. It didn't feel possible that I could have him, that something so good, someone so good, would see this much of me, the demon in me, and still want me. Maybe want me even more.

I could no longer hold myself back from him. He'd rendered me help-less. For the first time, I didn't mind that feeling.

Shadows hid our clothes strewn about the forest floor, but our skin soaked up the midnight sun, breaking up the dark, gleaming with the dim of twilight. It became a path for wandering and exploring. For knowing each other in a way time wouldn't allow and words couldn't share.

Though I'd learned the sound of his heartbeat thudding in battle, I hoped to remember it like this. With my cheek against his chest, not need-ing my power to hear the calm pulse of his heart. If I fell to the eclipse and woke in a world I didn't know and lost my hold on Nash, maybe the steadiness of his heart would beat in my dreams. Would drum with my own. Would tell me there was a man I'd always found before and had to find again.

We held one another. When the bright rays of morning light broke through the trees and woke us, we hadn't yet let go.

I hoped, beyond hope that beneath the eclipse we wouldn't let go either. The worst battles were ahead. Dr. Henderson would not go down so easily and neither would the Prophet.

CHAPTER TWENTY-FIVE

In the morning, we had ridden without stopping to the Prophet's village, where finally I would be able to free my innocents. I'd hoped to return here with my power, and even allies to help in the battle. Never had I imagined how much would have changed, though. In many ways, I was a different person. At least, I hoped I was. My track record on saving my world apparently was pretty lousy.

At least Dr. Henderson didn't have control of our world right now.

Straight lines of warriors stood ready for battle around the domineering walls of the Prophet's village. The perimeter was entirely surrounded by his army and by archers poised atop the wall. Though I didn't see his disciples, I was sure they were waiting for us.

We flattened ourselves on a nearby hill, watching.

The Prophet's stare loomed in my mind. I'd grown up with his inky eyes drilling into my own on the day of my death. I couldn't shake them now. Fear that had grown within me every day since I'd first slipped to my death choked me now. It was like a vine that had wrapped around every blood vessel and organ in my body.

"We can do this . . ." I whispered it to myself. Even with my medicine and Piercey's treatment, my anxiety was difficult to control. A voice inside told me that it was because it wasn't something that anyone could fix. It wasn't a problem with my mind. I should be afraid. That was the issue with my condition. It was hard to tell when it was my voice and when it was anxiety hijacking my mind. I still hadn't learned to listen to myself fully. Perhaps that was the worst way I'd always held myself back.

I ground my teeth down. When I went into battle, I destroyed all thoughts and lived in the moment, ready to deal with whatever came my way. Today was a day of battle. I had to shut myself up and focus on the only thing that mattered. Destroying everyone who stood in the way of me and my people. My family.

The rest of the mess I'd made trying to save them, that was for a different day.

But no matter how many times I told myself that, the unease hung inside me. My body knew what my mind had pushed away.

None of us were safe.

None.

That wasn't all, though. I still wanted to fight. That was who I was. Someone who knew the worst that could happen, feared the worst, and still chose the battle. Nash and Piercey were right to believe in me. They were right and I'd been wrong.

No more.

"It's time." I squeezed Piercey's wrist. "Tell your graduates."

My people were waiting and ready to attack, hiding in the woods west of the village. The Prophet must have had scouts watching the area, because they had fortified the west side of the village perimeter with twice the warriors as any other direction. I eyed the enemy fighters posted all along the wall.

Piercey closed his eyes. "It's done. I told them to tell your people to strike."

I wanted so badly to listen for Wren and Leif's hearts, but I couldn't alert the disciples to us. I had to control myself. I was just so desperate to connect with them in any way I could.

Nash must have felt my anxiety, because he slipped his hand over my back and whispered in my ear. "Your people will be free soon."

It shouldn't have been possible for any of the fear to ease from my tense muscles, but looking into his eyes did just that. Even here, even now, I longed to draw him to myself again. His heart already felt like a part of mine.

I had to protect Nash today.

A roar erupted from the woods where my people had waited. Though I'd expected it, it still shook me, reverberating in my bones. Their battle cry swelled like one booming voice that drowned out everything else in the Valley: the birds chirping, the Prophet's warriors readying their weapons, my own thoughts crying out in my mind.

The cry built in my own chest. My body flooded with energy so I could race down to my people and charge with them. But I remained hidden on the hill.

The first of our warriors broke into the field with the rest pouring out behind them. Though we were a small force compared to the Prophet's army, the worry tightening the faces of the Prophet's warriors made it seem as if they were the ones outnumbered.

I looked at Nash. How many of them were like him? Forced to fight for the Prophet when they really wanted to join my people in storming his village. Fervor shone from his eyes and tightened the muscles in his forearms. I could feel his desperation as viscerally as my own. The Prophet had used his power to carve his name into Nash's back repeatedly and forced him into service. What else had he done to others in the Valley? The man may have had more enemies than I realized.

We were ready to fight. It was time.

I searched for Leif and Wren and found them at the front of the charge, blades raised overhead. Please, they had to stay safe.

The Prophet's warriors sprinted for my people now. Archers on the wall unleashed their first wave of arrows. My people drove forward, even as arrows arced in the sky over them.

"Val." Piercey's face had gone ashen. I could practically feel his longing to return to the peace of the mountain.

She planted her hands on the ground and strained as a pulse of energy erupted from her, knocking into me like a physical force. The arrows exploded into a shimmering mist of wood and iron, each piece so pulverized that it fell like dark snow over my people. Our warriors charged unfazed while the Prophet's force all looked up to the sky.

We'd tipped our hand. The Prophet would send his disciples soon.

"You ready?" Piercey whispered.

My body buzzed. "I can hardly contain myself."

Nash grinned, but Piercey's brows tightened with worry.

A crack like thunder erupted from the field. Our warriors tore into the Prophet's line with no hesitation. Swords clashed against one another. I dug my fingers into the earth and focused on Leif and Wren now that Val had used her power.

A flash of energy tore my mind from them. Someone was coming. I felt their power like a gust of wind.

A haze of blue sparked at the front lines where the two armies clashed. Then it shot out in a beam that slammed warriors aside. A single woman was left standing in a small circle with a straight path out of the crowd. My people flowed around her like a rushing river, except for those who had been knocked over by her power.

She walked forward slowly.

My lungs tightened, burning in my chest. "An ambush." The words scarcely escaped my lips before I jumped into a crouch with my bow drawn. She was only a distraction from the real threat. I had to find the other disciples. I listened for heartbeats and unleashed my first arrow, focused on it as it curved for the heart I'd heard in the woods.

The arrow snapped.

Whoever was hiding had destroyed it.

The disciple walking toward us in the haze of blue had wanted our attention on her. Wanted us to see her. More were coming. It wasn't just whoever hid close by.

The other disciples must have been close.

"Val, focus on the warriors." I turned in a tight circle, scanning the perimeter. "Piercey, guard Nash."

"You hear them?" Piercey whispered.

I nodded. He should have been able to as well, so the fact that he couldn't told me his nerves had gotten the best of him. Piercey truly wasn't a warrior. His panic would make him sloppy. Not good.

I breathed out slowly.

We were surrounded. We just couldn't see them. I counted eight heartbeats, not including the disciple on the field who had stopped at the edge of the army, staring. No, waiting. Waiting for her time to strike. Studying us as we planned to study them.

"Draw them in!" I nocked an arrow, trusting Piercey to overcome his fear. He didn't move. Didn't even blink. His eyes subtly narrowed and the air around us warmed.

Cries ripped through the air. Three disciples came flying toward us from the woods, all forced over by Piercey.

They stopped midair and dropped suddenly. Piercey's nostrils twitched. Someone must have severed the tether of his power.

No matter. They were close enough to each other now. I unleashed three arrows, one that sliced through flesh and bone and cut the beating heart to silence. Another thudded against what felt like a wall. The third one snapped midair.

One of my arrows stuck out from a man's back. He must have stopped it at the last second from tearing through his heart. I could try to push it through, but I wouldn't waste my power on a battle of wills with an arrow that may splinter rather than kill him.

I darted down the hill into tall grass and raced for the disciples with Nash on my heels. All across the field behind us, the sound of snapping rang out like a song, one plucking chord after the next. I glanced back to see the Prophet's warriors gawking. Val had cut their bowstrings, drawing a grin from me.

It took all I had to keep my back to my people as they warred with the Prophet's forces behind us. I could hear their battle cries, their blades clashing, the shrieks of the injured.

Val had them. I had to trust her, because Piercey did, and that meant I should, too.

I turned my full attention to the disciples.

They raced for us, all seven of them still left alive, some emerging for the first time from the woods. The fear pumped energy into my muscles so I ran faster than I thought possible. Before we reached them, the two on the far end stumbled to a stop and strained to merely walk forward, their veins bulging against their muscles. Piercey was flexing his power and I couldn't help but be impressed. I'd been wrong to think his fear would hold him back just because he'd had a weak moment.

One of the women shot to me with an impossible speed and stabbed her knife for my gut. I parried with a gust of power driving my blade, nearly managing to wrench hers free of her grasp. Nash ran right past us. It took all of the discipline I had not to follow him and to trust that Piercey would protect him.

My senses honed in on the disciple closest to me.

I knocked my attacker back a step with a two-handed swipe. Followed it with a boot to her gut. Sliced through the tender flesh of her forearm.

The ground trembled beneath the strain of our power until it was quaking. The grass ripped open into a brown tear, like a massive smile. Nash leapt over the opening chasm and landed on the other side with the rest of the disciples.

Damn it, Piercey had better guard him well.

Instinctively, I balanced myself as I charged forward, but it took such little effort; I realized someone else was stabilizing me. Val or Piercey behind me. They must have been doing the same for Nash because he swept both of his blades in opposite directions with no issues, fending off two disciples who rushed for him.

I needed to make it to him and stop wasting time on this one.

Fury flooded me with heat as I feigned a lunge and kicked the inside of her knee instead. Before she could recover, I thrust my blade forward and caught her side, tearing through flesh and grating against ribs. Nails reached for me like claws. I slammed them with the force of my power.

Snap.

The nails ripped free in a spray of blood. A scream tore from her lips.

I shoved her back toward the growing crack in the ground with my power and she tumbled to the bottom. Clumps of dirt and rocks that had shaken loose fell over her as the ground swallowed her whole. The bloodied stump of her jagged nails reached up through the dirt. And then she was gone.

My heart panged as I leapt over the grave that had swallowed the disciple whole. I didn't even know her name. Fighting this way didn't feel the same as battle. Our power was unfair.

This was a war without honor.

But I couldn't spare a single moment mourning a woman who had given her life and power to the Prophet when my people were counting on me.

Ahead of me, Nash alone appeared to fight on stable ground, though the earth beneath him shook as well. Piercey and Val continued to stabilize us both as I ran and jumped to the other side of the gaping ground. Nash's blades didn't stop dancing for an instant. He held off two disciples as he slashed one blade toward one and blocked a hit with the other.

The disciples fighting him struggled for breath. That was when I caught the indentation wringing their necks. One of our people was trying to strangle them. And as they fended off the power, Nash launched a full-on attack. It really was working.

I swung my sword for the hip of one. The man caught it with his own blade, but Nash's twin swords snapped like a cobra and skewered him through the gut. Blood poured out of his slack mouth. The other disciple swung for Nash, but her sword caught midair and her body trembled as she tried to bring it down on him. I advanced for her when a powerful force wrapped around my arms and jerked me back a step.

The other disciples had learned from our example. We needed to regroup and launch the next stage of our attack. Growling, I broke free of the force, the pressure squeezing me right down to my bones. I shoved

Nash hard through the air toward the hill where we'd hid. Piercey would have to do the rest.

I threw my head back and screamed as I focused on throwing the disciples back. They all toppled, except for one, who dug her heels into the ground and snarled, managing to only slide a few inches.

Without hesitating, I rushed to retreat, eyes on Nash as an unseen hand pulled him through the air. He disappeared on the hill and within seconds I was there with him, helped along by Piercey.

The disciples rose off the ground from where I had flattened most of them and regrouped as we did the same on the hill.

"We took out three," I said. "Not bad for our first attack."

Nash wiped his forehead with the back of his arm. "I've never fought anyone like them."

"They're retreating, too, all except one." Piercey sat on his knees, not bothering to hide.

In the field, the woman who'd walked through the blue haze stood over the body of a fallen comrade, facing us. The others ran for the rest of the Prophet's warriors.

"She must be in charge," I said. "I couldn't knock her back."

"She's powerful," Piercey said. "I have a good feel for them now. Let me do the next part."

I nodded and twisted, looking for my people. I couldn't see Leif and Wren, but if I focused hard enough, I could hear the pounding of their hearts. The Prophet's forces had swallowed ours whole, so our warriors were surrounded from all sides. Sweat dripped down Val's face. She couldn't defend them all, but I knew she was shielding everyone she could.

Piercey climbed down the hill and walked out in the field, as if he wasn't in any hurry. "Surrender now, so I don't have to hurt you."

The lead disciple snarled. She reached her hand up and roared. Piercey swiped his own, deflecting a gust of wind that shot from her palm.

"Last chance." His hands tightened into fists at his sides. "Please. I don't want to do this."

He didn't. The weight of what I'd asked him to do by coming to fight the Prophet sounded as though it would break his voice.

"Die!" the lead disciple shouted.

Piercey lowered his head. The grass around him rustled. The wind shifted. Without warning, a gust shot across the field, nearly slamming me back onto my ass. Nash settled a hand on the ground, eyes wide.

The Prophet's disciples shrieked, every one of them except for the lead disciple. I whipped around to see that one by one, they collapsed onto the ground, halfway retreated to the warriors. Their bodies writhed. My gasp lodged in my throat and felt like it would burst. Blood beaded all over their skin. He was drawing it out through their pores.

The lead disciple finally collapsed to one knee. Her head lifted. Blood streamed from her eyes.

Beside me, Nash shook his head. "This death is too slow."

"He's putting immense pressure on their bodies." My stomach revolted against such cruelty. "The disciples are fighting him off. I'm sure a normal person would have died instantly." No wonder Piercey hadn't wanted to do this first. It wasn't just because he wanted to gauge their strength and plan accordingly. He didn't want to issue such a cruel death.

"Put them out of their misery," Nash said.

"I think he's trying."

"Then what are we doing?" He pushed to his feet and ducked down low as he ran down the hill.

"Nash!" I raced after him. "Let me go by myself."

Nash didn't even humor me with a glance.

Piercey stood unmoving in the field. As we ran past him, my oldest friend lifted his hand for me, eyes wide. Sweat doused his skin and clothes. Blood dripped from both of his nostrils from the effort. He needed our help. As powerful as he was, everyone with power was incredibly challenging to take on.

I focused on the disciple who knelt in the grass before us. Her body trembled and her mouth hung open as she whimpered. A thin glaze of blood covered her entire body. When she saw us, fear filled her eyes.

Nash already had his weapons poised to strike. We were warriors. It went against everything we believed to leave another fighter suffering like this. We gifted our enemies with swift deaths. And Nash was ready to oblige.

He could take care of her. I had to protect him. I focused on Nash, imagining an impenetrable circle of steel surrounding him, one only I could see, one that flashed only when he needed to be protected.

"You fought well," Nash said. His twin swords sliced through the air for her neck. But they slammed against air and bounced back.

The disciple gasped in relief, the tension melting from her body. Her eyelids fluttered and then she passed out.

There was only one person powerful enough to stop Piercey's attack like that.

"Nash," I whispered. "He's here."

Piercey swept past me and stopped directly in front of me.

The disciples all struggled to their knees and bowed. Turning, I saw the Prophet's warriors lower in a wave, even in the midst of battle. All around the battlefield, swords skewered warriors who made no attempt to defend themselves as they bowed down.

My people stumbled back from their enemies, ceasing their attacks as the Prophet's warriors made themselves defenseless.

Panic lurched in my gut. Nash moved close to me, hand coming to my back. I thought of the scars weaving down his spine. How many hours had he bled because of the Prophet? I wasn't the only one who understood his ferocity.

The black hood of the Prophet bobbed above his subjects as he walked through the crowd of warriors toward us. If he was willing to come out of his village to face us, why had he let three of his disciples die first?

My lips curled into a grimace. Of course. He needed his people to be afraid, so he would look that much mightier when he killed us. The Prophet let his disciples fight, knowing they may not be strong enough. The death of comrades spurred on any good warrior. The disciples would train more ferociously than ever.

This might be a loss for the Prophet's people, but it was a win for him.

As he drew closer, I could see his inky black eyes staring out from the shadow of his cloak. Only then did I notice the rope in his hand and the effortless way he dragged a bobbing form from it.

Tight fingers of panic strangled my heart. It was a man.

I didn't recognize him, but Piercey's composure wilted and I knew. This was one of his graduates.

"Jackson . . ." Piercey gasped.

The body was mangled, certainly just a corpse. Arms hung from the rope like loose sacks of skin, as if his bones had disintegrated. With every movement, his legs bounced at unnatural angles.

No one could survive this. The Prophet must have been delivering a dead body to us.

Only when the Prophet stopped and slung the body into the open space between us, did I see Jackson's wide eyes move to each of us. I pressed my fist against my stomach. He was alive.

Piercey walked toward him and then collapsed at his side, hands shaking as he slowly placed them on his back. The Prophet must have been actively keeping Jackson alive.

The man didn't respond to Piercey. He didn't cry or whine or even twitch. Nothing except wide, pain-filled eyes turning to his director.

"I'm so sorry," Piercey whispered. Then he drew his knife from his side and stabbed it into his graduate's neck.

CHAPTER TWENTY-SIX

Blood poured from the neck of the graduate who Piercey had put out of his misery. How could the Prophet have tortured him so barbarically? What he'd done to Nash had made my stomach churn, especially thinking about how many times the Prophet must have carved his name into his skin for the power to scar despite the healing. But this torment went beyond what I knew was possible.

"You bastard," I said, lunging for the Prophet.

"Max!" Nash clutched me around my waist.

Heat spread over my body in a flash. Nash recoiled, grabbing his hand.

"You didn't have to take it so far." The air around me grew hazy with heat. "You have the Valley. You won! Everyone fears your name. What's the point of toying with people like this?"

Piercey rose on shaky legs. "Don't, Max."

The Prophet wore a cocky grin I was desperate to wipe off his face. "You've seen it, too, haven't you?" He eyed me like a hungry lion would a piece of meat. "You've seen your blood pooling in the cracks of my stage."

It hit me like a punch to the gut.

"Time is given to the Prophets alone. And yet a foolish girl managed to sneak her fingers into the cracks of time and pry it apart." The Prophet moved forward. "I can still taste your sweet blood." A thin tongue snaked out of his mouth and licked his lips. "Tomorrow your soul will return to the gods."

Fear choked out my voice. I'd looked into his eyes so many times—the eyes of death. I couldn't ask what he meant about time. How he knew I would die. I could only see the life I'd never lead flash before me. A life I'd always known I'd lose and yet couldn't stop myself from hoping for, especially now that I'd found Nash.

Piercey lifted his hand to the Prophet. "You will not go near her."

"You have always been such a bright and optimistic boy." The Prophet clasped his hands behind his back. "Perfect qualities for a director. It keeps you blind and easy to control."

"Step back," Piercey said.

"You think your Sacred School makes Prophets?" He snorted. "You churn out loyal subjects. Demons who can control their powers. Who no longer cause chaos. The gods make Prophets."

My nostrils flared. "The gods train you once you leave the school. We should have known."

"Letting someone learn enough to think they have it all figured out is the best way to keep them in the dark." The Prophet glared at each of us. "The gods have no mercy left for you. I know what you did, thief. I won't allow you to steal this world for yourself."

Heat pounded in my temples. "Then you should rejoice in freedom, you coward, not pine for your precious gods to keep you in power."

"You all die here today. All of you except for her." His long finger pointed at me. "Tomorrow, Eclipse, you will finally surrender your power and the people will drink your blood and consume your power."

Piercey belted a roar and pumped his hands out to the Prophet. Blasts of air ripped his cloak back, but the Prophet didn't budge.

He snorted. "If you're so eager to die . . ."

Beside me, Nash gasped in a strangled breath. Piercey grabbed his throat, eyes round. Tears flooded Val's eyes.

He was choking them and even Piercey couldn't stop it. I tried to pry back his control, but it was like trying to move a mountain. The Prophet didn't even break a sweat. He looked into my eyes, smiling.

Beside me Nash fell to his knees, muscles straining as he gripped his neck. Terror shredded my focus.

I ripped my blade from my side and ran for the Prophet, roaring. With my arm wrenched back, I thrust it for his gut.

His power wound around my body and froze me in place. I struggled to break free, reaching within me for more power. It was as if it had been sealed again, only I realized that the Prophet was just that much stronger than me.

No.

I threw everything I had into breaking free of him but only managed to twitch my muscles.

Nash and Piercey had gone too long without air. They couldn't do this much longer.

All the power within me pushed against his in an eruption. My blade slid forward and then it turned slowly until it pressed against my own throat.

How could I lose now?

Piercey curled up on his side. Nash's head fell back. Val's body spasmed.

I screamed as beads of blood popped against the blade on my throat and I strained to break free of his power.

Two forms ran through the field for us. Pain flooded my heart. Leif and Wren had broken away from the war party and were closing in on where we stood. "Stay back!" I didn't need them to die, too.

Wren wrapped her arms around Leif and pulled him back. He skidded to a stop, desperate eyes on me. I shook my head. That was already too close. They stayed there, though I could see Leif struggling to hold himself in place. Anguish flooded Wren's face.

Behind them, the Prophet's warriors remained bowed down, and my people stood sideways with their swords ready, so they could keep their eyes on the warriors and the Prophet.

What a nightmare.

The Prophet didn't even glance at Leif and Wren. He probably planned to save them for later.

"The gods have given me visions of your destruction, Eclipse." Darkness crept over his face in a shadow as his head lowered. "You must be broken before your evil consumes us all."

Nash collapsed onto his stomach, fingers twitching against the grass. Tears poured down my face. Elsie needed him. I needed him.

"I don't care about what you're saying!" I cried out as I tried to strip away his control of my friends. "Let them go!"

The Prophet walked past Piercey's writhing body. Past Nash as his eyes fluttered. He stopped right where he could loom over me. "You truly are Eclipse. You won't stop until you consume our sun. Our gods."

"I will kill you," I said, voice straining.

His silence tore into me. Beneath the wrath in the Prophet's eye, I noticed a flicker of something. Could it be fear? Despite how he'd turned my own blade on me, he was the one who was afraid?

It occurred to me then that though the Prophet had seen my death, though he'd spoken with such confidence when he said he'd always had me, that he was afraid of me. Why? I wanted to ask, but I couldn't waste energy on any questions, not when I was searching for more power within myself.

"Do it," the Prophet roared. "Kill her. I can wait no longer."

Nash's fingers twitched as he reached for me. "N-No . . ." His tight voice was hardly audible.

The lead disciple ripped a dagger from her side. I stared into Nash's eyes, wishing we were connected with a neural link so I could tell him how sorry I was. I tried with all I could to break free of the Prophet, but it was like he had wrapped chains around my body.

As the disciple reared back, I could not even stop the knife from flying for me.

In a flash, she threw it straight for my neck. My senses sharpened, tuning in on it slicing through the air in the moment it took to reach me. The last sound I'd hear before I died.

The tip nicked my skin and then the blade snapped in half. It shot to the ground in two pieces.

I gasped so hard it felt as if it ripped my chest in two. Had I done that? Had I broken the blade? I hadn't felt my power increase or break free to the blade, though.

Suspicion filled the Prophet's eyes. Could it have been Piercey? No. He was barely conscious. What was this?

Something or someone had intervened to save me from death, but I had not felt power from anyone.

Another disciple pulled the bow from his back and shot an arrow at my chest. It snapped in half just like the dagger and dropped to my feet.

I looked down at the broken dagger and arrow.

Shock filled the Prophet's eyes. He grabbed a blade himself and shoved upward toward my gut.

The steel shattered and rained down over my feet as he clutched an empty hilt.

My heart stormed. Why couldn't I die?

I couldn't . . .

I couldn't die because I'd seen my death etched into the stone of fate. The universe itself bent to right the course of time. My entire life I'd feared and hated my visions of the future, but this was the greatest power I'd ever had. All this time and I never knew it.

I couldn't die.

Not until it was my time. The knowledge I'd gained from Piercey flooded my mind and I knew the experiments we'd studied had been right. Once an event had been observed by a conscious being, it couldn't be altered, even if it meant disrupting the laws of physics to change it. The universe would correct its own paradoxes.

Another arrow shot and burst into countless pieces before my face. The disciple nocked another and his bowstring snapped.

Fear darkened the Prophet's face as he lowered his head. "If you won't die, then your friends will!"

All this time I'd held myself back in fear. I didn't even know I had this power. Now my friends were dying on the ground. Piercey and Val had gone limp. Nash's fingers dug into the grass, clinging to life.

What was the use in living without them?

I couldn't fail them.

The field darkened, and in the distance, shadows dappled the Valley like the villagers had the day of the eclipse.

"Stop," I whispered, unable to draw breath as the Prophet strangled it from Nash and Piercey's lungs. Little Elsie had cried in her father's arms when we'd left her house. She couldn't grow up without him.

My father spoke in my ear. Loud and audible. "Do you feel it, Max?"

Nash's fingers went still.

I saw his eyes on mine in the twilight the night before when the heat of his body alone kept me warm.

I gave myself over to the slip, to the eclipse, to all that I'd hidden from. I stood in two places at once, in two bodies at once.

Her hands came along mine, the little hands of the girl I'd once been, on fire with power I had never felt before and hadn't felt since.

Daggers of heat cut through my skin, my bones, my soul. Cut me open so everything I'd buried inside poured out.

Black snapped over the sun and a ring of light pierced the moon's edges.

"Do you feel it, Max!" Dad's voice boomed in my ear.

Heat rippled down my spine. I felt it.

My voice came out guttural and low. "The gods aren't here to protect you any longer, Prophet."

I opened myself to the light inside.

The Prophet's body jerked straight and rigid like he'd been struck by lightning.

Every ounce of power that had sucked away the lives of my entire village exploded from me. This time it all poured into the Prophet.

In fear and in shame, I had locked myself away so deeply inside that I couldn't reach it or feel it. The moment in the past when I'd killed the villagers collided with the present in an explosion of power.

The Prophet choked, his body quaking. His skin flushed a red so deep it bordered on purple. A scream tore from the depths of me. It felt like the power ripped me open. But I let it all out, every last drop I could muster.

On the ground, Nash struggled onto his arms. The relief of seeing him alive only fueled me.

"Die!" I shrieked and gave myself to the endless energy inside.

The Prophet fought me, but I could feel his will bending and wilting and collapsing in on itself.

"Max . . ." Piercey reached across the ground for me. He shook his head. "Don't."

Even after all he'd seen today, all he'd seen when we connected, Piercey still didn't want me to kill the Prophet. His voice croaked as he begged me again to stop. Then, I felt his urging to let him in. To listen to him with the neural link.

I didn't. I shut him out. It didn't matter if this was right or wrong. It didn't matter if there was a better way to free the Valley or if in the long run this would only bring more chaos. There was only one way to make sure the Prophet never hurt my people ever again, and that was to kill him.

I gave myself over to the power that turned me into Eclipse, the Soul Eater, and accepted pure destruction—blind and all-consuming rage.

The Prophet coughed blood into the air. My nostrils twitched as I poured my power into his body.

"Okay." He clawed at his chest. "Okay! I'll spare them. All of them!"

The power rushed out of me.

"Release them." The Prophet doubled over and spewed another mouthful of blood. "What are you waiting for? Release the prisoners."

I struggled to finish him off and contain his power. He was losing the fight, but I wasn't sure I was that close to finishing him off.

The lead disciple sprinted down the hill toward the warriors who had finally risen from their bow. "Release the prisoners! Release them now!"

"Stop." Piercey coughed and pounded his hand against the ground. "Stop it now, Max! He's surrendering. This isn't the right way to deal with him."

This was the man who'd starved villagers until they succumbed to his power. Used the roads meant for trade and safe passage to send out bands of warriors to pillage and leave us all destitute. Who warred against us until every last village fell. This man carved his name into Nash's spine and left him permanently scarred.

He'd killed me over and over again when I slipped to the eclipse.

"He must die." My voice boomed with my power.

Piercey couldn't understand. He'd spent too long on top of that mountain, grown too powerful. There was no order, no justice in this Valley. Only power.

The gates of the village groaned loud enough for me to hear. My heart caught. Children sprinted out. Men and women followed behind them, helping our elderly. Our warriors raced to our innocents, and where once they clashed with the enemy in sprays of blood, they now wrapped their arms around family, clinging to one another in the red-stained grass.

Leif sprinted for the crowd, stumbled, and fell to the ground. He shoved himself back to his feet and ran with wavering legs for his family. Wren chased after him. Arn emerged from the crowd, carrying Rune as he sprinted for his husband. Safe. Finally, truly, safe.

A sob slipped from my chest.

Nash looked at me and stole my attention for a moment. I knew then that if he asked me to stop, I would. We'd planned this together. Were in this together. I wanted to kill the Prophet. I couldn't trust him, especially with his ego now wounded. But if Nash, of all people, thought I should spare him, I wouldn't have the heart to continue.

His resolute eyes stared into mine. "He'll come for your people. He'll come for Rune and Elsie." Nash nodded. "Do it."

The last barrier of my power, that I didn't even know I'd held on to, fell away. The Prophet slid back on his heels in a gale of my force and then slammed onto his back. I focused on containing his power that burst free as he finally started to die.

Veins bulged in Piercey's neck. "This makes you no better than him. Just one powerful person deciding the fate of everyone else."

I didn't need to be better. I needed my people to live. If that meant I had to be a demon, so be it. So fucking be it.

A voice barely reached me through the chaos of my power. A tone I would now recognize in any voice.

"Max."

My eyes shot to the right and my heart seized in my body.

Flare glared at me. And in her arms, she held a small child bundled in a blanket.

CHAPTER TWENTY-SEVEN

Little curls fluttered in the breeze, catching on the blanket.

The door within me slammed closed on my power. The Prophet stumbled up and stared with fear tightening his face. He shook as he wiped the blood from his mouth.

All I could see was the child in Flare's arms.

"Elsie." I gasped. "Give her to me." I reached forward, pleading. They were supposed to be safe at the cabin. Flare must have found them.

Nash's eyes fixed on his daughter, fingers digging into the earth. Dangerous, wild rage flashed in his eyes. His muscles strained and veins popped. He climbed to his knees and then to his feet and stomped one wavering step after another.

"Flare!" His hoarse voice roared through the air.

Fear widened Flare's eyes even though Nash would be no match for her, especially in his state. His rage was convincing, though, like he might muster as much power as I had, even though he couldn't.

Flare held Elsie tighter and backed up. "Stay there." Her eyes snapped to me. "You had better stop him."

I ran to Nash and pushed back against his chest. "Wait!" I grunted as he pressed against me, intent on Flare. "Nash!"

He stopped but a growl ripped from his chest, buzzing against my hands. "Do not touch my child!"

"I'll get her," I said. "I promise."

His body shook with a rage that emanated from him like my own power. "Why isn't Elsie moving?"

"I sedated her," Flare said. "She's fine."

"It's dangerous to sedate a child," I yelled.

"Undo what you did," Flare said. "You can have Elsie back then."

The grass rustled behind us. Val had managed to get her knees beneath her and Piercey wobbled on unsteady legs.

"I'll kill you," Nash said, his voice eerily calm now. "I'll find you in the next life and kill you there, too. You're dead."

Flare turned her nose up. "You primitive animals have no understanding of what the real world is or what we have made it into." Flare narrowed her eyes. "And no one out there in my world understands what this world means to you. They haven't seen it like I have. I'm trying to save you."

"You're delusional." I twisted for her. "You've kidnapped a little girl. Look at yourself."

"It's only a matter of time before someone from my world realizes what you've done and fixes it. I made it back into my avatar before you shut us out of the system. But if anyone realizes what has happened, they will end your world in an instant."

Time moved so much quicker in my world than theirs. Since Dr. Henderson was still in our world, she wouldn't be able to alert anyone. We may have had more time than Flare wanted to admit. But why didn't she just go back to her world and deal with us herself? Could she even get out now that she'd lost control? Maybe she was trapped here just like we were.

"Are you listening, Max? You foolish, foolish girl." I could hear Dr. Henderson's tone buried beneath the mask of Flare's voice. "It wouldn't be worth it for them to try to regain control of this world. It could corrupt the data. They already considered scrapping the project. You'll lose every-one you love. Good luck reconnecting with them after you wake up with no memory of this life."

I didn't want her to be right, but I couldn't deny what she'd said. Had anything I'd done actually helped my people? I looked down to the blood soaking into the grass where slain warriors from both sides gave up their lives. Beside me, Nash still breathed heavily from being strangled.

In my first two lives, I'd destroyed everything. I was doing the same thing again.

"I can't give up." I said it to myself more than I did to Flare. "You're hurting the people I love. How can I ever give up?"

"Your fight is pointless. What did you think would happen?" Flare asked. "Do you think we're powerless? We made this world. Either you give me back control or you destroy it all."

"Maybe it isn't so simple to turn us off when you no longer have access to our simulation." I stared at Elsie. "Maybe that is why you'd be so desperate as to steal a child."

"Nash said I feared you. Well, he's right. I do fear you. We all should fear you, because you're out of control. It doesn't matter that you know you can't win a fight. You'll raze everything to the ground trying to win. Piercey tried to speak reason to you but you're unreasonable."

I couldn't deny what she said, but I wouldn't let it break me like it had in the all-white room. "All I want is for us to have what every other world has. We don't deserve to be experimented on."

Flare clutched Elsie tighter. She didn't want me speaking of that which she'd forbidden. "Prophet."

He looked at her with his face pale.

"This demon's blood will quench the god's thirst. There's no need to take the rest." Flare patted Elsie's back softly. "You freed them, so let them stay free. All of them. Take only Max."

The Prophet's inky eyes turned to my own.

"If she resists, I'll take the child home to the gods." Flare's voice showed no hint of emotion. "Stop anyone who tries to follow me. I'll return the child once the demon is dead."

If I tried to take Elsie from Flare, it could hurt the girl. Did I feel confident that I could save her without risking her life? Besides, I literally hadn't been able to die because I was going to die during the eclipse. If that wasn't confirmation that it was unavoidable, then I didn't know what was.

Really, I'd accomplished my mission. I'd freed my people. Now, I could die in peace, like I always knew I would.

All feeling drained from me. This was it. What my life had led to. I almost felt relieved to get it over with.

"No," Nash whispered.

Flare whistled and a horse galloped from the Prophet's campground. She placed Elsie's little body on the horse, climbed up, and held the girl once more.

"Oh, and don't be foolish, dear girl. I'm linked with the Prophet. We can communicate. If you harm him or try to escape, I'll be forced to hurt her to save this world from you." Flare held my eyes a moment longer and then turned away. There was nothing I could do to stop her. I couldn't fight, not with Elsie in danger.

Flare faded from my mind. The Prophet and Piercey and Val faded. All the people and the disciples watching us were gone. It was only Nash and me.

"Nash," I said.

He shook his head, refusing to look at me.

"Nash." My hands slid up his arms softly. "Elsie needs you to be smart about this."

His jaw muscles bunched. His nostrils flared.

"I can't fight what's already happened. It's already happened to me so many times. I always die in the eclipse. Look at me. Say goodbye to me."

Nash's amber eyes locked onto mine and there was no gentleness there. No softness to be found. He had a warrior's eyes. "How dare you give up so easily?"

My voice got stuck in my throat.

"Fight for yourself like you fight for your people and your world. Max." He clutched my shoulders and shook me. "Fight!"

"She has your daughter."

"So find a way to save you both."

"I can't fight this, Nash. Neither can you. It's time to say goodbye."

I rose on my toes and pressed my lips to his, but he took my face in his hands and pulled me back.

"I'm not giving up," he said.

"I've ruined everything, Nash. Can't you see that? I don't know what I'm doing. I've been hot-headed, blinded by rage, too afraid to admit what deep down I've always known. I'm powerless."

"You're not. You could kill the Prophet right now."

"I don't want the power to kill." Hot tears rushed from my eyes. "What kind of power is that? I bring darkness to our world when I want to bring light."

Pain twisted Nash's face. "If you think your power is only good for killing, then find out what you can really do. You're not Eclipse." He pressed his forehead against mine and whispered so only I could hear. "Find your true name."

Piercey walked up to where I could see him in the corner of my eye. "Give us a second to think, okay? You're not dying."

"Flare could kill Elsie at any time." I wiped my face and stepped away from Nash.

"Then she would lose her leverage," Piercey said.

I stared at Nash. "She still has plenty of leverage over me. Who can defy the gods?" I smiled sadly. "Apparently not me." I looked at the Prophet. "Give me time to say my piece. I won't resist, as long as you free my people and don't hurt anyone else."

"Max!" Wren rushed for me with Leif a few steps behind her. What was he doing leaving his family's side when he just got them back?

There was no stopping them this time. I could tell by the look on Leif's face. They both came to my side.

"What's happening?" Wren gripped my hand.

I couldn't bring myself to speak the words.

Then, Nash pushed past me, chasing after Flare's retreating form. "Do the gods know you've lost yourself to your power?" His voice raised. "Turn and face me. Do they know?"

Flare stopped, but she didn't come closer. "I'm sorry it came to this, Nash. I really was always fond of you."

"Nash." My voice croaked. "Stop. This is dangerous."

"You said you're trying to save young worlds," Nash said. "Your people are supposed to be better. So what happened to you?"

She was quiet for a moment. "I've lived with perfect for so long now. There's something real in your world. Something in your humanity that shines only in tragedy and war. Something my people lost long ago when we evolved beyond death and strife." Her voice quieted. "Perfect can't stay perfect in a broken world. I think I've found who I was meant to be, if not for all the perfect I've lived in."

She gripped the reins and took off in a gallop.

Nash's jaw muscles flexed. "If her people are so perfect, they must have a place for broken monsters like her. They need to know that's where she belongs."

"We have no way of telling them. Please, don't get yourself killed for no reason."

Nash clutched the back of my head in his strong grasp and looked down into my eyes. "You're more than enough reason, Max." He kissed me hard and desperate. "I won't let you go. And I won't let that woman ruin our world and her own. She's a threat to everything she touches. Don't surrender. We need to figure out how we'll save Elsie, not waste time on sacrificing you."

"She told us how to save her. The fight is over."

What did he think we could do? Flare was already disappearing with little Elsie. I listened to their heartbeats until they grew too faint to hear.

Nash ripped away from me and strode for the Prophet. "Flare will use you to kill Max because she's afraid of her. Something about Max threatens her, not just in this world, but the next one. You must know this is true after what you've seen."

The Prophet said nothing.

"You've seen something, too. You want to kill Max, too, because you're afraid as well." Nash met him head-on. "But what you're too arrogant to see is that Flare has played you for a fool all this time. Once Max is dead, she'll kill you. She'll give everything you have to the Flatlander's Prophet."

"You're lying," the Prophet said.

"I'm a good spy." Nash didn't waver. "Flare told me she would choose one of you. You're too ruthless to lead a nation. She wants a more reasonable ruler. You're a blade she's using and then will throw away."

I stepped for Nash, but Leif caught me, holding me back. "Let the boy speak," he said.

"How will you keep yourself alive after Max almost killed you in front of your best warriors and demons? You surrendered and freed her people." Nash tilted his head. "Will sacrificing her be enough? Will it be when they all know it is really Flare killing Max? That it is only because of a little girl that Max willingly lowered herself for your blade."

"I could kill you now," the Prophet said.

"Does that make you feel powerful enough to overcome the shame of Max beating you?" Nash stepped closer so he nearly touched the Prophet. "Lay even a finger on Max, and we will make sure you lose everything. All these people who bow to you out of fear will bow to Flare. You'll be nothing."

Shame filled me that I had so easily surrendered my life. I never would have done that for anyone I loved, but I'd been convinced that I would die tomorrow. I'd been convinced of it for so long that I hesitated to live. Killing those villagers as a child and finding out that I'd failed in previous lives had made me feel like my life wasn't worth saving.

Nash was brilliant. And I was a fool. Flare's ploy had been desperate. The Prophet couldn't kill me unless I gave myself over to him. I was so convinced by my slips to the future that I was about to abandon Nash, my people, the entire Valley to this Prophet without any fight. We could walk away now and the Prophet couldn't stop us. The only problem was that he would tell Flare and she could kill Elsie. We had to keep him from telling her.

I couldn't give in. I couldn't abandon the people I loved.

This time, when I walked forward, Leif didn't try to stop me. "You said you've seen things." I slowly drifted closer. The fear that had led the Prophet to try killing me today rather than during the eclipse still burned in his eyes. "You've seen your death, too, haven't you?"

His eyes shot to me.

"Did Flare tell you that you could avoid it by killing me? Because you can't. I couldn't die earlier because the gods have already decided my fate. It's going to happen one day. Yours will, too. So don't let her manipulate you."

"It isn't possible."

"I promise you it is."

"How can you kill me if I've already killed you?"

My heart jolted. "That's what you've seen?"

His eyes narrowed to thin, dark slits. "I won't reveal the secrets of the gods to you. Either I kill you or you kill me. That's the only conclusion that I can draw."

"You've seen me kill you?" He was right. That didn't make sense. If he killed me during the eclipse, how would I kill him? What had he seen? Did we kill each other at the same time?

"Well." I lifted my chin. "Death will have to conquer me because I'm not surrendering to it, and certainly not to you." I didn't cower from his inky eyes. "And you aren't going to send a message to Flare, because if you do, I won't hesitate to slaughter you. You don't seem eager to take the chance that you can't die until it's your time, so we'll see if I can beat fate."

The Prophet's expression was still hard and filled with hate. "You expect me to believe you'll just walk away?"

"I'm assuming if I try to kill you that you'll alert Flare." I watched him. "Besides, my friend here thinks there's a better path to take."

"We will not kill you," Piercey said. "As long as you let us go now and say nothing to Flare. We'll return to the Mountain of the Gods."

"Prophet," I said. "You have our word. We will leave you in peace if you leave us in peace."

Fear looked foreign on the Prophet. He wasn't used to fearing someone, except for the gods, and they had shown him favor. Would he be able to live knowing there was a threat out there? No, even if he could, he wouldn't. He had to crush anyone who stood in his way, even if it ultimately sabotaged himself.

"I don't trust you." The Prophet spoke to me and me alone.

"I don't trust you. Still, it would benefit us both to save our battle for another day. You clearly need to gain strength. Don't humiliate yourself further in front of your people."

I looked out to his warriors who watched from their knees. Panic filled the Prophet's eyes. "Fine. You have your deal, for now."

I wanted nothing more than to kill the Prophet, but I would never risk Elsie's life. This was the only way.

"One more stipulation." The Prophet paused. "You stay on the Mountain of the Gods, demon. If you leave, I'll go after your people." He leveled his look at Nash. "Starting with him and his child. Or these two." He eyed Wren and Leif.

My stomach churned in disgust. "Don't give me a reason to leave the mountain and I won't."

"Then we have a deal."

Nash snarled. "You don't have shit until you tell me where Flare took my daughter."

The Prophet snarled and turned his face away. But Nash grabbed a handful of his cloak and jerked him a step forward. Fearless. "Tell me."

"Home." He turned his face to the side, voice tense. "She'll be waiting for you there. She didn't think there was any chance you'd defy her. Even if she did, Flare can't kill a child. She's bluffing."

Nash released him and took my hand. "Let's go."

Wren nodded. "I'm coming, too."

"It's too dangerous," I said.

Leif settled his hand on the hilt of his sword. "Don't dishonor us by stopping her, Max. I need to stay with my husband and child. Wren will be there for both of us."

"I'll look after her," Piercey said. I really didn't want her to come, but he was right. I couldn't reject their help. It would be like calling them weak. "Fine. I'm sorry."

There was no time to waste, but I couldn't leave without wrapping my arms around Rune and making myself believe that he truly was safe. I turned and looked at him, tears flooding my eyes again. "Rune." What if he was too afraid to come to me after seeing my power?

He let go of Arn's hand and sprinted for me in a mad dash. I fell to my knees and caught him against me, unable to hold in my sobs as I wrapped up his little body in my arms.

"I'm so sorry, Rune. I'm so sorry. You'll never be apart from your papa again." I kissed both of his cheeks and held his face as I looked at him. He'd come to me. He wasn't terrified. "You're safe now."

He wiped the tears from my face. "I knew you'd save us, Auntie. Don't cry. We're together again."

The pain of watching him get ripped away from us filled me, as though it was happening again. "Oh, Rune."

I clasped him to me, hating that soon I would have to let him go.

Chief Kaid walked forward with Beast at her side. They'd seen my true nature. All my people had. But the chief still met my eyes, raised her forearm to me like she would before battle, and spoke firmly. "My flesh."

Tightness gripped my throat. "My blood."

Beast lifted his forearm next. And if any of my people had turned against me, none would ever show it, because they all lifted their forearms as the chief had, every warrior, every man and woman, every child. Even Rune drew back to place his forearm against me.

"My flesh." Beast roared and the people shouted it in an echo after him.

I couldn't speak. So I only mouthed the words.

"My blood."

CHAPTER TWENTY-EIGHT

Our horses galloped up the long dirt path leading to what had been a sweet, peaceful home until Flare disturbed it. I should have realized that she might have stayed in our simulation and that Elsie could have been in danger. We had to find the girl before anything happened.

Nash had not spoken or taken his eyes off the distance since we left, only rode with his body as tense as when he first saw Flare holding his child. Nothing I said could comfort him, so instead of trying, I focused solely on trying to detect either Flare or Elsie.

As we drew closer to Trish's home, I didn't feel Flare or hear her heart beating. But I did hear someone else.

"Elsie's here," I said. "Inside."

Nash kicked his horse's side and sped for the house. He'd not stopped the horse completely when he dismounted and sprinted to the house. I followed closely after him.

"Elsie!" Nash slammed the door against the wall so hard the house shook. I thought for sure the door would break free. "Trish!"

The bedroom door opened. "We're safe," Trish said, moving aside as Nash burst into the room and swept past her.

There on her bed, Elsie slept beneath her blankets, looking unharmed. A man, who must have been Trish's husband, sat at the foot of the bed.

Nash collapsed at her bedside and grabbed her into his arms, cradling her head against him as he sat back against the bed. I pressed my knuckles to my mouth.

"Flare?" Wren asked, breathing hard in the doorway.

Trish shook her head. Her cheeks were stained with tears. "She placed Elsie at the door and disappeared."

"Disappeared how?" I asked.

Trish looked confused but there was no time to explain. "On her horse. She rode off too fast for me to even get a good look at her."

"She's a coward," I said. At least she didn't have the ability to travel instantly any longer. Surely, she would have used it today if she did.

"I'm sorry," Nash whispered, kissing the crown of Elsie's head. "I'm so sorry, baby girl. I'll never let her get to you again."

"Daddy . . ." Elsie's eyes opened slowly.

"Hi, baby," he whispered, a smile crawling onto his face.

"I'm sorry." Trish wiped her eyes. "I didn't stay at the cabin. We came home. It's my fault."

"It isn't your fault," I said quietly. "It's Flare's." Relief washed over me as Elsie nestled her head against her father. My people were safe now and so was Elsie. Still, what could have happened haunted me.

I turned to Piercey. "Take care of them." Fire burned within me. "Start for the Mountain of the Gods."

"Max—" Wren reached for me but I rushed past and continued through the door without stopping.

No matter how fast I rode, I couldn't catch up to Flare. She'd left plenty of clumsy tracks in her trail, but she was a fast rider, and her head start had really put me behind.

This wasn't working. I had to try something else, something I'd always failed at as a child, but might manage now that I had Piercey's knowledge and had unleashed my power. If ever there were a time to do it, now was that time.

I reached forward with my power, stretching myself in a search for her heartbeat.

My eyes slid closed as I rode. The woods rippled.

I heard the muffled beating and felt the distance between myself and Flare as if I could catch it and rip it away.

When I opened my eyes, I gave in to the pull of time and space, and the trees around me snapped shut.

I stood in a field facing Flare. She jerked back on the reins of her mare, so the horse whinnied and snapped back—nearly falling.

That was no slip. I'd propelled myself forward, ripped through space-time, and planted myself right before her.

The fire of my wrath burned so hot that nothing could survive its flames, especially not shock at how I'd yielded my power. The question was whether I'd ever be able to do it again, but at least I had this time. With steady hands, I ripped my bow and an arrow from my back and aimed right at her face. "Did you truly think you would escape from me?"

Flare climbed down from her horse, the anger burning in her eyes even more brightly than the fear. "Kill me and I'll have no choice but to break in from outside the simulation. It'll be almost instant for you and much more dangerous."

My fingers twitched against my arrow. "I'll let you live and play your games here, as long as you don't try to take back control."

Flare's shoulders shook as she laughed. "I can't blame you for trying, dear girl, but that must be your most pathetic attempt yet." She folded her arms over her chest. "And don't think that because it took Piercey years to figure this out that you'll have that much time with me. I helped create worlds like this. I know the code. I will have control back, whether I take it back from within the simulation or outside of it."

"You aren't good with your power."

"Not with the power you use. This world wastes the potential of the neural implant on war. You trained yourself for its most barbaric and primitive uses. I am a master of sophisticated technology you cannot begin to imagine."

"Maybe I should kill you, then. It'll be more dangerous for our world if you try to break in from outside the simulation. You may not risk it."

"Foolish girl." Flare narrowed her eyes. "I won't dust off my hands and walk away. You're lucky I won't, because you can never leave the closed circuit of this world to enter the afterlife until I release you. You'll slumber eternally. You need me to take back control."

My stomach tightened. "Slumber?"

"None of you are released to the afterlife when you die. I keep you here until we're done with the experiment. You're trapped here, Max, even in death. If I let you keep control of your world, no one will ever live again."

I coiled my muscles. "Is that your plan? To keep me here forever? To keep everyone who knows what you did here so we can never tell the council what you've been up to?"

A laugh burst from her. "When you wake up in the afterlife, you have no memories. You must seek out your memories if you want them. Most people never remember everything because they don't want to. Only a few seek and attain enlightenment over centuries. I don't need to strand you here in this world."

I refused to let her get to me. Even though it seemed certain she would regain control of the world, certain she'd lord over us and have total control of our life here and the one beyond, I'd come too far to quit. "You are the god of this world, Flare, but you don't have all the power. I've fought you in every life I've lived and I'll fight you in death if you steal this life from me. You're breaking your own council's rules and ethical codes. You're tampering with our world in ways no one should. I'll make sure everyone finds out."

Flare's eyes narrowed. "It's difficult to kill you given my current limitations. If you won't relent, which I know you won't, then I'll just have to get creative."

"So, it's war. Have fun trying to kill me, Flare. You may find the lack of amenities in this world distracting. All the war and disease can be a nuisance, too. I sure hope none of this detracts from the time you need to take back control."

There was hope. We had to keep her busy. In her hubris, she always gave me more information than she had to, just to see the look on my face as I witnessed her power and might. Today she'd given me something I could use, even if I didn't know how to quite yet. There was a way to reach the afterlife from this world.

One day, I would crush Flare—Dr. Henderson. I would stop her from ever controlling my world and all of us who lived in it again.

But for now, I needed to see my people to safety, and we all needed time to heal.

CHAPTER TWENTY-NINE

The sun shone overhead as the moon edged closer to covering it. The eclipse was nearly here and I could hardly breathe. Any moment, I expected to disappear from the field that I rode through with Nash and Elsie and to wind up on the stage where I'd witnessed my death so many times.

Flare's threats looped in my mind as I rode. I didn't believe her when she said she wouldn't trap me in the slumber of death in this world forever.

There was more on the line than I'd ever realized.

It distracted me as we continued on our journey. We all planned to return to the Mountain of the Gods and seek refuge in the Sacred School, but for now our group had split apart. Wren and Leif had returned to our people to help deliver them home. Trish and her husband had traveled to the council in the Prophet's village to confront them all for allowing harm to come to Elsie. I hadn't thought it was a very good idea and Trish hadn't wanted to part with her child, but her husband was adamant that they needed to make a strong show together to ensure nothing ever happened to their family again. They were bound to the Prophet after all.

That left Piercey with us and he'd volunteered to ride ahead to scout out the area and make sure it was safe.

Nash, Elsie, and I would have the day alone together. He'd been quiet today, though I could tell he was trying to smile when Elsie could see him. For years, he had served the Prophet to protect his daughter, and then he almost lost her. The rapture of being free of Eskel the Ruthless likely would not settle in until he had recovered from Flare taking Elsie.

It didn't feel right to leave the Prophet and Flare alive while we traveled out of the Valley. But everyone had agreed that we needed time to plan and that we couldn't help anyone if we died.

Besides, I had to make sure Elsie stayed safe. I never wanted to see such fear in Nash's eyes again.

Even so, I longed to return to my village with my people now that they were free. It might as well have been in a different world, unless I wanted to take on the Prophet, which I wouldn't do until I'd made sure everyone was safe.

So, I rode alongside Nash and his daughter on our way to the Mountain of the Gods, where I would stay until the others joined us, and Piercey's graduates arrived to guard my village. In the meantime, Val had stayed behind to keep an eye on the Prophet and alert us if he tried to strike.

"I'm bored, Daddy." Elsie gripped the horse's mane as they rode.

Despite the dread twisting my stomach, Elsie drew a smile from me. It felt good to hear that she could be bored after what happened the day before. If not for her, for how Nash's eyes lit when he looked at her today, the tether keeping me in my body might have snapped.

Fortunately, Elsie didn't remember very much of Flare. She'd come inside from playing to a woman she didn't recognize sitting with her mother. They'd all had tea and then she'd grown sleepy.

What had frightened Elsie the most was how the adults had acted when she'd woken up. Once we all realized it, we did our best to act normal, but it wasn't an easy thing to do.

Elsie looked up as we rode and her eyes widened with wonder. "Wow!"

The full moon darkened the sky now, cutting into the edge of the sun. Even though it looked like I really would survive it, I couldn't shake the dread. I waited for the gods to take back control of the world and for Flare to appear. I waited to blink and open my eyes to the inky black eyes of the Prophet. Waited to slip away from everyone and everything I loved.

Would I even dream in an eternal slumber?

I shivered.

"Let's take a break up ahead at that clearing," Nash said.

We pulled to a stop in a meadow marbled with the yellows and lavenders, the purest whites and deepest reds of the wildflowers. I hopped down from the horse and helped Elsie onto the ground.

"Look at all this room for running," I said.

Elsie squealed and sprinted into grass and flowers that swelled up to her shoulders. Nash grabbed my hand, standing close so he could hide it behind us.

"You're safe," he said quietly to me.

I gazed up at him as the breeze twisted his curls. "You were right. I'll always fear the eclipse."

"Just like you fear yourself."

Not only did death haunt me, but the threat that Dr. Henderson may never release me from it. Even if I survived the eclipse today, I had no reason to think anything good waited for me in my future. I'd made an enemy of a god. Nash would suffer for that if I let myself love him. So would Elsie. So would all of the people I called my own.

Still, I couldn't let go of him. I'd written it into the stone of fate just as when I observed my death. We'd always been together. If I did not fall during this eclipse, then it was still coming, because fate had refused to release me before my proper time.

There was no point in hoping to escape fate. If I couldn't die because I was going to die in the future, then I was destined to die beneath the eclipse, even if I lived through today.

Nash's hold on my hand tightened. He must have felt the sorrow gripping me. Selfishly, I couldn't bring myself to truly want to change a thing. My memory of our night together was so strong that I could still feel his arms around me when we drifted to sleep on the forest floor. The tension threatened to make my spine snap.

Elsie spun through a batch of dandelions, releasing a cloud of fuzzy petals that floated and spun and drifted down all around her.

"I don't know what to do with Flare." I worked my jaw.

"What if we could imprison her?"

"She could probably find a way back to her world, even if it meant dying."

"We have more power over her when she's here than we do when she's with the gods. Whatever we do, she needs to live as Flare in this world for as long as possible."

"True." The light had dimmed considerably while we spoke. The moon was halfway over the sun now. My stomach twisted. "We need to let her keep playing her game. Only we have to stay a step ahead of her until we can figure out how to beat her once and for all."

Nash nodded. "What do you think she plans to do?"

"She'll try to take control back from us while she's living in the world as Flare. But she'll play her politics, too. I'm sure she's already planning on how to kill me and how to create the nations she so desperately wants."

Nash watched Elsie as she played. "I want to give her a better life than this."

"We will." I met his eyes. "I promise. We will still kill Flare and the Prophet when the right time comes."

His gaze drifted down my face. "I won't let Flare kill you today, during another eclipse, or any other time."

He couldn't save me, though I wouldn't say it to him. Instead, I turned my eyes back to Elsie. "I have some ideas that I can't quite form. Things stirring in my mind. I need to talk to Piercey."

"Should we ride ahead after him?"

"No. We have a little bit of time. This world won't be easy for Flare to live in without her god powers." I made myself smile. "Let's forget about everything except for today." I wasn't sure I knew how to do that, and even though it wasn't fair to draw Nash close when I knew I'd die, I wanted it more than I'd ever wanted anything.

He kissed my temple while Elsie's back was turned. My arms craved him. One day with him was never going to be enough. We needed more of what we'd glimpsed.

The birds quieted as the meadow steadily darkened. Elsie sprinted back to us, hugged her dad around his legs, and looked up.

"Don't look at the eclipse," I said.

"Is it bad luck?" she asked.

"It will hurt your eyes, even though it doesn't look bright."

"Max is smart, Daddy."

He smiled. "Yes, she is."

Our conversation quieted as the day gave way to twilight. As the moon swallowed the sun whole and a thin ring of light shined from its edges.

"Look, Daddy!" Elsie reached her little hands up toward the black sun.

I shook off my father's own voice. Nash squeezed my hand between us, grounding me here.

Sweat beaded on the back of my neck.

"Wow!" Elsie hopped up and down in front of us. "It's dark out, Daddy! Like the winter!"

"Don't slip," Nash whispered. "Let yourself feel it, so you can stay in your body."

Villagers dotted the field. I blinked and they vanished. What if I slipped and took Elsie and Nash with me? I stepped back but Nash drew me back to his side, holding tight.

"Stay with us, here and now," he said.

I looked down at the ground, expecting to see my bound ankles, the strands of blood rushing down my legs. Or the little red books. But I only saw verdant green grass and dandelions and Nash's hand in mine.

All that I'd tried to bury too deep to unearth rose up to my surface—the people I'd killed, the power I feared, the pieces I'd broken my father into. No longer did I hold back the sorrow or turn from the memories, instead allowing the screams that had begun the day my father died to flow through me and settle into a moaning deep inside my bones. It hurt less to feel it than to hold it back. I was ready now to stop trying to escape, because ironically, avoiding it only trapped me in the inescapable loop.

I breathed out slowly and settled against Nash's arm. Years of tension unwound from my muscles.

Brightness pierced the edge of the moon and slowly the sun began to emerge.

"Do you feel it?" My father's voice whispered in my ear.

I did. I felt the power stirring inside of me—power that I'd squashed down and hidden from. Power that I held firmly in my hands now. The power to hold myself in place.

Elsie ran forward and clapped her hands. Nash drew my face to his while she wasn't looking and kissed me, his lips soft and warm and mine, at least for this moment.

The eclipse had swallowed my heart up with the sun. "I'll stay," I said. "With you."

"I know."

I wanted so badly to kiss him again, but Elsie was skipping back to us. So I settled for grazing his forearm and ran forward to chase his daughter through the meadow until she laughed so hard she couldn't breathe.

The sun shone down over us, free of the eclipse. The sun shone down over a world that was free and ours, at least for this moment.

CHAPTER THIRTY

The Valley looked so small below us as we stood before the Sacred School. Elsie had been enthralled with the trip up the mountain elevator. But she kept poking at the snow with her foot and a twisted expression.

"It's cold up here," she said. "Look at all the snow."

"I know, baby." Nash lifted her up. "It'll be warm at home when we return."

"When?"

"When it's safe. Until then, we'll be together every day."

"And Mommy?"

"Mommy, too, when she gets here."

"It's warm inside." Piercey smiled at Elsie. "Like spring. Want to go in?"

Elsie's eyes brightened. "Really?"

Nash patted her head and then waved at the Valley. "Say bye for now."

"Bye for now!" Elsie waved excitedly. "See you later!"

We chuckled as we turned and entered the school.

Piercey guided us to a hall that used to lead to the training rooms, which had been converted into personal suites with light yellow walls.

"I let everyone know we would have guests," Piercey said. "You'll have privacy here. If you need anything, Max can teach you how to use the phone. It'll connect directly with me. Our graduates and their families often stay here, so it should be comfortable."

"Phone?" Nash patted Elsie's back.

"I'll show you." I smiled.

Interesting that Piercey had connected a phone system to his neural link, so people without power could tap in. What else had he invented?

"Here." Piercey opened a door to a small living room with two bedrooms at the far end of the room. "The little room is set up for you, Elsie."

"For me?" She wiggled in her father's arms. "I want to see!"

"Say thank you," Nash said.

"Thank you, mister."

Nash lowered her to the ground and she peeled out in a run as soon as her feet hit the floor. He followed after her, leaving me with Piercey.

"Your generosity—" I squeezed my hands in front of me.

"Don't act like it's a favor. We're all fighting this battle together."

"Thank you anyway."

He shrugged. "No problem." His voice lowered. "Before you try to convince me that you should return to the Valley, you need to stay."

"I can't abandon everyone to whatever the Prophets and Flare will do. The Prophet of the Valley has been humiliated. He'll be ruthless."

"You're not alone in this, Max. Let's do this the right way. My graduates are already on their way. We can meet, talk, vote. Join us."

I didn't like the limitations that would impose. I wanted to be free to fight however I needed to. "I'll talk with you, but I'm making decisions for myself."

"I wouldn't have it any other way."

I snorted. "Yes, you would. You want order and justice. I do, too. It's for the best. But Dr. Henderson won't play by any rules."

"Just promise you won't leave without talking to me."

"I promise, Piercey . . . It doesn't feel right. My people are free now, but they aren't safe."

"Does leaving Elsie feel right?"

I shook my head. "No. Nothing feels right."

"Let me work my connections, okay? I'm sending people to protect your village. Everyone will be safe for now. It takes time to plan a war. Our enemies are doing what we are. Preparing."

"I suppose I can train while I'm here. Nash can work on battle plans."

Piercey clasped my shoulder. "There you go." He backed up to the door. "I have work to do before the others get here. Call if you need me."

I walked past the sofa and coffee table in the living room to Elsie's room. She knelt on a little bed by the window, gripping an armful of dolls. The bag with her clothes and belongings that we'd gathered had been thrown on the floor beside a small nightstand.

Nash sat on the edge of the bed.

"I've never had a room for Elsie." He chuckled and then looked up at me. "Strange, isn't it?"

My heart must have crumbled inside of me. Because of having to spy and battle for the Prophet, he'd never been able to really live with her, had he? That would change.

I left them to settle in while I explored the wing. There were three more suites identical to this one and four with only a single bedroom. It would give plenty of room for everyone to stay.

The closest one-bedroom suite was two doors down from Nash. So I picked up my bag of weapons and carried them to the door when I heard him.

"Are you lost?"

I paused and turned to him.

"You're going the wrong way." He pulled the bag from me and backed up toward his suite with a smile hugging his lips.

"I can't stay with you," I whispered.

"Why not? We need your protection. Who will look after us if we're all the way down here?"

I eyed his swords and then pursed my lips. "Because you're totally helpless without me."

He caught my hand and tugged. "We don't have power like you do."

"You're very safe here."

"You'll hurt my feelings if you don't come."

"You have a four-year-old, in case you forgot."

"Totally slipped my mind."

I jerked my bag back from him. "We could be here for a while. I'm not going to live with you."

"I don't see the reasoning behind it, but fine. It's your life."

"I've known you for two weeks."

"And multiple lifetimes."

"It's totally inappropriate for Elsie. It could confuse her."

"What's confusing about our own personal bodyguard?" He flashed that smile of his. Wasn't even fair, the weapons he used against me. "She's four. She'll believe anything."

"Nash. You can't be serious."

He hadn't lost the playful look. "Take your own room if you must, but don't tell me you're going to leave me all alone in a strange place. Stay the night at least."

I chuckled and lowered my head. "You're impossible. I'm going to my room. Alone. Get back to your kid."

He was looking at me, really looking, the longing I felt reflected in his eyes. His voice was quiet now. Instead of returning to his room, he walked close to me, lifted my chin, and looked into my eyes, so close to me that I couldn't draw in a breath. "I'll stop teasing you. Rest and settle in. Just don't run from me when you get scared. I'm right here."

My chest tightened.

He left me with that, walked back to his room, and gave me another look before he disappeared behind the door.

I fell against the wall and groaned. He made it hard to think with his ridiculous ideas like basically moving in with him and his daughter. Now was the time for me to plan.

Although, perhaps, it should have been time for me to live.

"Again," Nash said.

"It doesn't matter how many times I do it." I swung my sword with both hands and groaned. "I never break your defense head-on."

"You can't be good at everything instantly."

I tilted my head back and breathed out slowly. "Fine. Let's start over."

Nash glanced over at Elsie where she played in the courtyard grass. The temperature-controlled zone had given her the closest thing to home she could get while outside. "Okay."

When I'd imagined getting to know Nash better, I had thought it would be alone. Somehow I felt that I could never have glimpsed the true him without his daughter here. Sure, I'd be lying if I said I didn't want some child-free time with him. We'd had some time together while Elsie slept, but I'd quickly learned that I needed to sleep when she did. She was more exhausting than full days of training.

Still, I wouldn't trade the time for the world. I loved Elsie. Yes, already. She grew on me quickly. And her dad wasn't too bad himself.

I thrust my blade forward, knees bent. He deflected it again with only one hand holding the large sword.

"Damn it." I'd said I was ready, but frustration already clawed at my chest. "Not even close."

We trained until my arms felt too heavy to lift, and then met everyone for a lunch that Piercey had prepared himself. Leif passed a plate to his husband and son. Wren poured a glass of ale for herself. Piercey and Nash both took chicken from the platter at the same time. Trish and her husband sat down with Elsie, ready to eat their first meal since arriving at the school.

I let out a chuckle. One big awkward family.

Despite all that had happened, peace flooded me. I almost pushed it away, but denying joy wouldn't change what was coming. I couldn't change the future I'd observed any more than I could the past that I'd lived. Everything I'd experienced existed all at once—past, future, and present. So much so that I hadn't even been able to die.

Strange. I'd avoided thinking about it so much that I never considered that I'd never seen beyond my death, or everything leading up to it. Not that I had expected to see beyond, but I didn't know what was coming. I'd assumed I was powerless in my death because I couldn't prevent it. What if I had more power than I thought?

I might not be able to change that I could die. What if I could choose why I would die? Or what if I could fight for my world after I died? I told Flare I'd fight her in the next life. Like so much I said, I'd only uttered in anger. Could I really do that?

Piercey sat down across from me. "Tell me what you think of the potatoes. It's a new—"

"If there's a passageway to the white room, then there must be a passageway to the afterlife."

He blinked and lowered his fork. I thought he'd tease me for interrupting him with something like that, except this was Piercey. His expression went from intrigued to despondent in moments. Fear clouded his eyes.

"What?" I asked.

"Have you thought this through?"

"No. I was realizing it when you sat down so I blurted it out."

"It's not a good plan." He looked around as if to make sure no one was listening. "You'll want to enter the afterlife like you did the white room and tell everyone there about Dr. Henderson. You're right that there must be a passageway to the afterlife, but there's only one way to get there. You have to die."

"Well, I'm going to die. We know that. It works out."

Frustration leaked into his voice. "There's no way we're going to figure out how to break into the afterlife with our memories intact. It isn't possible."

"You've thought about it for about a minute. It's worth researching."

"No."

"This is because you don't want me to die."

"Yes." He lowered his voice when he became too animated. "Obviously, I don't want you to die."

"Let's meet in the library."

"The library?" Nash asked as he approached. "Are we making more war plans?"

Piercey stared at his plate. "That would be a better use of our time."

"What would be?" Leif dropped down hard enough on the chair that I worried it would crack.

"Stuff that stresses you out," I said.

Leif hooked both elbows on the table and scooped potatoes with his fingers. "Made up words about your power?"

"Yes," I said.

"Technology," Piercey mumbled.

"Made up words," Leif said.

Arn settled Rune's plate beside Leif while the little boy climbed onto his lap. "Good smells, Papa."

Seeing them together again made me feel whole.

Nash smiled at the boy. "Elsie said the same thing. Have you gotten to play with her yet?"

Rune nodded vigorously. "She hit me with two sticks."

Nash's shoulders dropped. "Oh. I'm so sorry."

"It was fun. She wants to sword fight like you."

I twisted around to watch Elsie run up and down the table of food, sticking her finger in dishes along the way to sample them. "Now that's something to be afraid of."

Leif clasped his son's shoulder. "It's good for him to get a few good whacks. Builds his pain tolerance for battle."

Piercey raised his brows but everyone else at the table nodded at the fair point.

My eyes lingered on Rune and the inexplicable joy shining from his eyes. Just looking at him, I would have never known he'd been separated from his papa and held captive. Freeing him wasn't enough. If I had to die, I had to know that he would live in peace. Rune and Elsie both.

"I missed you, buddy." I reached across the table and tapped his nose.

He giggled and squirmed. "I missed you more, Auntie." Then he twisted to look at Elsie as she sat beside her mother. "Is she your new buddy?" A hint of fear, even jealousy, tightened his voice.

"You're my only buddy. Always. But she is my new friend." I smiled. "My pal."

"I'm your buddy and she's your pal."

Nash and Leif both chuckled as Rune repeated the words to himself. But I could only watch, frozen by the thought of how close I'd come to losing him.

Never again.

The battle to free them from the Prophet had only been the first in a war and I could let nothing hold me back, especially not now that I had even more to gain.

Having everyone together for dinner brought so much fullness to my heart and flooded me with joy, but at the same time made me dread all that could still happen.

Piercey left his food only half eaten to make more potatoes when the children frowned at the empty bowl. They gleefully followed after Piercey to help him cook, or rather run around the kitchen while he did the work. I couldn't help but think that he looked incredibly happy having so many people around.

"Try this." Nash pressed a piece of chocolate to my lips. "I don't know what it is but it's amazing."

"Chocolate," I said, sighing when I ate it.

Leif eyed us across the table and Arn nudged him. "Stop it," the other man whispered.

"Seriously?" I asked. "After all that has happened?" It was Leif's first day at the Sacred School, and it had not occurred to me that he may not have accepted Nash yet. "Nash is on our side."

"That's only the first step to earning my trust." Leif anchored his elbows on the table and pointed at Nash. "What will you do when Max gets stubborn and refuses to listen to anyone?"

"She does that every day," Nash said, nonplussed by Leif's behavior. "Watch this."

He grabbed my cheeks, twisted my face to him, and plopped a kiss on my lips. My cheeks warmed.

"See? Distracted. Problem solved. Move on."

"Wow." I pushed him. "You don't do that, do you?"

"Sometimes."

I gasped. "I'm never going to trust your kiss again."

When Nash grinned, I realized he was messing with us, Leif and me both.

"Oh. More games." Narrowing my eyes, I looked back at Leif. "He's on his last chance. You may not have to worry about him for long."

Nash snorted.

"Mock me and see how that goes for you," I said.

Beneath the table where no one could see, he smoothed his hand slowly over my knee. "It goes quite well, generally speaking."

"The arrogance."

Leif groaned and shoveled more potatoes into his mouth. "Fine, so long as you understand that you'll answer to my blade if you hurt her."

"That sounds reasonable to me."

"It's not reasonable at all. I don't need you to coddle me, Leif."

Arn worked his arm around Leif. "He needs to coddle you."

"I do not," Leif mumbled, but then glanced up at me.

I could not fail at protecting this family I had pieced together.

Later, when everyone finished eating and became caught up in conversation, I led Piercey to the library to continue our talk.

"Time isn't linear." I folded my arms on the table. "We only experience it that way. Except, I don't always. I can't change what I've already experienced. It happens the same every time, but I change each time." I leaned against the table, eyes intent on Piercey. "Every time I relive something, it sticks with me."

Piercey looked like he was piecing together a puzzle with his mind. "Time isn't a barrier for you."

"Exactly. However long we have before Flare strikes, I have longer than that. I have more time. If I can learn how to control my slips, I can travel throughout my life for as long as I need to."

"What would you learn, though? You can't change anything. You're only observing."

"You love rereading books. Come on. You know what I stand to gain if I just stop fearing it."

Understanding lit his eyes. "You can look for different angles."

"And find out what the limitations of our world really are."

He straightened. "Max . . ."

"I'll only be able to find the passageway to the afterlife as I die. I'll have to die again and again until I glimpse it and learn to pry it open." I swallowed down the lump forming in my throat. "We are meant to travel to the after-life. There's a way."

"You can't get past Henderson. She's locked up that door. We're stuck here."

"Are we?" I picked at a loose thread on my sleeve. "I've avoided my death so far. But I've spent my life bouncing between these two eclipses and every experience tied to them. There's more here for me to learn. You found a way to break into the white room and take over our simulation. I think we can do the same with the afterlife."

Pain filled his voice. "We'll figure out how and I'll be the one to do it this time. It's too risky."

"This world needs you. Look at what your graduates are doing. You have students."

Piercey grabbed my hands. "You're the one with something to lose. You can't leave Nash and Elsie when you're just starting."

I swallowed hard and looked down. "I'm going to die, Piercey. That's why I can't die now."

"Reality is so complicated. You've experienced the eclipse, yes, but you did die in your first two lives that way. Maybe you're hopping timelines. Maybe you aren't going to die in the eclipse here."

"Then why can't I die otherwise?"

"You're assuming that's why. It could be that you subconsciously drew upon more power and saved yourself."

"I didn't."

"Why have you always stubbornly clung to this death?" He ripped his hands away. "You left me behind once. I know how it feels to lose you. That little girl shouldn't have to go through that."

"Piercey—"

"No. Nash was right. You refuse to give up on anyone. You refuse to give up on our world. But you jump at the chance to give up on yourself. I won't stand for it."

I lowered my head into my hands. "I need you for this, Piercey. After I relive everything, I need to connect with you again so you can experience it, and we can figure it out together."

"Fine. But I'll be the one to go to the afterlife. I'll train Val to take my place in case of the worst. There's no one to take your place for Nash and Elsie."

How must it have hurt him to say these things to me? "I can't let you die for me."

"I can't let you die for me either."

We stared at one another. No words could bridge this gap. We both meant what we'd said.

I settled my hands against the table, feeling too heavy to hold myself up. "Fine." I sighed. "Neither of us can let the other die. We'll just have to find a way to break into the afterlife and make it out alive."

CHAPTER THIRTY-ONE

I traced a crack in the table and avoided the eyes of Piercey's graduates sitting in the conference room with us. Somehow it reminded me that I belonged here and yet didn't, that it was true of everywhere I'd ever called home. I didn't fit in anywhere.

Piercey used his teaching voice as he continued with the end of his report. It grated at me today. "Flare has united six Prophets who have formed a council and agreed to work toward combining their lands. Others have refused, including the Prophet of the Valley. There's talk of war brewing." Piercey settled his clipboard onto the table. "We need to decide our next steps."

"I say we ally with Max." Val nodded at me. "She's proven to be very capable and she has the people's best interests at heart."

"I agree." Another graduate spoke up from the far end of the table. "Flare is an enemy to us all. If she uses the Prophets to conquer lands and create nations, they'll never be nations for the people. They'll be nations of terror and oppression."

I held my breath as the next graduate spoke. They were all in agreement. I'd assumed they would fight me, maybe because Piercey always had in his own way.

"Then it's settled." Piercey's eyes shifted to each person at the table. "We ally with Max against Flare. We'll need to keep her alive while sabotaging her efforts."

Nash gripped my hand beneath the table.

"It's tempting to kill the Prophet," Piercey said, "But Flare will use it to her advantage. It's better to isolate the major players and keep them busy defending against us."

I should have known Piercey would come up with an excuse to not kill. So, I rose and nodded at Nash. "Show them your back."

Piercey drew back at the interruption. "Max—"

Nash pulled his tunic over his head and turned so the overhead lights shone against the scars weaving down his spine.

"Eskel." I watched the graduates take in the devilishly elegant script running down the middle of his back. "Written in blood."

Piercey lowered his head. The table fell silent.

"I could tell you as many stories of Eskel's ruthlessness as there are days. Not only did he conscript Nash and use the threat of hurting his daughter to force him to serve a cause he didn't believe in for years, but the Prophet also tried to force Nash to bind himself to him."

The graduates murmured at this violation, because binding yourself was meant to be sacred.

"He used his power to carve his name into Nash's spine, healed him, and did it again. How many times must you do this before it leaves behind scars not even power can heal? This was done to one man. What else has he done? What will he do if left in power?"

Val looked at Nash as he put his shirt back on and sat down.

"The Prophet of the Valley, Eskel the Ruthless, must not remain in power. He is poison to the people. He uses his power against his people. Do not abandon them to suffer another day beneath his crushing rule. We should kill him now."

Piercey raised his head again with his eyes unyielding. "The Prophet of the Valley has refused to surrender or join forces with Flare. It'll mean war. He will be fighting Flare and keeping her distracted. That's the best chance we have of holding Flare off."

"Innocent people will die." My voice hitched.

Piercey's eyes shone with tears. "And if the Valley falls to the Flatlanders? Into Flare's hands? Are you prepared to handle the vacuum of power it will create while we also battle Flare?"

"I can't turn my back on my people," I said. "My chief agreed to hold off on attacking the Prophet until we all join, but they are prepared to defend themselves at a moment's notice."

"No one plans to abandon your people."

"You already did it once." I slammed my fist against the table. "Cowering on this mountain while the world is at war is unthinkable."

Piercey straightened, matching my stance. "Then don't cower. If you can control your power over space-time, you'll be able to travel anywhere instantly. Think of all you can do then." His gaze drilled into my eyes. "We will not help you with the Prophet until we know the Valley will stay out of Flare's hands. So focus on what you have power over."

It didn't matter that I understood Piercey or even whether he was right. Leaving the Prophet in power defied the justice and vengeance every ounce of my blood cried out for. I'd spent years fighting him.

Nash reached for me, but I stormed out of the room. I didn't need Piercey's permission to seek my vengeance, not when I'd vowed to Nash that I would kill the Prophet. The problem was that I couldn't say for certain that he was wrong. I had destroyed so much in my life and the two before this.

How could I trust myself?

It had taken me several days to stop shooting daggers at Piercey and even longer to warm back up to him during our training sessions. While I had not yet decided whether to kill the Prophet on my own, I did know I should not abandon my training sessions with Piercey. His knowledge had always helped me to control my power.

"Focus, Max." Piercey breathed out slowly.

"I am."

"No, you're obsessed and angry. It distracts you."

I slammed my palm against my knee. "I can't make myself slip through time."

"You've learned how to stop yourself. That's something."

I gripped the back of my neck as I bent forward and stretched my back. "Val said that Flare is trying to unite even more Prophets. She's using me and the threat of other demons like me to get them to join together. And who knows how close she is to breaking back into this world. I'm sitting here doing nothing."

"You're training for battle with Nash, Leif, and Wren for four hours a day and sometimes five with me. You're doing plenty."

I shook my head. "Not enough. Not fast enough."

"It's going to take Flare time to accomplish her mission. It doesn't matter that she helped create this world. The path we took to gain control wasn't easy to find. She's also having to live here full-time without the luxury of all the god powers she's used to and she's playing politics. She's a scientist. She'll play it safe to be sure. I'm sure we have months, at least."

"The Prophet doesn't need months. He's as impatient as I am."

Piercey nodded. "He has many eyes on him. We should practice teleporting more so that you can get to him quickly if you need to."

That I did need to do. Traveling was my skill set, though. I had unwittingly played with space-time repeatedly in my life. I could learn to do it on purpose.

I focused on Leif to search for his heartbeat and imagined peeling away the distance between us to travel to him. Heat swelled in my palms and I snapped forward. I opened my eyes in the hallway just as he slammed right into me.

"Ouch!" Leif sprang back and rubbed his chin. "Where did you come from?"

"Sorry. Practicing."

"Are you teleporting again? Make sure you know where we are before you do that. You terrified Wren when you popped up on her bed. She was napping. I think—"

His voice droned on as I listened for Wren and imagined myself standing in front of her. That was all it took to travel to her.

She screamed so loud I thought my ear drums would burst as she pulled her blankets over her head. "Max! Not again!"

"It's your fault for sleeping so much." I rubbed my ear.

"Teleport to Nash next time."

"I don't want to scare Elsie."

"Oh." She ripped the blanket down. "I'm glad there's someone you don't want to scare. Must be nice."

I grinned. This time, when I focused on Piercey, I hardly even had to think about it before I appeared in front of him.

"That's a record." He clapped. "Now we add in greater distances."

I didn't need to think about where I should learn to travel. My people were rebuilding our village, and I was long overdue for a talk with the chief about all that I'd hidden from her. Wren had already told me that as soon as I learned to travel that far, I had better speak with her. The chief would be an excellent person to discuss killing the Prophet with.

CHAPTER THIRTY-TWO

For the first time since our captivity, I stood in the home I had shared with Leif and his family since they'd taken me in. When the Prophet of the Valley captured our people, they'd set fire to dozens of our homes. I was fortunate that this one survived, but it was not without damage.

The chief had wanted to hear everything I knew and then desired time to think before discussing it further. So, I'd started from the beginning, during the time when I trained with the Prophet of my hometown to when I'd killed the villagers. I told both the chief and commanders of my time at the Sacred School, the binding of my power, and finally all I'd experienced and learned since captivity. While I did not attempt to explain the science, I even shared that the gods had created our world to test their power on us, and that I had stolen control of our world from them.

I knelt down to pick up the broken brush off the floor, the brush Rune had always used to brush my hair before battle. Our home was small with only two rooms, separated by a thick curtain. The house was nestled into the hill with small windows that peeked out like eyes. In the summer, we kept the door open, but in the winter, we closed it and covered it with canvas to keep out the bitter cold. Before all this happened, we would have likely been home cooking this evening, preparing for the battles ahead as we defended our village from the Prophet. Today, our door was broken and the curtain separating the rooms torn.

"Max." Beast stood in the doorway. "The chief is ready for you."

I held my breath for most of the short walk to the center of the village. I no longer recognized this place I had once loved, not with the homes burned and the ground blackened. It would take so much work to rebuild.

I met with the chief in a home that had not been razed and sat down on the ground before her. From her guarded expression, I could not guess at her thoughts.

"You have carried secrets far beyond my imagination," she said.

Shame choked my throat. I nodded.

"I wish you'd trusted us enough to tell us. Though, I understand your fear for our safety, since this god threatened the safety of anyone who you told the truth to. In the end, it was your power that freed our people. You did what no one else could."

My head lowered naturally, because I could not take praise when I had not accessed my power sooner. "I should have killed the Prophet long ago before he destroyed our homes and stole our people."

"I understand why you weren't honest and why you couldn't defeat him until now. It has challenged me to see that some without power are not hungry for it like the Prophets or wicked like many demons we have encountered. You only want to protect us. So, you remain one of us, and you are free of any guilt or blame."

My eyes closed tightly to cover the dampness spreading there. The chief could have banished me for simply having power, and certainly for deceiving them.

"We knew when you came to us that you had secrets. We accepted your silence and we cannot blame you for what we willingly participated in. I know that wherever your battle leads you, you will fight for us."

"Always." I opened my eyes. "I'm sorry I didn't kill the Prophet that day. I couldn't risk the child getting hurt."

"I understand. It's better this way. Once you kill the Prophet, there will be chaos. We need time to recover and prepare for the coming war."

"I want to kill him now." My voice deepened. "Piercey and his graduates voted no, but I am not bound to them. I could go to him now and finish what I started."

"Then what?" The chief tilted her head. "You'll have to kill the disciples. What about the one who takes their place?"

"I'll kill anyone who threatens this Valley and my people."

"When will you have time to train and become strong enough to ensure the gods never take control of our world again?" The chief leaned forward. "You're young and impatient. You're used to charging into battles. I plan for wars. The Prophet is weak and humiliated right now. This is the perfect time for us to gain strength rather than replace him with someone strong."

Was I really hearing this? Not only did Piercey want me to wait, but so did the chief? "What if he hurts people while we wait?"

"You won't let him do that. Will you?"

My hands trembled. "How can you say this? He would have killed all of the children in this village."

"Just like the Flatlander Prophet who will take his place if our Prophet falls. Use him, Max. Be smart. When you can kill your enemy at any time, you do not need to rush. I believe that you can stay stronger than he can. Right now, you told us you have preparation to do. So train."

I lowered my head, the tears that had threatened to fall before were now those of anger. No matter what anyone said, I could do it. I could defy them all to kill the Prophet. Nash would support me. There would be at least one person on my side.

"Max," the chief said. "You're powerful enough now to do what you want. You could take the village from me."

"I would never do that."

"You could. Think with your mind and not just your might." She rose, moved beside me, and knelt. "A few days will not hurt. Give yourself time to think. We'll speak again soon. Give us time to prepare. We're not ready for a war, even if you are." The chief clasped the back of my neck, looking at me with a warrior's eyes. "A commander and chief must know what her people need. Do not lower yourself to mere warrior or demon. Learn to lead. All of Skia Hellig will soon look to you to guide us and protect us. Are you ready to do that today?"

"Just because I'm strong doesn't mean I can lead the whole peninsula."

"It does and you can. Return to the Sacred School and become who we need you to be. You're not ready yet."

I dipped my head, unable to speak. Finally, I managed a "Yes, Chief."

After returning to the Sacred School, I dedicated myself even further to training myself, not just to hone my power, but to learn how to lead Skia Hellig. Two months had passed since we arrived here at the Sacred School and vengeance still pumped through my veins every day. I learned patience I hadn't thought possible.

On a day when I'd tirelessly trained on controlling my time slips, I finally quit for the night to be with Nash. I spent the last hour of daylight with him and Elsie, before he tucked her into her bed in Trish's suite while I waited in his. Traveling had exhausted me, especially since I had to face my people. Chief Kaid's acceptance of me stood, and no one would dare defy her, but I hadn't been honest. That wouldn't just disappear. Besides, even if people pretended to be okay with the fact that I was a demon, not everyone would be. Should I ever make it back home permanently, it would take time to rebuild trust.

When Nash walked into his room where I waited, I moaned about the long day I had, but he raised a brow at the bag I'd left on the foot of the bed.

"Hm." He crawled onto the bed over me. "I thought you desperately needed to keep your bag in that lonely room of yours."

My breath caught as he lowered over me. "It's only here for the night."

"And you?"

"For the night."

He pushed off of me and flopped onto his back. When I rolled over, he pushed me back with his hand. "No. You stay on your side. You have your own room, your own side of the bed, your own sad little bag."

"I'm not allowed to be near you because I won't move in? You think your tricks will work eventually but they won't."

"It's a mistake to challenge me. I'm going to prove you wrong now."

I groaned. "You know not to start a competition with me. Last time, we broke the bench Piercey made. He was so upset."

"And I won that sparring match."

"I won. Nash. Don't antagonize me." I reached for him, but he pushed away again. "This isn't even funny. It's our day. Elsie is with Trish."

He folded his arms beneath his head, gazing at me exactly how he knew would make my heart melt.

We'd grown so close. It hit me then, clearly, as he teased me. The smile fell from my face. I couldn't hold myself back from him, and yet still I tried, even now that I knew better. So with Nash looking into my eyes, I didn't want to hold back anymore, even if I thought I should.

"I have to tell you something."

He rolled onto his side, the joking, the annoyance beneath the joking, gone just like that. "What's wrong?"

My mouth refused to form the words. He'd be so angry with me. I owed him the truth, though, so I finally forced myself to speak. "Piercey is helping me learn to control my slips. I'm going to travel on purpose and relive my death until I learn how to escape our world to go beyond to the gods."

Nash's breathing froze. He stared. Silent.

"It's our only hope. Dr. Henderson has already reset our world twice. She's helping Prophets conquer our land. As long as she's in control, we die over and over without end. What will she do next? I have to stop her. And I didn't tell you because I'm a coward. I couldn't stand to hurt you."

Nash blinked, looked down, and then sat up, back turned to me as he slid his legs off the bed. He sat that way for torturous minutes until his hands gripped the sheets in fists and the muscles in his arms tightened. Nash glanced over his shoulder and the pain in his eyes sucker punched me. "You just didn't want me to get in your way."

"That's not it."

I tried to explain, but he rose to his feet and raised his voice over mine. "It's insane to torture yourself like this. You're doing it to punish yourself."

"I'm not, Nash. I really believe this will help me reach beyond Dr. Henderson."

"It's dangerous. Do you care about your life?"

We both yelled over each other, neither of us listening, neither of us able to stop as we spoke in circles at one another. Until finally, Nash sat back on the bed and hurt filled in the spaces anger had burned into minutes before.

"I don't want you to hide things from me like I'm a child," Nash said. "Even if you know I'll fight you, show me the respect of being honest."

"I said I was sorry." I scratched the back of my neck. "This is my decision, though."

"What if it were me? You would stop at nothing to keep me from doing it."

"And you would do it anyway."

We wouldn't agree. The more we talked, the clearer it was, until I curled up on my side, stomach tied in knots.

Nash settled beside me and twined his fingers with mine. We lay in tense silence, close, angry, together.

The chief had told me to prepare myself but I still was acting like a frightened girl. I rose, grabbed my bag, and dropped it in his closet. He watched me quietly.

I crawled back in bed beside him, heart pounding. "My bag can stay from now on."

He drew his arm around me. "You never leave your weapons behind."

A smile tempted me. "Never."

"I'm still mad," he said.

"Me, too."

Nash smirked, but it faded as he eyed me, until he whispered in a husky voice. "I love you, Max." His mouth was on mine before I could respond.

I whispered the words between his kisses. "I love you, too."

I took the happiness, not minding the hurt and anger that twisted in with it, and for once, I didn't push any of it away. It was just us, together, like one soul in two bodies that had been born and reborn, tangled together, in a thread between worlds.

CHAPTER THIRTY-THREE

Where my power had once been a drip I could scarcely control, it had evolved into a waterfall that I could shut off at will. The only problem with a waterfall was how difficult it was to control once it plunged into a river. When even a ripple could hurt the people around me, I feared the power of riptides and raging eddies could destroy my world.

After gaining control of my teleportation powers, I focused on my manipulation of time. I still needed to figure out how to break into the afterlife and keep my memories, but to do any of that, I needed to learn to travel to the moment where I would die beneath the eclipse. That moment held valuable data. While Piercey focused on academic pursuits and supporting me, I plunged into the experience of trying to travel not through the space around me, but through time. There had been progress, but not enough.

I steadied my breathing as I focused on times throughout my life that I felt connected to. I'd learned I couldn't travel to any point I wanted, at least not yet. But there were so many moments in my life that felt timeless, like they had dug so deeply into the fabric of existence that even time couldn't force me to let go, that I had never left. I had stayed in the eclipse for my entire life. Had never left my father on those long days of training. Never for a moment had let go of Nash's hand as he fell down the cliff in the landslide.

All this time that I'd nearly killed myself trying to hold back the waterfall of my power, I'd forced it to explode out of hairline fissures. I'd been wrong. Wrong for a very long time. I had to embrace my power and tame it and make it truly mine.

So as I sat in the grass beneath the towering tree where Piercey and I had long ago sat and talked, I thought of the points in my life I would like to travel to. Because why practice with the bad when I could drift off to the good?

That was the greatest power I had learned. To live in my joy rather than be trapped in my suffering. My mind was mine, as was my power.

Not that I never struggled with anxiety. But I would enjoy every moment of freedom, because it would be a shame to reject happiness out of fear that one day I might lose it.

"When will you travel to today?" Piercey asked.

"Probably the day when we were kids and I finally beat you at that puzzle game we liked."

A smile tugged my lips as I thought of memories I wanted to relive. I didn't slip as much as I drifted into the warmth of days I wanted to never end.

It would be harder to travel to the day I'd spent my life avoiding.

"You're sure about this?" Piercey knew the answer. I thought what he really wanted to know was whether he could stop me.

I breathed in deeply and smoothed my hands over the plush pillow beneath me. Piercey had surrounded me with pillows and blankets in the dim training room to make me more comfortable.

"It's time," I said.

"No one should have to do this."

I smiled sadly. "People have always done things they shouldn't have to do. I need you to be strong for me. If I try to quit, push me to keep going." He shook his head but I made my voice stern. "That is the least you can do for me. I'm the one who will be dying."

Shame flooded his eyes. He lowered his head.

I didn't soften my voice even though I wanted to. "You will not let me quit, Piercey."

He nodded, though he said nothing.

It had taken me weeks to reach this point, but once I began traveling at will, it all came to me quickly. There was nothing left to wait for. It wouldn't get easier. I just had to do it. Besides, Flare could take back control at any time. I had to be ready.

So I clenched my eyes shut and thrust myself toward the death that I had always run from.

Slipping to my good moments felt like floating atop a peaceful pool of water. This was different. I tore my way through my own resistance in burning fire that felt as if it melted the flesh from my bones and bored its heat into my marrow. Pain dug its claws into me and tried all it could to stop me.

I pushed through until I found myself trapped by thick ropes.

The pain consumed me. My head fell and I opened my eyes to my bound ankles. To strands of blood rushing down my legs. I would die here.

A crowd spilled out over every inch of the courtyard before me. Their screams tore into my mind. "Kill! Kill! Kill!" The voices swirled about me. Growing.

Stepping back, the Prophet raised up his bloodied spear against the dark sky. Black dripped from its tip.

"Oh gods, bleed this demon dry of the innocent."

His spear plunged into my gut.

I jerked off the pillow, my eyes bulging, the pain still clinging to my body.

Piercey knelt beside me and grabbed my arms. "You're safe. You're here."

"I . . ." I lowered my head, hating how I trembled. "I didn't mean to come back."

"Give yourself some time."

"No." I growled and shoved Piercey away. Stumbling to my feet, I kicked the pillows and blankets away and cleared an empty space of tile. "Soft won't help me. I have to do this."

"That doesn't make sense. Sit for a minute. Cool off and try again."

I narrowed my eyes and blocked out Piercey's voice as I plunged headlong through the agony of traveling to that day. I didn't care about how my soul reached for my body beside Piercey. I didn't care about what it would do to me. I didn't care that I'd slipped away while standing and would probably smack my head on the tile.

Rage was the only thing that would fuel me through these slips.

Rage against the Prophet who'd killed me so many times.

Against Henderson for engineering my death.

Against me for failing to face the inevitable.

Every time I tore my way to my death, my spirit threw me back to Piercey, until I was shaking on the ground, my nose and mouth bloodied. I didn't even know what from. My head pounded. My body was on fire. Piercey tried to stop me, tried to hold back my power with his own, but this was war. And war was one thing I knew.

It would hurt. That didn't matter.

In broken and shattered bits of memory of what would one day come, I witnessed my death and plunged myself into it once more. And then again. Again. Again. Again, until I awoke to my nails bloodied from clawing into the grooves of the tile. Again, until Piercey was screaming my name.

Again.

The Prophet's spear tore away bits of my life.

The crowd's chanting beat like a drum that throbbed in my temples.

Blood rushed from me in a river of sheer agony.

Like a star collapsing in on itself and exploding without control, death opened me up to the world, unleashing everything they'd put inside me.

Again.

Blood snaked down my legs.

Again.

"Kill the demon! Kill her!"

The Prophet's inky eyes drilled into my own.

Again.

Death opened me up to the world. Death, death, death. A single moment I couldn't quite grasp. A fleeting moment. A moment I needed to catch.

Again.

Flare tilted her head, the smoldering of her eyes bright against the all-white room. "You knew this would happen. Why did you never stop? The Prophet is waiting. The eclipse is waiting." Her voice dropped to a whisper. "The afterlife is not. I can't release you. You may not believe me, but I am sorry. I've never been sorrier for anything."

Again.

So many times, I lost count. Might have lost my mind. No, definitely did, at least for a little while. My consciousness waned on the tiled floor as Piercey's healing power flowed through me. It couldn't stop the pain of the future that still clung to me.

Then I felt the strong hand kneading the tight muscles in my arm. My eyes fluttered open to Nash holding me in his arms. Had I slipped away to another time?

"You see me, don't you?" Nash's jaw muscles bunched. "You have to stop. You're killing yourself."

"That's . . . the point . . . I have to die until I learn how to escape."

"You're going to die right now if you keep going."

"I won't. I can't." I smiled and slid my hand along his face, leaving specks of blood from the tips of my fingers. "I'll survive."

I dove back into death.

Eventually, I caught the moment I took my last breath, thought my last thought, felt the last shiver of life creep from my body. I lived in that moment for what felt like eternity.

Death bled into life. I'd learned to travel each but could never tame either. At some point, I lost my hold, and I slipped away to what my soul longed for.

"I love you," Nash whispered in a husky voice, mouth on mine before I could respond.

He loved me again and again.

When I finally awoke in a warm bed with the pain a distant memory, and realized I'd given up in the fight to continue traveling, I opened my eyes to Nash sitting beside me and Leif staring out the window.

"You're awake." Nash sat forward and brushed my hair back.

"Get Piercey . . . I need to share these memories. We've got to study the moment I died and figure out the code. I can feel it . . ." My eyes closed. I was so exhausted. "The way out."

I didn't want Piercey to suffer like I had, and taking these memories from me would hurt him.

We had to do this, though. Our powers complemented each other too well.

CHAPTER THIRTY-FOUR

It had taken me a week to recover from my slips until I could connect with Piercey to share what I'd experienced, and then another week for him to do the same after living through it all with me.

Despite sharing, we couldn't perform each other's skills, though our abilities did improve from the knowledge. I needed more than just to connect with Piercey to become a healer, and he needed more to travel through time or space. It wasn't something that could simply be known, but had to be practiced and mastered.

Though Piercey didn't want to admit it, that limited his ability to try to go to the afterlife for me. Would he even make it through the door?

My training turned entirely to breaking into the afterlife with my memories, but I longed so fiercely to leave the mountain and battle that the yearning turned into a dull ache that spread throughout my body. The Prophet of the Valley had not dared to cross me, but other Prophets were growing more powerful, and my people had fought several battles without me.

It was difficult to not let it distract me.

Day after day, in the somber quiet, Piercey and I meditated on that moment when death had taken me, Piercey studying it and tearing it apart and breaking it down into binary I'd never really understand, and me instinctively feeling along the jagged boundaries of our world.

I had begun to sense it before he discovered it, but in the end, it was melting my instinct and his studies that opened our eyes to the elegant little door that led from our world to the afterlife. The door that Dr. Henderson had locked.

Since we had control of the world and Piercey could work in the white room, we had everything we needed for him to learn how to crack the code.

Fortunately, Piercey had also been making rapid progress with the issue of potential memory loss. We'd decided that relying upon only one strategy was not enough. So, Piercey helped me back up my memories in the white room in the hopes that they would be accessible from the afterlife, considering it was distinct from my world. He'd also helped to compress and store them in my neural implant. But the last line of defense was the self-construction algorithm he'd been teaching me. If all else failed, I had to hope that it would be buried so deeply within me that I would remember to run the code and restore my memories.

As frightening as dying should be, the fear of waking up in the afterlife and remembering nothing was much worse. That would mean accidentally abandoning everyone I loved here without any help. I had to master this. So I couldn't worry about the battles happening in the Valley or about my guilt for staying here on the mountain.

This was a war only I could fight.

Every time we practiced, Piercey made sure to close the door to the afterlife when we were done, because Dr. Henderson couldn't discover what we'd learned if she regained control.

I practiced prying open the door until I could do it without even really trying.

Flare would be in control of our world again someday. I had to be ready and trust that when I escaped to the afterlife, I would know what to do. Someone would care about what was happening to us. Even in a young world like mine, there was always someone willing to help. I had to find those people and rally them to our cause.

As challenging as this seemed, I had found my way to people I could trust in every life. I would find my way to allies beyond this world. I had to believe there was good out there, because if not, we really were doomed.

Still, my dread only worsened as Flare made progress with uniting Prophets together. When the Flatlanders and their allies that Flare helped them form on the coast and in lands far beyond their own stole village after village from our Prophet, I could scarcely control the rage. We needed to act as soon as I had mastered these powers. Either I would kill the Prophet of the Valley and begin the war that would plunge Skia Hellig into darkness, or first I would travel to the afterlife.

The problem was that I couldn't die and pass through the door, even when we unlocked it. So, to go to the afterlife, I needed to actually live through my death during the eclipse. Piercey still believed that it may never happen, but I disagreed, because I could travel to it. I believed that once Dr. Henderson regained control of the world, she would find a way to send me to that day. When she did, I would escape from this world to fight her from the one beyond it. If that happened before I killed the Prophet, then Piercey had to watch over the Valley until I found a way to return. He promised me that even if I didn't, he and all of his graduates would come together to kill the Prophet. That would be my dying wish should I truly leave this world behind.

At this rate, Flare would have her nations in a few years' time. These wars would one day be forgotten as the wonders of plumbing and paved roads and maybe even factories elevated the life of everyone in the world. But whatever world she made would be built on a foundation of war, those with power crushing those without, a god who stole the lives of her own people. It would be a world that could never be fair and would always be at risk of this power unleashing upon the people. Prophets, demons, disciples, graduates. It didn't matter what any of us were called. We possessed something that could crush and torture and subjugate everyone else in the world.

And that wasn't even taking into consideration that when we died here in this simulation, we may remain dead forever.

We could not give up.

In the face of so much danger, Nash and Elsie, Piercey, Wren and Leif and Rune, my hope that one day they could be free, kept me grounded.

The morning I took Elsie out for a walk in the snow and watched her make angels in the white, watched Nash smile at his child, I knew better than I had ever known that I couldn't give up.

Enough time had passed that when the day came, it felt swifter than anything ever had. I was preparing for a training session with Piercey to practice opening the door again and then to study how to make it back from the afterlife alive, when he called out to me with his neural link.

I traveled to him immediately and froze. Piercey was doubled over, holding his head.

I pushed a hand against my stomach as I followed the trails of sweat slithering down Piercey's face.

"Don't know how long I can last." He grunted in pain. "She's forcing her way in."

"I have to do it now." My feeling drained from my body for that one moment. "There's no time to wait."

"Do what?" He grunted and wiped his forehead.

"Go to the afterlife."

"No!" His eyes snapped to me. "We have to figure out a certain way for you to return to our world."

"Hold her off as long as you can. I need to be in the right headspace to do this. I won't wait for her to take me and throw me off. I'll travel to the eclipse and I won't come back this time."

"Max!" Piercey reached for me as I slipped away to Leif and Wren.

"We need another group to patrol here." Wren smashed her finger against the map in the library. But Leif wasn't listening. He'd seen me appear behind her. Had seen the tears wetting my cheeks.

Leif watched me. "What are you about to do?"

Wren twisted her brows and then turned around.

They'd always known what I couldn't say. "Take care of them." I didn't stop the tears from coming. "Kiss Rune for me. This is the only way."

They stood and came to me, maybe to stop me, or just to hold me. I clung to my circle. "Goodbye," I whispered.

"Don't," Leif said. "Whatever this is, don't do it."

"Max." Wren clasped my face and looked forcefully into my eyes. "Stop it and tell us what this is about."

"Flare is about to take back control. There's no time." I kissed Wren's smooth cheek and then Leif's prickly one. "I love you both. Tell my little buddy I love him, too."

They uttered my name as they dug their fingers into me to hold me in place, but I forced myself to leave them.

I landed in Elsie's dim room where she played with morning weariness slowing her motions. She hummed as she lovingly placed the hand of one doll in the other and then groaned when they fell away.

I knelt down. She'd see my tears. A goodbye would only confuse and frighten her. So I gripped my hand into a fist and swallowed down the cry building inside of me.

"Goodbye, Elsie," I mouthed. "I love you."

When I closed my eyes, I didn't have to try to imagine Nash. He was all I saw. My heart broke in two. Back when I'd allowed visions of my death to rule over me and hold me back from living, I'd decided not to ever have a family, so I wouldn't leave them behind. How could I choose to leave now that I loved them and had let them love me?

I would lose them if I did nothing, though. Dr. Henderson would erase this life we created. She would erase me. Soon.

If I wanted to save everything I had, I had to let go. I had to go beyond my life, beyond the world that Dr. Henderson could control, and step into the unknown.

With my resolve fresh, I slipped to Nash, standing before him in the hall. It looked like he had been heading to find Elsie in Trish's suite.

Seriousness filled Nash's eyes immediately. He said nothing. Fear flooded him, tightening the muscles in his face, his hands, his arms. He was afraid to ask and I was afraid to say it. So we only stared at one another with the unspoken between us.

How could I say goodbye to him? How would that be possible when I didn't know if we'd ever remember each other? Or how long it would take to find each other in the next life? What if somehow Dr. Henderson kept us apart forever?

Hot tears flooded my eyes and spilled down my cheeks. The same heat built in my throat in a bundle that choked out my air and voice. I had to get a hold of myself. But I'd been slipping away my entire life no matter how hard I tried to hold on. Maybe people weren't meant to stay in place through things like this. Maybe grief was meant to sweep us away and I should finally accept it.

I'd always returned before.

This time, I didn't know if I would.

Nash rushed to me then and tangled his hands in my hair, tilting my head back, searching my eyes. "Tell me." It wasn't a question or suggestion. His words were forceful, almost prying the truth from my lips. We had traveled so far since that day in the cell when he'd been sharpening his swords or when I fought him in the woods after the Flatlanders had hurt Leif. The months had flown by, but they'd also felt like an entire life lived. I tasted the flavor of lives lost; dreams we could not remember but had fully lived.

I would find my way back to Nash like I always had.

I couldn't hold myself back from him anymore than I had been able to hold myself in time all those days the past and future stole me away. "I'm traveling to the eclipse." Resolution hardened my voice. "I have to die, Nash. I have to reach beyond this world. Flare is about to regain control."

"Let me." He begged. It didn't matter that he knew he couldn't. Nash couldn't accept what I told him. "I'll be the one to die."

I shouldn't have told him. I wasn't strong enough to face it. I should have run like a coward. "You don't have to let me go. Hold on to me so you can find me again in the next life."

His arms wrapped around me and smothered me.

"I've found you in every life I've ever lived." I wove my fingers into his curls. "I'll find you again."

"Don't let go."

"I won't, even when I die." I brought my lips to his and pressed closely to kiss him. Our tears mingled and smeared against our cheeks. "I'll hold on to you forever."

"I love you, Max." Nash kissed me hard.

"I love you, Nash. I always have, in the dreams we can't remember, and now, and in what comes next. I've always loved you and I always will."

I lacked the strength I needed, but that had never stopped me in battle. I reached within myself for something deeper and more real than my power. For the piece of me that told me I existed, that had been true in every life, the core of who I was, and I knew then that I could do this. I could do anything for the ones I loved.

"Goodbye, Nash."

I slipped away from him one last time.

CHAPTER THIRTY-FIVE

I opened my eyes after trying to travel to the eclipse and found myself lying on a white floor, suffocated by plain white walls with my arms tied behind my back.

Flare's face blinked in and out of view.

"Flare . . . ?" Her hair was a few inches longer than it had been when I'd last seen her.

"There you are." She tilted her head. "I thought it would be harder to bring you here, but you weren't responsive. It feels even worse when you don't fight back."

"I slipped to this time. I must have been unconscious."

She pushed my hair back. "You're burning up. Did you really just slip? Or are you toying with time?" She chuckled softly. "In your last life when you tried to learn to control it, you failed miserably. At least you're making some kind of progress."

"Why are we in the white room?"

"I took back control, just recently, actually. You must have been drawn to this event."

I squeezed my eyes shut. "How did you get control back?"

"I'm not going to explain myself to you. You showed me the error of such mercy. We should say goodbye for good this time, dear girl. You've caused too many problems. It's too dangerous to wait as you grow stronger."

I couldn't let her suspect I'd traveled here on purpose or she might figure out my plan. "Don't do this."

"Be a good girl and sleep this time."

"Don't hurt anyone else. Please. Be satisfied with me."

Flare tilted her head, the smoldering of her eyes bright against the all-white room. "You knew this would happen. Why did you never stop fighting me? The Prophet is waiting. The eclipse is waiting." Her voice dropped to a whisper. "The afterlife is not. I can't release you, not yet. You may not believe me, but I am sorry. I've never been more sorry for anything."

Flare rose and faded into the image of Dr. Henderson.

She smiled sadly. "Sweet dreams, Max. I'll send you and the Prophet to an eclipse that happened long ago. Like I did in your other lives. Only this time, you won't come back."

"Dr. Henderson." I strained against my bonds. "Dr. Henderson!"

She slid her hand over my eyes and then I opened them to countless snarling faces in a crowd. Screaming and cursing.

Ropes bit into my skin.

This was it.

I stared into the inky black eyes that had haunted me as long as I could remember. I was on the stage, bound to a tall post, like I had been so many times before, but this time I wouldn't slip back to reality. This was my reality.

Above me, the moon had nearly consumed the sun. A crowd spilled into the courtyard in front of me. And surrounding me stood ten figures wearing Prophet cloaks.

There would be no escaping if I changed my mind. Flare had convinced them all to join forces and kill me.

I focused on my arms to break my bonds anyway. Couldn't help it. I hated being unable to move. But my wrists only tugged uselessly at them. Power came at me from all angles. They were holding me down.

Fear sliced through me. It didn't matter that I'd chosen this. I couldn't shake it.

What kind of deal had Flare made?

"Kill her!" A woman shrieked and threw her shoe at the stage. "Kill the demon! Kill the bitch!"

The Prophet hypnotized the people with a speech so full of lies it made me sick.

And then he turned on me. Turned his spear in his hand as he stared into my eyes. Plunged the tip into my stomach.

Red hot fire seared my midsection.

The Prophet pushed the spear in deeper. I screamed and slammed my head back against the post.

"Vile demon." He stepped back and raised his spear to my face. Its sharp tip gleamed with blood. "Go back. Back to the pits of hell." Pain bit my neck. He pressed his spear carefully against my throat. "Spew another curse and I'll sever the head from your body."

"Kill her!" A man threw his mug of ale at me. It landed on the ground and splashed my ankles. "Kill the demon!"

"Kill her!" another shouted. "Drain her power! Bleed her and burn what remains! Hurry, before she devours our souls!"

"Kill! Kill! Kill!"

The voices swirled about me. Growing. I'd lived this so many times already and I was determined to do it one final time, but it felt different now. It felt so real.

The Prophet spat on my face. I grimaced in disgust. "We will show you no mercy." Blood beaded on my neck.

He slashed his spear and ripped my flesh open from my shoulder down my arm. Blood spilled onto the ground below. The crowd's roar swallowed my screams.

Stepping back, he raised up his bloodied spear against the dark sky. Black dripped from its tip.

"Oh gods, bleed this demon dry of the innocent."

He jabbed his blade deep into my thigh. My voice cracked as I cried out. The Prophet struck me again, and stabbed his spear straight through my shoulder, skewering me to the post behind me.

The pain consumed me. My head fell and I opened my eyes to my bound ankles. Strands of blood rushing down my legs. I would die here. I would die during the eclipse. I had so many times before but this time felt different. Felt final.

How could I leave Nash and Elsie?

"I'm human," I whispered. Tears poured down my face. My body trembled. It hurt so bad. Sobs shook my shoulders. Terror suffocated me. I didn't want to die. I wanted to stay with them. I wanted to stay with Nash. Not slip away for good this time. What if I didn't make it through the door to the afterlife?

"I'm not a demon!" I managed to raise my voice to a shout but no one could hear me. They'd deafened themselves by repeating the Prophet's lies.

He danced and chanted and kicked my blood up into the air from his feet.

Men and women and children fought to get close to the stage where they smeared their fingers in my blood and painted it in messy streaks along their faces. Some licked at their fingers, desperate for a taste of my power.

"He's fooling you!" My cry was lost in the chaos.

Coldness spread over me. My teeth chattered.

"I'm human! Just like you!" I didn't hide my weeping. "The gods are, too. They're humans sitting above, watching us burn. No better than the rest of us!"

"Blasphemy!" The Prophet spun his spear and raised his voice in a chant. But he couldn't come near me.

The burning I'd felt as a girl beneath the eclipse filled me again. If my power had been rendered impotent before, it had come rushing back at full force.

My father screamed in my ear. "Do you feel it?"

Both eclipses fully materialized now. Interwoven. I was myself in both places, both times. The child and the girl. The power that had once exploded from my body unraveled from me now, a long thread that twisted and turned between these two same moments. These two same moments in a very different time and place.

The force swept my blood from the stage and cast it over the people who cried in pain on the ground. It was only then I realized the power bursting from me was hurting them. A wave of it knocked everyone from their feet like it had back then. I was helpless to stop it.

"No!" I ripped at my restraints. Blood squirted from my wounds, flying into the force that was quickly killing them. It fueled it. It was my lifeblood, so close to being spent.

Like a star collapsing in on itself and exploding without control, death opened me up to the world, unleashing everything they'd put inside me.

I couldn't do it again, though. I couldn't slaughter these people.

"Live . . ." Despite the power, my words were only a whisper that rippled over the people. Soft and final. "Live . . ." I gave myself over to the power, funneling it not into the people, but into my effort to break into the afterlife and to save my memories. It took all my effort to contain myself and not accidentally hurt those surrounding me as my power swelled nearly out of control. They had to live. I wouldn't kill any other innocent people.

I was slipping away. Far, far away.

Live.

It was my last word. My last thought. And it carried out my last instinct, to reach my fingers into the seams of my world, and to pry it apart. There wasn't enough time for me to know if it had worked. If I could still open the door now that Henderson was back in control.

Beneath the eclipse, I died with the prayer on my lips. I died with nothing left to give. Died with no idea if I'd really go on to what came next.

Not until I opened my eyes to the face of a woman I'd never seen before. A face that looked kind and concerned. The pain was hardly more than a memory.

But it was a memory.

I'd escaped death and I'd kept my life for myself. I was in the afterlife.

CHAPTER THIRTY-SIX

I'd made it to the afterlife, whatever that really was. I wasn't trapped in an eternal slumber, at least. Unless, so much time had passed that my world had ended and I'd been salvaged from some kind of permanent death.

I shot up on lavender covers stretched tightly over the soft bed beneath me.

"Good morning." Soft eyes met mine. "Take it slow."

It wasn't Dr. Henderson, not unless she'd disguised herself. The smile was so genuine and kind, it was hard to imagine the god of my world managing it.

"Who are you?" I asked.

"That's what I wanted to ask you." Despite the concern on her expression, there was no malice in her voice. Any suspicion she had didn't seem to make her distrust me. I wasn't accustomed to such a trusting disposition. "Do you know where you are?"

The soft yellow walls closed in on me as I looked around. Natural light poured in from the floor-length windows and bathed the sparse room in so much life that it felt full even though there was nothing more than the bed I lay upon, the chair this woman sat on, and a nightstand with flowers.

When I didn't speak, the woman softened her voice even more. "Waking up can be hard on a person," she said. "My name is Dr. Drake. I'm here to help you."

I tensed at the title of doctor, and then winced, expecting the searing pain from my wounds. Except there was nothing. My injuries from the Prophet were entirely gone. My hands slid down my body, searching for the rips in my skin. Again, nothing.

"I'm healed," I said.

"In a way."

"I died." I didn't need confirmation. I remembered dying. Felt dead, like I'd left an entire life behind. Muted grief panged the hollow drum of my chest. I'd lost my life, my world. Lost Leif and Wren and little Rune. Lost Piercey and Elsie. Nash. Maybe I had a chance to win them back, but it didn't feel like it. Even though I'd chosen this and I planned to find a way back to my world, right now it felt like pure loss.

"Yes," Dr. Drake said. "Only people who have died come here. But you're safe."

"Here." I sat up, waiting to feel weakness or pain. I never did. "This is the afterlife."

"Yes. We call it different things for different people depending upon your cultural and religious beliefs. You came in unexpectedly. I didn't receive any information on you and I don't take memories without permission. It would help me a great deal if you could share a few things with me."

"First I need to know who you are." I stared into her eyes.

"I'm the supervisor of this realm of the afterlife. I help people wake up from death and serve as a guide for them as they live here."

I'd known that when I came here, it would be impossible for me to know for sure whether I could trust people, and that at the end of the day, I had to go with my instinct. Just like when I chose to ally with Nash.

"My name is Max. I come from a world that's at war and I have people there who need me to find my way back."

Even though I'd kept my memories in the afterlife, this place had a numbing effect on me, and I hadn't even realized until this moment, when the look of pain in her eyes drew upon my own grief lying beneath the surface within me. My emotions were tamer here. My memories in the backdrop. And Dr. Drake likely pitied me for thinking I could return home.

"I see which world you came from. From what I read, it does seem you've been through a great deal."

I shifted. "How much time has passed since I died?"

"Six days. It takes a person time to adjust to death. I woke you up slowly. Time is the same here for you as it is in your home world, so long as you want it to be. I can slow it for you if you'd like."

"Yes, please. Make it as slow as you can." Relief soothed the fire within me. She could be lying, but if she wasn't, it meant that my plan worked. I'd escaped from my world and remembered my life in time to help everyone.

Her brows piqued. "You don't want to tell me more. I felt that from you. You're afraid that you can't trust me." She eased a little closer. "It's okay. I would feel the same. Do you want to hear more about me and this world? Would that help?"

My eyes snapped to her. I searched for any sign of evil lurking within her. This was how Dr. Henderson should have been. Kind and wise and caring. I couldn't help but fear that this woman was only a more conniving version of the god lording over my world. Maybe she, too, had been cursed by death and lost her way. Only she was just better at covering it up.

"Max?"

"You're too kind."

Dr. Drake crossed one leg over the other. "Kindness is very important in my job. I usher people from death into a new life. I help them find peace."

"Peace and death don't go together. I don't think I could feel peace here."

"People normally don't remember their life. Not at first. The pain isn't so great and so peace is easier to find. It's very odd that you do. You traveled here unauthorized. You haven't been processed. It's very unique."

"Why do you steal people's memories?"

She sat back. "People can remember any time they want to. It's too traumatic to wake up here, remembering everything, and then figure out what's going on."

"Or they're too hard to control. They might figure out you're keeping them in this little bubble called 'the afterlife' while there's an entire digital universe out there."

Dr. Drake paused. "You know quite a bit."

"I do. Enough to know that stealing memories and saying people can have them back if they want is manipulative." The thought of Nash's arms around me flooded me with grief. "They don't know what it is they're missing. If they did, they'd want it back."

"They do have impressions of their life. Feelings they had. The sense of loved ones. The sense of memories they would rather forget. Each person has their own path to enlightenment. Some never want it. They are content to live here forever. But as soon as someone wants to remember everything, they can. And if they want to learn the truth, that this world is created and there's more out there, they can. They can leave the afterlife and join the rest of society."

I straightened. "Really?"

"Yes. This isn't a prison. It's a safe place to transition from the physical world and the short life of the flesh to the digital world and the eternity of our lives here."

As much as I didn't want to, I saw the logic. "I think it's better to remember, even if it hurts."

"We've tried that before. This intervention came about after a great deal of studying. Our current system was voted upon solely by people who currently live in the afterlife and who reached enlightenment and joined the rest of the Kethios. I don't make the rules. Although, I do agree with them. However, some share your views. Each person is unique."

I wanted to hate her so badly, because she shared the doctor in Dr. Henderson, and because she clearly was a part of the society that chose to make my world into an experiment. But my heart was slipping and I'd always lived by instinct.

"You care." I swallowed hard. "You care about the people here."

"I wouldn't do this job otherwise. I can have any kind of life I want. I chose this. I've lived a very long time, but I'm still a person. We all are. We're not so different from you. Only older."

"More powerful."

"There is power that comes with knowledge and access. Experience. So, yes."

"You're a god."

She quieted. "Some do choose to view me that way."

"In a way, people evolved into gods. Do you think some of those gods could be evil?"

The suspicion in her eyes grew. "Max, this is very important. You must have learned about our reality from someone. Was it a person like me?"

"You mean Dr. Henderson?"

It looked like she stopped breathing. "Do you know her?"

"I don't know her well." The lie burned on my lips. "But I am skeptical of people with so much power."

"Perhaps because you have power in your world. We allow people privacy, so I can't see everything about your world, but I do see that you were designated as one of the one percent to receive the neural implant. Did you know that's where your power came from?"

"Yes." I studied her reaction, probing her for authenticity. "I know your people created my world as a simulated experiment."

"Dr. Henderson is not supposed to tell you that."

I cast my gaze out the window, uncertain of how to move forward from here. I was playing a dangerous game. The most dangerous yet. If I didn't stop Dr. Henderson, she may never release the people I loved from the simulation. She could reset the world hundreds more times and destine the people I loved to endless versions of her hell. Even if she didn't do that, she'd wage wars against anyone who stood in her way. Nash, Wren, and Leif were warriors. They wouldn't stop fighting until they were dead. Dead and never allowed into the afterlife.

What if I was trapped here forever without them?

A shaky breath broke from my lips. The distant emotion welled within me again, within reach. "I can't mess this up." I squeezed my eyes shut. "Somehow, I find myself with a power no one in my world has ever had right now. What I say here . . . I'm deciding the fate of my world."

"You have a power that no one in any simulation has ever had. Souls are not released from the simulated worlds until the experiment ends. You're the first one to come here while it is ongoing and to have all your memories. I understand your trepidation."

"Are you a part of your council?"

"Supervisors are not on the council. Some of us continue to work our way up from this position to the council. Some stay here. This is the final step before reaching it. It is a very influential position, but neither I nor Dr. Henderson are part of the council."

I chewed the inside of my cheek. "You talked about privacy. Is our talk private?"

"Absolutely. Everything here is entirely private. You give consent for anything to be shared."

"Even if I tell you something you feel must be shared?"

"Yes. We don't have danger in the Kethios, Max. Privacy is of great concern, however. In such a connected existence, it takes great work to protect that freedom."

"Do you know Dr. Henderson?"

"We've met. I haven't spoken to her since the experiments began. We didn't see eye to eye on them."

I leaned forward. "You disagree with the experiments?"

"I do. I want to help people in the physical world as much as anyone else, but I can't justify manipulating people's souls in a simulation just because in the end it creates less suffering. How can a peaceful society create suffering?"

At least one of the gods made sense, unless she was trying to fool me. "Isn't it also wrong to leave people in the physical world to suffer?"

"Yes. That doesn't mean we should create another wrong."

"Apparently you're in the minority."

"I am. Some think that because I have spent so much time in the afterlife that I've forgotten suffering. I haven't. I'm reminded of it every day as I usher new souls into this life and as I watch them on their journey here. This power we have is sacred. It should never be used against someone."

Grief twisted my heart so terribly that I suddenly longed to draw her into a hug as if she was one of my own people. My voice came out quiet. "Your council let death into a deathless world. Instead of gods of life, you became gods of death. My world has paid the price."

Worry pinched Dr. Drake's lips. "I know you must be afraid to tell me what happened, Max. I have no way of proving to you that I'm trustworthy. I'm guessing, though, that you came here for a reason. So, I hope you can take a chance on me. I want to help."

I looked down to cover the tears that tempted my eyes. "Dr. Henderson has been corrupted." My stomach tightened. "I don't know when it happened or if she's always been this way. Only that she's fallen into darkness."

"She was a pure soul once. That much I can say for certain. Her fall must have happened during this experiment." Dr. Drake paused. "Can I trust you with something sensitive?"

"Yes. Please."

"She suffered a loss a very long time ago, during a time when so few died. Even later, when she was reunited with her child here, I sensed the pain that lingered. You wouldn't imagine that there could be any pain in such a perfect world. There is, at least, when we choose to remember it. I wonder if the loss made her susceptible."

The thought of Flare carrying Elsie away filled me with revulsion. "Loss doesn't have to corrupt a spirit."

"No, it doesn't."

"I did come here for a reason. I came to share my story. The story of my world. Except that telling you could end my world. If I had any other option, I would take it. I don't. I'm powerless. So, please don't betray me."

Dr. Drake took my hand gently. "You do have power, Max. I see it in you." She smiled. "Our system does as well. You were marked as a potential candidate for leadership here in this universe. You and a friend whose name I can't see until they come here."

"Someone with power?"

"Yes."

Piercey. I closed my eyes. "It would make sense that he would be. Not me. I'm impetuous and angry."

"Is that why you're here and not him?"

I smiled. "Maybe."

"Well, you weren't marked as individuals, but rather as a team. Together, your wisdom and courage make you rare souls who we might choose to recruit. It's very special."

"Would you have known I was a candidate if I never came here?"

"No. Only once you're in my system. I only know about your friend because I see that you're a potential team, not individual."

Flare's words ran through my mind. She'd trapped me in the simulation so I couldn't leave the afterworld. "Could Dr. Henderson trap someone in the simulation and conceal the record of them?"

Dr. Drake drew back. "That would be worse than murder."

"Is it possible? Is it possible because your people are so certain of themselves that they think you'll all stay pure?"

Understanding lit her eyes. At least, I hoped that was the look I was seeing. "We've evolved, Max. There's never been a need for precautions against crimes and evils. I'm sure if she had malice against someone, she could do that, though."

I buried my head in my hands, temples throbbing with each heartbeat. Dr. Henderson had planned to leave me dead in the simulation forever. Probably Piercey, too. It was the only way to ensure that we never recovered our memories in the afterlife. "Would Dr. Henderson know that Piercey and I were potential candidates?"

"Yes. As a supervisor, it's her job to watch over people like you who the computer identifies."

I bit off an angry chuckle. "She wanted me dead. Permanently dead. Because I knew too much." I lifted my hand to Dr. Drake. "Take it all. That woman cannot be trusted with my world. I don't know if I can trust you, but I have learned sometimes it is too dangerous not to trust the person who you need to trust."

She reached for my hand. "You've shared memories before. I give you my word I will do right by you."

Dr. Drake took my hand in her soft one. Her presence was so inviting that when we connected, I easily let all of myself slip away to her entirely. I couldn't even hold on to the fear that this was a mistake.

When she released me, sorrow filled her eyes.

"You're self-aware. You knew you were living in a simulation and you tried to make it here. This has never happened before, Max." Tears sprinkled onto her cheeks. Her voice was breathy and urgent. "We must take this to the council. This is worse than you know."

"What if they shut down our world? Dr. Henderson said our experiment is unethical, so if it doesn't yield results, it's only ethical to end it."

"Dr. Henderson has devolved. Her words are not to be trusted. This is evidence that the experiments were a mistake, a terrible mistake, and that we must make corrections. I know you've seen only evil from our world. That is only one grain of sand in a world of goodness."

I rubbed my chest. Sharing with her had brought it all back, so it couldn't be numbed. With my people on the forefront of my mind, I felt so close to the life I had just lost, that no matter how urgent this business was, my mind clouded with grief. I bent forward, memories zapping through me like shots of lightning.

"Hey . . ." Dr. Drake touched my back. "It's hitting you. Breathe through it."

"I don't have time for this."

"You do. Time is relative. It hasn't passed in your world since we paused the flow of time here. We have time for you."

I clutched my chest. I needed to ask, but I was too afraid of the answer. "Will I . . ." Sobs gripped my tight shoulders and shook them. "Will I ever get to go home to them?"

Dr. Drake's silence carved down my spine. When she spoke, her voice was heavy. "I don't know of any way to go home, Max. You died in your world. The physics of that world match the physical world. There's no way to resurrect the dead."

I scrambled off the bed, my legs desperate to run, though I had nowhere to go. Fear exploded in my mind. Dr. Drake stumbled out of my way as I pried the window open and clambered out. I landed on soft sand and sprinted forward, sliding with each step. Ocean waves rolled against the shore. I stopped before reaching the lapping water and fell onto my hands and knees. Fell and wept until I couldn't even utter a sound.

Her hand came to my back again and warmth flowed from it, easing me to sleep.

I tightened my arms around myself, back in the yellow room on the bed, tears filling my eyes again. "I'm not ready to leave them."

Though my emotions had been dulled again, the grief still tinged my thoughts. "They'll be here one day."

"They won't remember anything."

"It's very traumatic remembering your life. The memories come back when people are ready. But sometimes seeing a person you knew can help spark it. You never know. Nash may remember you quickly when he comes. Usually parents remember their children right away. Sometimes it's the same for lovers."

I didn't want to grieve. I finally had reached the gods. Gods who might be able to help. Right now, I didn't need to worry about Nash remembering one day. I needed to help him. It didn't matter that Dr. Drake said I had time. I had to see this through before I could do anything else, including mourn the life I'd lost.

"I can't fall apart now." I sat up and clutched my aching chest. "Dr. Henderson is in control of our world and she's fucked up. I have to help them. I can't leave them trapped with her."

"We'll report it. Right now."

"Who do we tell?"

Dr. Drake sighed. "I don't like to give so much information at once. You're already overwhelmed."

"Please. Please, the only thing I care about right now are my people."

"We could go to the Collective. They control forty-nine percent of the voting rights for the council. It's the easiest place to start."

"Okay." I nodded. "Who are they? What's that mean?"

"This is so much to explain." She pushed her dark hair behind her ears. "In the highest dimension, you experience all of time and space, as one. It's like you become one with our universe. And the people who want to live in that plane are unified as well. Collective consciousness."

I'd told her that I could handle it, but I couldn't wrap my mind around anything she just said. Piercey would have been all over this. "They're like one giant mind?"

"Yes. They have all the wisdom of humankind."

My breathing sharpened. "And they know about my world?"

She hesitated and then nodded. "The experiments never would have been approved without their vote."

I did slam my fist this time, hard against the bed. "All of the wisdom of humankind and they dreamed up this shitstorm?" I doubled over. "I just want to go home to Nash and Elsie."

"I can ease the pain," Dr. Drake said. "I can take it all away."

"The pain will keep me focused."

"Right now, it's going to make you lose your mind. Let me."

I closed my eyes. The acute panic and grief distanced from my mind, as if it had been locked away in a room inside me. "How did you do that?"

"We can do anything here, Max. Your world had to follow the natural laws of the universe for validity. There's no reason for that here. We can simulate anything."

"This is a simulation, too?"

"Everything is a simulation now, really. Except for the people still evolving out in the physical world."

I had so many questions, but with my grief now muted, I had the ability to focus on what mattered. I couldn't squander that. The haze of death cleared from my mind. "I know it probably doesn't make sense to you, because my world isn't even real, but I don't want it to end. I can't fail at this."

"I do understand. And it is real because you're real. It's your experience. I told you . . . I've lived so many lives, and only one of them in the physical world. Every life I lived is as real to me as the first."

I swallowed hard. "Do you really believe that?"

"Yes. You know, my world where I was first born is gone now." She smiled. "But it still matters to me as much as it did then. All the things I saw, the good, the horrible, it matters that it happened. For the Collective, my world exists today. All time exists as one. Every day you lived in your world was real and will forever be a part of the Collective. They can't access individual memories for privacy, but the sum of your existence is with them. Now it will forever be a part of at least one person's memory. Yours."

"I need to speak to the Collective. I'm going to ask them to send me back."

Dr. Drake shook her head. "We talked about this. They can't send you back. Your world operates under physical laws."

"Dr. Henderson's avatar doesn't."

Her eyes widened. "You want an avatar?"

"If she gets one, why can't I? It's my world. I'm the one who was unfairly experimented on. They owe me the chance to clean up the mess they made. If the individual is important, then the Collective has to see that my perspective is critical."

"We can't let what happened with Dr. Henderson happen to other supervisors."

"I'll petition them to leave our worlds alone. I used to hate the silence of the gods. Dr. Henderson showed me how much worse it can be when they listen."

"Let's go for a walk and calm your spirit before we see them."

Crystal clear water lapped over my feet as I walked along the shore of a gentle ocean. Dr. Drake walked with me.

"Dr. Henderson said Nash and I died as babies," I said.

"You did. Your world is populated by young souls who died as infants during a certain time period. It's best for the subjects to actually be from the same world and time. For validity."

"Validity. Of course."

She smiled. "You were born on Earth in 2027."

"And Nash?"

"I don't have access to his record, but it would have been within a three-decade span of your life."

Warm sand squished between my toes. "Why babies?"

"It's our policy that people live at least one life to adulthood, so that you can develop properly. Normally, we would place infants and children together in a simulated world just like their own. Of course, your world was different."

"Lucky us." I stuck my hands in my pockets, because, apparently, I had pockets in the afterlife. "Why didn't you just run simulations with fake people?"

"You can't fake consciousness. Either you have it or you don't. And conscious beings are very hard to predict. For valid results, we needed conscious people. The argument was that your life in the experimental worlds would probably be of a similar quality to your natural world."

"Except we don't get our lives reset in an actual world."

"That's true. Dr. Henderson has been lying in her reports."

A sliver of pain managed to slip into my heart. "I just want to go back home."

We walked quietly for some time.

"Am I healed enough to see the Collective now?"

"Already? You're strong-willed. Not everyone can come back from the afterlife, you know."

"When will you ask them to meet with me?"

"Already did." She smiled. "Come on. They're waiting."

"Thank you." I swallowed hard, palms sweaty. Time for another battle.

CHAPTER THIRTY-SEVEN

Dr. Drake and I stood before a window that stretched from the floor to the ceiling and opened to light blue water. Light filtered through from somewhere above I couldn't see, catching just right here and there so some patches looked teal.

"This is it?" I asked.

"Collective consciousness." Dr. Drake touched the glass. "You have the chance to teach the Collective something." Her voice was as tender as the hand she placed on my shoulder. "So be nice."

I breathed in deeply, staring into the empty room. "Why bother with this visual?"

"We need something. Religious people didn't want it to feel the same as praying. But how can you visualize the oneness of the multiverse? It isn't possible. But water is life, water transforms. Water can drip as individual droplets or crash together as raging waves. It can span the greatest depths."

"Okay. I guess." I shifted, strangely uncomfortable by the thought. "Can they hear me?"

"Yes."

I crossed my arms, looking down. "I'm here on behalf of my world. Not the one I was originally born into, but the one I came to know. The one you made for me." I looked into the blue. "It's all we know. So before I tell you more, I'm asking you to let the world continue and to grant the people the right to never be shut down."

Vibrations rippled the water before me. My eyes widened. I heard a melding of voices, young and old.

"We're sorry you have suffered for us."

Anger stirred within me. "Be nice," I breathed to myself.

"We're sorry we have not yet found a better way. The simulations have helped us get close to mastering evolution. Very close."

I straightened. "Does that mean you no longer need worlds like mine?"

"The data is valuable. We would like to continue gathering it."

"So, you'll let us live in our worlds?"

"Yes. The simulations are giving us billions of lifetimes."

Heat fueled my core, as fiery as when my power would fill me. "Don't you feel bad for what you've done? You created a world just to experiment on us. Gave us immense powers that we weren't ready for and then let us kill each other with them."

"Without the experiments, young worlds in the natural world would continue to suffer indefinitely. Now, we have proven what the best methods for helping to develop more peacefully are. However, with it, simulated worlds are suffering. We grieve the decision but we have mixed feelings on whether we regret it."

"It's not right . . . What you did isn't right."

"It is the last great evil of humankind. The last great evil of evolution." A pause. I'd imagine it was for me, not the Collective. "The reincarnation of your souls in the simulation had the same effect as if you'd lived in the natural. We bear the weight of the suffering. We bear the weight of our evil."

Tears sprang into my eyes. "Your words, many as they may be with so many speaking them at once, mean nothing."

"We are sorry for what we have done to you and your people. We only wanted you to live and for us to learn from your lives."

"Well." I bit off the word. "Despite the wisdom you claim to have, you overlooked an incredibly crucial risk. If you can guarantee that my world will continue without interference, I will share it with you. Dr. Drake told me that you don't get all of the information from our world without permission. You rely on data compiled by the computer. I'll give you all my memories, if you can make this promise to me."

"We promise. Please, share with us."

That seemed too easy. When I paused, the Collective seemed to sense my distrust.

"We're not looking to hurt you. We truly want what is best for you. If you, someone who lived in your world, wants it to continue despite its problems, then we must trust that it is only right to allow it to continue."

I pressed my palm against the glass. "Creating unethical human experiments compromises your social evolution. Did you never consider these risks?"

"We countered any risk of corruption with lifetimes of evolution and ethical mastery. Yet, you believe that despite this, we've failed?"

"Being capable of unethical experiments requires that you are unethical. There's no getting around that."

"It isn't so black and white. After making the decision, everyone involved in the experiments lived multiple more lives in simulations and were tested. Everyone was pure."

"Not everyone is pure anymore. Dr. Henderson devolved. Who knows how many supervisors this has happened to." The fury of my death rushed out of me. "That's why you people should have never played god with us."

"Share with us. We will listen to you."

I let my life rush into them as it had with Piercey and Dr. Drake. This time, I felt hollow when I was done, as though I had given away everything I'd ever had.

"Do you see?" I asked.

The voices of the Collective leaked out in a quiet and sorrowful moan. "We see." The words echoed, quieter and quieter, until all was silent.

"Dr. Henderson had me murdered. I believe she planned to trap me in the simulation forever. If I hadn't figured out how to escape, I'd be trapped there, dead. I know for certain that she has abused her power in my world."

"We did not expect these results."

I ran my hand over my mouth. "She sentenced us to lives we couldn't remember living. You left us with her. You placed us under untested conditions while she refused to intervene despite the dire consequences, all for the sake of your experiment. For the validity." Slips couldn't happen here. Even so, I feared that I'd open my eyes to the little red boots I'd worn as a child during the eclipse. That I'd be trapped forever in that moment, seeing the villager's bodies crumple to the ground like I'd sucked the life from them.

I didn't slip. But I was still there in my heart, beneath the dark of the eclipse, with my father listless at my feet. With his words hanging in my mind. Even after all these years, these lifetimes, still I didn't understand how he could make me kill those people and abandon me by dying with them. How could anyone do that?

"You're as guilty as my father." They'd know what the words meant. "Do you think that making an afterlife for the people I killed makes up for watching them die? You gave me such incredible power when I was a child and didn't show me how to use it. How can someone that has so much knowledge, so much power, still not have a better way?"

Their silence tore through me. I beat my fist against the window.

"Answer me!"

"We're trying to find a better way. We are not yet perfect. Even with how many people were injured in the simulations, it cannot touch the number which will be saved from that suffering from now. However, there were even more dire consequences than we had imagined."

I stared hard into the emptiness of the room. A lifetime of rage boiled over. These were ridiculous excuses. They really believed they couldn't find another way to gain the data they needed? "Fuck you! Fuck you from each and every one of us in every life we lived in the shit world you made for us."

Dr. Drake stepped toward me, lifting her hand. "Max!"

"Let her speak," the Collective said. "She deserves it."

"All the beauty," I said, "All the wonderful things like love." I lifted my hand. "It was worth the suffering. But that doesn't justify what you let happen to us either. So sit with that for eternity, assholes."

"How can we do better by your world?"

I'd almost let my anger blind me to the most important things I needed to say. "If you want to collect data on our world, fine. You've already set your experiments in motion. But do not intervene again unless people from my world approve it. Piercey can help create a fair system for evaluating your actions. Do not experiment on us. Do not manipulate our worlds. Make your supervisors simply watch."

"In your memories, you didn't like the silence of the gods. And yet now, you would rather that we ignore the prayers of the people?"

"I would, because your answers to our prayers, when you bother to answer, are deranged. Monitor us. Fine. But no one should be able to intervene in our world again like Dr. Henderson has."

"We will collect information from our supervisors and consider this."

I pressed my hands against the warm glass. "I lost my life because of your experiments going wrong. I want an avatar, just like Dr. Henderson has."

"Dr. Henderson lived many lives in preparation for being supervisor and having an avatar, so she could make ethical decisions. Even she fell into evil. You aren't ready."

"I don't need any new powers or any of the responsibilities Dr. Henderson has. Make my avatar exactly the same as I was before I died. I just need a body to take back to my world."

Dr. Drake nodded at me, smiling gently.

"Please." I wiped my tears. "I may be a young soul. I may be angry. But there's something inside of me that made the computer identify me as someone who could make a difference. So, listen to me. Let me go back to my world and I promise I will return one day with answers about how you can make things better for the people you experimented on."

I didn't like the silence that followed. Why was I asking? Begging? Sure, they could refuse, but I should stop acting like they were doing me a favor when their supervisor murdered me. With my eyes narrowing, I spoke in a low voice.

"Do you know what it's like to die? Can you even imagine how it feels for your life to be stolen? To be bled out on a stage while a crowd of ignorant people try to take your power for themselves? You owe me a body. Give me what I'm owed or you prove that you still aren't better."

"We can agree to this on one condition. You shared all of your memories with us. Allow us to watch over you for the rest of your life in your world. We'll give you reasonable privacy, but we want to see your decisions, and to look at your world through your eyes."

I hesitated. "Privacy?"

"Yes, we can filter out such things."

I rubbed the back of my neck. "Okay. As long as you filter things." My chest tightened as I realized what they had just said. "Wait, you'll really give me an avatar?"

"You're right that you deserve to return to your world. This is the only method available to us."

Tears flooded my eyes. Right now, everyone I loved had lived for nearly a week with me gone. They surely thought I was never returning. How must Nash feel? Elsie? Leif, Wren, and Rune? My chest ached with the horror of leaving them behind. I had to return.

"Is there anything else, Max?"

I struggled to keep my voice from breaking from the emotion. "Take away the power. It's only hurting people."

"If we alter substantial elements of your world, it may cause irreparable harm. If you want to keep your world, you must keep it as it is."

"What will you do about Dr. Henderson?"

"We have a great deal to investigate. We must understand what happened to her and if it has happened to other supervisors. We will look into how she hid this from us and exactly what she has done in your world. And we will rehabilitate her."

"Then you're taking her out of my world immediately, right?"

"We already attempted it as soon as you shared your memories. Dr. Henderson helped create our digital universe and understands it too well. She's woven herself into the fabric of your world."

Dread buzzed through my body. "Does she know you tried to remove her?"

"She shouldn't. We merely studied the code and determined that we may not be able to remove her without damaging your world."

"What happens if her avatar is destroyed?"

"We cannot condone murder and allow you to kill Dr. Henderson."

I snorted. "She's in my world. Mine. Our justice will rule. Self-determination, remember? I'll give her the chance to leave peacefully."

I expected them to argue; instead, they only paused. "Avatars follow physical laws. She would need to create a new one if hers were destroyed."

Where was Piercey when I needed him? He'd be able to genuinely tell the Collective he would go to Dr. Henderson in peace. I drew upon how I knew he'd feel, sensing him through our connected memories, and tried to have his heart for this moment. "I swear that I will do everything I can to be peaceful with Dr. Henderson."

Dr. Drake stepped forward. "I'll go into the control room and convince her to leave Max's world if all else fails. I can try to keep her from creating another avatar."

"What if she won't?" Fear tightened my voice.

"As a last result, we'll force her out, and attempt to repair any damage done."

"Am I authorized to negotiate with her?" Dr. Drake asked.

"Yes. Bear in mind the seriousness of her sickness."

She dipped her head. "I will."

"Thank you for sharing with us, Max. I hope that we will find a better path as we move forward. We will immediately implement security measures now that we know our supervisors are at risk of devolving."

I settled my head against the window, afraid to be finished. Afraid there would be something I'd later regret not saying. "I feel like I need to apologize for my rage so you'll grant my request. But it's how I feel. I don't think I should hide the suffering and pain of my people from you. So please, honor my request anyway."

Maybe in my next life I'd be ready to grow out of my anger. For now, I held it close as my longest and truest friend.

Because there was no way in hell Dr. Henderson was leaving my world alive. She needed to experience the death she'd forced upon us all.

I would kill her and she would never return.

CHAPTER THIRTY-EIGHT

A re you sure about this?"

I cocked my eyebrow at Dr. Drake. Was that a serious question? "Yes. Absolutely. Let's do this, now. I need to get back to my people as soon as possible."

"You can take more time to recover from what you've been through. You experienced death, Max."

"I'm ready to go home. Come on."

I tapped my fingers against the table. We'd just learned that the Collective gave all the worlds like mine the right to continue without being shut down while they conducted investigations into the supervisors.

I breathed slowly and met Dr. Drake's eyes. "Thank you for your help. When I come back, I'll remember what you did for my world."

"Be careful, Max. You've already felt so much pain. If you lose this body, they won't make you another."

"I will." I breathed in deeply. "You said Flare was with the Prophet in the temple. Are you sure there's no sign of her leaving?"

"I'm sure. I'll pull you back into this room after you confront her. If she can't be reasoned with, let me take care of her."

Reason with her. Ha! I had no intention of reasoning with Flare.

Dr. Drake took my hands and looked into my eyes with what truly must have been the look of a god. So full of wisdom and grace.

"Max," she said. "You have many lives to live. You're so young. Remember that what you do matters, in every life and every world."

I squeezed her hands. "See you on the other side, Dr. Drake." I lay down and closed my eyes, ready to wake up back home and deal with Flare according to my rules.

Dr. Drake did not disappoint. I woke up at the Door of the Gods with the promise that when I walked out, I would be wherever I wanted to be in the world. And I knew exactly where that was.

Dying hadn't been easy. Coming back to life wouldn't be either. I hesitated before the door, realizing I was trembling.

"It'll be fine," I whispered to myself. "Be strong."

Taking in a deep breath, I lifted my chin and stepped out of the door into the courtyard at the Sacred School. The smell of hickory and grass filled my senses. Home. For the first time, this had become home to me.

I wanted to run for Nash, but first I needed to see what was happening. They had all been through so much already. I had to be careful.

Dew wet my boots as I tiptoed into the yard. The sun had just risen. Quietly, I picked my way to the door and opened it slowly so it didn't make any noise. Silent steps carried me to the residential hall and into Nash's suite.

I steadied my breathing as I slid the door shut and crept to the bedroom. Standing in the doorway, my heart pooled in my stomach. Nash slept in the middle of the bed with Elsie bundled up in his arms.

If I was careful, I could wake Nash without Elsie stirring. But I didn't know how to do this without giving Nash a heart attack. Maybe I should have waited until he woke up.

My heart stormed. I couldn't.

Morning sun shone on the ground beneath the curtain. I stood in it, staring for a moment. His curls were a mess, his beard growing out, and the bed was covered in Elsie's toys and clothes. Imagining him here for this past week, likely more certain with each passing hour that I'd never return, grieved me deeply. My heart twisted as I slid into the bed beside him and placed my hand upon his heart, settling my lips against his ear.

"Nash," I whispered. "Wake up."

His eyes opened. I rubbed my palm gently against his chest, wanting so badly to erase the grief of the last week. For a moment, he didn't move, and then his eyes lowered to my hand, his fingers barely grazing mine.

"I'm dreaming." It came on a breath. Pain contorted his expression as he turned his face toward me and his glassy eyes met mine. "Don't make me wake up."

"Then walk with me," I whispered, kissing beneath his ear. "Quietly."

It wouldn't hurt him to believe this was a dream for a few minutes. I took his hand and pushed a pillow against Elsie's back when he stood.

Nash didn't move when I tugged his hand. His eyes were wide and his mouth open.

"It's okay," I whispered.

His hand was limp in mine. I led him out of the bedroom, down the hall, to the courtyard door, and out beneath the paleness of the morning sky.

"Shh," I said as we walked for the large tree where we could hide.

He looked like he sleepwalked as he followed me. I turned to face him, hot tears sliding down my cheeks.

"Nash." My voice hardly worked.

"This can't be real." Emotion shook his voice, his broad shoulders. "We waited as long as we could with your body. It's gone now. You're gone."

"Nash, this is real." I took his hands, keeping my voice calm and gentle. "I was with the gods."

"I've lost my mind, haven't I?"

"Okay . . . Okay, sit down." I tugged him toward the ground. "Come on."

I sat on my knees, close now. This time, he really looked at me, and I saw all the agony that had twisted him up. My heart broke. I had done this to him. I had left him.

"You feel me." I wrapped my arms around him and drew his head to my shoulder. "That's all that matters. I'm here."

Nash grasped me weakly. "You went unconscious. Dr. Henderson forced you into the white room. Piercey couldn't stop her. And then we found your body abandoned in the snow outside, bloody and cut badly." His arms tightened around me until it was hard for me to breathe. "Flare stood in the distance while I picked you up."

I ran my fingers through his tangled hair. "I'm here now. The gods showed me favor."

Nash dipped his hand into his shirt and pulled up the black burial beads of the dead. "We returned you to the gods. I buried you, Max. This . . ." He squeezed the necklace in his palm. "This is all that remains of you."

My stomach revolted at the beads. "They gave me a new body." I wanted to rip the necklace from him and throw it off a cliff. Shivers cut down my spine. That had once been me?

"I can't let myself believe this is real. It'll hurt too badly when I wake up." He drew back and looked at me, leaving the beads hanging at his chest. "I can't lose you again."

"The gods gave me an avatar like Flare's. You aren't losing me."

We sat together until Nash had calmed enough that I thought he could walk. I wasn't sure that he believed any of this was real. I would have thought I was losing my mind, too.

Once we were inside, I nodded toward the residential hall. "Wake them up. I'm afraid I'll put them all in shock like I did with you."

I twisted the bottom of my shirt and looked at each person as we sat on the grass together. Trish and her husband had taken Elsie away so she wouldn't see me yet. But everyone else was with me. And no one spoke.

Might as well start. I breathed in deeply. "I have no idea how to help you all cope with this except to be honest. I'm here to stay."

Nash leaned against his knees, holding his head. "I'm afraid I'm hallucinating that all of you are seeing her, too."

"We're all hallucinating if you are," Leif said.

"Flare took me to the eclipse," I said. "One in the past. I died and woke up in the next life."

Wren scooted closer and turned my hand over so she could trace her fingers along my palm. "You feel normal."

"I confronted the gods and convinced them to give me an avatar like Dr. Henderson's."

"Why did the gods agree to this?" Piercey asked, the first time he had spoken since seeing me.

"They apologized for the suffering they had caused and let me return because I only died due to Dr. Henderson."

"As a god? Have they returned you to us in god-form?" Leif asked.

"No. Besides, they don't see themselves as gods."

Nash lowered his hands, the look in his eye changing. His voice cracked. "This is real."

"Yes. It's real. It—"

Nash hooked his arm around my waist and dragged me down to the ground against him, his embrace strong, desperate. The shock had passed and I had him here, with me. Rolling me onto my back, he kissed the side of my face, my jaw, my lips. A laugh loosened the tension in my chest.

"You're here." He kissed me hard. "You came back to me."

His fingers dug into my sides like if he didn't keep a hold of me, I might slip away. It didn't matter who saw. Couldn't matter. We'd lost each other and now we were together again.

"We're still here," Leif said. "In case you give a shit."

I smiled as Nash's lips pressed against mine again.

They laughed and teased and I hardly heard a word of it. Soon we would need to fight the hardest battle of our lives. There had to be a moment to be reunited.

I knelt on the hill where I'd gathered with Nash, Piercey, and Val the first time we battled the Prophet when we were freeing my people. It felt like such a long time ago now.

Even though I'd agreed to this plan, worry sat like lead in my gut. Wren and Leif had returned to our village to gather our warriors to march to the Prophet's village, because when this was over, there would be chaos to continue. Piercey had sent word to his graduates, but I knew they wouldn't make it in time.

It should have only been me here, risking a life I'd already lost once. Instead, Nash and Piercey both knelt beside me as we eyed the Prophet's village.

I glanced over to the man who I had never expected to fall for and wondered how we'd ended up here. Only hours ago, he'd been silenced by the shock of my return. It didn't take long after I announced my plans that he quickly found his voice.

"We already lost you once," Nash had said. "You've just returned. Let us handle Flare and the Prophet. Piercey will call on his graduates and this time they will act because you carry the gods' favor. Rest and recover from what you've been through."

"We can't wait for them. Flare may already know I'm here. I've waited too long as it is by talking to all of you. Now's the time. Piercey can gather everyone, but I'm going ahead."

Nash had clutched my wrist and drawn me close. "Not without me."

"You don't have power. What can you do?"

I hadn't meant any cruelty by the words, but it had been clear from the pain in his eye that the words had cut him deeply. How must he have felt finding my body and grieving my death? The powerlessness surely haunted him now.

"I can fight." His voice had rumbled deeply. "Piercey and I will partner together again like we did before. Take us with you."

"I've never traveled like that before."

"Excuses. You can do this, Max. You will not fight this battle alone." Nash had clutched the back of my head and bent to press his forehead against mine. "Do not deny me this battle."

How could I when I would never forgive him for doing the same to me? "I'm scared of what could happen to you."

"Then you know how I feel about you."

The conversation kept playing through my mind without end. I hadn't thought I would be successful in bringing the three of us to this place, but Piercey had focused on me, trying to lend me his own power. I'd managed to teleport all three of us to the village.

The Prophet had been training and preparing and I knew Flare was with him, so it wasn't ideal for only the three of us to fight. We really needed more allies, but I couldn't afford to wait another moment. What if Flare knew that I'd returned? What if she knew the Collective wanted her out of this world?

There had been a time for waiting and that had passed.

"I'm ready," I said, rising. "It's time to end this."

"The Prophet and Flare won't be alone," Piercey said. "The disciples will be ready for us this time."

I nodded. "We'll have to kill them all. Together."

Nash held my stare, eyes determined. "Together."

"I'm not wasting time being evasive when I believe Flare will already know we're coming," I said. "We move fast for Flare and the Prophet."

"I'll focus on clearing a path and covering the two of you." Piercey nodded at me. "Max, give them all you have."

"Thank you," I said, my eyes on his. We had always made a good team. When this was over, I'd have to tell him about how we were identified by the gods as potential candidates. "You've always been there for me."

He smiled. "I always will be."

We sprinted down to the front gates. The guards shouted from the top of the wall, screaming their warnings as they aimed their bows at us. A wave of arrows rained down over us moments later. Piercey deflected them all without slowing down so the arrows splintered and rained down around us. I lifted my hands and threw the gate off its hinges with my power. It slammed onto the ground in a cloud of dirt.

Not slowing down to even look at the damage, we stormed into the Prophet's village, cutting right for the temple at the center.

Guards and warriors rushed to the streets, fighting against our unseen shields with thrusts of swords, with flailing arrows that burst upon impact, with spears that shattered. Doorways and windows clogged with normal men and women screaming the alarm, throwing chairs, pots and pans, anything that could do damage.

But between Piercey and me we blocked every last assault. I pumped my palm and shoved everyone on the road away. People flew back against buildings, through windows, into people crowded together.

My power flowed freely through my avatar, even easier to draw upon than before I'd died. Maybe it was that I had changed. Maybe this new body was just better. All I knew was that at my peak of training before I died, it never felt this natural.

I narrowed my eyes as the darkness within the temple door came into view. The towering stone doors of the temple were always open, but today they would close once we were all inside. I'd trap the Prophet and Flare with us and ensure they never left.

We reached the stairs and Piercey raised his voice above the screams in the village. "I've got it! Save your energy, Max!"

I snapped off my power as I slid through the huge doorway with Nash at my heels.

Piercey held back all of the warriors on his own with a protective shield around the temple that buzzed with his power. "Hurry!" His body trembled as he stumbled back to the door. It had been easy when we did it together, but the work had just doubled for him.

My eyes adjusted to the dim light inside and my muscles coiled.

The Prophet stood at the altar in his black cloak. The five disciples who'd survived our last battle circled him with their heads bowed and their hands lifted at their sides. A dozen warriors guarded them. No Flare.

"Wait. Turn back," Piercey yelled.

I twisted for him. He grunted as he reached for me with his power. The force tugged Nash and me a few feet toward him but his power was weak as he held off an entire village.

"They're meditating on the Prophet," Piercey said. "They gave him their power. Turn back now."

Alarm tensed my muscles. We needed to draw them out of this temple and try to separate them. Nash and I lunged for Piercey when a creaking started and then turned to deafening scraping. The heavy stone doors of the temple slammed closed and sealed us inside. The flames of the lanterns lining the walls flickered.

Piercey was still outside.

"Great." I drew my blade.

Nash turned, swords already raised.

In a flash, immense pressure clamped down on every fiber of my being—my limbs, my heart, the very blood flowing through my veins. Power erupted from my core as I fended it off from Nash and me. It took so much energy that it felt like I trudged through a river as I struggled toward the Prophet and unleashed my own power upon him. There was no longer any holding back. With a scream, the heat within me erupted and exploded out, all aimed right at the Prophet.

The incredible pressure on his body was immediately obvious as he knees buckled and his neck strained.

Still, panic rushed through me because Piercey hadn't come through the doors yet. I needed him to guard Nash. I opened my mouth to tell him to stay back when he took off in a sprint for the dozen warriors standing guard over the Prophet and his demons. Piercey wasn't here to block him. What was he thinking?

"Nash!" Energy rippled through me. I drew from deep within the well of my power and extended my hands like claws out toward the guards. Their heads shook. Eyes popped wide. One neck snapped. Another. Two more.

Without slowing down, Nash slashed one sword through a man's chest and blocked a swing from a quick guard with the other.

Snap. Snap.

I took down two more in the same instant Nash's twin blades wrenched a guard's sword free. Sweat dripped into my eyes and tickled the nape of my neck. Nash cut through another guard's neck like butter.

Only five guards left. Nash reared his blade back when it looked like he slammed against an invisible wall and then his body flew back through the air. I tried to soften his fall but he still bounced when he hit the stone floor.

The disciples moaned low, bodies trembling with exertion; some collapsed on their knees. The Prophet's eyes bulged. His face burned deep red.

So much power. A cry ripped from my chest as I struggled to break through their power and crush the Prophet.

It felt as if I had to shred my muscles just to walk toward Nash. Pain burned within my body and danced along my skin. Nash leaned against a knee, his determined stare on the Prophet. Blood trickled from his nose. My stomach tightened at that look on Nash's face. The brazenness. The fearlessness. His ferocity wild and almost inhuman.

It could get him killed.

No. I couldn't give in to despair or worry. Nash was fighting with everything he had. More than he had. All for me and Elsie. My nails pierced my skin as I dug them into my palms, turning my mind to the eclipse, when my life had rushed from me through my wounds, and I wanted nothing more than to stay with Nash. I had to find more within myself.

Everything inside of me stilled.

I looked at the circle around the Prophet and imagined that I could see the threads connecting them all. The threads of energy pulsating from the disciples to the Prophet. Trembling, I focused on that, my insides feeling as though they were melting.

Pop.

A disciple's wrist snapped. He fell back from the circle, panting as he stared at his wrist.

A woman screamed as she convulsed. All the veins in her body bulged against her skin, as if trying to escape. She was fighting so hard to stay connected, but I saw the fractures in the circle.

Nash took the distraction to move on the last guards. I ran with him, my legs finally flooded with energy now that I didn't need to use so much strength to hold off the Prophet.

We struck at the same time, my blade catching against a guard's and forcing his own against the soft of his neck, deeper and deeper, until it embedded in his flesh. I grabbed his sword and slid it all the way through, killing him. Nash blocked hits from two guards.

I focused on him to protect him, but two demons pivoted away from the Prophet to me. They blasted me with their unseen power.

I faltered. The Prophet's strength crushed my throat and the muscles in my body, immobilizing me.

Beside me, the tip of a sword sliced through the edge of Nash's bicep and flung his blood across my face. He was frozen in place, chest not even moving with breath. The guard raised her sword to strike him again.

No! I caught hold of the attack against us that had immobilized us. Broke free. Shoved my palm at the fool who'd dared to hurt Nash and threw her back with a force so hard her skull cracked the stone floor.

Her vacant eyes stared up while a pool of blood spread out from her head.

A strangled cough spasmed Nash's body. I'd overextended myself, giving the Prophet a chance to choke us once more.

Despite not being able to breathe, Nash blocked a hit on each side of his body. A third man stabbed for his back. A shot of heat burned from my chest, up my shoulders, and down my arm as I focused on the sword. It snapped in half before reaching Nash's spine.

With a cry, I regained control of the Prophet's power again and loosened the pressure on Nash's throat.

The effort left me helpless to stop two demons who rushed for me with swords extended. I screamed through gritted teeth. Blood dripped from my nose. I stopped one blade right against my throat. The other in front of my right eye.

I was doing too many things at once.

So was Nash. Blood pumped from his wound as he thrust his sword with his injured arm and pierced a guard's chest. This couldn't go on.

I planted my feet on the ground and tried to dig even deeper than the power I'd felt during the eclipses. There was more I hadn't tapped into. There had to be.

Pressure swelled in my chest.

"Go!" the Prophet roared.

The three disciples sprang from his side. The Prophet's pressure weakened considerably, but it only gave me a few moments of reprieve before I faced an all-new danger. Nash was still fending off the remaining guards while the disciples were all headed for me.

One of the women raised her spear, eyes on me, nostrils flaring. Beside her, a man reached his hands out, armored forearms catching the light of the lanterns. Gloves stretched over his hands, ending in sharpened daggers on each finger that looked like claws. His eyes shifted between me and Nash.

The third disciple knelt down and then the strength on the blades at my throat and eye intensified with her power. She was pushing them with her mind.

It all happened so fast, in just the time it took for the woman with the spear to steady herself.

Nash spun toward the disciples and jabbed his blade for the throat of the woman with the spear just as she released.

"Nash!"

As I snapped the spear in half, I thrust a wave of energy at the clawed demon behind Nash, but his daggers shot right through. The thin blades stabbed into Nash's shoulders, right above his collarbone.

Blood burst into the air.

Nash stabbed his right blade behind his back. I drove it with my mind so it swiftly carved through the clawed disciple's gut.

They both screamed as the claws tightened against Nash and the demon's bowels pulsed against his open wound. Nash grabbed the wrists on each of his shoulders and yanked the daggers out.

The sword nicked my throat, vying for attention that needed to be on Nash alone. I caught the blade before it could slice through me.

"Nash," I whispered. Scarlet splotches spread across the ten holes torn into Nash's shirt. Rivulets of blood fell from his fingertips and splashed against the ground as he stumbled toward the last two soldiers. He grunted and growled with every step toward them. It was my fault for letting this happen to him.

I screamed, pleading with myself to find more strength, but the blade at my throat only dug deeper against my skin. I couldn't help Nash. Couldn't even speak his name again. The effort to hold off the Prophet and his disciples hollowed out my core.

One guard broke into a run for Nash, but Nash only stopped in his tracks, watching. Watching until I thought for sure the enemy's blade would pierce his heart.

Nash fell back to dodge a strike at the last moment and impaled the man in his exposed side.

"Fuck this." The last man twisted and sprinted for the stone doors.

His neck snapped and his body slammed against the ground.

My heart jolted. I hadn't done that.

The Prophet looked at the remaining disciples. "You'll be next if you defy me!"

The Prophet wasted his energy on making an example of the guard. I shouldn't waste mine. This strategy wasn't working. I was wearing down too fast, and I'd already gotten Nash hurt. I needed something else, something better.

Instead of using so much energy on defending against the power that tried to crush our bodies and our windpipes, I let up on the effort to protect myself, and instead strengthened my own body. With the power pumping through my muscles, I ripped away the weapons aimed at my eye and throat and turned them on the two closest to me.

I couldn't draw in any breath. Had to do this quickly.

The woman closest to me drew a shorter sword just in time to block my first attack. Nash and I had trained together when I wasn't working with Piercey. My sword skills were better than they'd ever been. Twisting, I powered a two-handed slash for the disciple's shoulder and broke the sword she raised to guard, carving deep through muscle and tendon down to bone.

Two more disciples were running for me, but I had to finish this. With a roar, I pulled the blade free of the resistance of her body and skewered her through the chest. Black blood burst from the wound and soaked her shirt as she fell to her knees.

My lungs burned from the lack of air. I raised an energy shield to cover Nash and me as I focused on my airway to draw in a deep breath. A blade sparked against my shield while a fiery blast from another disciple ricocheted off.

Nash, under the cover of the shield, rushed toward me, his arms and chest covered in blood from the claws. I didn't have time to tell him to stay back. He should have known that he was too weak to fight any longer and would be in the way.

Only he reached his hand forward, slipping it through my barrier. I hadn't even thought about letting him in. It happened naturally.

He slid behind me. "Your bow and quiver."

Two more hard attacks slammed into my shield and forced me back a step. Quickly, I pulled them off and passed them to Nash. I dropped my sword to draw his twin blades from his sides. It felt surreal to swap weapons, but it was too dangerous for Nash to get close enough to these disciples to fight with his swords and this approach provided me more versatility.

From within my shield, he nocked an arrow, roaring through the obvious pain of using the bow, and fired at one of the disciples. The arrow broke before reaching her, but I knew how hard it would be to fend off attacks once I started to overwhelm them.

Time for another offensive.

I charged forward and abandoned my shield with Nash still inside as I lunged for a disciple. The blades danced as she blocked, evaded, struggled to keep her guard from breaking.

The Prophet, perhaps no longer content to hide behind his disciples like a coward and only attack my airway, sauntered closer to the battle. He raised up the spear he had used to kill me.

Vengeance flowed through my veins.

A glowing orb mushroomed from the tip of his spear, sparking like electricity. Had he been learning new tricks as well?

I feigned a strike and then teleported directly behind the Prophet. The twin blades pierced his sides but then stopped like they'd run into a concrete wall.

He spun and shot the orb at me, but I'd traveled again. This time, right next to a disciple. The orb of power burst against an empty stone wall, splintering it.

Meanwhile, I looked into the wide eyes of a disciple as I forced a sword between her teeth and out the back of her head.

The Prophet's attack that threatened to strangle my airway had weakened. I could see the fear in his eyes from here as he raised his spear again.

"You truly are a vile demon!" he shouted.

I gasped in a deep breath, exhausted from the battle, but hungry for the victory.

Arrows suddenly flew from the shield I still used to protect Nash. The remaining disciple warded them off, but it had stolen her attention and had given me time to summon my strength for a hard wave of energy to knock against her. It flattened her on her back.

I tried to teleport again, but my energy was dwindling and I remained in place. If I dropped Nash's shield, I could, but I didn't want to risk it.

The Prophet walked closer to me, the fear now looking wild and dangerous. His guards and disciples all lay scattered upon the floor of his temple in pools of their own blood.

The death did not faze me in that moment, though I knew that part would come later.

For now, I stared into the black eyes of the man who had stolen my life from me. I'd lived through it over and over.

I tightened my hold on the sword grip.

"There is nothing more pathetic than a man who kills only for the sake of power. You're weak." I raised my chin. "That's why you'll die today."

"You're losing energy." His stare cut to Nash and darkened with rage. "And you, traitor, serve only to hold her back. Leave your shield and face me like a man."

Nash only smirked, obviously not so easily ruffled. But the paleness of his face worried me. His arms shook as he struggled to draw back the bowstring and fire an arrow right at the Prophet. It shattered midair, but Nash did not show any sign of discouragement.

"Kill him, Max." Nash gasped as he nocked another arrow, voice as tense as the bowstring. "His blood is yours."

The arrow flew and I rushed forward just as fast, propelled by the power within me.

I skidded to a stop, hit by the Prophet's own power as he raised his hands to me. This time, I focused my power into two points like the tip of a sharp blade and drove them toward the Prophet's eyes. He screamed as he struggled to fend off my attack.

Nash fired two more arrows rapidly. Though the Prophet broke one in half before it reached him, the other caught the edge of his shoulder.

The overexertion ripped apart every fiber of muscle in my body, but I powered my way forward one step at a time toward the Prophet, until finally he was within reach of the twin blades. I slashed and he blocked with his spear.

We fought with ruthless hits powered by our energy. As I blocked a strike from the spear, I noticed that the Prophet managed to tear a hole in the shield protecting Nash.

The memory of the spear thudding into Nash's chest on the Mountain of the Gods gripped my heart with fear. I focused entirely on fortifying the shield to protect him.

Bright pain screamed from my side. The Prophet's spear stabbed deeply into my abdomen.

It was a pain I knew far too well. I didn't let it slow me down. With Nash protected again, I counterattacked with the spear still in me, and managed to cut at least an inch into the Prophet's arm before he stopped the blade with his power.

He ripped the spear free. I crossed the twin blades to slice at his throat, but the spear shot between them, catching the attack.

"Max!"

An arrow lodged into the Prophet's chest just below his collarbone. Out of the corner of my eye, I saw Nash struggle with another arrow and lose it as he suddenly collapsed onto one knee.

My energy seemed to flow as quickly as the blood from my side. I wouldn't come back this time if I died. There was no way I would fail.

I struck. He deflected. He jabbed. I sidestepped. With each passing moment, our powers waned, until we had to rely upon the blades of mere mortals.

My right blade cut through his forearm. His spear caught my thigh, ripping it open. The pain meant nothing to me. I'd felt so much in my life, had suffered so many times when I looped to my death repeatedly, that I easily ignored the draining of life and power.

I'd gotten so lost in the battle, I almost didn't notice that the shield had entirely dissolved. The Prophet's eyes snapped to Nash.

I defied all of my instincts and instead of protecting Nash, drove both blades forward into the Prophet's gut. His eyes opened wide. Though his power had managed to stop the swords from driving in too deeply, both ends had disappeared in his body.

All my strength went into forcing those blades in deeper.

But instead of the blow taking the Prophet down, I felt his power suddenly swell.

Shit.

I ripped the blades free and jumped between the Prophet and Nash. How could I have forgotten how dangerous it was to kill one of us? The instinct to survive was powerful, especially for a man with his strength.

Blood oozed from his midsection, from the arrow still sticking out from his chest, and the slash against his shoulder. He was dying and he wanted us to die with him.

I looked up to the stone ceiling above the Prophet's head. Hope flashed in my chest. If I could surprise him, maybe I could end this before he managed to do any damage.

My eyelids fluttered as I focused on pressuring the stone ceiling above his head.

The entire temple trembled with my power. My own desperation fueled me, so I could gather the remnants of my strength. Searing pain carved through every inch of my body like I was dying all over again.

Rocks shook loose and sprinkled all over us. My eyes rolled back in my head. My body went rigid. Power exploded from my body.

I felt the rock give way. Slabs of carved stone right over the Prophet dropped on top of him. The weight of it slamming against the ground echoed through the temple.

The weakness sapped the strength from my muscles and I collapsed, unable to even catch myself. My head whacked against the ground.

Dark spots popped over my vision. It was quiet.

Nash . . . What if I'd hurt him?

I moaned and turned my head, shutting my eye against the blood that slid down from my forehead.

Nash sat on his knees, eyes on me. Alive. I'd managed to protect him from myself.

The Prophet . . .

My arms were useless. I focused to strengthen my muscles but the burning pain blinded me for a moment. The wound to my stomach screamed for my attention while the pain of overextending myself with my power flooded my whole form.

Then came the sound of rustling and shifting beneath the pile of rubble.

Why wasn't this damn Prophet dead yet? I pushed through the pain, crying out as I rose to my knees.

A heap of broken stone covered the place where the Prophet had stood. The slab on top was shaking. And then it slid away.

The Prophet crawled out from the rocks. Blood gushed from his nose and mouth and ears. Covered his hands and torn cloak.

He dragged himself forward with his inky eyes locked on me.

Nash pushed to his feet and limply walked for him.

"Don't . . ." I managed to rise. Of course, Nash didn't listen. We both struggled toward the Prophet.

I dropped Nash's swords to grab my dagger. Dropped onto the ground before the Prophet.

He wheezed, clawing at the ground to pull himself away. "S-Stop."

With shaking arms, I lifted the dagger above my head and drove it down for his throat. I sliced through half an inch before the Prophet's power curled around my fist, threatening to crush my hand.

The blade thudded to a stop.

Nash's long arms wrapped around me, his chest against my back, his blood hot and tarry against me. He clasped my hands and pushed the blade with me, forcing it another quarter inch deeper.

Nash's blood flowed down our fingers onto the blade and against the Prophet's neck.

All of my strength went into the blade. Nash's did, too. I could feel it in his straining muscles. His shaking body. We both screamed and forced my dagger into the Prophet's throat.

A cry flowed out from the Prophet and wrapped around me like a physical force. As his life poured out, he surged in strength, and my throat felt as if it was being crushed by an unseen hand.

Blood gurgled from his open throat like a fountain.

I couldn't let him win.

Wrenching the dagger free of his power, I drove it right into his mouth, skimming his cheeks. His eyes widened in terror and pain. I kept going until he gagged. Until the tip touched his throat and then I broke his will to plunge it through the back of his neck. With a snap, his power was gone.

The life fled the Prophet's eyes.

He was dead.

Nash and I fell against one another. His bloody hands reached for my side. "How deep is it?"

"I don't know." I clung to him, eyes on the torn skin at his shoulders. "That's too much blood—"

Nash met my eyes, opened his mouth to speak, and then his body went limp against me. His deadweight knocked me to the ground.

"Nash . . ." I struggled to pull myself out from under him.

Listening, I heard his heart beating weakly. He'd just passed out. I had to get him to Piercey.

Before I could even try to move him, a streak of red flashed across the room.

A dainty form skidded to a stop in the middle of the room. Fucking Flare. She blasted the stone door with balls of fire. Two more blasts and one side popped free.

Her eyes caught mine briefly. She'd been here this whole time. Hiding.

"Coward," I growled.

I kissed Nash's face and rushed for the door, scooping up my abandoned sword on the way out.

Outside, Piercey still held off the entire army. Sweat doused his shirt. Flare was already dragging herself onto her horse.

"Max!" His bloodshot eyes found mine.

I stopped and looked at the crowd. I needed to go after her, but first I had to put a stop to this.

"The Prophet is dead," I said.

The shouts lowered until it was silent. Shock contorted the faces of the villagers.

"He's dead," I said. "His disciples are dead. Stop fighting. We aren't here to hurt you. But we will if you attack us."

Weapons lowered. Piercey's body relaxed. Murmurings broke the silence. Warriors looked to one another. They would likely attack again, but for now, the confusion of having their leadership wiped out would buy us time, especially since most of them probably hated the Prophet.

"Nash needs help," I said to Piercey.

He looked to my side. "You do."

"No time."

Frustration flooded his face. He grabbed my arm to stop me from leaving and pressed his hand to my wound. It felt like he shoved lava into my gut. I bowed forward, falling against him as I screamed through gritted teeth.

"Sorry," he said. "This is the best I can do for now. I cauterized your wounds and hit you with as much healing power as I could." His hands closed over my temples. "I can't give you my power, but I can calm your mind. It'll help your own recover faster."

This felt more like Piercey's power, soothing, instead of painful.

"Stay here," he said. "I'll get Nash."

Piercey ran into the temple and I sprinted for a horse. No one stopped me. The villagers were lost and stunned as I led the horse to the temple door. Piercey carried Nash over his shoulder, trembling from the effort. He must have used up all of his energy, too.

Once we got Nash onto the horse, I handed the reins to Piercey. "Take care of him."

"Wait. I need to go with you."

I couldn't wait, though. There was no time and I needed him to save Nash. I focused on Flare, focused on peeling away the distance between us, on ignoring the pain and exhaustion so I could travel. As afraid as I was that I would lack the strength like I had in the temple, I quickly found the worry to be misplaced.

"Max!" Piercey yelled the moment I disappeared.

CHAPTER FORTY

I transported directly in front of Flare, eyes narrowed as she skidded to a stop in front of me.

"You killed me." Hatred oozed from my words and deepened my voice.

"You already died on Earth as a baby." Fear strained her voice. "This life was never yours."

"It's certainly not yours. I've given the Collective all of my memories. It's over."

Terror flashed in her eyes, far deeper than even the bright fear that filled her eyes when I'd appeared. "You jeopardized your entire world. They could end everything now. You have to let me help you."

I snorted. "It's not that easy to fool me. I don't need you to save me from the Collective. You want me to save you."

"You think the Collective cares about this world? No one cares about any of you except for me."

"We're done talking. We've had three lifetimes of it." I winced as I drew my sword, the wound to my side screaming in pain. "Now have some honor and face me yourself this time."

Flare stumbled a step backward. She clenched her hands into fists. "You're playing right into their hands. Doesn't it strike you as odd that supposedly evolved beings would send you back here to kill me?"

I swung my sword and smiled when she stepped back again. "I told them I'd give you the chance to surrender." My lips tightened into a snarl. "Maybe I need to be rehabilitated, too. Because I'll make sure you taste death if it's the last thing I do."

"Stupid girl." Flames flashed between us, singing my knuckles. "The Collective knows that. You gave them your memories. That isn't all you gave them, is it? You're letting them watch this right now. You agreed to let them watch you for the rest of your life if it meant coming back."

My stomach tightened. "I told you that we're done talking."

"You're not the only part of the experiment. Your world isn't." Pain flooded Flare's eyes. "It's me. I'm part of the experiment. I should have seen it sooner. That's the only reason the Collective would let you come back here when they knew you'd kill me. So they can finish monitoring what they started."

I lowered my sword slightly.

"Don't you see, Max? The lack of safeguards to keep me from taking too much power in this world has nothing to do with my society being so peaceful it seems unnecessary. They wanted to see what would happen, so that when they implement interventions in the physical world, they already know how supervisors will act." She laughed bitterly and hung her head. "It isn't that I never considered it. I just never knew they'd want data on my behavior so badly that they'd send death to me."

"You brought death upon yourself."

"The Collective knew what you would do when they sent you here. This is a sanctioned killing."

My muscles ached as I wrenched my sword back up. "It doesn't matter to me if the Collective is just as screwed up as you are. That's a battle for another lifetime. Today, my fight is for my world to be free of your influence. To be free to choose its own path."

"Free to destroy itself like every other world out there. You're killing your only hope for salvation."

Her claims itched at the back of my mind. Was I wrong to let the Collective watch over my life like this? It had played into their hands if they wanted to observe Dr. Henderson's behavior until the end. Still, if that was the cost of freedom, I would pay it. I couldn't stop them from shutting down our world if they had tricked me and planned to do it. But I could kill this miserable woman standing before me.

I could kill her and I would.

I screamed and lunged. Snapped my blade like a cobra's bite.

Flare disappeared just as the tip nicked her side.

Instinctively, I locked onto her and threw myself through space-time, latching onto this thread that had always connected us through these lives.

I was as entangled with her as I was with Nash and the eclipse. It was time to accept that and seize that awful bond.

We appeared on a hillside I didn't recognize. Vanished and then stood atop a shore with lapping waves. Fear emanated like heat from Flare as I followed her each time she traveled and seamlessly landed with her. Any weakness I'd felt before burned up in the raging inferno within me.

The world around us peeled away and blurred as we sped through distances I could scarcely imagine. We landed on hard rock. Grassy plains. Soft flowers. Thick mud and dry desert ground.

I managed to lock my arm around Flare's throat before she took off again and we landed in front of the Mountain of the Gods as I aimed the sword for the tenderness of her throat.

"Hold still." I tightened my hold. "I might slip if you don't."

Her trembling hands grasped my arm. "We could agree this time." Tears spilled down her face and against my skin. "We both love this world. We work together this time."

"No," I whispered in her ear. "This time, you die."

"Max—"

"You helped the Prophet of the Valley, even when he tortured and slaughtered his own people. You manipulated Piercey and me when we were only children. Reset our world to try to get your way." I ground my teeth. "You stole little Elsie. You had me killed." My nails dug into her shoulder. "You locked the door to the afterlife and I know you were never going to let us through. You claimed this world as your own."

"I am the only one who can ease the suffering of this world."

"You're not the medicine we need." I expected her flames to burn against me, but they never did. Flare knew she'd been beat. I'd endure any pain to kill her. No matter where she ran, I'd follow. This was inescapable and I reveled in the joy of knowing that she couldn't deny it. "You've damned yourself to hell. I'll gladly damn myself as well to end you."

"I'll make sure everyone learns about what the Collective has done." Her voice raised, reaching beyond me to the ones who watched. "If I'm tainted, then you're evil incarnate. Her blade is yours. Any blood shed here is shed by the Collective."

"My world, my justice." I ripped my blade against her throat when she vanished from my grasp. "Damn it!"

I reached for her with my power and landed in the all-white room, facing Dr. Drake. Her sad eyes stared into my own. Dr. Henderson stood beside her.

How naive to think she'd accepted the inevitability of her defeat. She was only feigning helplessness until she could decide on her next move. I wouldn't let her escape so easily. "You can't take this from me." I spoke to Dr. Drake but raised my sword up toward Dr. Henderson. "She has blood on her hands. My blood and the blood of my people. The blood of lives stolen and banished even from memory."

Dr. Henderson clutched Dr. Drake's slender arm and whipped the other woman in front of her. "Stop her."

"She can't." I snarled. "This isn't her world. What power does she have here?"

"Max, please." Dr. Drake reached a gentle hand out to me.

I wouldn't be tempted by her grace and softness. Vengeance ran through my veins. "Do you know how many times I've died? It has haunted me every day of my life. Then, for her to threaten the people I love . . ."

"We need to make peace with each other." Dr. Henderson dared to speak. "One day we'll both be out of this world and in the rest of society. We must find peace."

"My blade will make peace with you." I tilted my head. "In this world, in my world, you answer to me because the people I love are still here."

"Max." Dr. Henderson lifted her hand. "Think about what you're doing. The Collective is watching."

"Let them see."

Dr. Drake's voice broke through, clear and calm. "If you cede control, Dr. Henderson, you won't be here any longer, and she won't be able to hurt you."

"Don't you dare run from me!" I ran forward and slid behind both women, grabbing a handful of Dr. Henderson's hair to rip her away from Dr. Drake. She shrieked.

"Stop it, Max!" Dr. Drake's voice commanded attention, but nothing could dissuade me now. "Dr. Henderson, listen to me. I'm authorized to negotiate. Instead of rehabilitation, you can heal in the afterlife under my supervision, but only if you leave peacefully."

The hazel of Dr. Henderson's eyes erupted into red and a ball of fire slammed into my gut. I skidded back across the floor.

The smell of fire burned my sinuses. Flames danced from Flare's hands. "This is my world. I'm not going anywhere."

Another ball of flames erupted from her hands. White snapped behind it. The walls closed in on me, trapping me. The fire swelled in the tiny space and bit into every inch of my body.

I growled and focused on Flare. Appeared so close to her that I knocked her back a step.

Dr. Drake shouted for us to stop and suddenly ran for us. I lifted my hand and pushed her back with my power so she couldn't come closer. I wasn't sure that we could even hurt her, but I wouldn't take the chance.

Fire erupted around Flare, spreading to the edges of the room, licking the walls, and quickly reaching the ceiling. I had to focus to keep it from consuming me and Dr. Drake.

This was the only way it ever could have ended between us.

I roared and swung my sword for Flare. Explosions erupted in the air between us. Knocked me back before I could reach her. Little sparks of fire popped like confetti.

Flare had plenty of tricks, but she didn't know how to fight. Not like I did.

Despite how my legs shook with exhaustion and my side screamed in pain, I stomped forward for her again. Flames shot against me, breaking through my defense. My clothes sizzled. I cried out but didn't let it stop me, even as fire burned away the flesh on my blade hand.

Flare was panicked. Terrified. I saw it in her eyes. "Barbarian!" Flare screamed.

I lunged, driven by a far worse pain. By Nash's pained eyes when I returned to him and he feared the hope of believing it was true. My friends choking under the Prophet's power. Elsie listless in Flare's arms.

The hundred times I had died beneath the eclipse.

I reached out and grabbed Flare's throat with my flaming hand. She screamed from her own fire.

Then she vanished from my grasp and I followed her without hesitation, gasping when we both slammed into a wall. The teleportation hadn't worked. Dr. Drake must have trapped her in the white room. It had been a mistake for Flare to travel here.

Grinning, I twisted her hair around my fist and slammed her face into the wall so hard it painted the white red. Flare tried again to transport away from me, but I followed, still gripping her hair. Blood gushed from her nose as she cried.

"Let me go," she cried. "Enough."

Pathetic.

"When did you show us mercy?"

Lifting my blade, I looked into Flare's eyes and drove it straight into her heart. I could hear her ribs crack and separate from the force of the sword and felt the resistance of her body against my weapon. With a final thrust, I forced it clear through her chest and out her back. The flames fizzled and died. The smoke burning my sinuses drifted up and curled against the ceiling.

Complete shock dropped Flare's jaw. Had she expected me to spare her?

"This isn't your world anymore," I said. The red faded until I stared into the hazel ones of Dr. Henderson one final time. Flare and the god melted into one. Terror and anguish warred in her stare. "If you hurt anyone ever again, I'll come for you in the next life."

One last flutter of fear flickered in her eyes, like a reckoning for all that she'd done. Maybe a recognition that she'd lost. Appreciation that after three lives, I'd destroyed her.

And then she was nothing, nothing but an empty body.

I had killed Flare and banished Dr. Henderson from this world.

CHAPTER FORTY-ONE

Dr. Henderson's body was gone. It had vanished. Like she'd never been here.

Dr. Drake sat down in a white chair, watching me with knowing eyes, but saying nothing.

"I accept the consequences of my actions," I said. The thrill of victory kept the adrenaline pumping through my body, or surely my wounds would have taken away all my strength. "Thank you and the Collective for giving me the chance to help my people."

The other woman averted her eyes with her jaw bunched. "Please, don't thank me."

I almost asked her if she truly had believed I would not seek justice for all Dr. Henderson had done. "You agree with her. You think it's barbaric." Sliding my hand over my wounded side, I eased forward. "It can't be left to your people to deal with her when you created this problem. She ruled over my world like a god. I have no regrets for what I did. Dr. Henderson chose a life of violence. She needed to taste her own blood for once."

"Don't pretend it wasn't for revenge."

"Of course it was revenge. But it was more than that. She needed to die by my blade. Now she knows the fear of death. She knows the pain of retribution by those she lorded over."

Dr. Drake was quiet for several seconds before meeting my stare once more. "I entered so many simulations and lived full lives in them. Do you think I've never wanted revenge? Or that I've never sought it? Do you think I've never been hurt or lorded over?" The pain in her eyes testified to what she'd experienced. "This is not the way to handle it."

"It is in this life. Maybe one day when I've lived as long as you, I'll be different. This is my journey and I needed to come to this place. Let go of what you can't change."

"Here's what I'm thinking." Her tone was sharper than usual.

"Yes," I said when she didn't continue.

"You've lived a hard life. These are unusual circumstances you're living in. You should live through a few extra lives before you try joining society."

"Seems fair." I hoped beyond hope that was my punishment for killing Flare. It was no small one. Still, it was worth it. I wasn't yet beyond revenge and I needed Flare to experience the pain she'd caused.

"Don't make me regret putting my faith in you."

"You still have it?"

"I would have done the same once. This is the world you live in. I just don't want you to have to suffer through a life of vengeance."

I rose and took her hand, looking hard into her eyes. "You're what I've been looking for beyond this door my whole life. I'll never forget that. From here on out, I'll do my best to honor what you've done for us. I swear it."

Her expression softened. "Be wise, Max. It's hard to fault you when an evolved woman attacked you, but I can't pretend that I'm not disappointed."

"My world is free of Dr. Henderson and Flare. I guess it takes a demon to kill a god. And I can't apologize for that."

Dr. Drake sighed and rose. "I'll be checking in on you from time to time. No one will have power over your world any longer, however. We'll watch. That's all."

"What about other worlds where experiments are happening?"

"The council voted on the same for them. We've identified other supervisors who devolved like Dr. Henderson. We're trying to remedy the situation."

Dr. Henderson's accusation buzzed in my mind again. "Is what she said true? Did the Collective study the supervisors as well?" I couldn't stand the thought of fighting more gods, but I couldn't pretend that Dr. Henderson was the only issue. The Collective had created these experiments. What if they had devolved, too? Fear trickled down my spine.

Dr. Drake lifted one shoulder in a shrug. "I don't have access to information like that."

"What do you believe, though?"

With a pause, her voice softened. "I believe we all need to investigate ourselves, especially the Collective, and that we cannot hope to help young worlds as long as we're willing to hurt simulated ones."

I nodded and smiled. "You'll fight for us until I make it to your world, won't you?"

She took my cheek. "I will. Promise me one thing, young soul."

I swallowed hard. "What?"

"Let the demon die today." Her voice soothed the irritated places in my soul. "Become who you were born to be."

The travel back to Nash and Piercey drained my remaining energy. As soon as I landed in the path of the horse, my knees buckled and I collapsed onto the ground.

Piercey had healed Nash enough for him to regain consciousness, but that effort had taxed my friend when he'd already used so much energy. They both climbed off the horse and rushed for me, also looking ready to fall over.

"Max." Nash took my face and searched for new injuries. "Is it—"

"It's done." A weary smile crawled onto my face as tears filled my eyes. "Flare is gone. I killed her and Dr. Henderson will never be allowed back in."

He drew me close and held me tight. "I was scared I would lose you again."

I looked over his shoulder at my old friend. "Do you hate me for killing her?"

Piercey glanced down, his face looking sour. "I hate myself . . ." He looked at me again with great pain in his eyes. "Because I'm happy you killed her after she stole you from us."

Nash and I both smiled appreciatively at him.

"Let's go back to the Sacred School. The kids need to know I'm alive." I touched my side, really feeling the wound now that my adrenaline was waning. "Piercey, do you have any strength left? I need help getting us back."

Piercey managed to help me enough that I could get all three of us back to the Sacred School, but we all immediately fell onto a bench in the hall.

"I don't know if we should see Elsie or Rune while we're like this." Nash and I rested against one another. "But I don't want to wait."

"I'll heal you both more soon," Piercey said.

"You're exhausted." Nash's voice was tense. "You held off the entire town and then you started healing me as we fled. The kids will be fine. They have to understand the way of things."

"I died. They don't need to be scared of anyone else dying."

"They need to know you're alive."

I swallowed hard and finally nodded. "But look at yourself." I caught a tattered piece of Nash's shirt, crusted with blood. "You want her to see you like this? We should cover the blood."

"Fine. You're right."

The holes all over his shoulders from the claws twisted my gut. As soon as we found the strength to stand, we stopped by our room to grab a blanket for each of us and then walked to the courtyard, where Trish waited with Elsie.

My legs felt numb as we reached the door, until we opened it to sunlight, and I saw her small form. Energy rushed through me.

A little purple skirt swayed with the breeze. Curls bobbed with each tentative step forward. Big, beautiful brown eyes stared wide at me in shock.

Elsie slowly drew closer. Slowly, until she stopped in her tracks, tears starting. And then she dashed across the grass with her fists pumping and sobs shaking her high-pitched voice.

I dropped to my knees and caught her in my arms, holding her so tight against me.

"Max," she sobbed.

I kissed her face and rocked her. "I'm here, Elsie. I'm here."

Lifting her, I turned to Nash and slid an arm around him, so Elsie rested between us both. She cried and cried until it all turned to sniffles. Her eyes slid closed as she fell asleep in my arms, with her head against her father. Soon, I would find Rune and set his world right as well. But for this moment, I held Elsie, focused on the little girl who I had never expected to have in my life.

I looked up into Nash's eyes, understanding fully in that moment that I wasn't who I once was, and I now held what I'd once run from, and how beautiful and dangerous that all was. Because I'd never had so much to lose.

CHAPTER FORTY-TWO

Dusty morning light bathed the green field before us, filtering through the dirt picked up by the wind. It hadn't rained in the two weeks since we killed the Prophet and the people called it a bad omen.

Nash slid his arm around me, unable to draw me too close because of my bow. "Ready?"

"You know I always am." Within a few days' time, I expected blood to stain this untainted field. Two armies were close to colliding, and I'd been traveling with Nash to scout out enemy territory and locations we might use for battle or ambush. "The Valley is in chaos. War doesn't wait on us to be ready."

"We wiped out the Valley's leadership. We knew it would be a rough transition."

"I understand why Piercey wants to vote on such major decisions. It's too much power for us to have."

"Does that mean your days of overthrowing Prophets and gods are over?"

I chuckled. "I don't know. That's a big commitment. The Flatlander Prophet claims that he should inherit the Valley now that our Prophet is dead. Piercey and his graduates are preventing anyone from taking charge, but we'll need a leader soon. I hope it can be someone without power. I hope it can be the first step toward a different way of life."

"Piercey loves voting. Perhaps we'll vote for someone."

My brow raised. "Our people vote in blood. It's hard to change so quickly. We did this. We'll have to help stabilize the region. It'll be the kind of war we've never fought, but we'll win."

"We will."

"Dr. Drake wants to meet soon, too. The gods want to hear from me again. They want to start making this right."

"Do you think they will?"

I paused. "It sounds foolish to place hope in the people who created the problems we're trying to solve."

"Dr. Henderson didn't have that much power compared to the Collective. They easily locked her out of the world once you killed her."

The words felt ominous. "If others are corrupted, they'll be harder to deal with. Who knows what is happening to other simulated worlds like ours."

We looked into each other's eyes until I thought I could see straight through to his soul.

"We'll fight together," he said. "We'll fight in every life we live and every world we call our own."

"Yes. I want to believe this is the beginning of peace, but Dr. Henderson is like our world. A symptom of a bigger problem."

"We have each other, though." He kissed one side of my face. The other. Voice husky. "Always."

My fingers crawled along his whiskered cheek, up into his hair. "No matter how many lives we live."

He grinned. "Let's get back to Leif and Wren."

I took his hand and teleported both of us back to our friends. Leif caught my wrist as soon as I appeared and whispered quietly. "Follow me. We have a target. Flatlanders are up ahead and we're going after one of their demons."

"I'll shield you," I said, heat already warming my palms as I listened for heartbeats ahead. The woods were crawling with enemies. I had to continue honing my power until I could protect this Valley from everyone.

These were the battles I had no doubt we could fight. What came next? Now that had made it hard to sleep at night.

No matter what, though, I wouldn't let myself slip away from this life and the people I loved ever again.

This was my world. I would protect it.

Epilogue

None of this was real. But life in my world had taught me none of that really mattered.

Even now that so much time had passed and everyone had reached the afterlife, I still would think about what Dr. Henderson had done to my world, my people, and to me. I could feel the blade cutting through her chest when I killed her. Would I do the same today? Was I still that same girl I had been?

I smirked and chuckled to myself.

Life was a strange thing. I never would have thought that I could lose track of years, but I had, and I didn't care to figure out how many had slipped away from me in the afterlife. So much had happened in our world before we passed on. Peace had been a nice change in this new realm. Although, I only wanted peace for so long when there was so much work to be done.

Nash held my hand as we walked through the yellow meadow for the gathering of all those we loved. It still felt strange that they didn't have all their memories like we did, but I had come to accept it. At least Nash and I remembered everything from our life. It'd been difficult waiting for Nash to regain his memories, but it was worth it. We'd fought so many battles. He deserved the peace I had never had. The peace of not remembering until he was ready. I was just thankful it didn't take him long to find me again.

As we approached our friends, Dr. Drake met us and took our hands. "It's the day. How do you feel?"

"Nervous," I said.

"I was nervous my first time, too."

Leif and Wren came to my side while I looked across the field for the kids. Rune picked flowers with his youngest daughter and smiled at me when I waved. Our lives had become full of so many people. "Good luck," Wren said and looped her arm through mine. "I hope you enjoy your new job."

"You better," Leif said. His eyes looked deeper. Like maybe he realized I was holding something back from him but didn't want to say in front of Wren. Even though they remembered everyone they loved now, they remembered little about our life so far.

"Things tend to be pretty enjoyable in the afterlife. I'm sure we'll like it just fine." I watched Nash as he slid his arm around Elsie.

Leif flicked my arm. "We should do some sparring before you go."

I grinned. That was something I would have to do. But first I made my rounds until I found my oldest friend sitting on a bench on his own, looking so content to watch everyone. Piercey had always been an old soul. His weathered fingers laced over his knee as he watched everyone in the meadow. We could be whatever version of ourselves we wanted to be here. A person's appearance often changed naturally depending on who they were with. Lovers might be young in one moment like when they first met and then middle-aged the next with their adult children. People could even become who they never had the chance to be, like children who died young, but found their adult forms here in the afterlife.

Piercey was always the same, though. I wasn't surprised that he chose this version of himself, this older and wiser man.

"Hello, friend." I sat down beside him.

He smiled at me, the wrinkles of so many past smiles deepening. "Max."

Like me, Piercey never lost his memories. We were potential candidates, but we hadn't chosen to continue toward enlightenment as a team. After all we'd been through, we deserved to choose our own path. And he loved it here in the afterlife. All he'd ever wanted was peace. Now he had it.

"You're going off to battle." Piercey's eyes glimmered.

"Not quite."

"Not like the old days, but still, a battle."

I watched him for a moment. "Do you wish I wouldn't?"

"No, Max. This is who you are. You could never stay here and be content, not until everywhere is as perfect as it is here. Neither could Nash." He smiled. "You're destined to do this together."

My chest softened. Buried beneath the years, my childhood friend still remained. "I guess so."

"Visit me when you're done."

"I will, Piercey."

We squeezed one another's hands and smiled. I walked to the top of the hill where Nash sat with all of our people. I couldn't blame anyone for staying here forever. It'd been all I wanted before, to be with the people I loved and never have to say goodbye.

But it was that yearning, that heartbreak we'd suffered in our world, that drove me to continue working my way to the council. Those who remembered were responsible to carry all that we had learned and suffered so younger souls could find comfort. One day, Nash and I would be ready to return to our family, for good. Or they would come out into society and live with us there. One day, we would all be together, and there would be no end. Maybe I would even let myself forget about the world we'd left behind. Maybe I'd let myself have the peace that Piercey so loved.

For now, I wanted to remember what happened, no matter how badly some memories hurt.

Surrounded by everyone we had ever loved, the land around us shifted into the blue of the ocean. Our lives flowed into one, like these gentle waters. Like our memories became one, looking like one, despite each droplet still being its own. Somehow, despite all I'd already experienced, I knew there was so much left for me to discover.

"We'll be back soon," I said to our family. To our little village. To our world. Leif and Wren nodded at me with gentle smiles.

My heart pounded as I settled back on the white table.

"You've waited a long time for this, Max," Dr. Drake said. "You two are ready."

I reached my hand out. Nash took it in a firm grasp.

My voice came out in a hushed breath. "I love you, Nash." The words mean multiple lifetimes of love.

"I love you, Max."

Then we closed our eyes and fell into a deep sleep, deep in another world.

Being born was so much like dying. A whole world in your heart and then suddenly a new one.

I'd held on to Nash's hand in the white room so tightly that I felt it every time something squeezed my hand after. First it was his, and then I was squeezing my own in the warmth of the womb. Squeezing my mother's pinky from the crib. Squeezing the sticky fingers of the kid down the road.

Squeezing the handlebars of my bike as I sped down the road with the wind whipping through my hair. And there I was. The autumn night crackled with the croaking of frogs. Coolness tickled my bare knees. Riding alone on the street, I wondered, for the first time, what the world was like before I'd been born into it. How it would be when I died.

My head fell back so the streetlights burned my eyes. Beyond them, the gaping black night stared back. The bike flew out from under me like someone had jerked it. In the moment before everything flashed impossibly fast, I felt myself slip, like I'd left the neighborhood.

Then the ground ripped across my body and I slammed onto my side.

I groaned, afraid to move and see how bad it was. My skin burned all down my left arm and leg.

"You trashed that mailbox."

I turned at the voice.

A boy held the splintered hunk of a mailbox post. A laugh tinged his voice, bubbling beneath the concern. "You okay?"

I glanced down. My skin was raw on my arm and my knee was bloody. "Fine."

"Here." He threw down the post and offered his hand.

I pushed it away and scowled. "I don't need some boy coming to my rescue." Wincing, I stood up, gasping at the burn in my knee. "I can take care of myself."

Standing now, I met amber eyes. My stomach tightened and the burning in my knee seemed to have moved to my belly.

"That's a stupid thing to say." He arched one eyebrow. "Helping you up doesn't mean you're helpless. My dad says people who can't take help are insecure."

The burning erupted in flames of fury. "Shut your mouth or I'll shut it for you."

"Oh yeah?" He looked down. Grass and dirt stained my clothes. "Good luck catching me."

He pivoted and took off in a full sprint. I ran hard after him.

I caught him, of course. And the next time he caught me. If time had moved so fast before that, so instantly that I didn't know it existed, it crawled through falls and winters and springs and glorious summers. It crawled until I'd come to expect that. Came to expect I'd never lose out on time to chase the boy who'd dared to help me when I fell.

When the slipping started and time raced faster than I could catch it, I understood, actually understood, that one day I would die. Those questions from the autumn night slipped back into my mind as I watched an older woman move down the aisle of the courtroom on her walker. I was twenty-five, and for the first time, for no reason in particular, I grasped that I wouldn't be here forever.

Harsh lights glared overhead as the woman made it onto the stand.

He stood up now, catching my eyes with the stare that could snap back time in an instant. He wore his curls differently in court. I wanted to pluck them so they'd fall over his eyes the way I liked, but he looked good like this, too. Especially as he smirked at me now and then shifted his stare to his witness.

The arrogance.

We'd fought our whole lives and we loved it. It was no wonder we wound up fighting each other in court. Even though I'd complained he copied me when he started law school a year after I did, it felt like fate. Even so, I didn't have time for him and his dimpled smile. If I lost my focus this early in my career, I'd be done for.

I'd been a fool then, though. I wished I could say I'd never been a fool again, but it wasn't long after that when I realized I didn't have the time to not be with him. Life was too fleeting. Time passed so quickly again. Even so it was a long time, a very long time, filled to the brim with wonder and heartbreak, before I felt myself slip far, far away from that life.

I awoke with a hand squeezing mine so tightly. I awoke in a haze, aware only that this had happened before, that we had never let go, that this wouldn't be the last time either.

As the memories slipped back in and I let my head fall to the side to look into Nash's amber eyes, I squeezed him tighter. "Good morning," I whispered.

He gazed at me like he had in the very long dream we'd just dreamt, how he gazed at me every night as we went to bed, and as we opened our eyes in the morning; like he had back in our first world when we fought our way through line after line of warriors; like he had when we sat with our family before entering this simulated life.

I figured no matter how many lives we lived, we'd always have each other.

Dr. Drake helped me up and I let her.

"It's not too late to go back to the afterlife," she said.

I didn't need to think about it, not after everything that had happened and that we'd learned. My world—my people—had shifted places, but it was still mine to protect. "Bliss is fine, but I'd rather clean this place up. We have a lot more lives to live before we're ready to do that."

It'd be the hardest battle I ever fought. That we'd ever fought.

About the Author

Lindsay French is the author of the Eclipse series, originally released on Royal Road. When she isn't trying to convince her middle school students to fall in love with reading, she's writing twisty science fiction and fantasy. There are few things she loves more than creating complex characters, dynamic action, and unforgettable adventures. French lives in the Midwest with her husband and one of the world's cutest dogs.

Podium

DISCOVER MORE

STORIES UNBOUND

PodiumEntertainment.com

9 781039 491281